The SECRET SON

JENNIFER BURKE

POOLBEG

Published 2013
by Poolbeg Press Ltd
123 Grange Hill, Baldoyle
Dublin 13, Ireland
E-mail: poolbeg@poolbeg.com
www.poolbeg.com

© Jennifer Burke 2013

Copyright for typesetting, layout, design, ebook
© Poolbeg Press Ltd

The moral right of the author has been asserted.

1

A catalogue record for this book is available from the British Library.

ISBN 978-1-84223-604-8

Typeset in Caslon 540 Roman 11/16

Printed by CPI, Cox & Wyman, UK

www.poolbeg.com

About the author

Jennifer Burke is a Dublin-based author and solicitor. Jennifer is an active member of the Irish Writers' Centre, where she regularly attends events and takes part in a monthly novel-writing group. She also writes shorter fiction. Having been shortlisted in the 2012 Cork County Council 'From the Well' competition, she had her short story published in the resulting anthology. Jennifer was also shortlisted in the 'Fish Publishing Flash Fiction' competition in both 2012 and 2013. This is her first novel.

Acknowledgements

I will be forever indebted to TV3 and Poolbeg Press for choosing me as the winner of their Write a Bestseller Competition 2013. Thank you to Paula Campbell, Gaye Shortland and all the team at Poolbeg Press for your hard work and belief in my book. Also thank you to all at TV3, especially Richard Stearn, Martin King and Sybil Mulcahy for your continued backing.

This book would not have been written without the invaluable guidance offered to new and aspiring writers by the Irish Writers' Centre. Thanks to Fergal and all the staff for being so welcoming. My gratitude to Conor Kostick and the other participants of the 'Finish Your Novel' course, especially Sarah Gilmartin for the extra time you gave me. Thanks also to Juliet Bressan. A special word of appreciation must go to my writing group for your on-going support.

A huge thanks to Dr Michelle O'Brien for all your help with the medical aspects of this novel and to Edel Hargaden for your advice on the legal side. Should any medical or legal inaccuracies arise in this work, they are entirely of my making.

As this is my first novel, I feel it is important that I thank all those who encouraged me in my writing during my formative years, including Sr Dempsey and my teachers in Mount Anville. I want to thank my extended family and my wonderful friends – I cannot express how your unswerving interest and faith in my ability to achieve this helped keep me motivated.

A few words in memory of my great-uncle Maurice Semple, author of many books on his beloved Lough Corrib: above all else and others, his encouragement throughout my childhood inspired me to keep writing.

Finally to my immediate family, to whom I have dedicated this book. Thank you, Richard, for being such a fun, thoughtful and supportive brother. To my parents, Denise and Michael, thank you for surrounding me with books as a child – for fuelling my imagining by reading to me, making up stories for me and being so enthusiastic when I began to create my own. Your whole-hearted belief in me is the reason I have completed this work.

*To my parents Michael and Denise,
and my brother Richard, with love and thanks*

Prologue

Liam

I stamp my foot onto the accelerator. The March dawn surrounds me in a blurry mist and I strain to find the slip road through the trees. My body shivers with frustration. I was stubborn for so long about avoiding the motorway, preferring the winding back roads. There was never any hurry.

Well, now there is a reason to rush and I can't find the shortcut that will lead me to the bloody motorway. I know that my destination, Cork, is only a few hours from Wicklow and even if I have to take these back roads the whole way I will still be early for my appointment. But that's not enough. I want to be there *now*. I cannot shake this feeling that it might be too late anyway.

Frowning against these thoughts, I surge the car forward. I want more than anything a successful result from this meeting. But then there will be no way to keep my secret from my family any longer. I cannot bear to imagine the look on Glenda's face. This is exactly why I couldn't bring myself to tell her all these years. The girls will be devastated.

As for my boy, Seán. He is now a man, living abroad and completely self-sufficient. Yet in many ways he is still so young. I wonder if he missed out, only having sisters. Maybe he would have gained something important if I had been able to give him a brother. I have failed him. Surely he will not see it any other way.

A choke escapes me and, to my disgust, my eyes prickle with tears. I don't want to think any more. I just need to be there. Growling, I pound my foot down, forcing the engine to roar.

My senses explode.

A deep horn and clunking smash of metal drown out my scream, taking my breath away. For a split second, the glow has a form: a dazzling headlight. It brightens to a beautiful degree I never imagined possible. Suddenly, instead of driving, I am walking towards it.

Part 1

Chapter 1

Seán

The tight-knit community of Ballyloughlin will of course be in shock at the unexpected death of such a favourite as my father. Yet I have no doubt that the tragedy will more than likely also spark a perverse interest in my return from America. I can just imagine the looks I will attract, walking down Main Street, from old friends, failing in their attempt at subtlety.

It would be a wonderful homecoming, if Dad hadn't just died. If the looks in my direction were engaging rather than searching for signs of grief so they can shake their heads and feel not just happy, but superior, in their own comfort. I know I should be grateful to be returning to the familiar intimacy of my childhood for consolation. But I really do dread those turning heads.

I knock back a third whiskey. It tastes unpleasantly tangy, tainted by the plastic packaging. The alcohol relaxes my muscles, allowing my body to slacken, easing further into my awkward position. My arms are trapped tight to my sides as I sit squashed between a large woman

5

and a snoring man on the flight home. As I gulp my fourth drink, I close my eyes, hoping for sleep, but the past twenty-four hours bounce repeatedly through my head. I watch the gold hands on my watch slide to noon, as it is in New York. Sighing, I twist the delicate dial to Irish time. It seems like a lifetime ago but it was only this time yesterday that Claire and I were on our way to an opera matinée. We had decided the night before that we should have a cultural day. Well, it was her ruling, a reaction to boredom with my favourite Irish bar.

"Enough with the pints!" she exclaimed, as I deposited a Guinness in front of her.

I grinned, pulling the pint back towards me. Her mouth twitched upwards as I handed her the spirit and mixer I had been hiding behind my back. I had even convinced the barman to rummage for an umbrella under the counter to dress it up like one of the fancy drinks she fawns over in hotel bars.

"Let's do something cultural tomorrow," she said.

Slurping back a mouthful, I cocked an eyebrow at her.

She cooed in the sensuous voice she knew I could never resist. "Come on, hon!" Seemingly immune to the sticky surface, her hand slid across the table to mine. "There are matinée tickets available for *Madame Butterfly* tomorrow. We could have dinner off Broadway afterwards . . ."

I gazed at her as she planned out the next day, hour by hour. It was not just unusual for Claire to initiate us spending an entire day together, it was unprecedented. I devote as much time to her as my job allows, but still she refuses to define herself as my girlfriend. Perhaps it is the stable family norm I have been raised to expect, but I would love to see more of her. She is without a doubt the most tantalising woman I have ever met. The refined posture of her tall, toned figure and the playful way she tosses her shiny black hair is enthralling. Bewitching, my flatmate once said, and I could not disagree. I sometimes wonder if she has any other men on the go.

Since it meant spending a whole day with her, I didn't complain that I had to wear a suit on a surprisingly warm March afternoon to a boring opera matinée. Claire radiated vitality as she glided up the steps of the theatre to meet me and I couldn't help but smile as she slid her arm coyly through mine, turning every head. She had booked us the best seats she could get at short notice, a box at the highest level. The lift – or 'elevator' as she makes me call it – had been so packed on the way up that when I reached out to hold her hand, I instead grabbed the fingers of a seventy-year-old woman. We laughed about it the whole way through the opera – much to the annoyance of the couple sharing the box with us – and well into the evening.

There were plenty of bars around the theatre so I don't know why we journeyed back to my apartment for our pre-dinner drink. But there we were, lounging easily on my couch, when the phone rang.

It was the worst conversation of my life. Mum barely managed to say hello before wailing uncontrollably. I sat frozen, not wanting to hear the reason for her hysteria. Yet when the worst was eventually confirmed by Pat O'Hara, who took the phone from my mother, the shock was as severe as if I had never suspected it.

"Seán, this is Pat. Are you there? Seán?"

I must have managed to squeak out a sound in the midst of my terror, because she continued in her gentle, comforting way.

"Seán, it's awful. Your father was in a car crash, on the old Cork road. A bad one. Oh Seán, he didn't make it. I'm so, so sorry, love."

Her words smacked my ears with their meaning, dizzying me. Denial engulfed me. It couldn't be. Dad was the most careful driver I knew.

"It happened around half six this morning," Pat went on gently. "We don't actually know where he was going so early in the day."

Even in my shock, I frown at this. Dad had told me only last week how he was enjoying more free time since scaling back on clients further afield. In any case, he shouldn't have any cause to be travelling the old Cork road at half six in the morning. There must be some mistake. I opened my mouth to object, but my chest constricted at hearing the desperation choking my mother's sobs in the background. I gasped in a loud, fraying breath. Claire's hand stroked my back, her soft voice questioning me, sounding frightened as I heaved in more air. I don't remember much after that.

I sat staring into space for a long time, barely conscious of Claire moving around me. Apparently she packed my bag, ordered takeaway pizza for us and organised a taxi to collect us early the next morning. But it was only when she sat down and enveloped me in her arms that I snapped out of my trance and pushed her back.

"I have to get home. My mother."

"It's all organised, Seán. That lady who rang said her son Kevin booked you onto the first flight tomorrow morning. He's going to collect you from the airport. Is that the Kevin who visited you last summer?"

I ignored her question, staring into her eyes. A sudden realisation of my good fortune hit me. I had people on both sides of the Atlantic who, at such a time, would take care of everything. But I did not feel lucky, merely unworthy. And anxious to be home, taking care of my mother. At least Pat O'Hara would be there until I got back. She would know what to do, what to say. Not only because she and Mum have been best friends since before I was born, but because she understands the pain of losing a husband. It is hard to believe it was a full decade ago when Kevin O'Hara Senior dropped dead of a heart attack and I – a lanky, awkward eighteen-year-old – tried to comfort my best friend with a few mumbled words.

It will be different now, I'm sure. Kevin will be able to express some sentiment I never considered, to ease the torment. Thinking about him now, with nothing else to distract me but the snoring man's head drooping perilously close to my shoulder, nervousness churns my innards.

I always found it strange to think of Ballyloughlin continuing as normal without me. Perhaps childishly, I felt that I was the one on a big adventure, experiencing life, while everyone at home was just plodding along the same as before. This assumption was challenged when Kevin O'Hara came to visit me last summer. I was determined to show off my new life and, to an extent, I succeeded. Kevin was fascinated by New York and took some rip-roaring stories back to his brothers, but I could tell he was not sorry to be leaving the buzz of the city for home. It was too much of a mystery for him to imagine an everyday life there. I had to laugh at him for embarrassing me with his tourist-like behaviour. He walked along the streets with his head tilted upwards towards the skyscrapers, gaping in awe. He guffawed loudly whenever anyone mentioned "garbage" or "sidewalk" yet could not understand why my American friends snickered when he overused such phrases as "thanks a million" or "grand".

I, on the other hand, am mad about New York and slipped right into the lifestyle. It is so different from the intimate small-town life of Ballyloughlin. I found from the start that the anonymity of the city suits me. While I miss the fresh air of home and security of well-known faces, especially my parents, it is not enough to drive me back.

I barely keep in touch with the two sisters closest to me in age, but my youngest sister has never given up on the romantic notion of my returning home and "reuniting" our family in Ireland. Her teenage ramblings have been a constant source of amusement during my time in New York. When I moved away, Lizzy was a typical, giggly fourteen-year-old. Life is, and always will be, full of drama when my little sister is around. Before social networking took off, she would send me letters on pink notepaper emboldened with a flouncy "*Elizabeth*" watermark. For the past year, I have been getting daily Facebook messages from her.

I smile now, as I think of Lizzy. She would find my current position – delicately manoeuvring a snoring man's head off my shoulder – absolutely hilarious. Of my three sisters, I think she will probably turn out most like my mother. Mum is a very intelligent woman, and has a reputation in the local community for being something of a feminist – a trait supported by the fact that she always uses her maiden name

9

despite having been married to Dad for nearly thirty years. Few people even remember that she has not spent her whole life in Ballyloughlin – that she is not even Irish but moved from England after marrying Dad. She's a real mover and shaker in the area, and Lizzy is very much like her, in miniature.

From the way Mum talks, I get the impression that Lizzy has been maturing and becoming more self-assured. She is now, at the age of nineteen, more a friend than a little sister. But she continues to wear her heart on her sleeve, and I imagine that the shock of the car crash that killed Dad will devastate her to the point of collapse. Picturing what little help my sisters are likely to be to my mother at a time of tragedy makes me all the more anxious to get home quickly. I stare out the window – or at least what I can see of the window past the woman on my other side – and urge the plane on.

I wish I could use my phone, as much to contact the people I have left in New York as to talk to those I'll see in a few hours. Claire had been so concerned and kind on hearing the news. She stayed with me that night, holding me as I trembled uncontrollably against the anguish, leaving my bedroom only to break the news to my roommates when they arrived home. I had pinched my eyes closed to shut out their whispered conversation in the hallway but sleep would not come.

It was still the middle of the night when Claire roused me from the bed and organised some last-minute packing. I showered, accepted firm embraces from my flatmates and walked out of my American home.

I realised that I had not given work a thought but Claire promised to contact them. I have taken her to a number of work functions and my boss Marx has a soft spot for her. He is less likely to throw a fit at the news of my impending absence if it comes from a beautiful woman. The American work ethic is somewhat manic compared to home, and LL&T, the large organisation where I work as a business consultant, tends not to factor family or personal time into the working year. I close my eyes and lie back against the headrest. I cannot think about them now.

It was not until Claire offered to travel to Ireland for the funeral that I registered her presence in the taxi. I allow myself a mischievous smirk at what she would have done if I had, in my grief, said yes. But just as quickly, my smile disintegrates bitterly. She certainly had not meant it. I know Claire would never commit to a serious relationship with me. Yesterday had been so perfect though. I lie back and focus on images of her for the rest of the journey.

As the plane touches down on the hard ground of Dublin, Claire slips away and I grunt against a painful tightening in my chest. I always imagined coming home would be a joyous occasion, with my entire family waiting for me at the arrivals hall with banners, ready to whisk me straight to the local GAA club where my father would buy everyone pints and insist on congratulations on the return of his son.

Instead, Kevin greets me with a sombre expression and a massive bear hug. I know it is unlikely that he had a growing spurt in the six months since I've seen him, but he seems even larger than before. Or maybe I just feel smaller.

I let him grab me and whisper condolences into my ear. Although I'll hear it all a million times over the next few days, the words of comfort are real coming from him. We have been buddies since we "shot out of our mothers' wombs within a few weeks of each other", as Pat O'Hara is fond of saying. I tried to be there for him when his dad died. I had hoped I would be an old man before he had to return the favour.

We slip into easy conversation as he lugs my suitcase across the arrivals area to the car park. The heavy darkness of the sky presses down on us, and I wish I could stop moving and drink in my homeland.

In less than half an hour we are on the road and the airport disappears from my side mirror. Kevin is already filling me in on the previous day and I try to concentrate.

"Well, I'd barely digested it but I knew we had to get you home. I was straight onto the internet booking you a flight. Mum was freaking out that you wouldn't be able to get home for days and I think I got you literally the last seat."

11

I smile, thinking of the snoring man and fat woman, but I do not tell him that he is probably right. I do not want to talk. I want to listen and watch the grey buildings give way to greener fields, artificially lit by flickering street lamps, as we speed along south.

"Your mum is only dying to see you. She's a mess to be honest, Seán, but that's to be expected, I suppose. Especially when she didn't get a proper goodbye. She hadn't expected him to travel that morning. She just woke up, and he was gone. I just can't believe it myself, you know? Your dad and Michael were only over on the farm two days ago giving us a bit of pro bono advice on the Loughend River. It's overflowed twice in the last six months and we can't be picking up the tab every time."

I feel him glance sideways at me but I continue to stare out the window. It has just hit me that I am in a car, which is unusual. It's all subways in New York. Aside from the taxi ride to the airport, which passed in a haze, I can't remember any recent car journeys. The last time my father got into a car, he didn't make it out alive. He is suddenly vivid in my mind, and I can practically smell his aftershave as I take a deep breath to steady myself.

"Tell me about the crash, Kevin."

He shifts in his seat, quickly changing gear to cover it up. "There's not much to tell. Head-on collision with an oncoming truck on the old Cork road. It was a narrow corner, you know. These things happen."

"But what on earth was he doing on the old Cork road at that hour of the morning? Out visiting clients?"

Kevin squirms again, sighing. "No, your mum was confused about that too. He rarely travels since giving up his clients from that neck of the woods. We just don't know, Seán."

"Which way was he heading?"

"Towards Cork."

"The truck driver?" I realise I haven't given him a thought, and am suddenly ashamed.

"He's stable. He'll be out of hospital in a day or two. The truck was so much bigger – it was your dad's car that was totalled."

As we approach the turn for Ballyloughlin, my mouth fills with saliva and a strange shiver runs through my body. "Are there many people at the house?"

"No one," Kevin replies quickly. "It was rammed to the rafters last night but Mum will have made sure everyone is out by now. Though it'll be some task – the whole of Ballyloughlin was over earlier. So far, there have been twenty-eight volunteers to do a bidding prayer at the funeral!"

My grin is forced, and short-lived. Before I am prepared, we are pulling up on the gravel driveway of my family home. Kevin leaves me at the door with a firm clap on the shoulder. I have to pause for a few moments to calm myself, staring up at the white, pebble-dashed façade. The three storeys loom over me as pale ivy trickles down the walls, and smoke billows from the living-room chimney.

As I gaze up at our impressive house, so different from my pokey New York apartment, I relive my boyhood pride at being a Murtagh. My family is one of the richest in Ballyloughlin. But whatever natural human tendency towards jealousy there might have been among the neighbours, it was overcome years ago by the warmth and generosity of my parents. My father's death will leave a hole in this community.

When I finally build up the courage to lift the brass knocker, it is Lizzy who opens the door. For a second she stares, then lets out a wail and flings herself against my chest. She has not grown an inch in height since I left, and I remember her crying in my arms on this exact spot as I departed for the airport five years ago.

Over her wild, bushy, brown hair, the hallway looms. My stomach lurches at the sudden realisation of what has happened since I was last in this house. The overpowering smell of home submerges me in a thousand memories as a torrent of heartache unsteadies me. I squeeze my eyes closed. When I open them I see my other two sisters walking slowly towards me from different sides of the hall, and my mother

13

standing on the stairs in the centre of the house, her hand pressed over her heart.

My siblings arrive at my side. Niamh puts her arms as far around me and Lizzy as they can reach and begins to weep, while Katie merely rests her head on my shoulder. I want to say something, anything, but my voice is choked by tears I can no longer stop as Mum comes towards me. Dropping to the floor with Lizzy, I move my arms wider to pull all three sisters close. My mother sinks to the floor to be with us and, in the half-light of the entrance hall, some silent, some weeping, what remains of my family gathers into a ball and mourns.

Chapter 2

Seán

People are unashamedly standing on tip-toes and craning their necks to gawk at me, the returned emigrant, as we enter the church behind the coffin, but most are disappointed. With Mum on my arm and the girls crowding around, no one gets a good look.

Our local parish priest speaks eloquently about Liam, a larger-than-life figure whose passion for, and devotion to Ballyloughlin has left an indelible mark. I try to hear it all but mostly I just sit in a daze, immersed in my own memories of him. Against my will, I keep coming back to the crash.

I speculate again about where Dad was going that morning. "Sure, he could have been going anywhere along the road or even as far as Cork – we just don't know." But this standard response from my family and the O'Haras doesn't answer my question as to why he was travelling anywhere at half past six in the morning, never mind in that direction. And why didn't he mention the trip to my mother? Or leave a note? I can't bring myself to ask them again. It sounds like I am accusing him of something. "The potholes on those old roads are notorious," my mother had sniffed. "No wonder he crashed."

When interviewed, the truck driver said Dad had come around the corner so rapidly he could never have swerved out of the way in time. Mum and Lizzy called him all manner of names for blaming a dead man. No one in the family gave any credence to the possibility that Dad might have been driving too fast. Speed was the reason he would never use the motorway.

I try to glance around without attracting attention. It does not seem real to me that this is my father's funeral, and that all my old childhood friends and neighbours are sitting just behind me, ready to descend on me when it comes to an end. The formal sympathising at the removal the night before, when they all filed quietly past the family with bowed heads and handshakes, had been bad enough. But after the burial there will be no holds barred and I will be expected to talk, reminisce and remember names and faces. The mere thought threatens to overwhelm me. I try to focus my mind on Claire again, but she is so far removed from my life in Ballyloughlin that her face shimmers indistinctly on edges of my mind, offering no relief.

Too soon, the Mass is over. The congregation keep their distance as we walk around the back of the church to the graveyard. I feel a desperate urge throw myself into my mother's arms as they lower the coffin, but Niamh and Lizzy are already clinging to her, and I find myself literally holding Katie upright. She retches a couple of times and I steer her away from the grave, wishing Dad was here to help me with her. She is an adult now; at twenty she is only a few years younger than Niamh and a full year older than Lizzy. But she feels like a child as she clutches at me for support.

The songs and prayers at the graveside pass in a blur, and after we have staggered back around to the church, I am, as expected, surrounded by sympathisers. Compassion presses in on me from all sides – wrinkled hands grip my own; my face is stroked by soft, womanly fingers; strong palms slap my shoulder vigorously. I meet their eyes, trying to remember names, smiling tightly and repeating thanks. I see my mother cocooned in a similar circle and feel another pang as I long for Dad to come and rescue us. I continue the shaking, nodding, acknowledging routine for what seems like hours. Just when I think I can't take it anymore, a familiar face appears in front of me and, with an authority none of the disappointed spectators question, my father's best friend steers me away from the thronging crowd.

It is strange how Dad's death has altered my perceptions of people. A week ago I would have described Michael Undersky as simply Dad's friend and long-time colleague. Now I see a man who, as a widower, will know how to help Mum through her loss. I visualise the religious Christmas cards he sends me every year in New York, despite never receiving one in return. A rush of gratitude for the support he always offered my father warms me. I remember Dad recalling how much he owed Michael for helping him set up his legal practice when he first returned from England all those years ago after marrying Mum. Michael has a quiet strength about him that I had forgotten but now deeply appreciate.

"Katie was feeling unwell," he says as he casually manoeuvres me to his car. "Your mother and the girls have taken her back home, so I told Glenda I'd give you a lift."

I sigh. Katie was always a sensitive soul but since Dad died she has deteriorated to a quivering mess. While the rest of us are at least attempting to hold ourselves together for Mum's sake, Katie veers between zombie and banshee. I am not surprised she was the first to buckle under the pressure of the funeral.

Within five minutes, we are on the road. I squint through the noon sun at Michael. I never exactly disliked him as a child, but he was not a favourite with any of us children. There was no good reason for this, except that he was a quiet and gentle man who never got excited or played with the kids. In fact, he was pretty boring compared to our father's other friends: the loud and hilarious head of the local GAA club Conn O'Shaughnessy, the entertaining Pat O'Hara, or even old

Mrs Boden who delighted in sneaking us sweets and chocolate behind our parents' backs.

I feel I should say something to Michael, but no words flow.

"How's the job, Seán?" he asks softly after a while.

Despite the fact that I had just been casting my mind about for a topic to break the ice, my head pounds at the expectation of small talk, especially about my life in America. I give a short, vague answer and he takes the hint. After another few moments, I regret dismissing Michael's attempt at conversation. But he does not seem to mind the quiet. I cannot help contrasting his company to that of my friends in America – they never shut up. Suddenly, the silence seems peaceful, rather than awkward. I allow my eyelids to sag but, just as I do, we turn into our driveway.

I had hoped for a few precious minutes with the family but the caterers have already arrived and Pat O'Hara is lining us up like soldiers – even a wan Katie – to hand out our marching orders. When her back is turned, I give a small salute and wink at Lizzy, who stifles a laugh.

The house is soon filled with well-wishers and the trauma of the funeral starts to catch up with me as I continue the greetings I started outside the church. I am relieved to see Michael in control. He moves seamlessly from the kitchen to the dining room to the living room, directing the caterers and deflecting people away from my exhausted mother. The house is buzzing, with half the neighbourhood eating and drinking more than their fair share.

Later, when the darkness is absolute and the crowd has depleted, I can relax with only those who are truly welcome remaining. Niamh is consoling Mrs Boden, who remembers when Dad was born and says she feels like she is burying her own child. "Liam was his father's pride and joy," she says, coughing loudly, nodding to a photo of Dad on the mantelpiece. She shakes her head tenderly as Niamh puts a reassuring arm around her.

I turn away, seeing Kevin distracting Lizzy, even making her laugh by telling some lewd and embarrassing stories involving his younger brothers. In the further corner, Pat is also talking of her sons, recalling for some of Dad's GAA friends the well-worn story of how her husband was content with just their son but she convinced him to try for one more baby, because she really wanted a girl. "Imagine our shock," she grins, "when they told me I was expecting triplets, and my three brutes popped out!"

"Are you talking about us again, Mum?" shouts one of her younger boys, busy playing poker in the corner with his brothers – Katie is also involved. She is the same age and a great favourite with the O'Hara triplets, probably because she is so shy they can talk as much as they want without interruption.

Michael is in deep discussion with Conn O'Shaughnessy and they beckon me to come over. I pull up a chair and join them.

"We miss you in the club, Seán!" Conn thumps me on the back and I have to laugh in return.

"Come on, Conn, I was never going to turn Wicklow into All-Ireland champions."

"No, if they ever manage that it'll be down to your Lizzy. You should see the paces she puts those lads through when I ask her to help me out with their training. They're terrified of her, you know! She's kinder to the horses!"

I catch Michael's eye and grin. Conn might be an eccentric but I'm sure he's not exaggerating about Lizzy. Unfortunately, he's also a gossip.

"So, Seán, is it all yours now?"

I stare at him blankly.

"The *land*!" he exclaims, exasperated.

I turn automatically to Michael who reddens before quickly shifting the conversation back to GAA. It's enough to distract Conn O'Shaughnessy, but not me. I watch Michael passively until he downs his whiskey as an excuse to send Conn into the kitchen for more. Shuddering at the aftertaste, he turns to me.

"Seán, your father made a will just after you were born and hasn't changed it since. He left everything to Glenda, rather than yourself, as I'm sure you understand."

I'm quick to put him at ease. My family's fortune is significant. But it is not, as is often assumed, inherited old money of landed gentry. My grandfather prospered from trade, as well as through farming, and invested most of what he acquired in the grounds we now live in. Almost one hundred acres of it is prime farming land, which we have let out to various families in the area. As far as I know, even the O'Haras run part of it, though they have their own land as well. But, surprisingly, most of Dad's money is kept in cash, stashed across every bank and building society in the state and beyond.

I remember a nasty article written about my father before I left for America. He was accused of hiding something, of being a shady dealer. There is definitely something dubious, they slandered, when a man keeps so much money in foreign banks. Dad went berserk, to put it mildly. He even released bank statements, though Michael advised him against it, and tax records, detailing everything. It proved he was clean so the papers took a different tack. Some called him an inept businessman because he refused to dabble in shares, or even low-yielding stock like government bonds. They deemed him a fool for not entering the property market at the height of the boom. He could certainly have afforded it. In hindsight, he was lucky to have avoided all those avenues, given how the markets collapsed. But it wasn't any genius strategy on his part. I often wondered if it was pure laziness. Ultimately, I think he was simply happy being a solicitor, and liked to keep his finances straightforward.

We had a fine house that was refurbished every few years to keep it fresh and modern. It would surely sell for a few million, even without the lands attached. Dad liked to have easily accessible cash for purchases like cars or holidays, though he and Mum never travelled far. They were happiest at home. In this way, I think I turned out a lot like my parents. I like the high life in New York – or rather, I like to be able to show Claire the high life – but I don't crave money for the sake of it. I earn enough in my job. I work the hours to justify the pay too.

Our estate is a large one, but I have no desire to manage it and would rather Mum maintain it, and with it her role as parent and captain of the family. Besides, the greatest asset is the house, and she deserves that.

Michael is looking at me strangely, even after I've done my best to convince him I'm not after my father's money. "I want to ask you something, Seán," he whispers uneasily. "Have you ever heard of a man named Roger Nestor?"

Feeling drained after the day, I half-heartedly cast my mind around but the name means nothing to me. I purposely yawn as I shake my head in reply, but Michael either ignores this or does not notice.

He sighs. "It was a long shot but I wanted to ask. Some years ago, your father gave me an envelope. He told me that in the event of his death, I was to open it immediately."

Taken aback, I straighten in my seat.

"Naturally," continues Michael, "I wondered why he was talking about death. I thought maybe something was wrong, that he was sick. But he assured me he was well and that he intended to live for a long time yet. He said he was just getting his affairs in order. As you can imagine, that confused me even more. I had made his last will for him years ago, before Niamh was born. I asked him if this will was still valid, but he said he didn't want to talk about it. He said that hopefully he would outlive me – as you know I'm a good few years older than him – but that if for some reason he didn't, I was to open that envelope and it would explain everything. I looked inside before the funeral, and this is all it was."

He pulls an envelope from inside his jacket pocket, carefully removes a slip of paper and hands it to me. There, in my father's delicate handwriting, are two short lines:

Mick – Ring Roger Nestor. I just hope to God they can somehow forgive me. Tell Glenda I loved her more than I ever loved another human being in my entire life.

Liam

I turn the paper over, hoping for more, but all that is written on the back is a telephone number. I sit unmoving, staring at the cryptic message. Michael's voice echoes distantly as he continues talking.

"I have absolutely no idea what this is about, Seán. I don't understand what could be so terrible that your father would keep it not only from Glenda, but from me. As your family solicitor, I know every detail of your estate. There is nothing financially or legally that could have happened without my knowledge. I haven't shown this to Glenda, Seán. I want to contact this man first."

As I nod, we are set upon by one of the O'Hara triplets inviting me to join their card game because Katie is too tired. Michael seizes on this excuse to throw all but the family out of the house. In the bustle, it is decided that Michael should drive Mrs Boden home and, unable to get out of this, he only has time to throw me an apologetic look before leaving with the rest.

Mum closes the door behind the last of them and, with my arm around Lizzy, I walk slowly into the living room where the older girls are already sprawled on the couch. We sink tightly into an armchair and sit in silence, as a family, without a dad. Luckily, Mum and the girls are too tired to talk much, so I am free to ponder on the note without interruption. Unfortunately this opportunity lasts well into the night, and it is long after the sobs filtering from my mother's and sisters' bedrooms turn to light snoring that I finally slip into a fitful sleep.

Chapter 3

Tors

"Okay, Jack, have you got everything?" I swivel around, watching him unbuckle his seatbelt and gather up his sports bag in his skinny arms.

"Yep!"

"Say thanks to Ethan's dad for the lift, won't you?"

He throws his eyes up to heaven, which makes me smile.

"Wait a minute, mister. Where do you think you're going without giving your sister a kiss?"

"Aw, Tors!" he whines.

"Well, you can give me one now or I can get out of the car and give you a big hug and kiss in front of Ethan and all the boys . . ."

I hear him tut as he bumps his soft little lips off my cheek.

"Good luck in the match!" I call, watching him bound over to where Ethan and his dad are standing with the rest of the team.

I grin to myself as I pull out of the car park. I love mortifying him like that. It's what Dad would have done if he was still alive, and Jack needs a bit of ribbing and fun in his life. I suppose I'm like an embarrassing second mother to him rather than an older sister, but what can he expect? I'm a full eighteen years older than the kid.

As I cruise along the familiar roads from the local GAA club back to our council estate, my mind focuses on the day ahead, making lists of things to do. Happily, today is relatively free. Andrew had dialysis yesterday and is not due back in the hospital for more of it until Monday. He's delighted to be home – the past month has been a nightmare. So we will take it easy today, like a normal family would on a weekend.

I usually bring Andrew to Jack's match on a Saturday morning if it's a home game, or not too far away. But today they have an hour-long drive, and I don't like Andrew having to take long journeys on the days he doesn't have dialysis, especially since he is still weak after the past month. Jack was disappointed he couldn't come; I suppose Andrew is the closest thing he has to a father since Dad died. Andrew loves mucking around with the boys, and some of Jack's pals don't even know he is sick. It never fails to amaze me how kids just don't notice when a young man is so pale and thin that other adults have to look away to hide their pity.

With Jack gone for the next few hours, I can think of one job that can't be put off much longer, and it will get Andrew out of the house for a short time. He is running out of clothes, so Mam is taking him shopping. He doesn't know it yet. I may not be very worldly but I know enough not to tell men in advance that they are being brought clothes-shopping. It starts up a tirade of constant moaning and they will always find a way to get out of it.

I smirk to myself. It's not my problem. Andrew's day-to-day, non-medical needs are Mam's department. I might be like a second mother to little Jack, but Andrew is twenty, just six years younger than me. I'm his big sister, but I'm also his friend. His best friend really, just like he is mine. Since I took over the role of official carer to him a year ago, we have become even closer. I'm not prepared to wreck that relationship by being the one who forces him to do the annoying chores, like shopping for underwear. So Mam and I agreed from the start that she would take that on.

I'll probably go along anyway. I don't like being away from him at the moment. Dialysis is a nuisance for him even on a good day because it takes us about an hour and half to travel from our home in Kerry to the hospital in Galway, sometimes longer if there's traffic. Then there's the dialysis itself which, even though they've got it down to a fine art, can still take up to four hours. By the time we get home, the day is gone.

But at least we do normally get home. When we arrived for dialysis a month ago, with Andrew feeling more poorly than usual, we discovered to our horror that his arteriovenous fistula – the permanent access point for dialysis in his arm – was blocked. I tried to keep calm but ended up practically yelling at Dr Jim, Andrew's consultant. "How is he going to get dialysis if his AVF is blocked? You can't give him dialysis without it! He needs it *today*!" Dr Jim told me firmly to calm down, that they could insert a temporary line near his shoulder to give him the dialysis. That did not reassure me. I'm not only a carer, I'm a qualified nurse and am well aware that temporary lines are prone to contamination. And my brother always has the worst luck when it comes to contracting infections. On top of that, the temporary line is just that – temporary. It cannot be used forever. And fitting a new arteriovenous fistula, or AVF as they call it to avoid scaring patients with complicated medical-speak, is not easy. So after the trauma of dialysis in his shoulder instead of his arm, Andrew was scheduled for surgery within the week to develop a new AVF in his other arm.

It took a long time to calm Mam when she was told he would need surgery for his first AVF. Even though she was constantly researching his illness, and the doctors explained it clearly, she would regularly turn to me with urgent desperation. "But why does he have to have an operation? Why can't they just *give* him the dialysis?"

"It's more complicated than that," I repeated patiently for weeks until she finally accepted that she was not going to get a different response from me. "He has to get dialysis three times a week, Mam. They need a long-term solution. They have to set up an AVF as a permanent point of entry."

She cried for hours last month when his AVF got blocked and was told more surgery would be required to set up a new one. Andrew was outwardly stoic, but I knew he was not ignorant about the extra strain this would put on his already wilting body.

The creation of an AVF involves the joining of an artery and a vein and needs a number of weeks to mature after surgery before it can be used in dialysis, so poor Andrew had to stay in hospital for weeks. Usually only a short hospital stay would be necessary, but with Andrew's typical bad luck, he was poorly after the operation and Dr Jim decided to keep him longer. Even now that he is home, the new AVF is still not fully ready – it could up to two to three months before it properly develops – and so the temporary one is still in use.

It's great having him back, which Dr Jim allowed since the temporary line has worked so far without causing infection, but we are all drained after the past month. I spent most of the time in the hospital, though for a few days I took over the running of the house so Mam could be with Andrew. She is lucky her job is so accommodating.

"There's no luck about it," she tends to argue back at me. "I've worked as personal secretary for that man for nearly thirty years and I always get my work done." There's truth in that. Her boss – the head of an Irish-owned printing company – does not allow flexitime for all his staff, but Mam has proven her worth over the years. Even when she has to leave early for Andrew or Jack, she'll go in before work or stay late at the other end of the day to make sure everything gets done. But she is still lucky. There is no denying that her boss is disposed to be overly accommodating when it comes to sick kids, having lost a daughter to cancer.

Mam found the past month particularly difficult. She worries, more than me and Andrew put together. The one night we both stayed at home to try to get a good night's sleep I heard her crying, and knew that was the end of my restful night. Out family is so small, we all have to take care of each other. Unable to leave her suffering alone, I sat cross-legged on her bed just like when I was a child while she confided in me that she was panicking about Andrew's long-term prognosis. If one AVF gives out, what's to stop the new one failing? There are only so many temporary lines the doctors can build. After a while, they will run out of ways to give him dialysis.

I tried to bolster her. "Someone will die, Mam – get out your cauldron and wand." This got a watery smile out of her. We need the right person to die, so Andrew can get his kidney. It's too awful to be wishing death upon someone, preferably someone young and healthy. So we have to make a joke out of it, pretending we're evil witches casting spells of doom out into the world. It's not really funny, but it's the best we can do.

"Yeah," Mam said, wiping her eyes and flicking the invisible wand in her hand, "someone will die."

I push these thoughts out of my head as I pull up outside our house. The old, battered family jeep takes up most of the driveway so I park my little Toyota outside. It's probably the nicest car on the street, even though it's eight years old.

Mam was flabbergasted when I first pulled up in my little speed wagon, as Andrew calls it, shortly after moving back home last year. "How on earth did you afford it, Tors?"

"Savings from France," I answered, vaguely. Only Andrew knows the real truth. He has to. We have a truth pact.

I call out to my family as I step over the threshold. Andrew grunts distractedly from the living room and I hear Mam shouting greetings from upstairs.

"What's she doing?" I ask, as I flop down beside my brother on the couch.

"Research," he shrugs.

I sigh inwardly. Poor Mam will never give up hope of a new trial or medical breakthrough that could save Andrew from having to have a transplant, and she spends hours on the internet every week, researching.

"Is that what you're doing too?" I ask playfully, indicating his laptop on his knee but knowing full well the answer.

"Come on!" he grins wickedly, and tilts the screen so I can see the cars zooming around a track. His arm, slightly swollen from the surgery, does not falter as he pounds the keyboard, directing his racing team.

I wish I could afford to get him a Wii or other games console, but there's no money. I offered to spend my 'France money' buying something like that for him, but when he heard how I got it, he insisted I spend it on myself.

The doorbell rings and I leave Andrew absorbed in the game to answer it. A tall, thin man with a sour face loiters sullenly behind a smaller, heftier man whose shoulders hunch almost painfully. I have always been proud that my mother, even with all the stresses of having an ill son, holds herself tall and strong as though she and hers would never let an ugly predator like kidney disease beat them.

The hunched man smiles politely. "May we speak to Karen Shaw, please?"

The taller man interrupts immediately from behind. "It's actually Andrew Shaw we have come to see."

I notice a cloud pass over the smaller man's face, as though they have had this argument already and he lost.

In an instant, he recovers. "Yes," he smiles back at me, "we are looking for Andrew Shaw, but perhaps it would be best if his mother is present when we speak to him."

My stomach swirls and I force myself to stay calm. When I speak, it is in a measured voice, but I wonder whether the hunched man saw in my face that emotion which I had, just moments ago, seen in his. "I'm Andrew's carer. If there is something I should know, please tell me now."

"Carer?"

The hunched man seems genuinely surprised, but I ignore this. People pretend to be surprised all the time to hear that Andrew is sick, when it could not be more obvious. The palms of my hands start to sweat.

"Yes. I am his carer, in an official capacity. Are you doctors?"

This time, the taller man in the dark black suit answers. "No. My name is Roger Nestor and this is Michael Undersky. We are solicitors and are here to discuss a legal matter with Andrew Shaw. When you say you are his carer, can I ask for what reason? What I mean is, is he mentally capable of speaking to and understanding me?"

I am so stunned by this question that I stumble into the answer without thinking. "There's nothing wrong with him mentally."

"Then I'd like to speak with him if he is here. As he is an adult, there is no need for his mother, or his carer, to be present."

The hunched man named Michael interrupts again, with a hint of agitation. "But given the sensitivity of this situation, I feel it appropriate that his mother be present."

The men glare at each other and, thankfully, Mam appears at the door. Seeing the nosy mother from three doors down crane her neck as she passes by with her buggy, I stand back to let the men in and introduce them to Mam. Michael is staring intently at my mother, but she shows no recognition at the sound of his name. She eyes them warily, taking Roger Nestor's business card reluctantly, as though it is a bomb.

I usher them into the sitting room and Andrew looks up from his laptop. He smiles and reaches out to shake the men's hands, but only Roger Nestor offers his. There is an awkward silence as we sit, except for Michael who stands transfixed in the centre of the room.

"Andrew," Roger Nestor begins, his voice somewhat softer than before, "I am here to discuss a legal matter with you. As you are an adult, I would prefer to talk to you privately. However, given the sensitive nature of the issue, Michael feels it would be appropriate for your mother to stay in the room. It is up to you."

"She can stay," Andrew frowns. "As can my sister."

"Sister?" Michael cuts in reproachfully. "I thought you were his carer? Do you have any other siblings?"

"I am his carer *and* his sister. And what business is it of yours if we have other siblings?"

My mother interjects. "We're all staying. Now will someone please tell me what the hell is going on here? Is there a kidney for Andrew? Is there some legal problem with the donor?"

Silence follows, and I realise that the two men honestly had no idea before coming here that Andrew is sick. A sideways glance at Michael is shocking: his eyes pop from his suddenly green face.

"Andrew," Roger Nestor casts a worried glance at his companion before settling his gaze on my brother, "you have been made the beneficiary of a will."

Andrew stares at him, perplexed.

He continues. "A man named Liam Murtagh died last –"

Mam is on her feet. "Get out. Get out of my house!"

I blink at my mother's reaction, as her visibly shaking hands move to cover her face. Her whole body vibrates, as though she is using all her energies not to scream. Instinctively, I shift closer to Andrew as Roger Nestor continues.

"Mrs Shaw, I'm sorry, I know this must be difficult for you. But Michael is the executor of the will and Liam essentially hired me, out of the proceeds of his estate, to be available to Andrew should he have any legal questions or to act for him should the will be challenged. In any event, as beneficiary of the will, Andrew has a right to be told sometime. Now, if you would like, we can give you a minute while you explain the situation to him."

Mam's breathing quickens as she looks at us, tears forming in her eyes. When she turns back to Roger Nestor, her voice is a whisper. "He's dead?"

Michael steps closer to her, his face dark. "Yes, he's dead. He died in a car crash last Saturday."

"Saturday." Mam's voice catches and she sinks back into the couch.

"Excuse me," Andrew's voice is commanding. "I want to know who this man is and why he is leaving me something in his will."

Michael sighs and turns to Andrew for the first time. "Not 'something', son. Everything. He is leaving you everything. And he was a wealthy man."

"Does this have something to do with my illness?"

"No. I don't think he even knew you were sick."

"He did know," Mam says with a shiver.

Michael spins around. "You've been in contact with him?"

Mam does not flinch. "Who are you?"

"I'm his best friend. And I never heard about you until this week. I am driving back to Wicklow this evening to tell Liam's wife that she has been left nothing. Well, not nothing – spouses always get a portion of the will whether they've been left it or not." He gestures Mam away impatiently.

"Hang on." Andrew furrows his brow. "Why would this man who I've never met and who doesn't even know I'm sick, leave everything to me and not his wife? Mam, who is this Liam Murtagh?"

All eyes shift to my mother, but she looks only at Andrew.

"He's your father."

A deathly silence pierces the air. Andrew's mouth drops open and the two strangers stare, embarrassed, down at the floor. I feel my head shaking from side to side. It doesn't make any sense. Andrew's father – *our* father – died three years ago. Suddenly, Roger Nestor is by my side, pressing another business card into my hand. I realise vaguely that my mother's fist has crushed the card he handed over on his arrival.

"We will leave you. When this has settled down, please have Andrew ring me. I will be happy to talk you through everything."

I look at him blankly.

"Do you have a copy of the will?"

I hear my mother, but her voice is fuzzy in my ears. I curl my fingers around Andrew's, as much to steady myself as him. There is a shuffling of papers exchanged, a murmur of goodbyes and the click of a door closing.

"Andrew," Mam's voice trembles violently. "I never wanted you to find out that way. I never wanted you to find out at all."

Andrew, ever the hero, finds strength from somewhere and stands to face our mother. Automatically I stand with him. His weight crushes into me as his legs start to give way but I hold him firmly upright. "Tell us now," he says quietly.

"Quickly," I add, urgently.

I can feel every word is an effort and it doesn't take her long. Snippets stay with me. *Trip to visit a friend. One-night stand. Regret.*

Never one to stall, Andrew engages, though his voice sounds oddly mechanical. "Did Dad know he wasn't my real father?"

Mam shakes her head, keeping her eyes on the floor. "I never told him. He worshipped you, Andrew. As far as I'm concerned, Liam Murtagh was one stupid mistake. Dad and I were having problems but we worked them out. You are as much his son as mine."

But Andrew has stopped listening. Letting go of me, he bolts upstairs to the bathroom. Mam and I stand listening to him throw up until she turns to me, desperately seeking an ally.

I hold up a hand to stop her, merciless, unable to contain my horror. "I have one question, Mam. Is Dad *my* real father?"

Mam has the decency to look sick. "Of course. I told you, Liam Murtagh was a one-time, idiotic mistake. I love all you kids. Can't you forgive me?"

I feel my face harden. "You've made Andrew my half-brother. I can never forgive you for that."

Chapter 4

Tors

It is almost a full day before I see my mother again, before I even come out of Andrew's room.

I spent the rest of that day and night with my brother, trying to coax him to sleep. He needs rest so badly. Every hour he does not sleep at night is an hour less his body spends building itself back up.

He just sat, staring vacuously ahead of him.

"Tell me what you're seeing," I probed gently but I could not get him to answer anything other than "Dad."

I sat with him on the bed, gazing into the past. Along with disbelief at Mam's revelation, I couldn't help but feel selfishly relieved that the lie didn't involve me, that Dad was still mine. As usual, it's Andrew who gets all the bad luck – kidney disease, a blocked AVF, a fake father. Even in the stillness of his rigid posture, I could tell his mind was racing. I rubbed his back gently and tried to convince him that Dad loved him. Andrew listened, or at least he didn't interrupt, but after a while he turned to me, his face pale.

"Do you remember Dad's cousin, Taylor, the one who lives in Texas?"

"Sure, I do. He might have been born in Galway but he was destined for America with a name like that."

Andrew gave me a half-hearted smile and I returned it gratefully. It was more than I had got out of him in the previous eight hours. I waited while he mused some more, and I tried to recall if I had ever actually met Cousin Taylor. We used to get letters from him every month, normally with mundane stories that Dad would embellish into a classic American adventure. Cousin Taylor rode a horse to the markets, but Dad described with gusto a wild-west race to the Alamo. Cousin Taylor bought a new hat, but it was a large white Stetson to match his cowboy outfit complete with tasselled boots by the time Dad was finished telling the story.

"Do you remember he had sons?" Andrew piped up.

My mind summoned up a story about two boys taking on a pack of wild dogs. In reality, it was probably just their next-door neighbour's Labrador. I smiled as I nodded in response; Dad should have been an actor.

"Then you'll remember Dad always referred to them as his *adopted* sons?"

My face crumpled as I was wrenched back to a long-forgotten argument when I berated Dad for always describing Cousin Taylor's boys as 'adopted sons' even though he got them when they were babies and they were years older than us. I forced myself to look at my brother, his face blurry through the tears I was trying to hold back.

"Dad could never think of them as his real kids. They were always outsiders."

"That's different, Andrew." I could hear the desperation in my voice. "He loved you. Nothing in the world could have changed that."

But Andrew had already rolled his head away. His vacant stare continued until his own drawing of Dad hanging on his wall caught his eye, causing him to vomit again. I put my foot down then, and made him lie down on the bed and close his eyes. I played some of my restful music – Adele, Sarah McLachlan – on his CD player, quietly, so as not to wake Jack.

Mam wasn't asleep. I could tell by the rustling of the sheets from the room next door. She hadn't come near us all day and I could hear her murmur on the telephone for hours. Even in my disgust with her, the sound of her voice was comforting. Jack bustled in the front door at some point later in the afternoon, but Mam must have told him Andrew was sick because he didn't come near us. Later in the night, in the early hours of the morning, when Andrew finally fell into a restless sleep, I could hear Mam weeping alone in her room but I didn't go in.

I hadn't expected to sleep, as my head was still pounding angrily against our new reality, but I must have drifted off at some point.

* * *

I am awoken by an aching in my right arm where Andrew's head has been resting. Carefully I untangle myself from him. The morning sun is streaming through the curtains. I look down at his sleeping face. He has been doing so well with the temporary line, but a blow like this could really drain him and weaken his ability to fight off the ever-present threat of infections. Worry for him only further fuels rage towards my mother but part of me knows he isn't the only one who needs protecting. It is easier to focus on Andrew's hurt than let mine in.

I slip out of the room as quietly as I can and pad sleepily downstairs to the kitchen. Mam is sitting at our kitchen table, fully dressed, rifling furiously through piles of paper and muttering to herself. Her eyes are slightly red and puffy, as I had guessed they would be, but they also shine with that hardened look she gets on the days we have to bring Andrew to hospital for something worse than dialysis. She looks up at me standing in the doorway.

"Sit down, love."

I obey, looking at her expectantly. She busies herself with the papers for a while, obviously to avoid looking at me. Eventually, with a sigh, she lifts her prematurely lined face. "Well, you must have some questions. Let's hear them."

I ignore the edge to her voice. "This man, Liam Murtagh, obviously knew he was Andrew's biological father, if he left him everything. Why didn't he try to contact us before? Help us before?"

Mam stands abruptly and I know she is wishing she never opened her mouth to invite such inquiries. She makes a meal of carrying her plate and cup to the sink, dumping them in dirty water that must have been sitting stagnant for hours.

"Mam, you're going to have to give us answers!" Her silence infuriates me. She just told me I could ask her about it, and then she clams up on the first question. I try to control my trembling lip. "Maybe not now, maybe not to me. But some day you'll have to explain it all to Andrew."

Shoulders tight, she turns slowly. "Liam Murtagh might be Andrew's biological father but that's where it ends. Stuart raised him, loved him. There was no need for Liam to be in his life."

I clenched my fists. "You're the one who's always harping on about how we can't afford to send Andrew abroad for tests. How it would make his life better – improve his health – if we could afford to move an hour up the road to be nearer the hospital. If the Murtaghs are so rich, he could have helped us. You should have asked. He should have offered!"

Mam shook her head. "That would have meant your dad finding out. Having him in our lives was more important."

"He would have stayed in my life. Jack's life. Even Andrew's life. It's only you he would have seen for what you really are – an adulterer."

Mam's eyes fly open and she sucks in a huge breath, gripping her stomach with both hands. "It was a one-time thing, my love. I promise you that. Why bring it up before when it would have destroyed our family?"

I stare at her angrily, then sadly, not knowing who I am looking at. I've seen her be gentle with Andrew, a buddy for Jack, a confidante for me. She's organised pickets with other parents when the government wanted to cut research-funding for kidney disease. She cried until she couldn't breathe when Dad died, and taught me how to puff and pant into a paper bag to keep from fainting with grief. She's my mother. But one who has made her son lose his father all over again.

Just when I think I'll never understand her, she proves me right.

"Listen, Tors, I never asked Liam Murtagh for money. I didn't want anything from him. When your dad died, I considered it, but that would have been . . . I don't know . . . insulting him and his memory when he raised Andrew as a son. But I've been thinking about it all night, and you're right. We need this money. I should have asked for it years ago. But now we don't have to go begging. Now it's Andrew's legally. I don't know much about Liam's estate but I know this – it's all in Wicklow. He hasn't spread his wealth around like a lot of the boom-time boys. He's kept it local."

"How do you know that?"

"He's wealthy. There are articles about him sometimes. I keep my eyes open. His assets are in Wicklow, so that's where we have to go."

At first, I don't understand. Slowly, very slowly, I lift my eyes to meet hers, gaping at her in disbelief as she ploughs on unashamedly.

"The hurt I've caused you and the boys, it can't be fixed in a day. It's going to take time. But in the meantime, we have to think about Andrew."

"I always think about Andrew!" I glare at her, stung.

"I know that, sweetheart. You more than anybody knows the problems we have. As sure as I am of anything, I know the wife is going to fight this will. She has four children of her own. She will not want to give up everything she has for her husband's illegitimate child."

"What are you saying, Mam?"

"We need to be there. I read the will and spoke to Roger Nestor for an hour on the phone yesterday evening. He will help us if they contest the will. But we need to put up a good fight. Show that Andrew really needs the money, which he does now. You know what a setback like a blocked AVF means."

Of course I know. It means time is running out. It means his body isn't in prime condition for a move across the country. But that's not how she sees it.

Mam continues without a pause. "We need to be on the ground, in Wicklow, near Liam's property, his assets. If we put enough pressure on the wife, insist on the house, maybe she'll move out. Maybe she has family elsewhere and will put up the fight from afar. I don't know, she probably won't." Mam waves her hand almost impatiently. She mutters, as though trying to convince herself: "But we have to try. We can't let this drag on for years. Andrew needs attention now! I've just called Mary Kelly – you know she has that summer house in Wicklow?"

"The one by the sea?"

Mam's eyes are bright. "It's only about half an hour from the Murtagh family estate in Ballyloughlin. Mary said we can have it, rent free, for a few months."

"A few months! Wicklow is the other side of the country, Mam!"

She pays no attention to me. Her voice is alive with the enthusiasm of youth, like this is the quest she's been waiting for, the one that will save Andrew.

My voice starts out as barely a whisper, but before I know it I am on my feet, shouting. "You want us, including your terminally ill son, to move to some draughty, wooden summer house in Wicklow! At this time of the year?"

Mum nods curtly, her face like stone. "It's done. I've taken a leave of absence from work for three months. Unpaid, but I've been up for hours going through the finances and we've enough saved to get by. Anyway, money won't be an issue once this will is sorted."

"Andrew's new AVF won't be properly developed after the surgery for another few weeks. He's still on a temporary line, more prone to infection. Mam, you can't be serious about moving him!"

"There's a hospital near Ballyloughlin. St John's – it's a really good one. Dr Jim is going to arrange for Andrew's dialysis to take place from there. And it's only an hour from the centre of excellence at Beaumont in Dublin. Dr Jim vouched for one of the doctors in St John's, a Dr Stevens, in particular. I'm going to meet with him when we arrive. You should come too."

My head is spinning. I sit again, my words laboured. "Jack? School?"

"He'll be fine for a few months. Worst comes to worst, we'll enrol him in a local school."

I walk around to my mother and take her hand. "Mam, I'm angry. We all are. But we have to be reasonable. If the family fights this will, who knows how long it will take to resolve? Months? Years maybe? Are we supposed to just sit around Wicklow? We don't know anyone there, we've no support system. Andrew is used to the hospital in Galway. He likes Dr Jim and there is a real community in the dialysis unit – he has friends there. It's not fair to move him like this, especially when he's still on a temporary line and vulnerable." I try to keep my voice steady but it falters, high-pitched, at the end.

Mam ignores the panic. "We need to be there, Tors. You don't understand what it's like to be the mother of a family who has lost a father, a husband. Liam's wife will be grieving and she won't give in to this will. Polite solicitor's letters won't deter her – she will fight. We have to show her – really show her – that we're not going away. That we will win. For Andrew. It has to be this way. I'm still the head of this family. Andrew might be twenty, legally an adult, but I am his mother and he is coming with me."

She sits with a thud of finality back on her chair.

There have been many times, when I have been sad or lonely or curled shivering in bed with vivid memories of Paris keeping me from sleep, that I wished my dad was still with us. When Mam was panicked about Andrew's deterioration, he could soothe her. If money got tight, and she made unfeasible plans to work two jobs, he would talk her down. I remember sitting in my favourite mermaid pyjamas on the stairs, peeking through the banisters, watching him comfort her. Within minutes she was wiping the tears away and laughing tenderly at some awful joke. Dad would have known what to say to make Mam see the sheer stupidity of this Wicklow plan. But would he want to help, if he had known about her deception? Would he have walked out? Would he have taken me and Jack with him? What about Andrew?

My mind thuds with such circular and unanswerable questions. Eventually, I rise from the table and walk slowly, like a zombie, past Mam whose sudden boundless energy only deflates me further.

The rest of the day is a blur. I ring Roger Nestor from my bedroom and he insists he told Mam over the phone last night that there is nothing to be gained from relocating to Wicklow. He makes a shrewd observation. "Your mother sounded highly agitated on the phone. Almost manic. I can't see how your moving will solve anything. In fact, putting yourselves in such close proximity to the Murtaghs is likely only to exacerbate the situation. You are better off leaving it to the lawyers."

I nod frantically into the phone as Roger Nestor continues.

"But I have seen clients fall apart before and people do not always act rationally in these situations. My guess is that your mother must feel guilty about Andrew finding out about his real father in this way. She probably needs to do something, anything, no matter how counterproductive, to try to make amends."

I beg him to talk to Mam again but he seems reluctant to interfere beyond the calm advice he already gave to her last night. I want to scream at him. She doesn't need calm advice. She needs to be forced to listen. But I hang up the phone. It's not Roger Nestor's job to sort out Mam. As usual, there is no one but me.

So I tackle her again, with logic, pleas and threats. We argue, we cry. Mam explains it to Andrew – I refuse to do that – and she makes it sound like a road trip to Jack. We pack. We fight again. I can't get a word of sense from her. She contradicts herself, going round in circles vindicating herself for not seeking help from Liam Murtagh years ago, then insisting Andrew can't survive without his money now. She promises he can handle a move to Wicklow but a minute later is willing to curse the Murtaghs if they foist a legal challenge on his delicate state.

Eventually, I realise I have lost, at least for now. Hopefully she will see sense once we arrive in Wicklow and this will all have blown over in a few days. Resigned, I sit on the couch waiting for Peter, our mentor from the Family Support Network, to arrive with his van and drive us to Wicklow. Once we get the will sorted, Mam argues, we can buy our own wheelchair-accessible van, instead of the twelve-year-old jeep that just about accommodates the family. Andrew hasn't had to use a wheelchair in years, but the few times he did it resulted in uncomfortably squashed journeys in the jeep. I remember Dad complaining indignantly that all cars should be designed to fit a chair. I wonder how he'd feel about us using Liam Murtagh's money to buy a van.

Jack is acting the maggot again. He's Tarzan, Darth Vader, Superman . . . all at once. Running and jumping around the house, reaching into the depth of his suitcases looking for treasures. Suitcases I have just finished packing. I'd usually find it funny but, after yesterday, I wonder if I'll ever laugh again. Still, I don't want to yell at him. It will only be a matter of time before he realises this trip isn't going to be any fun. None of his little mates will be in Wicklow. I grab him around the waist and fling him upside down. He screams with glee and wriggles away from me, then runs upstairs to hide, finally out of my way.

As I flop back down on the couch, I glance through the open living-room door to see my mother sitting in the kitchen, close to Andrew, leaning in towards him desperately. Dad used to say that when I got thoughtful, I'd tilt my head to the left. I'm conscious that I'm doing it now. It's easy to spot a mother: she looks at her child with such longing, as though if only she could get him back into her womb, she could protect him.

A familiar, jaunty beep alerts me that Peter is here. I watch Mam leap up, almost excited.

"Jack!" I call, wondering how she is ever going to break the news to a hyperactive eight-year-old that he won't see Ethan, or play on his GAA team or sleep in his own bed for months to come. "Come on, the adventure starts here!"

Chapter 5

Seán

My sleep was erratic again last night. In the week since the funeral, my dreams have been punctured with caricature images of my boss Marx towering over me, laughing, while Michael's voice booms from all around that I would have been much better working for Roger Nestor. I come to in a sweat, relieved to be awake.

As I clamber out of bed, the sun is spreading over the horizon. I watch it for a while. It is remarkable that I could have forgotten how beautiful the view is from my bedroom window. Maybe I was just too young to appreciate it. Or maybe five years in a concrete city has provided just enough of a contrast to catch my attention. The massive oaks in the woodland across the road are still obscuring a proper sunrise when I hear Lizzy's bedroom door creak quietly and I know it is time to go downstairs.

I weave my way through the contents of my half-unpacked suitcase and the bits of stuff from my teenage years that Mum likes to keep lying around the room "so it feels like you're still here when I'm in doing a bit of cleaning". My old guitar, not played for years, lies crookedly against the massive CD rack that lines the wall. A pile of hurleys teeters in the corner by the door. I must have knocked them over at least three times since arriving home. What did a teenage boy need five hurleys for anyway?

I find Lizzy in the kitchen pouring us coffee. As always with my youngest sister, she is dressed according to necessity rather than fashion, and her mish-mash ensemble of light-pink tracksuit bottoms clashing with a red sleeveless puffa jacket over an orange long-sleeved T-shirt makes me smile inwardly. Without saying much in our sleepy stupors, we automatically make for the front door. I open it and we stand for a minute, blinking furiously against the pool of sun flooding in from the outside, as though it had been pressing up against the door for hours, just waiting for us to welcome it.

We move, stumbling, the gravel path crunching under our feet. That gritty noise, along with the fresh, morning air finally rouses me from my morning lethargy and we set off down the garden path around the side of our house. These early-morning walks have been a regular occurrence since Lizzy and I met at dawn the day after I arrived home, neither of us able to sleep.

"Your boss from work called again last night, Seán," Lizzy ventures after a while, her voice still croaky. She pulls back some wild brambles for me to pass, indicating the trail she wants us to take. Always the outdoors type, Lizzy knows our estate and the surrounding woods and fields better than anyone in Ballyloughlin.

"Thanks," I squeeze through the tight lane, made all the more narrow by the hanging branches, bare from some harsh winter months. Still, an elegant fineness seems to emanate from their spindly offshoots. "What did you tell him?"

"Just that you had gone to the graveyard."

I turn around, frowning, but Lizzy is smiling slyly. "Well, I thought they might feel less guilty about pressuring you to go back if they knew you were out boozing with Conn O'Shaughnessy!"

I can't help but grin. Last night, Mum and I called over to Mrs Boden, to find Conn O'Shaughnessy already there. After much reminiscing and squeezing of cheeks by Mrs Boden, Conn stood to leave and insisted I go back to the GAA club with him, where he had some old photographs of Dad and us kids from years back. We ended up staying in the clubhouse bar for a drink, just the two of us. I knew I should be working from home on my laptop but the chance to escape the house of memories was too strong. Not that it was a memory-free evening. Conn wanted to reminisce about my dad, "man to man" as he put it. Thankfully, he did most of the talking and I escaped after a couple of hours. Still, Marx would not have deemed it an acceptable excuse for abandoning the laptop and I am thankful for Lizzy's quick thinking.

We reach a high wall that leads into neighbouring farmlands. The smell of dew-covered primroses wafts over the wall, and I strain in vain to see the O'Haras' house, hidden out of sight over the hill. Just like when we were kids, I automatically put my hands out to boost my sister over the wall, and carefully manoeuvre my way over after her. I take the lead, setting off down another narrow lane with Lizzy closely in tow.

"Claire called for you too!"

Though she is behind me I can sense the cheeky grin spreading across her face and I laugh out loud, something I have barely done once since arriving home. Just the idea of talking about girlfriends and lovers with my baby sister is enough to set me off. I know I have to be careful though; I can almost see my mother's expectant face at the notion of my settling down, even if it is with an American. But I am a realist. With Claire, that could never happen. That is not what she wants. So I distract my sister.

"Quite the popular guy, I am. Anyone else call for me?"

"Just Michael. He said he would come by this afternoon. He wanted to talk to you about something."

I stop abruptly, and Lizzy walks right into me.

"Sorry," I mumble distractedly. "Did he say what about?"

"He didn't mention. Why?"

"Oh, no reason." I try to keep my voice even. "I just wonder whether he will take over any of Dad's clients."

"I guess so. Didn't they have some arrangement in case one of them died, that the other would take over his practice? But I suppose the clients would have to agree and it probably depends on what the will says. When is Michael going to go through Dad's will with us anyway?"

"Whenever he's ready." My tone is a little too aggressive and Lizzy notices.

"Seán, are you all right?"

"Of course. Sorry, Lizzy, I suppose I just don't want to think about all that stuff. Let's talk about something else. Tell me how Lilly is getting on."

Mercifully, she seizes on the opportunity to rave about her horse, Lilly, allowing me to mull in peace, with her expecting no more than occasional murmurs of agreement.

No one was surprised when Lizzy got a job at the largest equestrian centre in the country. She has the air in her soul, Mrs Boden likes to say. If she is not horse-riding or taking care of Lilly, she is helping Conn O'Shaughnessy plan fitness routines for the teenage players, or organising sports competitions for our mother's pupils at the local primary school. Dad initially wanted her to go to college or at least do some course or further study like the rest of us, but the chance of working with the best equestrians in the country, especially when the centre is so near Ballyloughlin, was too good an opportunity to pass up. He conceded to me shortly after she started there last year that it was the right decision for her. He used to ring me every week for a "man to man" chat, just like Conn O'Shaughnessy tried to have with me last night. I want to focus on those times with Dad, the good times, but my mind is consumed with the mystery of Roger Nestor. Michael better have an explanation this afternoon, I muse darkly.

Lizzy chats away animatedly, occasionally sobering her naturally jovial conversation by references to our dad, but I don't listen. I am now almost frantic to know if Michael has discovered anything about the note. I don't know what it could possibly be, but I try to believe that the tension and endless speculation running through my mind has to be worse than anything he could learn. I had tried to contact Michael a number of times over the few days since the funeral but he never answered the phone.

When Lizzy and I arrive back at the house, faces flushed from the exercise, Mum has cooked a fry for us and I make an effort to act casually as the three of us breakfast together.

I try to block out the conversation around me. Niamh and Lizzy are arguing about who gets custody of Mam's car for the day. It amazes me that none of the girls have their own cars though, of course, Niamh currently lives in Dublin and gets chaperoned everywhere by her live-in boyfriend.

"Niamh, why don't you just walk to the library – it will only take you half an hour," says Lizzy.

"With all my books!"

"Oh for God's sake! Fine, I'll drop you as far as the library, but I'm going to be working late in the stables so you'll have to find your own way home."

Niamh opens her mouth to retaliate and I slam down my fork. Both girls are so headstrong that I feel the beginnings of a dull pain throbbing at the back of my head, as tends to happen when they get into their stride.

"Where's Katie?" I interrupt pointedly just to shut them up.

"She spent the night at the O'Haras'," Mum responds, stroking my hair as she passes me while clearing off the dishes.

We lapse into silence as the girls storm off. They arrive back downstairs some time later, hauling two large bags of books each. I wave them off vaguely from the kitchen, ignoring Lizzy's moans about the weight of the bags and Niamh's sniping reply.

"Are you all right, Mum?" I venture tentatively as she plops down heavily onto the wooden chair opposite me.

She gives me a small smile. "It's best they keep busy these few days. We're all still feeling it. Are you working today, love?"

I nod as I swallow a prickly piece of toast. "Technically I only get three days leave, so I should be back in the office."

Mum's eyes bulge at this but I laugh off her obvious worry. "Don't stress, Mum, I'm not going anywhere soon. If I'm not there, they'll just have to deal with it. I'll do what I can on the laptop and they can sort out the rest. I'll let them take it out of my annual leave if needs be, or they can convert it to unpaid leave. Whatever." I shake off the concern; I don't really care at the moment.

"Are you sure you won't lose your job?"

Mum's concern sparks some in me. I start clearing my own plates to give my hands something to do. "No, they'd let me know if they were considering that and my boss, Marx, hasn't given me the impression that it would go that far. He'd prefer if I came back, but he's a decent guy and he'll cover for me where he can." I want to believe my own words – the alternative would mean returning straight away and that's not on the cards, at least not until the identity of Roger Nestor is determined. A brief Google search brought up a number of men with that name in Ireland, including a solicitor in Dublin and a dentist in Wexford. The solicitor is the most likely candidate, what with Dad and Michael both being lawyers, but I agreed to let Michael make contact first, as that was Dad's intention.

Mam is still harping on about America. Her questions are innocent but I am sure she is looking for reassurance that I won't be returning there soon.

"Do you not want to get back, Seán? To your friends, and to Claire, as well as work?"

My eyes snap up at this. Lizzy has clearly been gossiping about Claire, the fiend. The truth is I am somewhat eager to get back to America but I don't feel strong enough to leave Mum right now. I want my family around me, something I haven't needed for a long time.

I am spared the need to reply by a knock on the door. Mum throws her eyes up to heaven. "What are the odds Niamh has forgotten a book?"

I laugh – second time today – as she pulls her dressing gown tight around her to open the hall door.

Michael is standing there with a large beefy man who he introduces as Eddie Edwards, a solicitor.

I try not to snort dismissively at his ridiculous name.

Mum, embarrassed to be seen in her state of undress, greets them in a somewhat confused manner. She had not expected Michael until the afternoon. Ushering them into the sitting room, she hisses instructions at me to entertain while she dresses herself.

"Just give me a moment," she says to the men and hurries out.

Michael calls after her. "Take your time, Glenda. We're very early."

"My fault entirely," Michael's companion booms out. He lowers his voice as he shakes my hand. "Sudden meeting this afternoon. Couldn't get out of it." He speaks with his head bowed in towards me, conspiratorially.

I don't know quite how to respond so I settle for introducing myself. But before we can converse any further Michael dispatches me back to the kitchen to make coffee. He doesn't meet my eye and I notice that he looks pale. My stomach churns suddenly. Does this man have anything to do with Roger Nestor? I fumble about in the kitchen putting together a tray of tea, coffee and the fancy biscuits I remember my mother will only let us eat when visitors call.

Mum returns just as I re-enter the living room, and Michael purposefully moves up on the couch to let her sit beside him. I feel an odd mixture of apprehension and relief that the mystery is presumably about to be solved.

"Glenda," Michael takes her hand and looks at her very solemnly, "Eddie is a solicitor too, and an old friend of mine – we go back years."

Mum looks expectantly at the man, who doesn't look away. "Did you know my husband as well then, Mr Edwards?" It pains me to see her wide-eyed look of anticipation, as though any new story might be told, bringing him somehow alive again.

Our visitor smiles sadly, his loud voice echoing around the room. "No, Mrs Murtagh, I never met your husband, which is precisely, I think, the reason Michael asked me to meet you today. And you can call me Eddie."

"And I always go by my maiden name which is Wilson. But we might as well stay on first-name terms here. I'm Glenda," Mum pauses. "May I ask what this is about?"

"Oh Glenda!" Michael's voice cracks with emotion.

Every muscle in my body tenses in morbid expectation and Mum automatically reaches out her hand.

"Michael, what is it?"

We all wait anxiously as Michael composes himself. Then he begins speaking and, with his words, my world slips away.

"Glenda, as you know, I drafted Liam's will, years ago. Well, it turns out, Liam made another will some years afterwards and I never knew about it. He left me a note, telling me to contact a man called Roger Nestor who, it turns out, is a solicitor too, from Dublin. Liam left his most recent and valid will with him. I have been named executor of the will, which means that I am essentially the person who will be making sure it is administered as Liam wished. This is why I have brought Eddie to meet you."

"I don't understand." Mum's arm twitches nervously.

Eddie leans forward, his expression a mixture of pity and embarrassment. "Glenda, I have had a look at the will. You might want to challenge it. If so, Michael can't advise you. As executor, his loyalty has to be to Liam. His duty is to make sure the will is adhered to. So, if you want any legal advice, Michael trusts me and I would be happy to help. Of course, you might not want me, or any other solicitor. It's totally and completely up to you, and your children."

My pulse quickens as I wait for Mum to ask the inevitable question.

I shiver involuntarily. But she says nothing, continuing to look at Eddie in open astonishment. Feeling a sudden urge of protection, I move to stand behind the couch, putting my hands on my mother's shoulders. She does not seem surprised by, or even aware of the gesture. She stays silent, so I ask the question.

"Why would we want to challenge my father's will?"

Eddie opens his mouth to speak again, but then stops. He stands abruptly, his large physique filling the room oppressively. Pinching the bridge of his nose, he sighs loudly, pacing for a few steps before lowering himself back into the chair. Michael watches him with a stony face, Mum in wonder. When he speaks again, it is less soothing, and more professional.

"Apparently your husband and Roger Nestor met at a conference in the Law Society in Dublin in the late eighties. They hit it off and exchanged small pieces of work in the months after the conference. According to Roger Nestor, they did not see each other again until your husband showed up at his offices unexpectedly in January 1993.

"Now, at that stage, your daughter Kathleen was only a few months old. Your husband told Mr Nestor that he wanted to draft a will to supersede his current will and that when he eventually died it was likely that the beneficiary – that's the person who gains under the will – would need legal representation. He had a clause drafted into the will that, if the beneficiary agreed, Mr Nestor would be his legal adviser, and he left a sum of money for this purpose. He said he had arranged that Mr Nestor would be contacted on his death, at which stage Mr Nestor was to reveal the will and offer to represent the beneficiary. The contents were to be kept absolutely secret until his death."

He pauses dramatically, and takes a sip of water. No one else has touched the tea or coffee from the tray. The fancy biscuits lie forgotten.

I shake my head and try to focus. "Wait a second. If this Roger Nestor is to act for the beneficiary, why isn't he here?"

There is silence, and it is Michael who breaks it. "Because, Seán, your mother is not the main beneficiary, and neither are you kids."

Before I can respond, or even take this in, Eddie stands and paces again. "While you were pregnant with Kathleen –"

"Katie, we call her," Mum interrupts, with the air of someone trying to put off the inevitable.

Eddie acquiesces with a nod. "When you were expecting Katie," he continues, "your husband had a one-night stand with a young woman while on business in Galway."

There is silence. Except for a buzzing. A strange buzzing between my ears.

My mother's arm shudders violently and she gives a nervous laugh. "Eddie, with all due respect, there must be some mistake."

The solicitor is suddenly in a hurry, as if wanting to get this unfortunate business over with as soon as possible. "I assure you, Glenda, there is no mistake. The woman's name is Karen Shaw, and though your husband insisted to Mr Nestor they were only intimate once and that he sincerely regrets having ever been unfaithful to you, Karen Shaw bore his son. His name is Andrew, and he was born nearly three months after Kathl – Katie, on the first of November, 1992."

In a work crisis, this is the moment – the moment when all seems lost – that many of my colleagues crumble. I always try to stand strong. But at the stranger's words, I feel my knees tremble beneath me, and I lower myself onto the arm of the couch. Eddie continues without stopping, looking anywhere but at my mother, who is leaning far back into her chair, with a look of mingled shock and disbelief on her face.

"Karen Shaw, who was married at the time with a six-year-old child, made it clear to your husband that she needed nothing from him, and that he was to have nothing to do with the baby. When your husband came to Mr Nestor, he had seen Andrew only once, when he was just a few weeks old, and had made an oral agreement with Karen Shaw that he would have no more contact with the boy. Andrew was to be brought up by Karen Shaw and her husband Stuart who, as an aside, died three years ago. Your husband confided in Mr Nestor that he was racked with guilt that he could have no part in Andrew's life. His solution, and apparently Roger Nestor tried to talk him out of it, was to provide for him in death."

Michael stands, and takes my place behind Mum, hands on her shoulders, as Eddie continues.

"His will provides that his entire family estate, including any real and personal property, is to be left to, in his exact words 'my natural son Andrew Shaw'. He also leaves a trust fund for you, Glenda, with the equivalent of fifty thousand euro, and a separate fund to be administered by Glenda, with the monies to be used at her absolute discretion for the benefit of Seán, Niamh, Kathl – Katie, and any other children Glenda would subsequently bear by him, which of course now includes Elizabeth."

He stops speaking, almost gratefully.

"Lizzy," whispers Mum. "We call Kathleen 'Katie' and Elizabeth 'Lizzy'."

Michael, who has been gripping Mum's shoulders with unintended vigour, appears jolted back to reality at the sound of her voice. He comes around the couch to kneel beside her and takes her hand tightly in his own.

"Glenda, none of this matters." He looks anxiously at his friend. "Tell her, Eddie. There is legislation – the Succession Act. You won't lose everything – you have the legal right to a share."

Before I can demand further explanation, Eddie cuts in. "Michael is right, Glenda. Under Section 111 of the Succession Act 1965 you, as Liam's wife, will automatically gain one third of his assets, no matter what his will provides. Roger Nestor told Michael he all but throttled your husband trying to make him understand that because he was married, leaving everything to the boy wouldn't work. To be frank, Liam should have known that anyway, as a lawyer. But he was adamant. He insisted that the will was to be drafted that way."

Mum is out of her seat suddenly. A memory flashes in front of me at her action. I was ten. I pushed Niamh over and she fell on top of

Lizzy. They both screamed and Mum stood up with such conviction that I knew I was about to feel her full wrath. I have a strange urge to bury my face in the cushion beside me now, as I did back then.

"You!" Mum speaks quietly, yet with unparalleled force, to Eddie, who looks suddenly small. "You come into my home and tell me my husband cheated on me, had another child, lied to me about it, and now, after bearing his children, raising them and looking after him for nearly *thirty years*, he is throwing me out of the house he promised me was my home, and leaving me *nothing*?"

Michael tries to take her hand again but she shakes him away. Undeterred he moves in front of her and speaks urgently. "No, Glenda, didn't you hear what we said? Liam left a trust fund for you but, as his wife, you are in any case entitled to one third of this estate. While the boy will get something, I'm sure you won't lose the house."

Though not fully understanding, my breathing eases somewhat at Michael's tone. But my mother pulls away from him and walks to the door. She stops, turns and looks directly at Eddie. Nothing could have prepared me for the words she utters.

"My husband knew what he was doing, sir. There is a reason I always use my 'maiden' name. We are not married. We have lived together as man and wife for twenty-nine years, but we never had a ceremony, we never got a certificate or marriage licence. Tell me now, what am I entitled to under this Succession Act?"

Eddie's bushy eyebrows fly up into his sandy fringe but he answers immediately. "Nothing. I'm sorry, Glenda, you are entitled to nothing." He looks at Michael for any possible solution but Michael just gapes at Mum, and does not contradict him.

"I'm sorry, Seán," she whispers without looking at me.

I watch in disbelief as she runs from the room, leaving me with another loss, another crack in the family I thought I knew.

Chapter 6

Seán

As the Murtagh women sob in the living room, I get into the car without thinking about the destination – without really thinking at all – and speed three miles until I reach the local GAA club. The gate to the car park is closed so I pull in to the side of the road and bundle myself out of the car, practically gasping for air. Leaning against the bonnet, staring into the dark, reminds me of the teenage nights when Kevin and I, with a few other lads, would sneak into the grounds and sit in the centre of the pitch, downing cheap cans of beer. We had felt like such rebels.

Automatically, I find myself walking about fifty paces to the left of the gate and to my amazement discover the same strip of fence that had been ripped apart when I was a kid still torn, though now covered by a wild growing bush. Pulling the greenery away from the fence violently, I squeeze through the hole, tearing my jeans in the process, and walk around to the pitch. It is weathered, I observe, brown and dry. I make my way out to the centre of the field and sit down, staring up at the north goals.

More clearly than in years, my father's voice chimes loud in my head. "C'mon, Seány lad, get it over! Yes . . . *yes*! My son, Seán Murtagh, scores the winning point for Wicklow!"

A childish laugh of delight escapes my lips, as though Dad is really lifting me above his head again, just the two of us, practising after dark. Then just as abruptly, silence descends once more and the sound of my father's voice is just a memory ringing in my ears, fading further with every second. Only the blackness of the night remains, with no answers.

I feel the blood pulsating through my veins, rushing to my brain, as question after question spits from my mouth. "Why did you *do* this?" I grip my hair in my fists. It hurts.

I don't know how Dad could leave this boy – Andrew – without a father during his life and his acknowledged family without support when he died. There was no justification for him leaving everything to the other son. He could have left him something, a token. But to expect Mum to give up the house, to cast me and the girls from our childhood home, is nothing short of cruel. He must have known this day would come, that the truth would emerge. I picture him, driving away from Roger Nestor's office and slipping that secret note to Michael. He surely realised the hardship it would cause everyone, yet he chose that the secret would be revealed only when he was dead and would not have to deal with the consequences.

"*Coward!*" I scream into the night.

Curling my knees into my chest, I bury my head deep into my hands, as my accusation reverberates throughout the stadium. Was this the reason he kept his money in a form that was easily accessible? In case this Karen Shaw woman backed out of their oral agreement and demanded support from him? Was it so he could quickly put the money out of reach of the other son, or so he could get his hands on it immediately to give to him? Neither answer would make me feel better. Not that I could ever get an answer, to that or any of my hundred other questions.

At the funeral, people said I was so lucky to have enjoyed a good relationship with my dad. Kevin O'Hara Senior was a decent man, but was always working so his boys never really got to know him. Some of my school friends had stories of being beaten, ignored or bullied. But Dad was always there for me, from supporting at the sidelines of football matches to teaching me how to shave, the way every boy should learn.

There are so many questions I crave to ask him, but none more than whether, if my mother had been Karen Shaw rather than Glenda Wilson, would he have stayed away from me too?

Now I will never – can never – find out. Because he orchestrated it that way. He chose to leave me in this darkness for the rest of my life. He never prepared me to handle this kind of a situation.

On top of all the other emotions, a sense of misuse swaddles me. He might have betrayed us all but I am the one who will be expected to look after my mother and the girls. Fill my father's shoes. How could he leave me alone with this?

The blame comes easily as I drag my exhausted body from the pitch. As I cross the kicker's line, the memory of the two of us practising echoes once more in my head.

I spit on the ground and walk from the pitch, without looking back.

Chapter 7

Tors

I keep an eye on Jack in the rear-view mirror while racing to keep up with Mam and Andrew's car as they zoom through a quaint village somewhere in the midlands. Mam would never be driving this fast if she wasn't trying to keep up with Peter, who speeds like a maniac. Jack has been playing with his Lego in the back seat, but more slowly and with less energy than usual. Now his small face is screwed up in concentration and I smile sadly. I can almost see the cogs whirring in his brain, trying to make sense of our earlier conversation.

"So, do you understand, Jack?"

He had been listening hard. His Lego castle, which resembled more of a disused shack the way he had built it, lay forgotten on the back seat.

"Two daddies!" he repeated in amazement. He scratched his ear absentmindedly, exactly the same way Dad used to, trying to rationalise this phenomenon. "Because Andrew's special," he reasoned eventually.

58

That's right, I thought. Not sick, just special. I explained about Andrew inheriting the house and who knows what else – according to Roger Nestor, Andrew's biological father was a wealthy man – but Jack didn't really understand, and tried to bring the whole scenario back to his level.

"Who would get my stuff if I went to heaven?"

I grinned in spite of myself. "You mean your Lego and your CD player? Well, who would you like to get them?"

He thought about that one seriously. "My best friend Ethan."

"Ethan! What about me, or Mam, or Andrew?"

"You don't like Lego. And Andrew already has a CD player."

I had to laugh at his logic.

He has been quiet now for a while and sure enough more questions soon come pouring out. Will he have to support Wicklow in the football instead of Kerry now? Will the house by the sea be bigger than our house? Is Peter going to drive him over and back to Kerry for school every day?

The last one presents a real problem. Home schooling seems to be Mam's plan for the immediate future. Enrolling him in a local school will only be considered "down the line", whatever that means. But I am not sure how home schooling will work. Mam is qualified, having taught Andrew at home for a while during some of his worst years. But this is different. There's a lack of routine and Andrew and I will be around, distracting Jack. Well, I think bitterly, that's Mam's problem – she can sort it out.

* * *

We arrive at the sea house within a few hours. Jack has tired himself out thinking and is flopped over his safety belt in the back seat. When I pull up to the bungalow, I realise it is, quite literally, on the beach front. As I step out of the car, my face scrunches up against the pungent smell of salt on the air, but the wind is not cold. In fact, it is surprisingly refreshing. I stand for a few minutes in the dark, listening to the small waves crash on the shore, each one seeming nearer, as though they are creeping towards me, one by one.

The two lads are already doing most of the heavy lifting. As I carry a sleeping Jack past them in the dark, I call to Peter not to let Andrew strain himself. Mam is standing in the open-plan space, which encompasses both kitchen and living room, with her hands on her hips, surveying the house.

"Oh Tors, good," she whispers as I ease my way in the door. "Follow me – you can put him in this room."

The second door to the left down a narrow corridor opens to a wide, square room with two single beds.

"Jack and I can stay in here. I'm giving Andrew the main room with the en suite – you know, in case he needs to throw up. That leaves you with the smallest room, Tors, but it's right next door to Andrew so you'll be near him if he needs you."

I nod. It is the best arrangement of the three bedrooms, though Jack will not be happy about sharing with Mam. Our semi-detached house in Kerry might be pokey and narrow, but at least there are four small bedrooms.

While she goes out to help Peter and Andrew bring in the rest of our belongings, I change Jack into his pyjamas. He doesn't wake. I sit looking down at his face, totally relaxed in sleep, until I hear Peter's car pull away from the house. I leave the room before Mam can come back in.

"Andrew?" I poke my head around his door. "Do you want me to sleep in here with you tonight?"

His expression is unfathomable as he shakes his head. I notice that he has sourced a duvet from somewhere, and is curled under it like a child. A part of me wants to make him talk about it, to cry, to swear. But I have been his carer, and his sister, long enough to know that forcing him into confidence will only diminish him further. A sense of control is the best incentive for him to keep fighting.

His whole sense of identity has been shaped by this illness. He was always a sickly child, in and out of hospital. But it was only in his late teens, when his kidneys started shutting down, that it became his life. If he wants to be alone, I will not impose my company on him.

My own room is definitely the reject of the sea house, even smaller than my bedroom in Kerry. The double bed squeezes into the corner, barely allowing space for the doors of the cupboards to swing open. The bed creaks when I stand on it to scan the highest shelves and sure enough I find a stack of bed linen. The covers are cold with the damp and I flick a few dead moths off the pillow cases before making up the bed. The staleness of the air is to be expected, a result of the place being abandoned since the summer, but it is depressing. I force open the window above the headboard, scraping off the moss festering on the sill. Breathing in the briny air, I find myself alone with my thoughts at last.

I close my eyes, listening to the comforting rhythm of the waves lapping against the shore and hugging my knees close to my chest. I don't like moving to new places. Since coming home from France, I have been perfectly content living back at home with my family. Sighing, I reach over and thrust my arm deep into my suitcase to pull out my day planner when my hand falls on three photos, still in their frames. In our rush to pack, I grabbed them from my dresser and flung them into the suitcase without much thought. I place them now on the windowsill and stare at each one in turn.

The first is of me and Dad, just a year before he died. We had been walking up the mountains when we asked a man with a four-year-old girl to take our picture. The child was grumpy and clearly unimpressed at the delay. As the man took our photo, she pushed him from behind with all her might, trying to get him to move along. Her little body had no effect on the man, who took the photo without even realising she was trying to shift him. It was such a comical moment, and the camera captured our laughing faces perfectly.

The next is an older, more faded image of the five of us in the hospital just after Mam gave birth to Jack.

The final photo is of my best friend Debbie, holding her little sister. I think about the other close friends I have had over the years. I do not keep in touch with many of them now. Even those I see regularly in Kerry are really just casual acquaintances.

I hesitate before pulling out my day planner and sliding my smallest finger deep into the lining. Eventually, the tip of my finger brushes what I am searching for and eases out a small, dog-eared photo. I know I should have got rid of it. I have certainly thrown out every other reminder of him.

Claude.

But, in my weakness, I kept this one photograph of the two of us at a ball in Paris. His full black hair is slicked back and he stands with his arm around my shoulders as I beam up at him. He told me that night that my dress was beautiful, but nothing compared to the sparkle of my eyes.

Looking at the door guiltily – Andrew would be furious if he thought I was reminiscing about Paris with any sort of pleasure – I close my eyes and cast my mind back to my initial hesitation about Paris and how quickly I became captivated by the city, and by Claude.

I had been shocked when I got the offer of a job in Paris, because I had not applied for it.

"What do you mean, you applied on my behalf?" I was furious at Mam for interfering and also because I could not believe she would want me to leave. Dad was barely dead one year.

"Of course I don't want you to go, Tors," she said slowly, as though explaining the logic of two plus two equals four to a tantrum-throwing child. "But you've been floating around Ireland for the past year, not holding down a job for more than a few weeks at a time, and coming back here as often as you can."

"What's wrong with that? You're my family, I want to see you. And you need help with Andrew."

"The new carer is moving in next week. She was recommended to us."

"The last two were recommended as well," I muttered bitterly.

"Tors," Andrew interrupted then, in his usual straight-talking way. "You've been taking French classes since college. Why not go to France?"

I knew they were right, of course. Though nursing was my profession, French was my passion. After my final year in college, I spent months travelling around the south for France, working typical student jobs in pubs and restaurants, just to practise the language. I got quite good, almost fluent. But, with Andrew deteriorating and then cancer hitting Dad hard, I ended up coming back to Ireland and working any short-term nursing jobs I could find in Ireland – locum work, covering maternity leave. They were generally well paid, and I felt justified in spending long periods at home between jobs. I didn't begrudge it. Andrew was always sick and Jack was a colicky baby and clingy toddler. My parents were glad of my help.

When Dad died, I didn't want to be anywhere else. I didn't care about a career – I just wanted to be with my family, especially as Andrew was only getting worse. My friends thought I was mental. Even Debbie, whose sister had been ill as a baby, could not understand why I didn't want to get out of there. "You need to live your own life, Tors." I remember the worry in her eyes that I would regret my decision to stay.

Paris was my chance. It was a private hospital for the higher echelons of Parisian society, the kind of hospital we used to rail against in college for its snobbery. I certainly used ideals as an argument against going. Proper healthcare is a universal right – it should not belong to a privileged few. I thought Mam would have agreed, given our personal experience of struggling to afford decent treatment for Andrew and Dad. But she hurled back the counterarguments. Rich people are human too – they need support and care like the rest of us. It would be fantastic for improving my French.

But none of her reasoning convinced me because it did not address my real concern about going. I was terrified something would happen to Andrew and I wouldn't get home in time. He told me to get over it, but that didn't motivate me. Mam said Dad would have wanted it, but that didn't help either. No one understood. In the end, it was little Jack drawing a picture of me underneath the Eiffel Tower holding a stick of French bread the size of the tower itself that turned the conversation from an argument into a comedy, and slowly the idea grew on me.

We compromised. One year, and they would never keep anything bad that happened to Andrew secret from me. If I sensed they were hiding something, I would be on the first plane back. I remember Andrew throwing his eyes up to heaven, saying I was the only girl he knew who felt she had to take on a father's role in the house. So I went, on that wonderful and awful year.

I close my eyes and allow my mind to drift back to the good times with Claude, before it all went horribly wrong . . .

Before I realise it, it is the next morning and Jack's screeches from the room across the hall are jolting me into consciousness. "I want my own room!"

Though cursing the paper-thin walls, a horrible part of me cheers on Jack for giving Mam grief. She deserves it. I hear Andrew mooching around next door, and quietly slip out of my room and into his, ignoring Jack and Mam hollering at each other. He is sitting dejectedly on the edge of the bed, fully dressed and staring at his shoes. I drop down beside him, ejecting a puff of dust from the duvet, and sling my arm around his shoulder. He does not shrug it off.

We sit for a few minutes before he speaks to me for the first time since leaving Kerry. "Whenever I got scared about dying, I always thought: Dad's dead too. Whatever it's like, he'll be there. But does he know now? That I'm not his? Will he want to see me?"

I try to keep it light. "He's probably up there now having an auld scrap with this Liam Murtagh!"

Andrew does not respond. Instead he just lies back on the bed and stares at the ceiling. I start to get worried. Andrew knows the reality of his situation. But he makes a conscious effort not to become despondent. Aside from knowing that all the research points to a positive mind-set aiding recovery, he finds people treat him more normally when he is not wallowing in self-pity. I expect him to be upset – God knows I am – but I can't let him spiral into depression. I snap into my carer role without missing a beat.

"Andrew . . ." I lie back beside him and we look at each other. "Dad loved you. And obviously this Liam Murtagh loved you too, even if he couldn't show it while he was alive. You've got to work hard to adjust to this situation."

He nods, closing his eyes. I lift his feet onto the bed and throw the musty duvet over him and, making a mental note to open the window the second he's gone from it, leave the room to find Mam and Jack unpacking the box of food Peter has been sensible enough to leave for us.

"Breakfast time, baby!" Jack says, imitating our mother.

I wink at him. Ruffling his hair, I ease myself onto one of the high stools beside him and look around. The bungalow is small, but the open-plan living area saves it from feeling claustrophobic. Mam has opened the doors and window wide and is poking around under the sink for cleaning products.

"Andrew will be freezing in here," I moan, thinking he won't be the only one.

"There's nothing wrong with this place that a good airing won't fix," Mam says firmly. "See, the windows are double-glazed and the electric fire will keep us going."

I know she's right so I don't reply, strolling instead over to the windows to take in the view by daylight. It's quite picturesque. The morning sun floods in through the wall of windows at the front of the house, reflecting off the white, squishy couches in the living part of the room. But with a further step I feel the wooden tiles bubble up under my feet; trapped air from a sloppy build pressuring the floor upwards.

I move instead to the kitchen, tasting dust, and as I brush my hand over the high, wooden countertop, sticky cobwebs mesh into my palm. I scrap them off, my temper flaring. It might look pretty, but this draughty sea house is no place for a dialysis patient.

Now that she has distracted Jack from the room-sharing conundrum, Mam is in flying form. I watch her potter around, humming while she opens presses and wipes down the sink. I speculate as to whether she told Mary Kelly the reason why we need to take over her sea house.

Jack is still rummaging through the bag of food looking for Coco Pops but finding only porridge. Food-shopping is top of the to-do list for today, I think, extracting three large oranges from the bag. I crinkle my nose in disgust at their sickly sweet aroma and throw them at Jack who starts chasing me around the room with them. I squeal playfully, dodging his attacks and eventually distract him by picking up the food bag, pretending to find something delicious. Jack shoves me out of the way, digging deep for a tasty treat, without success.

As much out of sympathy for him as to give Mam and Andrew a bit of space, I turn to him. "Tell you what, buddy? If you get everything unpacked today, what do you say you and I go get a drink of Coke in one of the bars after dinner?"

Leaping with excitement, he dashes off to empty the entire contents of his suitcase onto the floor.

Alone at the kitchen counter, Mam and I smile, or grimace, uneasily at each other.

"You're going to take him to a bar? To give me and Andrew a bit of time?"

She looks so worried at my reaction that I almost feel sorry for her. Almost.

"Yeah, I think it's important that Andrew stays positive during this. Depression is more likely to cause a relapse than the physical move. So talk to him. But don't say anything that will cause a spike in his temperature. I won't be here to read the signs." As I slip off the chair,

I catch her looking at me in a motherly way.

"I'm meeting the solicitor tomorrow," she calls after me, but I keep walking.

Popping my head in Andrew's door I am relieved to see him asleep. I throw myself down on my new bed and stare at the bumpy, whitewashed ceiling, my day planner beside me.

We don't have to bring Andrew to the new hospital for dialysis until tomorrow, but I might drive by and see what it's like. My strongest argument against the immediate move to Wicklow was the extra strain it would put on Andrew's dialysis timetable. Especially since he is still recovering from surgery and using his temporary line, which is more likely to become infected than a mature and functioning AVF. But Mam had an answer for every concern. St John's Hospital is resourced for dialysis and is only a ten-minute drive from the sea house, unlike the hour and a half journey from Kerry to Galway. Dr Jim's recommendation was enough for Mam but I insisted on speaking to the new guy – Dr Stevens – on the phone before we left Kerry. He seemed approachable and will take Andrew for his first dialysis tomorrow. It's a day later than he was scheduled in Galway but that's still only three days since his last dialysis, certainly doable in a crisis. Dr Stevens said if there are any problems to bring him in straight away.

Unable, or unwilling to believe we would be staying in Wicklow for long, I didn't pack a large suitcase and it does not take me long to sort most of what I brought. When Andrew wakes up, I tell him that I'm going to pick him up some T-shirts and trousers when I head into the town to do some grocery-shopping later, since we never went clothes-shopping after all on Saturday.

"Do you want to come with me for the spin?" I know he ought to be resting after the physical journey and emotional whirlwind that he has been through over the past forty-eight hours, but I think he could use a distraction.

However, he refuses, saying he just wants to sleep some more. I don't believe him.

"Truth pact," I say pointedly, crossing my arms and leaning against the door frame. "This isn't just your way of avoiding clothes-shopping, is it?"

He smiles sadly. Andrew and I tell each other everything, no matter how embarrassing or even inappropriate for brothers and sisters. It's the only way we can stay on an even footing, and it makes me less his carer and more his friend.

"This is a small town, Tors," he says quietly. "Everyone will know who I am, what I am here to do. I don't want them looking at me."

I sigh. Now is not the time to force him into the open so I turn around to leave him where he is. Then he blurts out my name to call me back, visibly agitated.

"Tors, I don't want to do this. Mam cheated on Dad with this man. I don't want anything from him. I mean, if it was the other way around, if Dad had left everything to some sprog he produced from a one-night stand, instead of to Mam and us, I'd hate that other guy. Those people must hate me."

Tears spring to my eyes. I don't know whether I'm getting increasingly empathetic as I get older, or if I'm just more in tune with Andrew's feelings because we spend every waking moment together, but I physically ache at his pain.

I try to keep my voice level. "You didn't ask for Liam Murtagh to leave you everything. It's not your fault."

"Of course it is. If I hadn't been born, none of this would have happened. I have to tell them I don't want this." His eyes focus on me now. "They have to know. Please, Tors, I can't bear to be that kind of person."

I touch his arm gently. He can't go running off to the Murtaghs. Mam will be just behind, contradicting everything he says. I convince him to stay put for the moment and I try to conjure up ways of putting his mind at ease while I drive around the town, getting my bearings. The GAA club is not far from the centre of the town, which is surprisingly busy for a Monday. I pass a primary school with screaming children running around on their lunch break, and a secondary school. There is a massive library and a mere fifteen-minute drive from the centre of town brings me to the outskirts, with rolling green fields and luxurious houses. I wonder if one of them is the Murtaghs'. Close to the GAA club, I see a homey-looking pub and decide it will do as a place to bring Jack later.

* * *

The inside of Keogh's is pleasant and there is a decent crowd. Jack got so excited when I told him we could have dinner here as well as a Coke. We settle into a small booth and I tease him as he tucks into his sausages and chips like a total savage. After a short while, I notice something odd. A man is staring at me.

At first I find it irritating, then I begin to panic a bit. But that's ridiculous. He doesn't look like a murdering psycho. Quite the opposite, in fact. He is tall and broad, with a strong jaw and neatly cut dark hair. If I had found a man as handsome as this staring at me before I went to France, I would have been flattered and intrigued. It must just be the events of the past two days making me nervous. Still, there's something in the way he's looking at me that's strange. He's not trying to catch my eye, or make a move, yet I can feel his gaze wandering in our direction repeatedly. I urge Jack to eat up. Even though the sea house is in the middle of nowhere, I know I will feel safer once I'm there.

As Jack slurps back the last of his drink, I sense movement from the man's direction. I chance a glance at him as he makes for the door. He doesn't look away, but I do, quickly.

I ignore Jack's ramblings on the journey back to the sea house, my mind still full of the strange encounter.

Chapter 8

Seán

The sun has risen fully over the rolling hills beyond the O'Haras' land, drenching the fields in its warm, hopeful glow of a new day. Stopping to soak up the rays only for a moment, I decide against the route I normally take with Lizzy and start down a different, less overgrown lane leading away from the house. I am used to having my little sister for company on these early-morning strolls but this morning I am glad she is too tired to join me. For once, I want to be alone with my thoughts and the memory of two nights ago.

I had not been in the mood to go to the pub, especially since Michael Undersky hinted he might call over. But Kevin insisted and Mum nagged until it was easier to just go. As soon as we got to Keogh's, I was glad I had made the effort. I always feel better having chats with Kevin. Having learned all about the will from Pat – there are no secrets between the Murtaghs and the O'Haras – he acted like it was his mission to distract me. He poked and prodded for information about Claire, although he had already heard it all. He knows my friends from his visit to New York and eagerly discussed them, and it wasn't long before I felt the weight lift off my shoulders.

"Hey, Seán," he whispered after a while, "who are they?" He nodded his head at the bar, where a young woman in her mid-twenties was ordering, with a boy of about ten years old clinging onto her and trying to get her attention.

I shrugged in response. Kevin returned to his pint, but I continued staring at the woman. For some unfathomable reason, she reminded me of Claire. Yet she was so unlike Claire in every way: she was short and scrawny whereas Claire is elegantly tall, her dirty blonde hair fell messily past her shoulders while Claire's shiny black locks are always perfectly combed, and her long coat hung unflatteringly off her shoulders, unlike Claire's always-pressed outfits. It was as if I knew her from somewhere, but I was certain I had never seen her before.

I could tell that Kevin was not impressed enough to take heed of her, other than to comment on the fact that she was a stranger. My eyes kept darting to the table where she sat engaging the boy in conversation. As I reluctantly followed Kevin out of Keogh's a little while later to go meet the triplets in town, I threw her a fleeting glance. She caught my eye briefly, but looked down again so quickly I wondered if I had imagined it. To my own utter incomprehension, I wondered about it all night and all day yesterday.

Striding around a bend in the trail, I am still mulling over the incident when I collide with another sister. After initial jolts of surprise and apologies for barrelling into each other, we smile self-consciously, unsure of what to say.

Katie is the one person in our family who I have not talked to properly since arriving home. She keeps to herself so much that I haven't felt the need to engage with her. Although I started out the walk content to be on my own, I am suddenly overcome with an urge for company. I sigh inwardly. Since arriving home, I have been switching almost hourly between wanting to be with others and craving solitude.

71

Without discussing it, we walk on together, and I cast a sneaky sideways glance at Katie. She is staring at the ground as we walk – nothing new there – but I notice things I hadn't before, like the deep purple of the bags under her eyes and the drawn tint to her usually pale skin. Tall and athletic by nature, her shoulders are crouched over, as though she is trying to protect herself from something.

These observations are not the result of brotherly concern alone. A couple of nights ago, Mum pointed out her worries to me. Katie had been particularly close to Dad – he was one of the few people with whom she would open up. Since his death, she has become very withdrawn, even more so than usual. The O'Hara triplets, who are great friends with Katie, called to see Mum a few days after the funeral to say they were concerned that she was not handling it well. I shrugged off Mum's comments at the time, feeling like I had enough on my plate. But now I do appreciate the vulnerability Katie exudes.

Slightly irritated at having to take on the big-brother role once more, I decide to be direct. "How're you doing, Katie?"

She casts me a sharp look and keeps her silence for a moment before answering in a way that appears to be an attempt to distract me. "I'm fine, Seán. It's just so weird about Mum and Dad not being married, isn't it?"

I draw in a long breath as I nod in agreement. To me, and Katie too apparently, that particular revelation has been the oddest so far. Telling the girls had not been a pleasant conversation.

Niamh and Lizzy did most of the interrogating – Niamh brashly, as though Mum had set out to intentionally offend her second-born by not marrying Dad. Lizzy sniffed and gulped her way through, not wanting to upset Mum but not being able to control herself either.

It turns out there was a simple reason why my parents never officially tied the knot. Mum was married already. "To a man my parents chose when I was eighteen because his father was rich," she explained. "Things were all right for about a year, until his father was indicted for tax fraud, and George took to the drink even worse than he had before we were married. It made him violent. I wanted out but that was not how it was done in those days. My parents and even my friends didn't want to know. When you married someone, it was for life. Your father saved me from it. We met when he saw me crying alone at a bus stop and he approached me. It wasn't long before I realised he was the man of my dreams, not George. But we couldn't stay in England so we came to Ireland, telling them all we eloped to Scotland."

"You always said it was so romantic," Lizzy interrupted, looking devastated.

To our surprise, Mum laughed. "Well, so it was. We really did go on a holiday to Scotland in case anyone had any suspicions. My own parents disowned me and I was happy to move to Ballyloughlin. It took me years to win over your Granny Murtagh though. She was beside herself at having missed the ceremony. Your dad's brother died years ago without marrying, as you know, so she never got to plan a wedding."

"Did you ever see your parents again?" Lizzy asked.

"No." Mum's voice trembled then. "They died years ago and left everything to some distant cousin. As for George, he died of a drug overdose just after Seán was born. Seemingly the drink wasn't enough for him any more. Your father and I thought about making it official then, but there seemed no point. Everyone in Ballyloughlin thought we were already married. It didn't make any difference to our day-to-day lives. We were careful not to do anything that would have demanded legal proof that we were married. We used separate bank accounts and I kept my maiden name on the grounds of feminism. The house was never transferred into both our names, though when your grandfather left it to Liam, Michael suggested it many times. I guess the only way it would have made a difference would have been if we had separated. Unmarried fathers' rights aren't absolute, and back when you kids were small they had even less. But that wasn't an issue for us. We loved each other. We felt as though we were married and what difference would that piece of paper have made?"

"Well, apparently, it would have made all the difference in the world, Mother!" Niamh snapped.

The conversation got quite heated from there on, but neither Katie nor I made much of a contribution either way.

It is clear from the haunted look in Katie's eyes as we rounded the garden back to the house that the news has affected her significantly. I have an urge to confide my inner musings to her – like whether part of the reason Dad kept the other son a secret was because he was afraid Mum would take us away from him. But something stops me – a deep-seated sense that Katie, above the others, needs to be protected. I try to sneak another glance at her, wondering if she is really so fragile. She surprised us all by being the first to return to work at her job in the local library. Apparently encouraged by this, Lizzy also returned to work at the equestrian centre. It is odd to me that while Lizzy and Katie never fight, they don't appear to be close either. It is almost as though they live two separate lives, never realising that as the only sisters still living at home, a friendship could be forged.

I am daydreaming about this when we reach the hall door, and before I can decide whether or not to engage Katie in further, perhaps deeper, conversation, we hear gentle sobs coming from the kitchen. I catch Katie's eye, recognising the same look of pity mixed with resignation I have come to feel whenever one of the girls breaks down.

Tempted though I am to ignore the sound, I do not get the chance to sneak away. The kitchen door is flung open and Lizzy storms out, her dressing gown askew and her hair even more tousled than normal.

"Lizzy," I grab her arm as she tries to push past us up the stairs, "what is it?"

"Ask your other sister," she growls, glaring back at the kitchen before wrenching her arm out of my grip and marching dramatically on.

Tentatively, we walk into the kitchen to find Mum crying gently with her head in her hands. Katie immediately goes to her and strokes her back.

"Mum?" I ask from my place on the threshold, and she looks up.

74

"Are you all right?"

Suddenly, from the corner, Niamh emerges. I hadn't noticed she was there and from the way Katie's head snaps up, it is clear she hadn't registered our oldest sister either.

"Mum's upset because I'm going back to Dublin this afternoon. Mark is coming to collect me at four o'clock."

Stunned, I can only stare at her and I notice Katie's mouth drop open in surprise. Taking a few deep breaths to calm myself, I motion for Niamh to follow me. I expect a fight, but she obeys. Ushering her inside the living room, I shut the door forcefully.

"What the hell, Niamh?"

"Don't you give me a hard time as well, Seán. Katie and Lizzy have been back in work for days. I need to get back too. My PhD won't write itself, you know."

Flabbergasted, I run my hands through my hair and take a step towards her. "Niamh," I say, hearing in my own tone the falseness of the attempted placation, "the girls both live in the house. It isn't a big deal for them to go back to work. But for you or me, it would mean leaving Ballyloughlin. In the middle of all this?"

"Seán, be realistic. Dad's will isn't going to be sorted in a day. There won't be a resolution for months at the earliest. That's what Michael said anyway. I can't put my work off that long. And I don't believe you can either." She looks at me craftily.

"No, of course not. But Niamh, Dad hasn't even been buried a week. We still have to decide if we are contesting the will. For God's sake, Eddie Edwards is coming over tonight to discuss it – the least you could do is be here." She doesn't reply and I push on, hoping to persuade her. "And we haven't heard anything from Dad's other child yet, but we're bound to soon. We need to stick together, at least until things are a little more secure and Mum is ready for us to go, which she clearly isn't."

"I don't see what I can do for her here, Seán. Anyway, you're here to look after her."

"That's so unfair!" I spit out the childish words bitterly. Then I pause. "Is Mark pressuring you to get back to Dublin?" Part of me knows this is a cop-out – it would be so much easier to blame the outsider. But I know before she answers that if anyone is selfish enough to do this without encouragement, it's Niamh.

"This isn't about Mark, Seán, it's about me."

My temper, always so close to the surface these days, flares. "Why am I not fucking surprised, Niamh?"

I turn from her and pound up the stairs, two at a time. Niamh is, and always has been, that type of person who knows she is self-centred without perceiving it to be in any way wrong. Her loyalties lie in her own development and ambitions, and she views any suggestion that she alter her priorities as a direct attack on her lifestyle.

For Mum's sake only, I stand at the door to see Niamh off at four o'clock with an ashen-faced Katie and glowering Lizzy. The day has taken a turn, and low-lying clouds have begun to descend over the house. Mum wipes away a tear as Mark's BMW speeds out of sight without so much as a backwards wave from the occupants.

"She was right to get back," Mum's voice quivers. "Our lives have to go on. Seán, I hope you know we understand that you'll have to go back to America soon too."

I pat her shoulder softly as we walk back into the house, all too aware of the stares of my sisters, frightened of losing yet another family member. "Don't worry," I sigh, "I'm not going anywhere."

Mum and I attempt to make light conversation over dinner, but Lizzy's anger at Niamh has not abated and Katie seems even more dejected than earlier. Frustrated with them all, I go straight to my room after dinner to try to get some work done before Eddie calls over.

After half an hour, my laptop is still lying fruitlessly in my lap. Work is not going well. Marx has sent me eight emails since I checked my account this morning, only one of which I have replied to – badly. Giving up, I flop back onto my bed and after a few attempts at the international dial code, manage to get through to Claire.

She greets me with a high-pitched squeal of my name. I am surprised and chuffed at how delighted she is to hear from me. I had assumed that her many friends would keep her distracted while I'm gone and, though I don't like to think about it much, probably some men too. But she chats away, asking no questions and filling me in on all the news from New York. At first I'm relieved. The last thing I want to do is have to start talking about everything that has happened since I got back here, especially to Claire whose gasps and shrieks would only have made it worse. Somehow though, I can't get interested in what plays our friends are going to see, and what couples are going on holidays together. My mind drifts: back to Michael and Eddie, Dad and his other son, and again inexplicably, the girl from the bar.

By the time Eddie arrives, I am glad of the excuse to get off the phone, though also pleased by her reluctance to say goodbye. She gushes that she misses me and can't wait to see me. I wonder if I'll ever get back to my life in New York. Suddenly, I am jealous of Niamh, but I shake off the feeling quickly.

Everyone is standing in the living room when I come down. Eddie looks perfectly at ease, bouncing on the balls on his feet and humming to himself. I certainly wouldn't be acting in such a nonchalant manner if Lizzy was throwing such disgusted looks in my direction. We know Eddie is only trying to help us, but none of us like him being here. I suppose it brings home the seriousness of the issue. Lizzy barely reaches Eddie's elbow, making her disapproving looks comical to watch. Mum and Katie are almost as tall as I am but even they seem tiny in his presence. I find myself wondering how tall Dad's other son is.

Mum has the fancy biscuits out again. She is disappointed that Michael cannot be here too.

Eddie does his best to put her at ease, but I am not able to warm to the man.

Eventually, we all sit and Eddie begins to speak, unprompted. "Glenda, if you decide this isn't for you, I can go at any time. Today, all I am going to do is explain a bit about how the will works and what your options are. I can come back again if you want to discuss any of those options in more detail, all right? Andrew Shaw will have Roger Nestor on his side, but don't forget, you're not alone. You have me."

Mum nods and visibly relaxes a little. I catch Lizzy's eye and see the burning sentiment echoing mine. He's a pompous know-it-all.

Eddie starts off by saying what we all expected. The law only protects a proper, legal spouse. Mum is entitled to nothing under the will. Eddie emphasises that the law on this is very strict. But there is some hope. "Without a marriage cert – without that particular bit of paper – it used to be the case that you were flummoxed. Luckily for you, a new law was passed in 2010 which gives some rights to people who have cohabited. In other words, couples who have lived together, but who never married."

"Wait," Katie cuts him off, and we all look at her, surprised. Katie never interrupts anyone. "Isn't that the Act that gives rights to same-sex couples?"

All eyes fly back to Eddie, who looks impressed. "That's right, young lady. But it also gives certain rights to heterosexual couples who live together. To be honest, Glenda, it was more designed to give rights to young people who lived together before marriage, rather than for your situation, but it still applies."

"What does it say?" Lizzy is almost breathless at the thought of a solution.

Eddie grins. I think he's a showman at heart. "Well, it doesn't guarantee your mother anything. But it does give her the right to apply to the court for something out of the estate. I'd say that if Andrew wasn't around, and Liam had left everything to, say, Michael Undersky or someone else, then she would have a real chance. I mean, Glenda, you and Liam lived together as man and wife for thirty years! That's got to count for something."

Lizzy nods furiously.

"However," Eddie gestures firmly, "if the court decides to make changes to Liam's will, it will take into account the circumstances of Liam's children and that includes Andrew."

Mum's face creases suddenly in anger. "So I have a chance under this new Act because I 'co-habited' with Liam and the Shaw boy has rights under my husband's will – but what about Liam's other children, *my* kids? Don't they have any rights of their own?"

"Well," Eddie looks thoughtful, "I'm probably not the right person to discuss that with."

We all stare at him, disbelieving.

"Look, there are ways for children to challenge a parent's will in court. But Michael asked me here to help you, Glenda, not your children."

"Why can't you do both?" Mum demands.

"Look, Glenda, you are going to look for as much as you can from Liam's estate. Presumably, if one of the kids challenges the will, they'll also be looking for as much as they can get. So who gets what? You'll both need to argue your cases to the judge and you'll essentially be arguing against each other. I have to put my client first, and I can't do that if I have two clients both asking for the same thing."

I watch Mum biting her lip and know she's thinking the same thing I am. We never intended to be fighting amongst ourselves. We just want the estate back from the other son. It doesn't really matter which of us gets it.

Lizzy bristles. "Only Mum should challenge the will then."

Eddie tilts his head. "It's important to understand, Lizzy, that I cannot promise success. We are not helped by the fact that the Co-habitants Act has not been tested in the courts. No one, to the best of my knowledge, has made a claim under it since it was brought in. We don't know how the judge might respond to Glenda's challenge, especially with Andrew Shaw arguing his case."

Seeing Lizzy's face darken, as though he is deliberately being unhelpful, he hurries on. "Of course, if all you kids stood by her, telling the judge you weren't going to ask for anything for yourselves because you wanted your mother to have everything, that might help persuade the judge. But you might not all want to do that."

"Of course we will," snaps Lizzy, clearly forgetting about Niamh's likely response. "Mum should go for it herself." She looks around for support.

"Well," I frown, "not if one of us has a better chance."

Mum holds up a hand before we get into a flow. "Look, Eddie, I really don't want to get *more* lawyers involved. Just tell me what the kids challenging the will would mean."

Eddie looks slightly hesitant but answers her. "It would be easier for the kids to get something from the will if they were minor, underage. Because then they would really need to be looked after. But they can still try. Issue can rely on Section 117 of the Succession Act, so Seán, Niamh, Katie and Lizzy could challenge the will on that ground."

Lizzy and I rush in with our questions together.

"What's an 'issue'?"

"What does Section 117 say?"

Mum smiles sadly. "Yes, in English please, Eddie."

"Sorry!" He laughs obnoxiously, as though our ignorance elevates him. "Issue is a legal word for 'children'. But not just Liam's own children. Any grandchildren, great-grandchildren, and so on. In this case, obviously, it just means the kids . . . unless . . . ?" He raises a questioning eyebrow.

"Just the kids." Mam seems insulted at the implication.

Lizzy and I exchange grins.

"Of course," Eddie smirks. "Section 117 allows issue – children in this case – to challenge a will of a parent if that parent did not make proper provision for them in the will. It can also be used if a child feels they were not adequately supported while the parent was alive. Imagine," he turns to me, "if your father had bought you a house and paid for your education, but refused to give Katie any financial help when she asked. She would have a good chance of being awarded something under his will, on the grounds that she ought to have received just as much as you during your father's life. Judges are often sympathetic to such fairness claims. But, again, nothing is a sure thing in this game."

I hear Lizzy whisper "Game!" murderously under her breath.

"Michael never mentioned this Section 117." I hear the bitterness in my voice.

"Of course not, son. I know it sounds strange, but as executor his loyalty is to Liam. If he were to suggest you challenge the will he is protecting, he could be deemed negligent. Now, arguing that your father hasn't made proper provision for you will be a hard sell given everything he did for you when he was alive, compared to what he did for Andrew. If Roger Nestor is worth half his salt, he will argue that Liam made this will to try to even out the provision he made for all five of his children. Andrew was born out of wedlock, but I suppose, so were all of you! Anyway, that distinction doesn't make a difference nowadays. In the eyes of the law, Andrew Shaw is just as much Liam's child as you four."

"God!" Mum puts her head in her hand and sniffs quietly. Katie moves to sit beside her while Lizzy glares at Eddie.

"Maybe that's enough for tonight," he says awkwardly. "You have my number. Feel free to ring any time." He stands and turns with an afterthought. "By the way, it's important to know that for the executor to administer the will, he must take out what is known as a grant of probate. It's essentially a lot of form-filling on Michael's part. But once the grant is issued, you will only have six months to challenge the will either as co-habitant or under Section 117. So get thinking. Of course, with an estate this large, it will take Michael months to gather all the information about assets and liabilities, which is one of the first things he must do to go about getting the grant. So you could have up to a year before the clock starts running. Contact me any time."

We stay in the living room after Eddie leaves, but one by one Mum and my sisters retire to their bedrooms. It is not long before I hear weeping echoing throughout the house. Too many girls to comfort. For the first time in my life, I wish I had a brother.

I had told Pat O'Hara I would ring her if Mum was upset after the meeting with Eddie, but instead I phone Michael. I just don't think I can stand another woman in the house, even one as formidable and unlikely to succumb to tears as Pat. Michael says he will call over straight away and, while I wait, I email Marx to inform him that it will be another week at least before I can consider going back to New York. I know I am pushing my luck, but there is no way I can return to America at the moment. Aside from the fact that they need me here, I have a feeling that if I leave home with my family in this state, I might never come back, and that is not a reality I can face right now.

Michael arrives quicker than I expect and, after I call out to Mum, we walk together into the living room. Anyone else would ask for all the gory details straight away, but Michael would never pry like that. He sits, adjusting his jacket, damp from the light drizzle that has begun to fall outside. I tilt my head and stare at him, wondering how he feels about having to stay loyal to my father's will, knowing that Dad lied to him. But a different question is out of my mouth before I realise it.

"Did you know that my parents never married?"

Michael does not seem surprised by the question. He exhales deeply and looks me straight in the eye when he answers. "No, I didn't. Liam met your mother in England, and returned with her as his bride. I remember your grandmother was very upset that she had played no part in the wedding, but by that stage it was too late. No one ever questioned the validity of the marriage. Why would we?"

I believe him. "They always told us of their wedding as if it was the most romantic thing in the world." I lean my head against a clenched fist, trying to recall every childhood mention of marriage. "An elopement, was what they called it. Just a private ceremony in Scotland. Mum always said it was a beautiful adventure . . ."

"I'm sure she will explain it to us all in time."

As if on cue, Mum arrives in the sitting room with Katie trailing after her. Lizzy sticks her head in the door to greet Michael but leaves again immediately to get some fresh air. We sit for close to half an hour, discussing what Eddie had to say. While careful not to advise, Michael seems satisfied with the information his friend gave us, and I concede reluctantly that Eddie might be a decent ally to have around.

After a while, the conversation peters out and I watch Michael fidgeting and shifting in his seat. I open my mouth to question him but he blurts it out before I can speak.

"Glenda, I have a confession to make."

There is a tense silence. I suddenly want to shout at him to shut up. Whatever Michael has to say is clearly not going to be pleasant and I don't think Mum can take any more disappointment right now. But somehow, when she locks eyes with him, one of her oldest friends, she sees what he is too scared to say.

"You knew!" Mum gasps.

"About the affair," Michael stresses, his voice shaking. "Not about the boy. I swear, Glenda, I never knew about the boy."

Katie's mouth falls open. After a moment's silence, Mum turns to us. "Seán, Katie, do you remember that the day Michael brought Eddie Edwards here to tell us about the will I spent the evening looking at old photographs?"

I nod, uncertain where this was going. Katie remains motionless in her seat. Mum turns back to Michael.

"Well, I spent the night looking through boxes of old postcards, diaries, calendars of school events, church occasions. And I remembered something I had forgotten. Michael, you and Liam had a falling out just after Katie was born. I remember you swinging her around on her first birthday and saying how you were sorry you'd missed so much of her first year, because she was getting so big already."

Michael lowers his head. "You remember that?"

"I remember everything to do with my kids. And I remember that Liam told me you had a fight over an old friend, but refused to go into any more detail. That was when we were having problems so, to be honest, it was the least of my worries. It started to get better between us just as you and he made up. Everything was falling back into place and I never questioned further why you two hadn't spoken for nearly a year."

"I was so angry with him," Michael says softly. "Maggie and I had gone through our own rough patch a couple of years earlier when we were trying for a baby. But I never, ever, for a second considered doing that to her. And I couldn't understand why he wouldn't confess to you."

"Well, now you know, don't you?" Mum is clearly struggling to keep the level of bitterness in her voice to a minimum. "It would have meant confessing about the Shaw boy too."

"Eventually, I realised that you and he were back on track, and I decided that if you could work through your problems then it was none of my business. But he never told me about the boy. That was just as much a shock for me as anyone else. I feel now that if I'd been more compassionate with him when he confessed to me about the one-night stand, maybe he would have confided in me about the child."

"His name is Andrew."

We all turn to stare at Katie, who bows her head, embarrassed.

Ignoring her, the conversation continues.

"Why are you telling me this now, Michael?"

"Things are going to get tough, with the will. I want you to trust me, Glenda. You can trust me, you know."

She smiles, though it is sadder than the smile I remember. "I know."

There is a light but definite knock on the front door. Mum frowns questioningly at me, but I shrug my shoulders – I am not expecting anyone. Thinking it might be Pat O'Hara, worried about Mum after Eddie's visit, I go and open the door.

There stands the young woman from the bar.

She is the last person I expect to see at my door and I feel my mouth fall open in astonishment. She looks fresher than she looked in Keogh's – her clothes are more becoming, revealing a dainty yet curvy frame, and her dirty-blonde hair is pulled back into a casual but elegant bun. Her wide eyes bore into mine, and I feel a strange swooping sensation somewhere around my stomach as she gives a small smile. She seems to recognise me too but from the way her eyebrows arch upwards, it is clear she hasn't called to see me.

"I'm looking for Glenda Wilson?" She talks so quietly it is almost a whisper, and every word seems to be causing her tremendous effort.

Still rooted to the spot, no words escape my mouth. I physically shake myself and stand aside to allow her to come in out of the rain. Slightly reluctantly, she walks through the door, and I lead her silently to the sitting room. Her eyes search around before coming to rest on Mum, who stares at her blankly.

"You must be Ms Wilson?" She tries to smile but it is clearly a difficult task and her face twists into a painful contortion.

Mum, always the caring type, takes pity on the uncomfortable young woman before her and stands to shake her hand while smiling at her.

"Yes, I'm Glenda," she answers gently and, seeing me move closer, carelessly adds, "and this is my son."

The woman merely nods in response and a hot stuffiness pervades the room as silence lingers on.

"I'm sorry, dear," says Mum eventually, clearly noticing as I do that the woman's large brown eyes are slowly filling with tears, "but I don't know who you are."

"I'm Tors Shaw." This means nothing to me, but Mum's eyes almost pop out of her head and she actually takes a step back, her bulging eyes starting to water.

Frustrated by a lack of understanding and the constant flow of tears I've had to deal with recently, I am jolted into speech for the first time in the presence of this stranger.

"I'm sorry, do I know you?"

She looks back at me with a mixture of surprise and embarrassment. "No. I shouldn't even be here. If my mother knew . . ." She pauses, as if trying to find the courage to go on.

"My younger brother is called Andrew. Actually," she tilts her head at me as though only seeing me for the first time, "he's your brother too."

I can feel the blood drain from my head, and I think I might be swaying a little on the spot. Of course: Shaw. The woman is still talking, addressing herself to Mum again. "I'm sorry I just arrived like this. I know it is totally inappropriate, but I'm not happy at all with the way my mother is handling this whole affair and I wanted to talk to you before she does. Would you mind if I sat down?"

She breathes the last question quickly as though she might collapse if she doesn't sit.

Despite her shock, Mum seems to realise that this young woman is genuinely upset and gestures her to a seat near Michael. The Shaw girl, whose name I didn't quite catch, smiles shyly at him.

"Michael, right?"

Mum scowls at them. "Do you two know each other?"

"We met last week," Michael soothes her. "I was there when Roger Nestor told them about the will. This is Seán and Katie." He gestures at us and the girl gives us a small smile, her eyes lingering ever so slightly longer on me.

Michael addresses her. "How are you, dear? Tors, isn't it?"

"Yes, Tors." She pronounces the name distinctly, as though used to explaining her unusual name.

We all sit, watching her take a large gulping breath. She begins talking, twisting her hands self-consciously in her lap.

"I'm sure I'm one of the last people you want in your house, so I'll just say what I've come to say and then leave. Until last week, neither Andrew nor I knew that he isn't my father's child. Dad died three years ago without knowing. Mam seems to feel that Andrew is owed whatever your husband left him, but we disagree." She stops here and

86

looks at us in earnest. "Andrew asked me to come here. He doesn't want to take anything from your family. As far as he is concerned my dad was his as well, and he doesn't want your money. But my mam sees differently. I've never seen her this way – she's so angry. She insisted we leave our home in Kerry and we've been staying locally since the weekend. She wants to take possession of your house immediately. In fact, she would have come here already but we're concentrating on settling Andrew into the new hospital."

"Hospital?" I cannot help but interrupt.

"Oh. Yes. Andrew has kidney disease. He's been on dialysis for nearly two years now. He's on the transplant list but so far there's been no suitable donor. Medical fees keep going up. I think that is part of the reason Mam is so insistent on getting every penny she can from your family. Andrew's getting his dialysis in St John's now."

My mind reels. After Eddie Edwards had left after revealing the truth, Michael had tried to describe his meeting with the Shaws but Mum had cut him off with something close to viciousness. She wanted to hear no details about Andrew Shaw, or his mother. I glance now at Michael who is looking down at his hands, apparently unsurprised. I wonder what else he knows.

"Anyway," the woman with the strange name continues, "once Andrew has adjusted a little bit I think Mam will want to call over to you. She isn't going to be nice about it. I think she expects you to just vacate the house for us. She's not usually like this, but she's really fired up. I told her she shouldn't be taking time off work like this but she said once Andrew gets your estate she won't need to work."

She pauses, looking embarrassed. There are no longer any tears in her eyes, but she looks as uncomfortable as when she walked in the door. Mum is gaping at her in awe, as if she does not know what to make of her. To be honest, I don't either. Just as I'm wondering whether it's a trick, we hear Lizzy shuffling in the door muttering curses about the rain. She marches into the living room, still shaking herself off, and halts suddenly at the sight of the stranger.

Tors stands abruptly.

In her typical style, Lizzy thrusts out her hand in welcome, eyebrows raised inquisitorially. As though anticipating a fight, we all rise slowly.

Tors takes Lizzy's hand tentatively but lets go almost immediately, tears swimming once more in her eyes. She turns back to Mum, backing out into the hallway as she does so.

"I don't even know why I'm here – there's nothing I can do. Andrew wanted me to come. He wanted to say all this himself but he's just not up to it at the moment. I'm sorry."

With a tentative glance in my direction, she rushes to the front door and we hear her open and slam it closed behind her.

"Who was that?" Lizzy asks, fresh rainwater dripping steadily from her hair. In the short time that Tors had been with us, the rain increased from an inoffensive shower to plump, wintery drops.

Mum does not answer but lowers herself slowly back onto the couch beside Katie.

I move to the window and watch Tors Shaw run down the driveway. I continue to stare until, as if to make her still more interesting, she disappears into the early evening mist.

Chapter 9

Tors

As I glare down at him he smirks back, which only infuriates me more.

"Don't make me play the 'when I'm dead and gone' card, Tors!"

I lightly smack his right arm in response and the nurse glares at me in disgust. "They're not using his arm today!" I gesture impatiently at the wires sticking out of his torso just under his left shoulder.

Still, he winces, clutching his old dialysis entry spot around the inside crook of his elbow. As soon as the nurse stalks away to the nurses' station, he lets go, grinning wickedly at me again. Before I know it, we are both laughing.

It's only his second round of dialysis in St John's, but I have to admit I'm happy with the hospital so far. Dr Stevens spent about half an hour with us on Tuesday, discussing the temporary line and Andrew's medical history. It turns out he and Dr Jim went to college together and he is under strict instructions from his former lab partner to take special care of his favourite patient. This is a real comfort to me. I was worried that the staff here wouldn't give Andrew the royal

89

treatment he gets in Galway, where he is practically like family.

We talked to the patient in the next bed for a while, a chatty middle-aged man who left about an hour ago. I look around at the quiet ward at the mostly older patients, hoping the next time Andrew is in there will be a younger crowd. His immune system is so low that he has to stay indoors a lot and hospital is his only chance to regularly interact with others his own age. Still, Andrew seems comfortable enough here. The layout is the same as in Galway, with a ward of ten beds encircling a medical station in the centre of the room. The nurse who thinks I'm the worst sister ever gives me another filthy look as she walks away and I laugh as much at Andrew's snickering as at the joke itself.

Though there hasn't been much of it over the past few days, I've noticed how much more I've laughed since coming home from France. A few years ago I would never have believed that I'd be happier living with my mother and caring for a sick brother than swanning around the streets of Paris on Claude's arm, being bought diamonds and shown off as one.

Thrilled that Andrew seems to have snapped out of the dangerous depression I could sense settling over him since we found out about Liam Murtagh, I banter back and forth with him for a while until he remembers what he was trying to get out of me. He wants to know everything – about the house, the wife and, of course, Liam's other children.

Andrew's form improved significantly when I suggested talking to the Murtaghs on his behalf. He would rather have done it himself, but he understands why I don't want him to go charging off to confront them while he's still coping with the news. Besides, he can be too direct for his own good, and the question he reluctantly asked me to put to them could have come out all wrong – the question I couldn't make myself ask when it came to it. He might have sounded demanding, rather than desperate.

The initial shock of learning that Liam Murtagh is his real father has worn off slightly, and his natural resilience is shining through. The last thing I want is for him to spiral so I'm tempted to play down the whole visit. But aside from the fact that this is a reality from which I can't protect him, I remember our truth pact. I've told him worse things than this. He's the only one who knows the truth about France, and Claude.

So I describe Glenda Wilson and the house in detail, but don't dwell on the other son. It's not to spare Andrew. There are other – unexpected – feelings I'd rather not think about right now.

Andrew's voice cuts across my thoughts. "So do you think you got through to them that I'm not a total bastard?"

"What, only half one?" For a second I think I've gone too far, but he lets himself smile.

"Yeah, something like that." He reaches over to the bedside table with effort to take a sip of water. I know better than to help him. He looks at me hesitantly as he replaces the glass with a wobble on the bedside table. "Did you tell them I'm sick?"

I glance at him sharply. "It came up."

"And? Did you ask them?"

I sigh and shift closer to the bed. "The whole thing was a bit overwhelming, Andrew. I got upset, and they were in total shock that I was even there. They were completely taken aback when I told her you were in hospital. What was I supposed to say 'My family just moved across the country so my brother can take your children's inheritance. Oh, and can he also have –"

"Jackie-boy!"

I snap my mouth shut as Andrew calls out to our little brother who bounds into the room and springs up onto the bed. He is off it again just as quick, ogling the large haemodialysis machine with its array of dials and screens, and colourful tubes connecting to Andrew's temporary line. He has seen it all before, but it continues to fascinate him.

"Can I touch?" he asks, as though asking for a treat.

Andrew takes Jack's hand and presses his fingers to his skin, just under his line. The tingly sensation, like a thousand pulses whirring, makes Jack jump even though he was expecting it. He grins as he leaps back.

"Careful now, Jack!" Mam is just behind him, beaming.

A quick glance tells me it's a genuine smile, and I exhale slowly, relieved she didn't hear the conversation. She would have had a fit if she knew I'd been to see the Murtaghs. That's one aspect of the whole situation I'm refusing to get involved in. I'll move county, deal with Jack's schooling and Andrew's new hospital, but I won't take part in the legalities of extracting money from Andrew's biological father's estate.

And it does appear to be an 'estate', in the Jane Austen sense of the word. If Glenda Wilson could see our tiny house in Kerry, she'd probably give us the money out of pity. But what we really need, what Andrew had hoped I would discuss with the Murtaghs, is something I am sort of surprised Mam hasn't brought up herself. I suppose it is a different matter. Andrew has been left Liam's estate legally so it's easy for Mam to play the righteous owner card. Asking for what I was supposed to ask the Murtaghs, on the other hand . . .

"So you've got the room to yourself this time, love?" Mam bends over and kisses Andrew on the forehead.

He nods and, though staying silent, he leans into her embrace.

I can see the relief wash over her. She is terrified that Andrew will die, but his own worse fear is that he'll die after arguing with one of us, and leave us to struggle with something worse than bereavement. I ended up taking Jack to the pub again last night to spare him their blazing row.

Andrew's anger had clearly been festering so he was slightly wild-eyed when he'd tottered into the kitchen. "I need to talk to Mam," he said, without looking at me.

As I ushered a confused Jack into his new bedroom, I threw Mam a significant look but she looked past my warning face, focusing on my brother nervously.

The SECRET SON

I tried to distract Jack with story-time, and by blaring his favourite music in the new CD player Andrew bought him for Christmas. But the voices in the living room continued to rise as Andrew demanded answers, challenged her rationalisations and dismissed apologies. Jack's eyes kept darting to the door.

Andrew and I have standard jokes we use to lighten the mood whenever one of us gets upset about Dad dying. One of these is teasing Andrew that, since Dad is gone, he is going to have to explain the birds and the bees to Jack when he's old enough. To be honest, I think Mam had that conversation with the kid last year, but I suddenly got uncomfortable when Jack asked, his eyes fixed on the bedroom door, why they were fighting.

How was I supposed to explain that this is all the result of a one-night stand? He thinks we're on a holiday but there are no other kids for him to play with. He can sense the tension but the 'two daddies' explanation just confuses him more. Knowing I had to get him away from the sea house, I suggested the bar again. I wondered whether the man from the other night would be there, but it was empty apart from a handful of local farmers.

As Jack munched on his chicken pieces with less enthusiasm than usual, I began to plot ways to help him. After listening to him tell me over dinner that the goal Ethan scored in their last GAA match was a result of his own skilful pass from the wing, a plan with potential began to form in my mind. Andrew is my responsibility, not Jack, but our family is so small, we're all in it together.

Though I would never admit it to Mam, the first two days here have not been so bad. The sea house, once aired and cleaned, is just as comfortable as our house in Kerry. The hospital seems to be working out. The main problem is Jack. Since Mam is insisting on us staying, I want to see about enrolling him in the local primary school until the end of term. But Mam is determined she does not want him anywhere near Glenda Wilson.

"How do you know she is a teacher in the school?" I yelled at her

93

in frustration. Apparently, it was mentioned in Liam Murtagh's death notice, which took up practically a full column in the *Irish Times* newspaper.

Mam's solution is still to home-school Jack until the end of the school year. It's not something I have much of an argument against except that I don't think it's healthy for a hyperactive kid like him to be stuck with his mother all day, especially when Andrew and I will be in and out of the hospital.

"It's just temporary." That's Mam's answer to everything.

Having spoken to Andrew about it, he came up with idea of asking Mam to join us for his dialysis today so I can escape for a few hours and do something for Jack. Now that we are all in the hospital, I catch Andrew's eye and he nods. On the pretext of me going shopping for the summer house, Mam is happy to take the rest of the dialysis shift. Mam isn't suspicious, even though I always stay with Andrew. Only on a rare occasion would we trade places and I mind Jack so she can sit with her first-born son. While we are in Wicklow, the most important thing is to make sure he has someone with him at all times. He has been going to the hospital in Galway for so many years that he has a clatter of friends there, between the nurses and doctors and other regular patients. Here, it will be lonelier for him.

I stop Dr Stevens on the way out for a word about Andrew and, in an attempt at off-handedness, ask directions to the address I found in the Golden Pages this morning. The drive does not take more than twenty minutes, but already I am paranoid that this is a bad idea. I am doing this for Jack, I tell myself over and over. I park the car a little away from the house, which is certainly smaller than the Murtaghs', but still large enough to fit about three of the houses from our estate inside. Imposing trees, though bare from the winter, still manage to block out the neighbouring houses on the wide country road and I feel a little safer, sheltered, as I make my way swiftly up the garden path.

Michael Undersky's mouth drops unflatteringly when he opens the door. He recovers quickly and invites me in before I can finish the speech I've been practising all the way here.

He leads me down the hallway, narrowed by spindly writing tables, into a sitting room decorated with patterned wallpaper and frilly curtains. I recognise a woman's touch, but one from many years ago.

An older lady, probably in her mid-sixties, stands up from the couch when I enter. Her eyes widen in surprise when he introduces me, but her handshake is cordial. "Should I go, Michael?" she asks bluntly, as I take a seat.

"No, no. You stay, Pat. I'll just pop into the kitchen and get us some tea."

"So," Pat's eyes bore into me as she plonks herself unceremoniously back into the sofa, "I hear you have moved over to the east of the country for a while."

I stare back at her, but can detect no malice in her looks or snide tone in her remark. She actually seems to be trying to put me at ease. I swallow. "Yes. Just for a little while."

"Glenda told me you called to her last night."

"Oh, you know the Murtagh family?" I don't know why I'm surprised. Their estate must be the largest in the town, if not the county.

"Oh yes, we go way back," she says easily, as though this is the most pleasant conversation she has had all week. She settles herself back into her chair, fussing at her skirt and pulling her cardigan around her. "My boys are great pals with the children, and Glenda and I have been best friends since before they were born."

I take a deep breath. "Then you must have known Liam Murtagh too. I'm sorry for your loss."

The lady gazes at me, expressionless, as Michael bustles into the sitting room carrying a laden tray.

"Oh, my dear, you see he's using the good china in your honour! Why, just half an hour ago I was choking back tea in a common or garden *mug*. And look at this array of snacks – Michael would have left me to starve if you hadn't arrived!"

Pat's humour indicates acceptance, and relief washes over me. We all smile and I accept everything Michael presses on me. Their kindness makes me feel considerably calmer. Michael pours tea from the delicate pot without saying anything but, once he sits, the legalities begin, as I suspected they would.

"Look, Tors, you must know that as executor my interest can only be in ensuring that Liam's will is properly administered. I can't offer you or your brother any legal advice and outside of my legal duties my loyalty will always be with Glenda. You should speak to Roger Nestor if you need –"

I hold up a hand to stop him, uncomfortably aware of the lady watching me with hawk-like eyes. "I know all that. I'm not here to talk about the will."

"Oh. Right. Then what can I do for you, my dear?"

To my horror, I feel tears welling up and concentrate angrily on forcing them down. Taking an extra-long sip to tea to steady myself, I begin to speak. I tell them about Andrew being in hospital and my responsibility to be with him as much as I can. How that means poor Jack is going to be left alone with no one but his mother for company until we go home to Kerry.

"He's only little and he needs an outlet, some other kids to play with. We don't know anyone here, though I'm sure everyone in the area knows of us by now. I can't imagine there are many places that would welcome us. I thought – Andrew and I both thought – you might know of a football club or, I don't know, any kind of activity that Jack could get involved in. If you could talk to them, they might be persuaded to accept him. It would only be for a few months at the most, but I think it's important for him."

Silence stifles the room while the two of them share a look of significance. I rush on, scared they will be angry.

"I think we can all agree that whoever is in the wrong, whoever is to blame for the situation we are in here, it's not an eight-year-old kid. I'm asking just for Jack. My mother would never know you helped."

"Of course, Tors." Michael sounds awkward, but sincere. "Pat, maybe you can talk to Conn O'Shaughnessy. He's the head of our local GAA club," he explains to me. "I'm sure we can sort something out. Give me your mother's number and I'll make sure he rings her. He can say it was his idea and that he got the number from me," he adds, seeing my hesitation. "I have all the relevant contact information because of the will."

I'm so grateful that, as I type her number into his phone, I realise my hands are shaking.

"So, have you cared for your brother for a long time?" Pat asks.

"I've only been his official carer for a year." I hand the mobile back to Michael, a strange feeling of contentment relaxing me.

Pat raises her eyebrows and nods encouragement to continue.

I choose a large biscuit and dunk it in my tea. "We all pitched in until my dad passed away three years ago, then Mum got a stream of professional carers to help. But they never stayed for long. I don't blame them. They always ended up getting better-paid jobs within months of starting with us. But it was disrupting for Andrew. When I came back from Paris last year, we decided I would be Andrew's carer. It's better for all of us. And he's in much better spirits since I've been taking care of him." I can't keep the note of pride out of my voice.

"So he's improving?"

I open my mouth to answer, but snap it shut again immediately. I sense the danger of be-friending Michael and Pat, confidants of the Murtaghs. Pat's question could be purely conversational, but it would be a sort of betrayal to go into detail about Andrew's health with her. How his AVF shut down. How this move can only make it worse. How Mam is starting to panic that time is running out for her son, and how she will grasp any sort of potential lifeline, even the Murtagh inheritance. At the end of the day, these people aren't on our side, and I suddenly wish I had never come here.

Michael seems to think that the answer is self-evident, and instead of waiting for me to reply, turns to Pat. "Speaking of illnesses, you know who isn't doing so well? Mrs Boden. Jeanette is talking about flying home from London."

"I know. I've drawn up a visiting schedule for the neighbours so she will have someone spending some time with her every day for the next two weeks. Just to check in, you know. Keep an eye on her. Glenda insisted they be involved so Lizzy is doing tonight."

"That's great, Pat, having the four Murtaghs will make a huge difference."

I zone out as they talk, feeling increasingly uncomfortable. I don't want to listen to how kind everyone is to elderly neighbours and what an amazing community they have here. It makes me feel like the villain of the piece. I try to think of an escape plan, but they are soon involving me in the conversation again.

"It's about the only positive of sickness, or a funeral, that people you love come home, if only briefly," said Pat. "My boys have missed Seán Murtagh – I'm glad he's staying around for a while." She turned to me. "Did you meet him when you went to visit Glenda?"

"Yes," I answer, curtly. The last thing I want to talk about is my visit to the Murtagh estate, or the reason for it. Still, I can't help asking a question about Seán, now that Pat has brought him up. "He doesn't live in the country, then?"

"No, he has been in New York for about, oh, what would you say, Michael? Four years?" Pat starts counting on her fingers, but Michael answers swiftly.

"It'll be five years at this stage, Pat. I always thought he'd be one to come home eventually – he's a real Mammy's boy. But he seems to be well settled in his job over there. I don't know whether he'll ever move back permanently now."

"The boys say he's loving it. My eldest went to visit him last year," she adds for my benefit.

I try to imagine staying five years in Paris. It was certainly an attractive option, at least when I first met Claude. The act of leaving home for Paris was difficult and threatened to ruin the entire experience for me. I wanted to stay where Dad used to live. Where sometimes, if I climbed up to the attic where he used to spend hours sorting boxes and attempting to re-decorate, I could still get the smell of him. And I felt so bad leaving Andrew.

So it was in tears and dramatics that I waved from the window of the plane and with sobs that I touched down to a grey Paris evening. Still weepy, I must have looked utterly pathetic trying to heave my massive suitcase off the carousel. The tall, muscular man who helped me with a smile left quite an impression, and I was shocked when he arrived into the hospital three weeks later with a twisted knee, and remembered me. Thinking about Claude in those wonderful first few months, I could never have imagined how we would end, and I shudder now at the thought of what my life would have been like if I had stayed with him for five years.

It was wonderful at the beginning. He wined and dined me, and he used to laugh at the simple things that amazed this small-town girl from Ireland. But I just could not find trips on his private jet to vineyards in the south of France 'simple'. His high-powered job in one of France's most prestigious banks had made him a fortune already, even though he was only in his mid-thirties. He also came from a wealthy family where money was no object. So we took in weekly opera visits and frequented extravagant cocktail parties. I didn't have the clothes, but he bought me sparkling red dresses and gold earrings. Even in the painful high heels he insisted I wear, I only reached his shoulder, but I felt taller as we paraded around and he flaunted me to his colleagues, to politicians, to all kinds of important people.

In hindsight, I don't know why I didn't see his true colours earlier. On all those lazy mornings in his king-size bed and afternoon strolls by the Seine, he never asked about my family or my past or even my plans for the future. It was always about how beautiful I looked and how much fun we were going to have at the next dinner party. For the first six months, we did not fight. It was, I suppose, a honeymoon of sorts. But I did have the experience of seeing him angry with others.

There were heated arguments with business colleagues on the phone and harsh words with powerful men at functions. But during those exchanges, I was never uneasy. He would always have his arm firmly around my body, pulling me protectively towards him. It was only later I came to recognise that for what it was, a gesture of ownership.

". . . ownership . . ."

"What?" I bark at Michael's words, before sense catches up with my wandering mind.

He looks startled by my interruption. "Well, I was just saying that Seán has responsibilities here too, to his family. He's used to only looking after himself in America, but he's going to have to take ownership for a lot more now."

I can never snap quickly or easily out of my painful memories of Claude, and I find I am rubbing my wrist as I try to take in what Michael is saying. My vague interest in Andrew's new half-brother has evaporated and I feel crowded. I sense my breathing becoming shallow and it is with great effort that I remain composed and use Andrew as an excuse to bustle out the door.

I manage to drive a short distance before pulling in and scrambling for the paper bag I keep hidden in the back of the glove compartment. I gulp in and force air back out, allowing so many of my Paris memories to wash over me, the exquisite and the terrifying. I am so consumed I don't check my phone (which I had set to silent so I would not seem rude in front of Michael if it rang) for another ten minutes. By then, I have eight missed calls from my mother at the hospital.

Chapter 10

Tors

I ease the car as slowly and quietly as I can up the narrow road in front of the Murtaghs' house. I don't know why I have come here of all places. There's no space to pull in without turning into their driveway so I just edge the car as close as I can to the bushes lining the side of the country road.

Tears stream down my cheeks. In the dark with no one around, the freedom to let them spill overwhelms me and huge gulping sobs escape me. Andrew is so sick. There is no explaining why he took such a bad turn during dialysis. Dr Stevens doesn't think his temporary line has become infected but has yet to offer any alternative explanations. There's always the fear that his body has just gone on as long as it can on his failing kidneys.

He's stable for now. Well enough for me to leave the hospital for a few hours. The others have gone back to the sea house, but the thought of being cooped up in there with Mam and having to put on a brave face for Jack is too much for me. Images from the day haunt me now. Andrew's ghostly-white face shaking from side to side as they injected him with yet more painkillers. His grip loosening and his hand finally slipping out of mine when sleep took over at last. Fearing that one day, and possibly one day soon, he could let go of my hand forever, my breath catches. I reach into the glove compartment and, for the second time today, fumble around for the paper bag. Grasping it around my mouth with shaking hands, I draw deep, unbearable breaths until it's just the tears again.

Out of nowhere, the passenger window shakes with a loud knock. A tall, shadowy figure bends to look in the window. I gasp audibly and my body reacts by jerking violently, causing me to knock my elbow off the side of the car door.

"Tors?"

I hardly recognise the muffled voice from outside but, as the face peers closer to the window, I see it is Seán Murtagh. My body trembles with a mixture of relief and humiliation. With a quivering hand, I reach over and unlock the door.

He pulls it open hastily. "It's me, it's Seán. Sorry, I didn't mean to scare you. I spotted you from my bedroom window and wondered why you weren't coming in."

As he slides into the car I'm still breathing heavily, one hand pressed against my frantically beating heart and the other against my bumped elbow. I try to smile, but it's watery.

"Is your arm okay?" He has the beginning of a smile on his lips, but looks unsure whether that's allowed.

"Yeah, I'm fine. You just startled me!" I try to keep my voice light, but I know I sound like I have a head cold, and I try to wipe my cheeks without him noticing. I think I'm unsuccessful.

"I have to ask you a serious question," he sounds grave. I look at him apprehensively. "What sort of a name is 'Tors'?"

A burst of relieved laughter escapes me and, for the first time in hours, I feel myself physically unclench. He smiles at me with familiarity, as though we are old childhood friends.

"It was the most Andrew could make of 'Victoria' when he was younger and it just stuck. Once, Jack heard Mam call me Victoria and asked who that was!"

Seán grins. "When Lizzy was small we just called her 'The Baby' for ages. Until Mum and Dad realised Niamh thought 'The Baby' was her actual name, and she got really confused when Mum tried to convince her to call her Lizzy!"

We both laugh, and a comfortable silence descends over the car.

"What brings you here anyway?" he asks after a while.

It doesn't even occur to me to lie. "I don't know. Andrew took a bad turn during dialysis. The doctors wanted us to leave the hospital so he would have a chance to rest, and I needed to be on my own. I just ended up here. Here, at this house, the reason we're in Wicklow instead of at home." Mortified, I start to well up again.

"Tors, please don't. Let's go to Keogh's and have a drink. It's only five minutes away. I'll even drive you home if you feel like something strong."

I glance at him. "I saw you there the other night."

He looks awkward as he nods. Neither of us knows what to say. Clearly embarrassed, he gets out of the car. I stay still, thinking he's about to leave, but he comes right around to the driver's side of the car and opens my door.

"Come on." He's smiling now. "I'll drive."

I stay where I am. "I can't drink in case the hospital calls. I have to be able to drive."

He reaches in and takes my hand from the steering wheel. "Then I'll drive you back here after a lemonade."

His coaxing is gentle so I let him lead me out of the car and over to his.

"How did you know who I was?" I ask as we click our safety belts into place.

"Sorry?" He glances at me, puzzled, as he revs the engine.

"The other night in the pub, you kept looking at me. How did you know I was connected to Andrew?"

"Oh, I didn't, I just thought you were pretty." He shrugs, as if it's the most natural answer in the world. I watch with fascination as, realising what he has just said, his whole face flushes red.

We don't say anything more until we arrive at Keogh's. It's quiet tonight. I try to figure out why, and have to strain to remember what day of the week it is. Thursday. The day of Andrew's second dialysis in Wicklow. Seán calls up to the barman who swiftly bustles over with our soft drinks.

When we start talking, I am amazed to find that the conversation flows, as though we are picking up from an earlier chat. I wonder if it is real to him that, because of my family, his might lose everything. We talk a little about Andrew, though I'm not inclined to. I don't know why, but I feel like I don't want to give too much of Andrew away. He's my brother, not Seán's. That's not strictly true, but I don't want to think about Andrew being any less mine than he always was, so I try to steer out of the conversation when Seán asks about his health.

"I'm his carer. I can't really talk too much about it. Confidentiality issues, you understand."

"That's your job?"

"For about a year now. Mum pays me what she can, and I'm entitled to a carer's allowance from the government."

"And he's that bad that he needs a carer full time?"

"Yes, he's sick. Very sick." I wonder if now is the time to ask him the question I intended to ask Glenda yesterday. I can't explain why, but I stall. "I trained as a nurse. Not that you need to be qualified to care for a relative but, in my case, it helps. Some weeks Andrew is better than others, but with dialysis three times a week and his general health being so poor, it's really a full-time job."

"Is that why you became a nurse, because of Andrew?" He seems genuinely interested.

"Not directly, but I suppose living with a sick brother had an effect. Most people hate the smell, the whiteness, everything about hospitals, but I am so used to them that I'm perfectly comfortable there. One summer, when I was about fifteen or sixteen, I did a carers' course. It was better than sitting around waiting rooms for hours on end. I think that's when I decided to become a nurse."

Seán's eyes are out on stalks at the effect a sick sibling can have, and I feel guilty now that I was so underwhelmed by the course at the time. Andrew being ill wasn't anything new, and I was seething at being pulled from summer with my friends every other day to sit in hospitals with only my parents for company. Initially, the carers' course was the last thing I wanted to do – class in the middle of summer! But it turned out to be the best thing that could have happened to me. That's where I met my friend Debbie. She didn't have any other brothers and sisters and was terrified her little sister was going to die. She took the class seriously and, as a result, I started to pay attention.

"I still keep in touch with Debbie. She lives in Donegal. Her sister has some recurring health issues but is loads better. She's starting secondary school next year – I can't believe it!"

Seán grins. "I know what you mean."

He talks about his youngest sister, Lizzy, but hardly mentions the other two. Maybe it's because one of them is the same age as Andrew. Or perhaps I'm just being paranoid. He talks animatedly about his job at LL&T Consultancy in New York with the same passion I used to exude during my first six months in Paris. I feel a massive urge to confide in him about Paris, about Claude. I shake myself mentally. What am I thinking? I haven't even told my closest friends and family, aside from Andrew. How could I even consider sharing that with this man, who is part of the Murtagh family?

We are interrupted by the barman, coming over with more drinks. Seán engages him in friendly chat for a few minutes and I watch with interest.

"It must be nice coming home and seeing people again after so long," I offer when we are alone again. "Even if, you know . . ."

"Yeah. It's hardly the best circumstances to be coming home in. It's great to see my friends again but it's weird in a lot of ways. Seeing Lizzy so grown up. And Pat O'Hara's hair is almost totally grey now. I've only been away for five years, but it seems like I've missed so much."

"There's a great sense of community here."

He nods animatedly. "You know, there really is. I'm only seeing it now that Dad's gone. Everyone really rallied around us. A list has been drawn up of people willing to call in to an old neighbour of ours, Mrs Boden, because she lives alone and hasn't been well since Dad died. But no one told us about the roster, because they thought we had enough to be worrying about. Anyway, one of the triplets let it slip and Mum insisted Pat put our family on the list. Lizzy will be over with her tonight and I'm on duty in a couple of days." He pauses and looks at me strangely. "You know, we really shouldn't be talking about stuff like this."

I freeze. "What do you mean?"

"You know, about our families. About our lives."

I don't know what makes me do it, maybe the torturous guilt in his voice, but I reach over and grab his hand. He looks surprised, yet doesn't hesitate to squeeze it. His eyes are boring into mine. I feel my heart start to race. I can't look away. Slowly, so slowly I wonder if I'm imagining it, he begins to move towards me. But just as I dare to lean in, our mobile phones start to ring, simultaneously.

I grab mine, thinking immediately of the hospital, without even registering that Seán is pulling out his phone too.

"Victoria Maria Shaw!" I don't have time to panic at the fact that she is clearly furious enough to use my full name. Right at that second, I hear a woman screaming the name "Shaw" through Seán's phone and I realise, as Seán's wide eyes lock with mine, that our sudden popularity is not a coincidence.

* * *

As Seán screeches into the driveway, neither of us saying a word, I cast around wildly for some plausible excuse as to why we are together.

A stand-off is in session. Mam and Glenda Wilson are hovering a few feet away from each other in the driveway, glaring at us as we approach. I see one of the other daughters standing beside her mother, gripping her arm, and for a second my sense of dread melts into fury as I see my little brother ducking out of sight, clearly terrified, behind Mam in her long flowing skirt. I pull him to me as he runs to me, and march over to my mother.

"You brought Jack here?" My voice is hard and yet it shakes with barely suppressed rage.

Mam doesn't seem to hear me. "What are you doing with *him*?"

A ripple of anger flows through me, and I turn, seeing Seán bristle as he puts his arm around his sister's shoulder. I try to push Jack out of earshot but, though not crying, his arms remain fastened tightly around my waist. Rubbing his back gently, I try to keep my voice soft.

"We went for a drink – is that a crime now?"

"Don't you speak to me like that, young lady!" Mam's voice continues to rise, growing slightly hysterical. "I got a call from a man named Conn O'Shaughnessy to say he heard we had moved to the area and if Jack wanted to come to GAA training on Sunday morning, they'd be glad to have him. Of course, Jack got so excited he couldn't wait, so I took him out for a drive to see the clubhouse and what do I see outside this house as we drive by? *Your car!* You told me that you wanted some time alone, and to give me and Jack quality time together, when really you were colluding with the Murtaghs!"

"Mam, what are you talking about? Listen to yourself!" My delight at the phone call from Conn O'Shaughnessy and my fear that Mam will find it was because of me are both overtaken by alarm at her behaviour. "'Colluding with the Murtaghs'? What's the matter with you? I was driving and got upset, so I pulled in. Seán saw me in the car and we went to have a drink. In case you hadn't noticed, I don't know anyone in this county. Seán's someone I can talk to, so don't you

107

give out to me for spending time with him. What has got into you, bringing Jack here and fighting in front of him?"

For a second, she stares, apparently torn between screaming at me and apologising, then her phone rings. I chance a glance at Seán as she whips it open. Within seconds, her face drains of colour, and she grabs Jack from my side.

"Andrew!" she chokes out, before running past me, pulling Jack behind her.

For the second time today, I dash towards my car. Somehow, Seán is beside me, ignoring his mother and sister's calls. He touches my arm lightly and asks me something I don't hear. I feel a tinge of regret as I slam the car door without responding, but I cannot stop myself. I feel my body move of its own accord, rushing, as always, to my brother's side.

Chapter 11

Seán

I watch her speed off after her mother's car for a few seconds before Lizzy's angry voice echoes through the grounds.

"Who does that woman think she is? She had a *child* with Dad – you'd think she'd be too ashamed to show her ugly face!"

Inexplicably, my eyes are drawn up, and I see Katie staring down from her bedroom window. Catching my eye, she retreats at once.

Lizzy is still venting. "And what is Conn O'Shaughnessy doing, trying to get them to fit in here? Does he think they're going to stay? Does he think we're going to give up the house?" She turns to our mother for an explanation, but Mum is standing rigid, as if rooted to the spot.

Cautiously I inch forward and put my arm gently around her shoulder. "Come on, Mum." I find I'm whispering. "Let's go inside."

She lets herself be led into the house but when Lizzy closes the front door she shrugs herself out of my grip and turns to me, looking older than I have ever seen her. "What were you doing with Tors Shaw, Seán?"

Though I probably should have expected it, I start at her accusatory tone. "I saw her sitting in her car outside the house."

When both women continue to stare at me, I find myself stammering. "I was supposed to be working on my laptop but I couldn't concentrate. I was staring out the window and saw her pull up." I hear my tone becomes defensive. "She was upset, we went for a drink. She's a nice girl, Mum . . ."

"Oh Seán, what does that matter? Her family is trying to ruin ours! What will we do if we lose the estate? For all of Michael and Eddie's efforts, I don't see how we're going to be able to keep it. What judge in the land will feel more sorry for me than Andrew Shaw, after I lied to everyone for years about being married? What can I expect? And why should you kids get anything when a terminally ill boy with no father needs all the help he can get? I don't have a back-up plan, Seán – your father was supposed to leave us everything. Tell me, son, how should I feel about you fraternising with Tors Shaw?"

I don't know why it starts to flow from me now. Maybe because talking with Tors reminded me what it is like to have a normal conversation with someone, without worrying what family tragedy will befall us all next. Whatever the reason, every bad thought I've had since the will was discovered bubbles right up from my stomach to my lips and tumbles out.

"The will isn't Tors' fault. Mum, no one is more angry at Dad than I am. Do you think I want to be here, worrying about your future? What about my life in New York? You're all expecting me to fill some father-role here. Well, if I want to have a drink with a girl, I will! She's a good person, and she doesn't want this to be happening any more than you do!"

I'm cut off by Lizzy.

"Don't you defend her, Seán, and don't talk to Mum like that! You're making out that we're keeping you here against your will – we're your family and we all have to pull together."

For some reason I'm glad Lizzy is fighting back at me, it makes it easier to spit out all of the pent-up hurt and anger. "I don't see anyone telling Niamh we have to pull together! No one cares that she's gone, because good old Seán will pick up the pieces. Well, *I don't know what to do!* And what about Katie? Does that girl ever make an effort with this family?"

I hear a door creak closed upstairs but with the atmosphere buzzing in my ears, I really cannot care less.

"Katie is delicate at the moment," says my mother.

"So what, Mum? Don't you think I'm fragile? Dad's dead, my boss is emailing me every five minutes, I just found out my parents aren't married and that my father cheated on my mother and has another son. What kind of a family is this?" I fling my arms into the air and turn my back on them.

"Now look here, Seán –" Lizzy continues to bicker.

"That's enough!" Mum's voice suddenly deepens, and reverberates through the house with an authority I have not heard since I was a child. "We're all emotional. This is hard for all of us, and yelling about it won't get us anywhere. We'll just say something we regret. Lizzy, stop crying. Seán, calm down. I'm going to bed, and we'll discuss this in the morning."

Without saying another word, she storms up the stairs. Immediately, I feel my righteous anger drain away into guilt. But even as I turn to apologise, Lizzy is already charging up the stairs to her room. I hear her door slam angrily. Barely aware of what I'm doing, I slowly walk into the dining room, open the drinks cabinet, and pour myself a double whiskey. I think of my friends in America as I drink it. My flatmates would join in, or scoff and pour a beer. Claire would probably drink me under the table. I caress the glass slowly as I meditate on her. I don't think I have ever gone this long without thinking about her. I pick up the whiskey bottle again.

* * *

111

The next day, my family don't speak to one another. More correctly, we don't see each other. I stay in my room, curled up in the warm duvet, feeling all the more snug for the rain pelting against the window. I do a bit of work on my laptop, drop Claire a quick email and sneak downstairs for food when I hear the front door slam shut in the afternoon. I don't try to contact Tors but I wonder about her constantly. Sleep comes easily that night, even though I haven't done much all day. I doze off hoping that by tomorrow morning tempers will have dissipated and the rash words of the night before will be forgiven.

* * *

The next morning I am munching toast with Pat O'Hara's famous home-made raspberry jam and reading yesterday's leftover newspaper when Mum appears in from a morning walk, her cheeks rosy-red and her eyes full of the vitality I remember from my youth. I smile at her. This is the mum I know.

She shakes off her jacket and lowers herself into one of the wooden chairs opposite me. Sighing, she casts her eyes around the small, dainty kitchen.

"You know, your father never understood why I wanted this small room to be the main kitchen. It used to just be the pantry."

Hearing her talk about Dad in the past tense still hurts.

"The house is so large and before you kids were born it seemed even bigger. This room gets the early morning light and the size is just right for a kitchen – it's cosy, and homely."

I sit through the pause, waiting for her to get to the point. I know her long enough to know not to push her. She changes the subject again. "Are you still okay to visit Mrs Boden tonight? Pat was with her last night and thinks she was looking a bit peaky. But she insisted to Pat she didn't need a doctor, just a good night's sleep. So, just check that the house is warm enough and ask if she needs anything. You don't have to stay longer than ten or fifteen minutes."

112

I nod. It's the last thing I want to do. Not because of Mrs Boden who I have always loved, but I know she'll want to talk to me about Dad and I can't bear to think of happy memories of him right now. It's easier to hate.

The talk comes more suddenly than I expect. She stares me straight in the eye and does not flinch when she says it.

"Seán, I don't want you spending time with Tors Shaw. Do you realise that your father cheated on me with her mother? You know our families can have no future together – don't get caught up in something you'll regret. You can bet her mother is giving her the same advice."

Keeping my head down, I stuff another slice of toast into my mouth to keep myself from answering straight away. I should have known the fight wasn't over. I cannot blame Mum for what she is saying. The thing is, I do not want anything to do with Karen Shaw, and I have no desire to see this half-brother of mine. But I don't know how to explain to Mum that Tors does not feel like part of the drama. She is just someone I connected with and I wish I could put into words how much I need that right now.

But I have a feeling Mum is right about one thing – Karen Shaw is sure to be telling her daughter not to have any further contact with us, unless it is through a solicitor. I need to talk to Tors.

The sudden arrival of Lizzy makes us jump. She can usually be heard coming a mile away and has obviously been listening at the door. Her mouth is stretched into a thin line and I stare at her for a moment, trying to figure out what is wrong. She continues to glare at me and I feel my stomach drop, sure she is about to join in the conversation on our mother's side.

But to my surprise she turns to Mum. "Why didn't you and Dad marry?"

"Not now, Lizzy, please." Mum shakes her head wearily.

My sister does not pursue the issue, but turns to me. "Seán," she says, more calmly than I expect, as she slides into the chair next to

Mum, making me feel like I am sitting in an interview across from two very stern taskmasters, "I read Dad's will again last night."

Mum's head snaps up.

"I found the copy Michael gave you in the middle drawer of the dining-room cabinet where you keep all the important documents."

Lizzy is clearly talking to both of us but keeps her eyes on me. I squirm uncomfortably.

"Do you realise that I'm not in it?"

"Yes, you are," I answer immediately. "Dad left a trust fund for all of us. It's not worth much, but . . ."

"No," she replies, stubbornly, "he left it to you, Niamh, Katie and any other children."

"That includes you, you big eejit!" I try to keep my voice playful.

Lizzy's voice is suddenly shrill. "I know that! But I'm not named personally!"

"What the hell? You weren't born, Lizzy!"

"Seán!" Mum casts me a warning look. "But, sweetheart, Seán is right. You weren't born at the time, so how could Dad have named you personally?"

Mum puts a comforting hand on Lizzy's back but she jerks away as though burned, the chair scraping loudly against the wooden floor.

"Exactly! That's the point, Mum!" We gape at her as she begins pacing the kitchen. "Dad didn't even bother changing the will after I was born to include my name. I only sneak in under some chance catch-all phrase. I don't care about the money or anything else he might have left me –" she waves away the notion of inheritance impatiently, "but every year on my birthday, you and Dad make a toast, Mum. What is it?"

I crease my eyebrows, but Mum answers immediately. "We toast to you, our beautiful baby, who completes our family."

"Yes. But I wasn't enough, was I? If Dad had really loved me, if he really felt I completed this family, maybe we would have been enough for him. But he didn't and now we're left with next to nothing. Mum, you know Katie and I don't even make enough money to be able to afford to move out of this house. Niamh will probably want to do a post-doctorate after her PhD, and Seán lives all the way in New York. None of us can support you. Dad just abandoned you, and I wasn't enough to convince him to stick with us."

Mum stands and, I can tell, with some effort smiles at my little sister whose eyes are sparkling with tears. "Lizzy, sweetheart, I'm not going to starve! None of us are. I am a teacher with a salary, you know, and Dad did leave us some money. Ignore what I said the other night, I was in a rage. I have savings. We have plenty of friends here in Ballyloughlin who'll make sure we're taken care of if things get really bad. We'll be fine."

"I'm not giving in!" Lizzy says fiercely. "I thought about it all last night. Seán, I don't know why you were with Tors Shaw yesterday but you have to decide where your loyalties lie. I'm not going to take this. I loved Dad, and I was a good daughter but I won't let this one stupid decision of his ruin the rest of our family."

"Sweetheart, we're not going to be ruined –"

"I'm not talking about money!" Lizzy cuts across her. "I'm talking about being let down, being passed over by Dad in favour of the other son. We're going to fight this will. And I'm going to tell Karen Shaw exactly where she can stick it."

"No, you are not!" Mum's tone is firm.

She takes a step towards Lizzy and I can feel a screaming match coming on. I know my own temper will not be able to resist joining in. I hold my head in my hands as Mum continues.

"This is a sensitive legal issue, Lizzy. You can't just go barging up to Karen Shaw demanding that she convince her son to renounce his rights. You saw what she was like last night."

"I have a right to talk to her, Mum." Lizzy is determined, and her voice cuts the air with a high-pitched frequency that jolts me out of my seat.

"I'll talk to her," I say. A silence follows, so I continue. "I mean it,

I'll do it. You're right, I've developed a – a friendship with Tors. I can find a way to talk to Karen Shaw, *calmly*," I stress, looking directly at my sister, "and explain our situation. But, Lizzy, after the run-in you and Mum had with her last night, I think Mum's right – if you confront her you'll only exacerbate what may well turn into a court case. They are probably still at the hospital with Tors' brother. I'll go this afternoon." When no one objects, I realise how much my mother wanted this.

The last thing I have a desire to do is talk to Karen Shaw. The way she just showed up in Wicklow to demand the house is not just aggressive, but slightly demented. She can't honestly have expected Mum to just hand over the keys. Is she just trying to bully us? A very small part of me wonders if Tors lured me away on purpose to give her mother a chance to accost mine. But the memory of the frantic phone calls we received convinces me otherwise, and makes me embarrassed to have even suspected her.

Patting Lizzy's shoulder awkwardly, I walk past them, my head down. My mind is so full of what I really wanted to say, that not a word is spoken between Katie and me when we pass on the stairs. I'm ashamed of my cowardice, at being unable to comfort Lizzy for what was really upsetting her. But, unlike my frank sister, I cannot bring myself to say out loud what we are all feeling – that none of us had been enough for our father.

* * *

The house Karen Shaw has taken is a small cottage by the sea. The area is a massively popular holiday spot in the summer when all the Dublin 'bathers' flock to the beaches for the months of July and August. But in the semi-light of a cold March afternoon, the whole vicinity looks dull and gloomy. It is too blustery to consider venturing to the beach but I watch in fascination as the wind whips the sea into a frenzy, wave after wave smashing onto the shore. I would have had trouble distinguishing Tors' bungalow from the many others in the row along the seafront but for Karen's car, the only one parked for miles around. Tors' Toyota is nowhere to be seen.

Suddenly, I begin to lose my nerve. I had half-hoped that Karen would be at the hospital to give me some time alone with Tors, or at least that Tors would be there to calm her mother should she respond as she did last night. Steeling myself, I get out of the car, which I reversed into the driveway so I can make a quick getaway if I need to escape.

I have to walk right around the bungalow to get to the door. The front faces the sea and is mostly glass, offering a full view of the inside of the house. A hammock lies limp on a damp, wooden porch swing by the doorway.

The boy is playing alone on the floor just inside the door. I stare at him. It takes me a second to remember his name and I speculate, not for the first time, whether Karen has also been dishonest about the paternity of this boy, and even of Tors. But then the ever-connected question of whether my own father was guilty of the same offences arise and I push the thought away.

Jack raises his head as I knock gently on the door, then scratches his ear almost inquisitively, his other hand paused in the motion of slamming one truck into another. I smile, imagining his little mind at work. *This man looks familiar, definitely not a stranger. But where have I seen him before? Is he a goodie or a baddie? He's smiling nicely and waving – maybe I should let him in. But since we moved to the sea house, Mam gets angry so quickly.*

I clench my teeth in frustration as Jack jumps up and runs to get his mother rather than answer the door himself. It might have been easier if I could have got the boy on side first. When Karen sees that it's me, she halts abruptly and Jack mirrors the motion, skidding to a stop. Her dainty, even pretty face distorts painfully as her eyes narrow and her mouth becomes pinched, the anger positively rippling out of her. I swallow, with effort, realising that even if I had managed to befriend the boy, Karen would still be looking at me as though *I* was the one who abandoned her and Andrew all those years ago.

A thought flashes, unwanted, through my mind. I would have been Jack's age when my father and this woman met to break their wedding vows. Of course, in Dad's case there had been no wedding. I take a breath to recover myself, knowing I will only get this one chance to convince Karen she should back off. I have to get it right. I am also well aware that I have no intention of cutting off ties with Tors, and that although this woman is nothing more than the adulteress trying to destroy my mother's life, to Tors she is a mother. I have to tread carefully.

I extend my right hand as Karen slowly and deliberately opens the door.

"Mrs Shaw, I'm Seán Murtagh. I need to talk to you privately."

To my surprise, she pauses only for a second before letting me in, though she does not take my proffered hand. The house is surprisingly warm and snug. I drink in the detail of the pleasant surroundings as Karen gently ushers her youngest son into another room. The house is small, but would suit holidaymakers perfectly; it reminds me of the way my own mother had talked about the cosiness of our kitchen earlier.

"How is Andrew?"

She stares at me.

"You got a call last night –"

"He's fine," she interrupts, crossing her arms over her chest.

Desperately, I cast my mind back to a Networking and Relationships course all the newly recruited graduates had taken a few years ago. First rule, find something in common with the person with whom you are conversing. It's weak, pathetic even, but anything is worth a shot. "I've never been down to these holiday cottages – they are lovely, real cosy. Mum was just saying this morning –"

She cuts me off. "Have you come to tell me that your mother has moved out of the house?"

118

I abandon the rules of networking immediately. "No. She is not going to move out of the house. She has lived there practically all of her adult life and raised her family there."

"Well, I raised my family between a shitty box of a house and hospitals. My son is taking what's his. His solicitor is in the process of drafting a letter to your mother. It's probably best if we don't discuss it. Is there anything else?"

I stare. There has to be a way to make her engage with me.

"I want to know the truth about you and my father." I shock myself – this was not the question I had intended to fall from my lips.

She starts, looking uncomfortable rather than militant, for the first time. Releasing her arms from her body, she runs a hand through her hair. I am startled to see her let her guard down like this. She perches herself on the side of the worn sofa, as though for support.

"Come on," I take the opportunity, somehow more belligerently than I had planned, "I'm sure if your children have not asked you that question yet, they will. I don't need to be placated – I want an honest answer."

Her face sharpens again ever so slightly at the mention of her children, but her eyes betray a mixture of guilt and pity. "What your father and I did was stupid and irresponsible. It was only once and we both regretted it. But it gave me Andrew so I have to think it was one of those mistakes that was meant to happen."

"Mrs Shaw," I soften my voice, "please, I need facts. I can't ask my father. Please, just tell me what happened."

She looks at me suspiciously. I know what she is wondering – is this just a ploy to trap her into saying something that my family can use against her? Or am I, who can't be much older than Tors, simply looking for a way to excuse my father for betraying my mother? My mouth is dry and I realise I am holding my breath.

She twitches, then starts speaking. "Look, there really isn't much to tell. I was in a very bad place. About a year before, when Tors was four years old, my late husband and I started trying for another baby.

But it didn't work straight away, as it had with her. It put a strain on our marriage. Then my mother died. She was my rock, I was lost without her. I withdrew into myself, and became depressed, I think. It was hard on Stuart too, but at the time I couldn't see that. Then Stuart's mother died six months later. I was still too low to offer him any real support and I don't think he wanted to lean on me at that point. We were drifting apart and we stopped even trying for a baby."

Now that she has started, she seems unable to stop. Her face is knotted with angst as though she knows she shouldn't be speaking these words aloud to anyone, never mind to me, but she can't stop them leaking from her mouth. I stand frozen, terrified of breaking her train of thought, drinking in every word.

"About six months after my mother-in-law passed away, I began to feel the need for a connection again, but Stuart was still deep in his own grief and not inclined to forget my recent hostility, because that's what it had been: I had been hostile towards him. Don't think for a second I didn't realise the effect all the negativity was having on my sweet daughter. It compounded the guilt and I started to spiral back into misery.

"Then one night, I went to Galway to have dinner with an old friend from school, who had emigrated but was back in Ireland for a short while. We had a long talk. Old friends are the best for being able to see straight through your bullshit to your heart, and she insisted I go home and try to fix things with Stuart. To be honest, I agreed just to get her off my back, she was so headstrong. But as I was walking back to my car, I was attacked.

"Your father saved me. The attacker, whoever he was, knocked me down and was towering over me when your father appeared. Maybe he just wanted my purse but you never know what could have happened. When your father came upon us – he lunged at the man and dragged him away from me. I could do nothing but cower on the ground while they scuffled and eventually the man pulled free and ran off.

"I was very shaken. Liam took me back to his B&B which was only around the corner. He cleaned up my head and made us tea. He was kind. There was nothing planned or premeditated about what we did. My friend, who I'd met earlier, had been so opinionated about what I should do that I hadn't had the chance to get everything off my chest as I'd so badly needed. So it all came pouring out then to Liam, all the problems with Stuart, how worried I was about what it was doing to Victoria, our mothers dying, not being able to conceive. Your father was sympathetic, he listened. Then he tried to comfort me using stories about his own life. He was having troubles too." She pauses. "He and your mother – they were going through a rough patch. We had a connection. It just happened."

I steel myself to ask the one question to which I know neither a confirmation nor denial will make me happy. "Did Dad want him?"

A cloud passes over Karen's face and once again it only takes an instant for her naturally beautiful features to contort into an ugly sneer. "Andrew is my son. Your father had his own family."

"But did he want him, Karen?"

She stiffens. "You can address me as 'Mrs Shaw', thank you. And it is none of your business."

I stand up a little straighter and raise my voice. "It is absolutely my business. This is my father's son we are talking about."

"No, he is *my* son, my child," Her voice is hard.

"Then why are you trying to take my mother's house from her? Why are you doing this to us?"

We are both shouting now.

In the same second, we each take a step closer, as if to assert our authority.

We are almost touching and I hear the threatening pulse to my words. "Leave my mother alone."

Something seems to snap in Karen. Angrily, and forcefully, she slaps me across the face. Stumbling, I back away.

"I never asked your father for anything in his whole life and I never took a penny off him, even though he had the big house and the fancy car and the stables for his children. We live in a tiny house that gets so damp in the winter that it makes my boy feel worse. And he's dying. I mean it, young man, my son is not just sick, he's dying. Your father had everything when we had nothing. So I'll take what's rightfully mine for my son – fuck you and fuck your mother!"

"*Mam!*"

I whip around so fast my neck cricks.

Tors is standing in the doorway, with a wide-eyed Jack at her side.

Chapter 12

Tors

I'm running. My swinging arms propel me forward and my legs stretch each step into a leap. My breath thins to ragged gasps, but I keep going. All too aware that I am not fit enough for this, the damp sand further hampers my stride. It's not long before he catches up. I don't hear him over the crashing waves and whistling wind, and even though I know it must be him grabbing my arm and swinging me around, I'm suddenly back in another place, another memory of shouts and grabbing. Claude pinning my struggling body to the wall, his voice bellowing in my ear.

Then a voice that's just as loud, yet infinitely more tender, breaks through. He's angling my face up towards him as I'm still pulling from Claude. Misunderstanding my tussle, he's shouting over the smash of the waves that he's sorry, my mother's okay, my brother is fine. With his words, I'm back in the present.

Poor Jack. I left him open-mouthed on the doorstep and ran. I only heard the last sentence my mother screamed at Seán Murtagh, but that was enough. What has she become? What has our whole family become?

I bury my face in his chest. Knowing a whispered apology will be lost in the roar of the sea, I say nothing. It takes a few minutes, but I control my breathing and make myself look up at him, scared of what I might see, of what I used to see in Claude's face – anger, or even hatred – but there is only concern. Something more than relief washes over me.

Suddenly, I am kissing him. He staggers in shock, but then responds urgently. I can't believe how natural it is to feel his lips on mine, our hands finding only heavy coats and scarves, but searching anyway. The wind on the exposed shore almost knocking us sideways, he takes my hand and pulls me against the force of the gale to the refuge of a hollow in a nearby dune, where we collapse together and lie nestled in an ineffective cranny.

I don't want to say anything. No words can explain or improve our impossible situation. We're on different sides of a bitter divide, with Andrew caught in the middle. I imagine trying to explain to Andrew my feelings for Seán Murtagh and my body shivers. He pulls me closer, thinking it's from the cold.

He says something, but it is caught in the wind. "I said," he tries again, pointing, "what about back there?"

I squint through the sandstorm as he pulls me to my feet and leads me by the hand around the back of the dune. It takes about five minutes, but eventually we end up off the beach entirely, at the back of a long field. Here we are more sheltered from the wildness of the shore. The back of the dunes and the bushes provide a buffer, the sea's crashing now strikingly distant. We sit, controlled this time, on a mossy stretch of damp grass facing each other.

He makes no move towards me, and I sit paralysed by the reality of what we just did. I sneak a look at him after a few minutes. He's looking down at his hands, seemingly lost in thought. I wonder what else my mother said to him, but the idea of asking fills me with dread so I look away again. Suddenly, he's speaking directly at me.

"Let's just say it!" His voice is determined.

"Say what?" I can hear the reservation in mine.

"Everything we're thinking! About the other's family. It's not something we're going to be able to avoid. We might as well confront it now. I've spent a lot of time thinking, over the past couple of weeks. If my father had been upfront with us, it would have saved us all a lot of heartache. I won't make that mistake. I'll start. Your mother is a conniving wench."

His words hit me with force. "Seán!" How can he say that? He must know I'll defend her.

"Go on! You must have some choice words for members of my family!"

Raging at him, I can't help but retaliate. "Well, about your father anyway!"

"Yes? Say it!"

"He abandoned my brother! And my mother! Why isn't your family completely mortified? If you had any sense of decency, you'd have handed over everything you had to Andrew on the day your father died!" I jerk my face away. I can't believe I just said that. I didn't even know I thought that.

Seán is ready. "Mum didn't know Andrew existed. None of us did. But your mother knew about us. She could have asked for help from us at any time. But she waited until my father died and we're all alone before she came here."

"You really don't get it, do you? This isn't about our mothers, or fathers. Or you or me or a will. It's about *Andrew*. He's the only one who should matter here."

"Why? Just because he's sick?"

The incredulity in his tone infuriates me. "Let me ask you this. Your youngest sister, Lizzy? You get on well with her, don't you?" I barely give him time to nod. "Well, suppose someone put a gun to her head and told you they would shoot her unless you did what they asked. You'd do anything, right? Well, Andrew's not just sick. He's dying. He's got a gun to his head. And like it or not, money can open doors, give us options. It could buy better specialists, a more comfortable place for him to live, cut his commute time to the hospital by half a day. It's not much, but it's something. Something to make it easier on him and maybe hold off the gunman a little longer."

I stand up and turn away from him. It's my mother's argument, not mine. But it's starting to become clear to me what his family sees when they look at me. They see my mother. I never asked him, or Glenda, or any of the daughters the question I should have – the real reason I first visited their house that rainy afternoon. I don't know why I haven't asked. I believe what I just said: Andrew is the most important person of all. Yet something is stopping me.

I feel his hands brushing my arms. "I liked it better five minutes ago."

Despite everything, my body tingles under his touch. I turn into his embrace and we kiss ardently. His cold, smooth fingers interlock with mine and we stand there a long time, just being.

When we begin to talk again, it's easier, like it was that night in Keogh's. The worst is out, and we move on to lighter topics with relish. He describes his Irish flatmates and discusses Kevin O'Hara's trip to visit him in New York. I tell him, briefly, that I lived for a year in Paris. I don't say any more.

We sit for hours, then walk, saunter, back to the beach and beat our way against the wind along the shore, hand in hand. It's easier now to talk to him about Andrew. In Keogh's, I felt I was betraying my brother, but today is different somehow. Interestingly, he seems reluctant to talk about Andrew, but also unable to hold back his curiosity.

"What happened to him two nights ago, when your mum got that call?"

My chest tightens. It had been horrible. Though we try not to dwell on it, we have all been on tenterhooks since Andrew's AVF got blocked. It's not unusual, it happens. But it cuts off a route to dialysis, takes away an option, increases the worry. The urgency about the need for a transplant is growing.

That night, his temperature spiked and he was asking for me. It looked like the temporary line under his left shoulder might be infected. Luckily, they determined that was not the case, that Andrew might have just contracted a virus. His body is so vulnerable, so susceptible and the trauma of the move hasn't helped. There's an extra burden he's shouldering as well. He is right-handed and since the surgery to install the new AVF in his right arm, he's worried that his drawings will be affected. Dr Jim told him not to be too concerned and Dr Stevens has been very encouraging about him keeping up the art, but I can tell he's scared he'll lose one of the few joys in his life, one of the only activities he can take on independently.

"What does your brother do? Has he ever worked?"

"His dialysis is three days a week – his new schedule here is Tuesday, Thursday and Saturday. Either way, it's not very conducive to work. Luckily he got through his Leaving Cert. Probably not as well as if he had been in the full of his health, but the kidneys only really went that year so he got his education. He is doing a distance art diploma with the London Art College at the moment. It's supposed to be a one-year course but they are allowing him stretch it over two years. He's only six months in, and he loves it. It gives him a real focus."

"Is he good at art?"

"He's brilliant. You should see his watercolours." Again, I can't help the tint of pride that resonates through my answer like he is my own child. "We're hoping that he'll get a transplant soon, so once the course is done he'll be able to go to college full time. Some kidney patients do manage to structure their dialysis around work or study but we don't live near enough to the hospital for that to be realistic. We leave early in the morning and don't get home until late. It just wouldn't be feasible."

"Did you ever think about moving nearer to the hospital?"

I look at him strangely. He really doesn't understand what it's like not to have money. "We live in a council house. We can't afford to move. Most of my carer's allowance goes on petrol but it's the best we can do."

There's a silence as Seán digests this.

It is clear from the massive support he has received since his dad died that he does not appreciate what it is like to literally just have the four of us. The Family Support Network will help if we ask. The hospital is wonderful when we're there and we have a few friends we can call on in an emergency. But on a day-to-day basis, no one looks in, no one helps. We do it ourselves. We are not the heart of a community like the Murtaghs.

Tentatively, I ask Seán about that, whether he misses the resounding sense of community when he's in America. For some reason, he appears a bit embarrassed.

"It's just different," he explains. "I have my own freedom in New York, my own space. But I'll never be able to escape Ballyloughlin – I'm too tied up in it. 'Escape' probably isn't the right word – it's not that I want to go away and never return. It's just that when I'm here I don't have a separate identity – I'm just part of the jigsaw puzzle." He looks down at me anxiously, like he's just admitted something awful. He continues quickly in an attempt to redeem himself. "Look, I don't mean to complain. Our friends and neighbours have been so wonderful since Dad died." He goes on to tell me about his grandfather who farmed the land while running two businesses in the town. He made his money and ploughed it back into the local community – building halls and revitalising the GAA and hurling clubs. Passionate about music himself, and of course religion, he instigated a folk group to sing every Sunday at Mass and sponsored prizes at the local Feis Ceoil. He involved his son in every aspect of the community.

Seán's mother has admitted to him that his grandfather was not immediately impressed when Liam arrived back from England with a new bride. But I can imagine Glenda, even though young and uneducated, charming her new in-laws with a lively spirit and an obvious love for their son. Seán tells me how she threw herself into the culture and community and how, with his grandfather's financial help, she graduated as a primary school teacher after giving birth to Seán.

"My family helped make Ballyloughlin what it is. When I'm here, I feel like I should be living up to everyone's expectations. Of course, it's a bit different now that Dad's a disgrace. Of course, I can't help imagining what else they are hiding since Mum admitted she never even married Dad –" He claps a hand over his mouth in horror, knowing he should not have exposed that particular secret to me.

The wind whips around us as we stop moving against it. "Relax, Seán, I already know. The solicitor told us."

I had refused to discuss the legalities with Mam but she blurted out that juicy piece of information earlier this morning. At Mam's insistence, Roger Nestor had contacted Michael Undersky for some basic details around the benefits under the will. When no marriage cert, or even details of a wedding, could be obtained, Roger Nestor finally twigged why Liam had insisted the will be drafted with no regard for the legal right of his apparent spouse.

"I suppose your mother is over the moon."

I glare at the malice in his words and he has the grace to look ashamed. But the truth is he is right so I decide to let it go.

"You can't keep a secret for long in this place," I say. "I can't believe you didn't know who I was by the time I called to your door that day."

He tells me how utterly shocked his family were when I turned up at their house, and confides to me, in detail, Michael Undersky's revelation that he knew about my mother.

I am not as surprised as Seán that his father would confess to his friend. What interests me most is that Katie, the sister who is the same age as Andrew, insisted the Murtagh family call my brother by his name. I ask Seán about her, but he just shrugs.

"Katie's quiet. She doesn't get involved in what's going on. To be honest, we haven't spoken much since I came home."

We are within sight of the sea house before I know it but I can't bring myself to go in just yet. I don't think I can stand any more drama. Seán squeezes my hand, understanding this one great torment we have in common.

Then it happens again. For the third time since we moved to Ballyloughlin, it happens. I know it as soon as I see my grief-stricken mother bolt from the house with Jack tripping over himself in a frantic run. I teeter a little on the spot, as another memory, but a beautiful childhood memory this time, envelops me.

My father is standing behind me moving my arms back and forth, trying to loosen them, but I continue to jerk the long fishing-rod haphazardly. "Dad!" I whine, as I let my body go limp. "It's too big, I'm too little!"

"Tors, you're eight years old. Come on now, you can do it! Never ever say you can't because I know you can do it!"

With a swish, he casts the line out, me still holding on, laughing with delight.

I don't remember if we caught anything. But his words hit me now, and I suddenly want him there to do it for me. I don't know if I can keep doing it like this, without him.

Holding onto his belief in me, the adrenaline kicks in. I'm running faster than Seán this time, reaching them as Jack jumps into the back of the car. As though the scene in the house had never happened, my mother looks deep into my eyes, hers brimming with tears.

I turn to Seán to apologise but my words are whipped away by the wind. As we speed away, I watch him in the rear-view mirror staring after the car, suddenly wanting to leap from the car and run back to him. The longing does not last as my mind moves to our destination. It never gets easier. When Andrew takes a turn the shock never lessens, the worry never decreases. My little brother is dying and I still haven't asked the Murtaghs for what he really needs.

Chapter 13

Seán

I am waiting for her at the front door when she swings the car almost silently into the driveway. The sun is barely breaking through the oaks across the road but I know my youngest sister will be up soon.

Having Tors here is not an act of defiance. I really don't care what they think. The look on her face as she dropped my hand to run to her mother has had me up all night. I sat in my car by the sea house until late into the night, and when I eventually surmised they weren't coming back, I drove home. I waited by the house phone for hours, just staring at it, willing it to ring. We had not swapped mobile phone numbers. My American friends would not believe it; that is the first thing they would do. Luckily, she did ring the house phone, about half an hour ago, to say that her brother is stable for now.

I insisted she come over, just to talk. She did not need persuading.

As she trudges to the door, I am glad to see she is not crying. I kiss her lips quickly and lead her through our large entrance hall into the homely kitchen, where I think she will be more comfortable. Immediately, I feel like a snob.

"So your brother is okay?" I ask, pulling some sparkling water from the drinks cabinet and pouring us each a glass.

She stays standing, looking at me curiously, and watches me gulp down my drink before answering. "Actually, no. He's worse."

This is not the answer I expect and I clumsily spill some of the water down my front as I take a step closer to her. "I'm sorry. What happened?"

She does not move, but continues to stare straight at me. "Nothing happened. He's just been getting steadily worse. It's taking its toll – all the stress of realising my dad isn't his natural father, and moving hospital. He's deteriorating."

I don't know what to say. Tors keeps talking, never taking her eyes from mine. She looks slightly dazed.

"It's been getting worse for a while, even before your dad died. I told you about his AVF. He's been bad before, but he recovered. So I have to keep believing he'll pull through again. He's resting now. Mum is taking Jack home for a few hours. I'll go back to the hospital soon."

Her sentences are short, clipped, spoken in a deadened tone. Suddenly, I realise the lack of tears is not because everything is all right. It is the opposite: she is in shock. I do not know what to think, I certainly do not know what to say. I reach out awkwardly, intending only to hug her. But instead of her body, my hands take her face. Gently, I caress her cheeks, knowing if she looks away, I would probably stop. But she never takes her eyes from mine, and does not push me back. My mouth finds hers, and I pull her into a strong, one-armed embrace, my other hand cupping her head, keeping her locked to me. She wraps her arms around my body and returns my hold with passion.

I pull away. I could kiss her all day, but I am scared she will think that is all I want, that I do not care about Andrew. She stares up with an intensity that scares me. Her mouth opens, she looks as though she is wavering on the verge of the most important thing she will ever say . . .

We wrench apart as a piercing voice shrieks from upstairs.

Fear charging me, I shove Tors aside and race to the stairs, taking it three at a time. Lizzy's voice rings out again, calling for me, calling for Mum. I follow the sound of her cries, not registering that they are leading me not to her room, but to my other sister's.

My lungs empty. The world spins.

Katie is lying very still, half drooped over the side of her bed, with a pool of vomit curdling on the floor beneath her. Three empty bottles of pills lie on their sides on the nightstand. Blood rushes to my head and my knees lock in terror. I grip the door frame to stay upright, a pathetic groan escaping my lips. My mother brushes past me and runs to Katie screaming, while Lizzy sinks to the floor, crying noisily.

Suddenly, Tors is there. She pulls Katie back onto the bed, keeping her on her side while brushing her tangled hair off her face. Katie flops, unresponsive, onto her back. Tors checks for a wrist pulse with her fingers.

"She's alive," she nods. Her voice is commanding, steady. "She has to get to a hospital."

She is addressing me now, but I barely hear her. I watch in a trance as she scoops up the empty pill bottles.

"There's no point waiting for an ambulance to come out since we're so near St John's," she says calmly. "We should go in the car."

Mum nods frantically, never taking her eyes off her daughter, and reaches out for Tors' hand without questioning her presence.

"*Seán!*" The panic in Lizzy's voice steadies me somehow.

Tors repeats my name, solidly. As though miraculously thawed, my legs move me swiftly to the bed. I lift my sister gently, carry her out of the room and start down the stairs with her. The women shuffle frantically behind me, and I allow Tors to overtake me at the front door to lead me to her car.

Within minutes Tors is speeding towards St John's with Lizzy beside her in the front. Mum and I don't look at each other in the back

133

seat, but stare down at Katie's limp body sprawled across us. Mum smooths her mangled hair with desperate, loving caresses. I remember stroking Tors' face that way only moments earlier in our kitchen. It seems like a long time ago.

Tors screeches up to the ambulance bay at the door of St John's A&E. The engine is barely off when she is out the door. She bends down and looks in the window at us. "Get her in here – I'll find someone."

Mum and Lizzy help me jostle Katie's still-limp form out of the car and hoist her back into my arms. I register dimly that I must look so strange, bursting through the doors carrying an unconscious girl with two hysterical women at my side. The thought is fleeting and then, again, all I can think is that Katie hasn't made a sound or stirred since we found her. To stop myself imagining the unthinkable, I look straight ahead, focusing on putting one foot in front of the other. I've never needed to concentrate on that before.

Tors is running towards us with a doctor, who is calling back for assistance.

"Glenda, this is Andrew's doctor! He's not an A&E doctor, but I just found him down here! Dr Stevens, this is –"

But the doctor cut across her, looking down at my sister, "Katie Murtagh!"

Our eyes snap up from Katie to stare at a doctor we have never encountered before.

"We found her like this just over ten minutes ago," Tors is saying. "She seems to have taken these pills – there were three empty bottles . . ." She presses the bottle into the doctor's hand.

He looks at the label, hesitates only for a second, then shouts for help again. A trolley appears in front of me. Knowing I could not have held onto her dead weight much longer, I lower my little sister onto it and watched helplessly as Katie is pushed through a set of swinging double doors, Dr Stevens calling back to Tors to keep the family where we are.

We stand together for a few seconds, breathing heavily as we watch the doors swing back and forth. In a gentle but controlled manner, Tors manoeuvres my shaking mother and crying sister into orange plastic chairs by the wall. I am still watching the double doors through which Katie disappeared when Tors walks back to me. At her touch, I look down at her vacantly.

"Come and sit down," she murmurs, and I let myself be led to sit beside my family.

Lizzy buries her head in my chest. Tors sits on my other side and squeezes my trembling fist with her small, strong hand.

The next few hours pass in a haze. I am vaguely aware of nurses coming to talk to us. They ask questions about how long Katie had been unconscious, if we know how many pills she has taken. We tell them again about the three empty bottles, and Mum becomes increasingly distressed. So they turn to me for other, easier questions, such as Katie's age and medical history. Patients and visitors pass in and out of the door, but I am too dazed to register more than blurry shapes.

At one point, Tors goes to check on her brother, and comes back with a different doctor. Mum stands up immediately, but he beckons her to sit down and pulls up a chair facing us.

"Your daughter is alive," he states bluntly. "We've had to pump her stomach, and she's sleeping at the moment, but you can go in and see her if you like."

Mum breaks down completely, and Lizzy buries her head in her shaking hands. I hiccup a laugh.

"I'll need to sit down with both you and Katie at some stage and discuss the reason this happened. Now is not the time. I know you've had a huge shock. But it is important to remember that just because she is alive, that doesn't mean this is over. To be perfectly frank, you are lucky you got her to the hospital when you did."

My mother nods frantically as she links Lizzy's arm and makes to follow the doctor.

I hold back. "I'll follow you in, Mum."

As soon as they have disappeared through those swinging doors, I turn to Tors, and take her hand. "Thank you. It's because of you we got her to the hospital so quickly. You saved her life."

But she shakes her head, blushing.

"If you hadn't been in the house this morning . . ." I shake my head. "God, when I saw her lying there . . ."

"Welcome to my world."

Before I can even begin to comprehend the enormity of what she has just said, I hear someone call out my name. One of the O'Hara triplets – I have no idea which one – is walking hurriedly toward me. Without even pausing to realise there is no way he could have known what happened to Katie, I immediately begin to assure him that she will be fine.

"Katie?" he repeats, his heavy eyebrow creasing. "What's wrong with her?"

I stare at him. "Isn't that why you're here?"

"No. What's the matter with her?"

I pause, but know that we cannot keep this a secret from the O'Hara family. "She overdosed," my voice is expressionless, "but she's alive."

I watch as the colour drains from the O'Hara boy's face, and he lowers himself into one of the plastic chairs. Tors looks down on him with pity.

Gripping his head in his hands, he looks up at me, a cloud of resentment spread across his face. "We told Glenda to keep an eye on her. We told her there was something wrong."

My insides squirm with guilt, but there is a more pressing question. "If you didn't know Katie was in hospital, why are you here?"

But even as I speak the words, I see Pat O'Hara rush in the door. My stomach contracts with fear. There is something wrong here, something else is going on that does not concern my sister. Tors clearly realises the same and puts her hands gently around my arm just as the O'Hara boy spits out the truth.

"You ought to know. Mrs Boden is dead."

Chapter 14

Seán

The few bluebells and daffodils poking up through the earth, still hard from a harsh winter, radiate colour I didn't think could still exist in this world.

I discovered the Reflection Garden at the back of the grounds as I staggered from the hospital. "*A peaceful space for quiet reflection*" the engraved stone informs me. I snort. I don't think I will ever be at peace again, and further reflection on my abandonment of Mrs Boden will certainly not help. Still, my family is unlikely to look for me here so, finding it mercifully empty, I pick a bench in the farthest corner, and sit brooding for hours.

Pat O'Hara had recruited fifteen people for her rota to visit Mrs Boden. All I had to give her was fifteen minutes last night. I remember Mum's words, reassuring me that the visit would not be too much of a nuisance: "*Just check that the house is warm enough and ask if she needs anything.*" How could I be so selfish, so caught up in my own desire for Tors to return to the sea house, that I would forget that sweet old lady who was like a grandmother to both us and the O'Hara boys?

The cold nips at my extremities and my cheeks alone feel warm from the tears. I don't care. I don't deserve warmth, or comfort. Mrs Boden and all her eccentricities are vivid in my mind: her famous collection of cures for scraped knees and bumped heads, including her assortment of pink and blue plasters; the way we used to fight to be the first to Mrs Boden's house on Hallowe'en because she always had the best selection of goodies; how she was the only person who didn't recite the generic "I'm sorry for your loss" at Dad's funeral – she merely gripped my wrist in her small, shaking hand and whispered that he was proud of me.

A dreadful spasm rips through my shoulders. Dad would be proud of me all right – another abandonment by the Murtagh men. Lizzy had said Mrs Boden was in good form the night she was scheduled to visit. I should have called to see her. Not just last night to comply with the roster. I should have popped in just to see how she was coping. Instead I retreated uncaringly, pining for America and wallowing in the revelations about Dad, as though I was the only one affected by his death.

"There you are!"

A body appears by my side. Lizzy.

"We've been looking for you everywhere. You just ran off."

I shake my head, but cannot think of anything to say.

"You know it's not your fault, don't you?"

A hollow, bitter laugh escapes me.

"Look, Seán, you forgot, okay? It was a mistake, but you didn't do it on purpose."

I stare up at my sister's eager face. "You're not angry at me?"

She shakes her head as if disappointed. In me, or in herself, I don't know. "Our sister nearly died today. We don't get to be angry, only grateful. Even if we lose the house to the Shaws, even if I have to give up Lilly and the other horses, we're all still alive. Wouldn't we all give up everything to spend just another day with Dad?"

I can't help it, it's too much. My body heaves with the tears that fall again, and Lizzy sits, taking my hand in hers. "Look, Seán, they have to do a post mortem to be sure, but it looks like Mrs Boden died of a heart attack during the night. There's a good chance that even if you had gone over to her last night, it wouldn't have made a difference."

"Maybe. But she wouldn't have spent her last night alone."

She can't dispute this and we sit in silence, hand in hand, for a long time as the guilt festers in me, seeping into every part of me like the blood running through my veins. Eventually, she pulls me up and leads me slowly back to the hospital.

*   *   *

The curtains are drawn in the room where Katie lies in the only bed, artificial light thrown across her body by a dim lamp in the corner. I move slowly, unsure if she is asleep. She looks so small, and young. As I stare down at her, I find to my surprise that the memories flow easily.

Dad is passing a pink bundle to me. I can tell he is staring into my eyes as he gives me a serious "big brother" speech but I'm not looking at him. Niamh is playing on the floor at my feet, unimpressed, but I concentrate hard, trying to hold the baby both gently and tightly: an impossible combination.

Another memory. Kevin and I are baby-sitting, begrudgingly. We're playing poker, or gin, or something manly and serious with a deck of cards. I don't see Niamh in my memory, but Lizzy is sitting on my lap, while Katie and the triplets tear loose around the sitting room, squealing and shouting. Then there's a crash, and a cry. One of the triplets is screaming, "Blood, blood!" while another comes running to us, "I didn't do it, I didn't do it!" Katie doesn't cry as I pick her up and carry her past the boys into the kitchen, but as soon as I close the door – as soon as it's just me – she starts to wail. With the very beginnings of my facial hair, I make her laugh by giving her a whiskery kiss.

There's a laughing memory too. And we're not merely giggling, we're in convulsions. Tears stream down our cheeks. I'm keeled over, clutching a stitch in my side. I don't remember where we were, or what set us off. But I do remember it was just the two of us. I must have been about twenty, her age now.

Looking down at her delicate body, I wonder what happened to take that laughter away. As gently as I can, I brush a long strand of her brown hair from her face. She is pale and drawn-looking, but she stirs at my touch and smiles up at me.

"Seán." It's a whisper, a croaky one. It sounds as if it hurts her to talk.

I feel a rush of tenderness towards her, and I start to well up again. I lean right in over her, so our cheeks touch.

"I'm sorry," she begins hoarsely, but I shake my head into her neck, whispering that it's okay, even though, just like Mrs Boden, it's not.

We curl like that for a long time, half rocking on the bed. I don't know how much time has passed when I feel her push against me to sit up and look past me. I turn to see Tors standing in the doorway, backing away.

"I'm sorry, I can come back . . ."

"No, come in." I shift around to sit on the bed beside Katie, placing my arm around her. She looks sheepish as I introduce them.

After some small talk about how Katie is feeling, Tors leans forward in her chair.

"Katie, I told my brother what happened to you."

Unexpectedly, Katie snuggles closer to me, and takes my hand. "What did he say?" She sounds strangely nervous.

"He's angry. He's clinging to life with every ounce of strength. He'd give anything to be like you, healthy and strong. He doesn't understand why you would do this."

"Tors!" I can't believe she's lecturing my sister, she doesn't know anything about Katie.

"No, it's all right, Seán." Katie tries to sit up straighter but her voice remains weak. "Tors, I wasn't trying to hurt myself. Honestly, I wasn't trying to kill myself. I just haven't been able to sleep. Since Dad. I can't remember the last time I slept for more than a couple of minutes at a time. I've been taking sleeping pills but they don't do anything. I just got so . . . tired. So I took an extra pill last night but it still didn't work. By four in the morning I was still awake. So I took more, and more, and more and . . . suddenly I'm here."

She slips back into the pillow heavily, as though even talking exhausts her. I'm wondering whether I should call a doctor, when a scene from earlier in the day flashes through my mind. I turn in towards my sister.

"Katie, we met Andrew's doctor when we brought you in. He knew your name. How does he know you?"

Katie lowers her eyes and, after a minute, Tors speaks up.

"She came to see Andrew. Yesterday. He just told me. While we were at the sea house, Seán. Dr Stevens met her then."

I gape down at my little sister in awe. "Why?"

She looks back at me, confused. Exasperated, I almost forget Tors is there as I sit back around to face Katie properly. "Why did you come here looking for Andrew Shaw?"

"Why haven't you?"

I splutter an indignant, incoherent reply, but Katie is already addressing Tors. "Will you please tell him it was an accident?"

Tors nods and stands up to leave.

"Wait," Katie pushes herself further upright, with some difficulty. "How is he?"

I'm suddenly mortified that I haven't asked her that myself. I've been so consumed with Katie I forgot it was only this morning that Tors stood in our kitchen in shock at her brother's rapid deterioration.

Her smile back to Katie is weary but genuine. "He's doing well, Katie. Thanks. He had a temperature last night, but I called in to him and it's broken. They might keep him in for another day just to be sure, but he'll be fine." She brushes her hand lightly and discreetly against my shoulder as she leaves.

Once alone again with Katie, my mouth is burning with a million questions. But seeing her body sag and eyes begin to close, I settle for just one.

"Why did you need to see him? I'm your brother." I know I sound childish, selfish.

"It's not about that. He's my age. We're like, twins. Dad loved me, didn't he, Seán?"

"Of course he did."

"I know. But still, I can't help wondering now, if all he ever saw when he looked at me was Andrew."

* * *

For the second time today, having watched my sister fall back asleep and tucked her in, I find myself sitting in the Reflection Garden. I couldn't stay in the hospital and am happy to let the afternoon hours slip away in solitude. I know the entire O'Hara family are lurking around the building and the last thing I need right now is to be confronted by them. I should be exhausted, but my mind is reeling.

The Garden is not empty this time – by now it is late afternoon. A few elderly people sit in apparent contemplation, though they might be dozing, and a young mother sits breastfeeding a small bundle wrapped in blue – a baby boy. Absent-mindedly, I wonder where the father is, and for an awful moment imagine a man with another family, already having abandoned these two, and feel a jolt of pity for Karen Shaw.

At that moment, a burly man, with a boy of about two years asleep on his shoulder, comes to sit beside the woman. A fresh thought occurs to me, but offers no comfort. Andrew does, in fact, have a family. He had parents growing up, an older sister who takes care of him when he is sick, and a little brother to play with. Suddenly, Karen Shaw's insistence that Andrew is owed everything by my family seems like a crime again.

I stare over at the two little boys. I never wanted a brother. After Lizzy was born, I remember comments that I must have been disappointed that I didn't finally get a brother. But I wasn't. Dad always told me I was special, being the only boy, and I liked being the one to take care of my sisters – it made me feel important. Somehow, in moving to America and building a life for myself away from the girls, I have lost that need to take care of them. Since being back, it has seemed like a burden. But now, having nearly lost Katie too, that feeling of triumph when Dad announced that Lizzy was a girl stirs once more.

I think about Tors. She is just like me, looking after younger siblings, but she seems to relish it. Somehow, this makes her even more attractive – she is something I was a long time ago, something I am ashamed to have lost. Katie asked why I didn't want to meet Andrew, when it had been the most natural thing in the world for her to do. My confident sense of self that sustained me in New York is disintegrating.

A wailing ambulance pulls up to the entrance of the hospital. The couple immersed in their boys look up at the sound, and catch me staring at them. I give a half-smile and they beam back.

I hear someone call my name but I don't have to turn around to see who it is. A mother's voice is known anywhere.

"Lizzy said you might be out here."

I take her hand as she sits beside me. "How are you, Mammy?"

I haven't called her that since I was a kid, but it feels natural now. She doesn't even seem to notice. It's all about my sister right now.

"The doctors said she should sleep for a while. Tors Shaw is going to drop us back to the house so I can pick up some pyjamas and bits of things for her."

I offer to go instead, aching to be useful. But she shakes her head.

"Katie's sleeping, and the triplets are going to stay with her.

Anyway, I'd like to go back so we can get our own car and I can have a quick shower."

"Mum," I begin awkwardly, feeling I owe her an explanation, "Tors' brother took a bad turn. She was upset, so I told her she could call over and talk if she wanted. That's why she was there this morning."

She looks at me blankly. "She saved Katie."

Needing more, I open my mouth but she cuts across me. "Pat rang Jeanette Boden this morning. She managed to get a flight home from London today."

A knot tightens in my stomach and I have to lean over to ease the physical pain. "I'm so sorry." I don't deserve her comfort yet I crave it. She does not offer it.

"There's Tors. Let's go."

Her words are monotone and I know it is useless to plead any further.

None of us speak on the journey home. Taking the front seat this time, I cast sideways glances at Tors. She looks drained. She makes to drive straight back to the hospital when she drops us off but, to my surprise, Mum insists she come inside. Directing Tors to the kitchen to make herself some tea, she wearily shoos me and Lizzy upstairs to pack a bag for Katie while she takes a shower. We move quickly, saying nothing, listening helplessly to Mum's keening sobs over the gushing water.

Mum is showered and ready by the time Lizzy and I have got Katie's case together. As I come back inside from throwing the small suitcase into the boot of the car, Mum and Tors are embracing. Stunned, I catch Lizzy's eye. She shrugs.

"Tors, thank you for what you did today." Tors starts to shake her head but Mum is firm. "You saved my daughter. I don't know what we would have done if you weren't there to help us."

I feel a jolt of resentment but immediately recognise her words as justified.

"Can I ask you one more favour? Can you bring Seán back to the hospital for about eight o'clock this evening?"

Tors nods her agreement but I cut in. "What? That's two hours away – why can't I come with you now?"

"Jeanette Boden should be arriving in the hospital shortly. She knows about the visiting rota and will undoubtedly want to speak to the last person to see her mother alive. I think it's best if you stay away from the hospital for a while."

"Mum, I'm sorry . . ." My voice cracks.

"I know, Seán. I just don't want there to be a scene around Katie." Mum's words are comforting but she won't look me in the eye.

Lizzy throws me a sympathetic glance before shuffling after Mum out the door. As it shuts, I hear a small movement behind me.

Tors and I are alone again. Standing in our large entrance hall, in an empty house. I never noticed before how loud the clock above the door ticks. We smile awkwardly at each other and move in time towards the kitchen. In one gulp, she swallows what's left of her tea. I take the mug from her and place it with a steely clang in the sink.

"I'm sorry about your neighbour." She stares at me.

I whisper thanks and meet her gaze. The kitchen feels balmy, although it's late and the afternoon sun has long since left it. My mind is full of Katie, Mrs Boden, Andrew. Yet something more stirs inside me. Her face is searching mine, and suddenly everyone else disappears. There's no one but her. Before I know it, we are in each other's arms, the warmth of the room pulsating through us. Her lips are as soft as I remember, but there is a renewed urgency to her embrace.

Not wanting to be interrupted by another call with bad news, not wanting to dwell on our pathetic lives, we claw and pull into each other, as though we can each burrow far enough into the other's world to remove ourselves from our lives.

Struggling to stay locked together, we fumble our way towards the stairs. Stumbling, her feet tangle in mine and we trip on the first step.

"Sorry!" she gasps as my body takes the brunt of the fall.

I brush aside her apology, desperate not to lose the moment. I pull her to her feet and we scramble clumsily to the top of the stairs. Smiling down at her, I guide her into my room and shut the door. She closes her eyes to the sound and lets out a soft breath. I know what she's expressing. I feel it too. Finally alone, behind a closed door, we are safe.

I watch her lean back against the door, her eyes still firmly shut. I seem to shrink inches as my shoulder muscles relax and my body sags with relief. We do not break eye contact as we undress, separately and untouching. Finally, we stand before each other, our breathing coming rapidly now. She closes her eyes again. Falling forward in the moment, my body presses against hers, her skin burning like a midsummer sun against mine. She does not open her eyes. My name falls softly from her mouth into mine.

The world is gone. There is only her. As I lay her on my old, single bed, she moans with pleasure and, seemingly not wanting to wait any longer, pushes herself up towards me.

Chapter 15

Tors

Mercifully, we are moving together, as one. It's not just about the release, it's about him. It is as though he is all I have been waiting for: Seán! Seán! I cry out his name, whether aloud or inside my head I don't know. It doesn't matter, I know from his gaze as he moves gently, rhythmically, that he hears me. The heat rises and every second I've ever spent with him plays over and over in my mind. My fingers fix fast to his back, clasping a lifeguard. His eyes focus on mine, never straying.

We collapse together, still clinging to each other in the heat. As the ecstasy ebbs away into contentment, images of our world come flooding back to me. Andrew, Katie.

Seán's mouth is still roving over my body, but slower now. I watch his face tense and his shoulders clench as the cruel clutches of reality sink once again into his being. Soon he is looking at me with the same pained expression I know I too am wearing.

Yet we both smile, genuinely, knowing what has happened is more than just an escape. We lie together for a long time. Holding his head to my chest, I feel my heart beating against him. I wonder if he is counting the pulse.

After a while, we peel from each other and dress in silence, casting shy glances at each other. We know this is over for another day. We have to get back to the hospital, to the people who would see us separated forever. But it won't be forever. I can feel it in his touch as he takes my hand to lead me from the bedroom. This has changed everything.

Still not a word is spoken as we glide, hand in hand, down the winding staircase. I look around at the vastness of space, the landing that just continues on and on, the number of doors, each leading to a large room.

As we reach the bottom of the stairs, he moves to kiss me but I back away. The question I was supposed to ask him days ago rises inside me. Now is the time. He trusts me. He has been vulnerable with me. But I am afraid he will think I have been using him, when nothing could be further from the truth. I realise in that moment the real reason I have not asked him is because I care for him too much. I have felt a connection to him from the start, and I want to spare him. But I force myself to picture my brother's face. I have always put him first, and cannot let that change now.

I know in one way I shouldn't ask Seán today, what with everything he has been through. I worried when he ran from me at the hospital that he might blame me for distracting him, making him forget that he was to visit his neighbour. But he takes another step towards me, clearly wanting me as badly as I do him. I have to say this. I have to think of Andrew.

Just as I open my mouth to speak, Seán's mobile phone rings. I let out a groan of frustration. This is the second time today that, after building up the courage to ask the question, I have been stopped. He does not move. We stand like statues, not wanting to know what fresh tragedy awaits us. But its shrill ring continues, and he touches my arm briefly.

"It could be about Katie or Andrew."

Knowing he is right, I nod. It's Lizzy, telling him their neighbour's daughter has been and gone from the hospital. He ushers me out the door, still talking to her and I have driven us almost as far as the hospital by the time she lets him hang up. My mouth feels dry as I try to keep my concentration focused on the road, but just as I start speaking, Seán does too. He's saying wonderful things: how he feels about me, how we will make it work, how we will bring our families around in time. In a way, it's all I want to hear, but I force my own wants, my own needs down, as the question bubbles furiously towards my mouth.

"Oh look, Tors, there's a spot, just by the door!"

He's right. We have arrived at the hospital and there is a free parking space beside the main entrance. I am never lucky enough to get a space like this, I think, as I turn the car in slowly.

Then he is opening the car door and taking my hand as we walk quickly into the hospital. People of all ages and injuries mill around, some with crutches or bandages, others looking worried or bored. Nurses and doctors pace briskly in and out from behind the reception desk. As we enter, Seán drops my hand and I know this is my last chance. The moment is about to disappear and I cannot let it pass without asking the question.

"Seán."

He turns and looks down at me. Even in the bustle of the hospital reception, his attention is solely mine. He turns up the corners of his mouth into a smile just for me, his eyes crinkling happily, his whole being relaxed. It is a calm, beautiful moment – one to look back on in slow motion.

Suddenly, I feel myself knocked aside. A vision in red is barrelling into Seán's arms, squealing with delight.

I blink.

I blink again. Seán is pushing her back as if to take a proper look at her. That friend of Seán's, Kevin O'Hara, is standing at the door looking on, his expression unreadable.

"Claire? *Claire?* What are you doing here?" Seán's tone is accusatory but the woman doesn't seem to notice as she throws her arms around his neck and, to my horror, kisses him fiercely.

A choking sensation rises in my throat. I want more than anything to look away but I am frozen, transfixed. Seán looks embarrassed as he pushes her off him again, but not quickly enough. I am painfully aware of the sudden drop in volume around us as people freeze mid-stride and even stop writing on their clipboards, their mouths agape at the dramatic love scene unfolding as though from a film.

Then she is turning towards me, her thick black hair flowing out behind her, the swishing motion mirrored by her blood-red coat. I notice it is exactly the same colour as her lipstick and even in my shock I am suddenly conscious that I am not wearing any make-up. I can't even remember if I brought any make-up with me from Kerry, apart from basic foundation. Why am I thinking about cosmetics? She is almost a foot taller than me and I automatically take a step back.

"Hi!" She grips my hand, shaking it with vigour, ignoring my limp response. "You must be one of Seán's sisters . . ."

Fury and despair clash as I summon all my strength to control my voice and answer the beautiful woman beaming down at me. "No, I'm not Seán's sister. I'm just . . . a family friend."

"Oh!" This does not seem to faze the woman in the slightest as she continues wringing my hand. "I'm Claire. I'm Seán's girlfriend," her voice booms. "From America!" she adds brightly, as though it was necessary.

"Right," I breathe, finally extracting myself from her grip. "Well, I'd better go." I duck around Seán and head for the door.

I hear the woman call "Bye!" as I swerve around a young couple, nearly crashing into an elderly man in a wheelchair just coming in the door.

I continue without looking back but, just as on that day by the whirling sea, he catches up, touching my arm. Once again, the sensation triggers a memory of Claude and I wrench violently out of

150

his grip. He holds up his hand defensively, bewildered at my extreme reaction, but I don't care. His shock gives me the split second I need to get away.

Stumbling backwards, I turn and run, stifling the sob that I know will erupt at any second. He is calling my name but I am already in the car, reversing out of the lucky space with a screech, not looking back.

Part 2

Chapter 16

Seán

The key has to be jiggled slightly to the left. I can't believe I forgot that after less than a month away. Can it really have been such a short time since I last turned my key in this lock, drunk from the bliss of spending a day at the opera with Claire?

From the street the apartment had looked empty and oddly alien but, as soon as the door opens, I am greeted by a roar of welcome as Jerry's burly figure engulfs me in a bear hug. I am back where I belong. I let out a raucous laugh as he shakes me enthusiastically and stubbornly refuses to step aside as Sam tries to reach me too.

Eventually, after much hugging and cursing, I am pulled inside and a beer shoved into my hand. The apartment smells the same – like new fabric – and I sit with my eyes closed for a second taking in the warm scent. It's not the smell of my childhood home, but it is recognisable and comforting and suddenly Ireland seems a lot further away than it did only a few hours ago.

The lads are chatting away at a million miles an hour and I nod

155

along, not hearing much but relishing the vitality, the normality of it all. After being home in Ballyloughlin, the apartment seems even smaller than usual, and I realise with a shock that I am even comparing it to Tors' sea house, which is slightly larger than here. Shaking her out of my mind, I force myself back to the conversation which, as I had guessed it soon would, has taken a turn.

"We're so sorry we couldn't make it home for your dad's funeral, Seán." Sam's eyes bulge with sincerity as Jerry nods furiously. "It's just the jobs wouldn't let us off, boy."

I grin mischievously. "Jesus, Sam, they don't get as culchie as you anywhere! I've been home for a month and haven't heard as thick a Cork accent!" Sam thumps my arm as Jerry barks out a laugh, and I ignore the jarring sensation stirred up by a mere mention of Cork. "It's okay, lads, really. I wouldn't have made it either if it had been the other way around."

"You know," Sam speaks tentatively, "Claire wanted to call around this evening, but we told her we wanted you to ourselves, just for tonight. I don't think she was too impressed. But we got the notion, when you sent her back as soon as she arrived, that you mightn't want her here?"

He looks nervous, and a familiar sense of guilt swims around my midriff. But I smile appreciatively. If any of my friends would be astute enough to know I'd want to keep Claire away, it's Sam.

"Thanks, *boy*," I stress, trying to keep it light. "It's a bit complicated right now."

"We barely heard from you, Seán – what's the story?" Relieved that I'm not going to explode at them, Jerry is in on the action now. "Claire just said there was trouble with the family."

I recognise that this unusual reserve on Claire's part would have taken some effort, and though I don't feel much else towards her right now, I am immensely grateful for this. I wonder if she has forgiven me yet. My plan is to keep the family secret just that, a secret, but I made the decision on the way back to tell Jerry and Sam. Since Claire arrived in Ballyloughlin, my temper has been on a very short fuse. Better to have some people who know what happened. In case I need to erupt, I only have to make sure it's around them. So I take a deep breath and throw caution to the wind.

"Lads, it's a long story, but here's the gist. We discovered Dad has another son, from a one-night stand he had when we were kids. He's willed everything to him, and Mum is left with nothing. She would still be entitled to something, as his wife, but it turns out they never actually got married. We can contest the will but we doubt that'll work, because the other son is seriously ill and anyway my sister Katie has taken it so badly she ended up in hospital from an overdose so we're not even sure she's up to a legal battle. Oh, and I've fallen in love with my new brother's sister."

I hold my breath, watching their faces twist in alarm.

Jerry breaks the silence. "Fuck."

I give a small smile. They continue to stare at me in unflattering disbelief but my mind has already focused on the most shocking part. This is the first time I have spoken aloud the extent of my feelings for Tors. I know I am in love with her, probably right from the beginning, but I didn't expect Jerry and Sam to hear it before she did. I miss her. I haven't seen or spoken to her since the day she ran from me at the hospital.

"Yeah," says Sam, his eyes still wide. "What he said."

"Well, he put it so eloquently." I'm grinning now at their scandalised expressions.

"Your little sister. Is she okay?" Sam's voice is soft and Jerry gives me a frightened look.

"Yes, she's out of hospital," I rush to reassure them. "She'll be fine," I add, partly to convince myself.

I wait, watching with half-amusement as they shift in their seats, shaking their heads while trying to digest my loaded speech.

"So you've a new brother," Sam shakes his head. "Have you met him?"

"No," I answer, a little too defensively, but they do not seem to notice.

Jerry lets out an amused snort. "But you've fallen for his *sister*?"

Suddenly, when I'm talking about it with the guys, it does seem ridiculous, hilarious. Within seconds, we are all keeled over in hysterics. I grip my stomach, howling, and I want stay here forever, just laughing with my friends.

"Jesus! In love with his sister!" Sam is wiping away tears as he reaches into the fridge for a beer. "I need another after that! Jer? Seán?"

I catch the bottle he tosses in my direction. "Let's get one thing straight. She's not my sister. She's my half-brother's half-sister, on the other side."

Jerry chokes on his beer. "Oh, well, that clears it up nicely!" he splutters, as Sam doubles over, holding his side.

I know I'm never going to be able to talk sensibly about this with them. In fact, I suspect every time the word *sister* is mentioned from now on, I'm going to get an earful. I instantly regret ever mentioning Tors to them.

"Hey, Sam," Jerry can barely blurt the words out through his fit of merriment, "I'd give anything to be a fly on the wall at Christmas dinner in Seán's house, wouldn't you?"

Sam slaps his leg in delight. "Wouldn't like to go on a family holiday with his lot! Seán'd want to bunk with his sister!"

Jerry almost slips from the chair in convulsions. It is as if they have forgotten I am in the room and it is not until Sam catches sight of the anguish I am not quick enough to smile away that his eyes widen, seeing beyond the joke of his last remark.

"Oh Jesus, Seán, you didn't, did you? I mean, you didn't actually –"

"Shut up, lads!" I try to keep my voice in the same light tone, but his question stings. I don't want to talk to Jerry and Sam about Tors. Somehow it's different than making them jealous with lewd stories about me and Claire. I feel like I'd be betraying Tors. My whole body stiffens and there's a bitter taste in my mouth. I stand up, willing myself to keep it together. "I think I'll leave you boys at it," I say, arranging my mouth into a grin so they won't think I'm angry. "That sister joke should keep you going for the rest of the night."

The cushion hits the side of my face as I finish the sentence and I use the excuse to duck into the hallway and drag my bags across our little apartment.

"Hey, Family Man, you're not going to bed now?" Jerry looks at me, disgusted. "You're only home! It's Saturday night, let's have a few more. You're not going to work tomorrow, are you?"

I am expected to work long hours at LL&T, and it wouldn't have been outside the realm of possibility that they would expect me in the office on a Sunday, on the day after my flight back from my father's funeral.

"No, I'm avoiding work tomorrow. I've no desire to get in there."

"That's not what you said to your new sister!" Jerry almost chokes at his own genius and even I can't help grinning, more at his red face and inability to breathe than the sick joke itself.

I use his momentary disability to slam the bedroom door shut in his face, shouting goodnight to Sam as I do so.

My room is exactly as I left it. The sheets are musty and dust bunnies cling to the stack of books piled in the corner. A stale smell wafts from the wardrobe as I open it. Resolving to get my suits dry-cleaned first thing in the morning, I pull a T-shirt from my suitcase and flop gratefully onto the bed. The curtains are cheap and light from the street streams into the room.

I close my eyes, ignoring the rush of traffic and city life buzzing outside, hoping sleep will come quickly after the long flight and charged farewells. Instead, images float in front of my eyes – Dad, Mum, Andrew (or how I picture him, at least), Katie, Tors. I wonder who it will land on. Every night for the past week, a different mistake of mine has haunted me. Tonight, it is a tall, longhaired woman with piercing blue eyes and a low-pitched, penetrating voice.

I roll over, pulling the sheets tightly around me. This one is the worst of them all. At least my family problems are not all my fault. But the guilt of this one tears me apart.

* * *

Mrs Boden's funeral took place two days after Claire left. The clear sky disguised the biting cold and the sun seemed to mock the tragedy as the entire town filed into the church to say goodbye to another Ballyloughlin stalwart. I tried to make myself as inconspicuous as possible. I sat with my family about halfway back, horrifically ashamed at my own relief that Katie, rather than me, was the centre of attention. There was no mention of the visiting list, though everyone on it must have known I was due to see her that night. I wondered if it had been hushed up for Mum's sake.

Katie had been discharged from the hospital last night and came directly to the removal service. Though desperate to avoid any contact with Jeanette, I knew I could not avoid the obligatory queuing to sympathise with relatives at the end of the service. Mercifully, the line shuffled with relative speed through the front row of mourners and Jeanette shook my hand with a blank expression and generic "Thank you". It was only when I had moved on to her husband beside her that she seemed to belatedly realise who I was. I could sense her stare following me but I kept my head down and walked quickly back down the side aisle.

Her purposeful gaze made me certain she knew about the list, and my abandonment of her mother on the last night of her life. Despite Lizzy's attempts to comfort me, the fact remains that if I had visited her, there is a chance I might have spotted a warning sign. Jeanette Boden, I was sure, must hate me.

Mum was worried Katie would not cope well at the funeral after memories of Mrs Boden's kindness caused her to weep uncontrollably for an hour after the removal. But my sister insisted on attending to pay her respects and say goodbye. She was improving daily, but was still pale and tired-looking. Sitting as close to Mum as possible, she accepted good wishes from those who approached her with small smiles.

The funeral service was long, with hymns and prayers from a queue of neighbours and friends. Mrs Boden's long life and service to Ballyloughlin was recounted in detail. The photo of her that stood on the coffin had been taken some years previously and showed her grinning directly at the camera, her eyes sparkling behind her round glasses. I did not realise until it was mentioned in her son-in-law's short eulogy that she was eighty-nine years old. I suppose that explains why she seemed ancient even when we were kids. Staring at the photo, I half expected her to pop up from behind the pews and press a chocolate sweet into my palm with a "Hush, now, don't tell your mother!"

Lizzy kept close to me during the funeral. But afterwards, as we stood around the front of the church, waiting for the immediate family to come back from the private burial her family had requested in the graveyard just behind, I found myself standing alone and accosted by a longhaired woman. At almost six foot, her shining blue eyes looked down on me in anger and revulsion.

"Seán, do you remember me?"

"Of course, Jeanette. I'm so, so sorry about your mum."

"I was going to come home, you know. When she told me last week that she no longer had the energy for bridge and she stopped meeting her Active Retirement group because she was too tired, I was worried about her being all alone in that house without seeing anyone all day. But then she told me the neighbours had organised a rota. That at least one person was calling in to see her every day . . ."

"Jeanette . . ." My throat constricted and my voice was a rasp.

But she was towering over me, her voice rising steadily. "Shut up. Shut up, Seán. Don't you dare try to defend yourself! You were on the roster and you weren't there. If you didn't want to help, why didn't

161

you just say so? I would have come home. I would have come home, Seán . . ."

Aware of a few heads nearby turning to look at us, my heart pounded roughly against my ribcage as I tried to placate her. "Jeanette, I really . . . I'm just so sorry . . ."

But she was practically screaming then, pulling at her hair like a woman possessed. "I would have come home, Seán – *I would have come home!*"

Suddenly, Michael Undersky was there. "She knows that, Jeanette – it's not your fault."

I felt him push me back as she collapsed in tears, wailing uncontrollably. Then Pat O'Hara was there too, and Jeanette's husband, all leading her gently away from me, back towards the church. Immobilised with shock, I stood until I felt a warm hand press firmly into mine, and I let my little sister lead me back towards our car without a word.

* * *

I twist in the sheets, letting it take me over. I thought my own remorse was the worst part. But knowing Jeanette Boden will be writhing in guilt for the rest of her days too, because of me, is too much. I bite the pillow to keep from groaning in agony. It'll be better in the morning, I tell myself over and over. Because it has been, every morning this week. It has been better until the night comes upon me again.

I fall asleep many hours later and don't wake up until late Sunday morning. My eyes open to a bright room and a sense of relief that I have a whole day before another nightmare invades my mind.

The apartment is empty and I have to think for a minute before I remember that both Jerry and Sam work on Sunday afternoons. Jerry, the chef, has left me a plate of cheese and ham with a stack of bread. I eat my sandwiches slowly, feeling slightly achy with weariness. It must be the jet lag.

After an obscenely large brunch, I load my arms with as many shirts and suits as I can heave around the corner to the drycleaner's.

Alek, who has been cleaning my suits for at least three years, wrings my hand gleefully. "I thought you deserted me, old boy!" His Russian accent is familiar on my ear and I pump his hand enthusiastically in return.

"Of course not – you know me better than that! I just – I had to go away for a few weeks. But I'm back now and need you badly, mate – look at the state of these!"

"Wow, so many, my friend! I will charge you an even better price than usual."

"You're a decent man, Alek!" We smile at each other, both knowing I'll tip him the discount he gives me.

I'm in a better mood as I continue down the road towards the supermarket. The friendliness of New Yorkers surprised me from the beginning. At home, the city was always spoken of as a lonely place, where people looked out for number one. But within each few blocks, there are little communities that are as close-knit and kind as the familial bonds of Ballyloughlin.

After some grocery shopping, I head to the park at the end of my street. I take a seat on my favourite bench, under an enormous willow tree. Usually if I come here it is on a Saturday afternoon when both Jerry and Sam are home with their girlfriends and it's too crowded there. I'll bring my laptop and work during the summer, or in the winter I'll grab a tea from one of our many local coffee shops and sit reading, wrapped up in my woollies. Sam and Jerry think I'm mad, but I like the fresh wind and bite in the air. Today, there is still a touch of winter in the air, even though it's almost April and I don't need a book to distract me.

I took Kevin to this park when he visited last year. We borrowed a picnic rug from Claire and spent the day lazing in the sun "like a pair of auld women" as Kevin put it, sipping beers and trading war stories from the night before. In a way, although I want to escape

Ballyloughlin in its entirety, Kevin is the one person I wish I could take with me. He might still be angry with me about Mrs Boden and, if I'm honest, I'm still fuming about the part he played in collecting Claire from the airport and bringing her to the hospital, but I would only have to look at Kevin for him to know what I'm going through.

He brought me to the airport and, despite barely speaking on the journey, he gave me a genuine, brotherly hug before waving me off. In a way, I had been glad of the quiet. My last conversation with Mum and Lizzy was still ringing in my head.

I hadn't been able to keep my temper when Lizzy started hassling me again, just as I was lugging my bags downstairs. "I still can't believe you're leaving, Seán."

"Oh for God's sake, Lizzy, we've been through this before. Kevin is coming to get me any minute – do you really want to have this conversation again?"

"I'm just saying, it's not too late to change your mind. You could always stay."

"And do what, Lizzy? I mean it, baby sister, tell me. What am I supposed to do here? Katie is out of the hospital, she's fine. She's going back to work next week. Mum is talking about starting back at the school in a few weeks as well, and you've been working in the equestrian centre for weeks. I need to get back to my work, to my life."

"And to Claire?" There was no trace of a smirk on her face.

"Don't start."

"Tors is only down the road, you know. Are you just going to leave her?"

At first, Lizzy's devastation that Tors and I were no longer talking amused me. After all, she had been so adamantly against me having any kind of contact with Tors in the first place. But since Katie's overdose, Lizzy's aversion to the Shaw family, like Mum's, no longer extended to Tors. I never told my family that Tors and I had even kissed, never mind made love, but Lizzy's not stupid.

She couldn't wait for Claire to be gone. I never expected them to

164

be best friends, they are so unalike. But Claire made a real effort to be friendly with Lizzy, asking her about her horse Lilly and feigning interest in her job. Lizzy treated her just a little short of rudely. I got the impression that unless Claire somehow managed to save Katie's life, she would never live up to Tors.

"Lizzy, I'm not *leaving* Tors. She doesn't want to speak to me. And she has enough on her plate at the moment without me harassing her. Anyway, this isn't about Tors, or Claire. I have to get back to work."

"You know we're not done with the will?"

"We'll talk on the phone, all right? Look, one of us has to keep a decent job. You're not exactly making millions in the equestrian centre and Katie's barely earning a junior librarian's salary. Based on what Eddie Edwards had to say, any challenge is shaky at best. If Mum is left with nothing, one of us has to look after her financially. I need to keep my job."

I impressed myself with this argument, since it had nothing to do with the real reason I was returning to America.

Unfortunately, Mum chose that moment to walk in on the conversation. "I don't need you, Seán, or any of you, to look after me. I'm fine. Seán, we're not upset because you have to get back to your job. We're upset because we'll miss you. We understand why you have to go. We'd just like you here. That's all."

"Well, I'd like to be anywhere but here. I thought you'd be happy. No one to consort with the Shaws. No one to abandon family friends in their hour of need or embarrass you at funerals. I'm surprised you're not jumping up and down."

"Oh shut up, Seán!" Lizzy said. "Your pity party of one is just pathetic!"

Mum spun around. "Lizzy, don't talk to your brother in that way. And Seán, don't you *dare* speak to us like that. We understand you need to get back to New York, but you have to recognise that it's hard for us here, left behind. We've got to stick together as a family."

"Yeah, right!" I spat. "Unmarried parents and hushed-up affairs. Secret brothers and overdosing sisters. Some family!"

A double beep sounded in the driveway, not quite drowning out Lizzy's growl.

"Let's . . . let's not leave it like this . . ." Mum's eyes flickered, panicked, from me to Lizzy.

But blood pulsated through my veins and I whipped away from them, strutting to the car without looking back to the door or to the upstairs window from where I knew Katie was looking down, waiting for a wave that never came.

By the time I was sitting on the plane, of course, I wanted to turn back. I wanted to apologise for what I'd said in those moments, for everything. I wanted Mum to hold me and tell me it wasn't my fault Mrs Boden died.

Before I left, before that confrontation with Mum and Lizzy, I talked to Katie. She was more engaging than she had been in years, and confessed that she wished we could all just go back a month, before Dad died, to when things were normal. Surprisingly, though I didn't tell Katie, I could not agree. I do not want to go back to a time before I knew Tors Shaw. Even though she won't see me, or talk to me, I would still rather it this way than not to know her at all.

Claire was very intrigued by the woman who left us so abruptly at the hospital. I had watched Tors speed away, momentarily distracted by the way she pulled away from me: more in fear than in anger. It took all my restraint not to knock Claire's hand from my arm when she caught up with me, having watched me run through the car park, calling Tors' name. I was so angry with her, I could not even speak. I knew it was not her fault, but she had ruined everything.

"How did you get here? Why did you not tell me you were coming?" My voice was demanding.

She looked confused. "I decided to surprise you. Your roommates gave me your friend Kevin's phone number and, when I rang him from Dublin airport to ask for directions, he insisted on collecting me. I thought you'd be happy. It's been weeks, Seán, and I can never get you on the phone. You're not responding to emails. Aren't you pleased to see me?"

She sounded so disappointed at my reaction that I managed to control myself. Wrapping my arms around her, I breathed in her scent and nearly choked. Either she had changed her usual perfume or it was just not the same away from the busy city of New York. "Of course I am, Claire, of course. I'm sorry, it's just . . . my sister has been taken into hospital. And a family friend passed away last night. We're all a bit of a mess."

I took a step back, wondering if she could smell Tors on me. She responded kindly with the usual platitudes but I felt no comfort, merely annoyance. Her words rang hollow. She couldn't understand what I was going through, not like Tors could.

That night, as we grieved for Mrs Boden and tried to make some sense of what had happened to poor Katie, Claire was the last person I wanted around. She didn't fit in, that was clear. She expected an American-style welcome with lots of attention and being paraded around, not an exhausted mother and sister who barely acknowledged her and a boyfriend who could not hide his frustration at her unannounced visit.

At around ten o'clock that night, I left Claire in the living room with an unimpressed Lizzy and sneaked upstairs to my room to ring Tors. She didn't answer so I left a message trying to explain. But it sounded so unconvincing, my stammered excuses about Claire just being a girl I see in New York sometimes. With Claire downstairs, it felt dishonest. I needed to see Tors.

The next morning, Claire awoke late, despite having gone to bed early. I had never been so glad that my childhood room contained only a single bed. I couldn't have dealt with either trying to convince Mum that Claire stay in my room or, even worse, having to explain to Claire that I didn't want her in the same bed as me. She must have slept well in the spare room because she arrived in the kitchen looking immaculate. Mum and Lizzy were already at the hospital.

"So, Seán, what will we do today?"

I took a deep breath. "Claire, I'm sorry. But I'm going to have to spend most of today in the hospital. I'd bring you with me, but Katie really isn't up for visitors, and Mum just doesn't have the energy to be making small talk right now."

She looked down. "I'm in the way here. I shouldn't have just arrived like this. I should go back."

Knowing that was my cue to tell her to stay, I stood up, biting my tongue. "I'd ask Kevin to hang out with you but his family was very close to Mrs Boden and he's going to be busy helping to organise the funeral."

"I'll go back," she whispered. "I'll book myself on the earliest flight I can get."

Massively relieved that she picked up on the barely disguised hint so quickly, I felt at the same time like an absolute bastard. "Claire, I'm sorry but I do think that's best. You're amazing coming over like this. It's so unfortunate that you landed in the middle of all this mess." I enfolded her in my arms and pulled her into me. "Look, book yourself first class, on me."

She smiled sadly and nodded as I removed my arms from her without a kiss and left for the hospital.

I stayed for nearly an hour talking to Katie, or rather listening. For once, she would not shut up. She talked about Dad and her feelings of depression, but would suddenly divert into a hilarious story involving her and the triplets, or blabber on about exhibits the library was running in the coming months. It was great to see her lively and looking so much better, but afterwards the doctor had words of caution.

"People do not just recover from the feelings she went through: they are a part of her now. We'll have her on anti-depressants and you'll need to watch out for extremes in her behaviour. Not just excessive sadness or anger, but the other end of the spectrum too. If you can't get her to stop laughing, if she's in the best mood she's been in for months –"

"You don't want her to be happy?" Lizzy interrupted indignantly.

"Of course I do," he smiled. "I'm just saying to be aware that her emotions are all over the place at the moment. We want to settle her, give her a sense of balance so she can deal with everything that has happened. Just watch her."

Using Claire as an excuse, I left shortly afterwards but did not return home. Instead I drove, my pulse quickening with every second that passed, to the sea house. To my immense frustration, I saw only Karen's car in the driveway. As I pulled into a quick U-turn, I heard her call my name. Half-tempted to speed away, I forced myself to think of Tors as I cut the engine and stepped out of the car.

Karen was upon me before I even closed the door. I backed away, remembering what happened the last time we stood that close.

"What are you doing here?"

Her voice was full of the malice I remembered.

"I want t-to see Tors." I tried, unsuccessfully, not to stutter.

"Yeah, well, she doesn't want to see you, kiddo!"

I did not flinch. "Is she at the hospital?"

Karen tilted her head and surveyed me with narrowed eyes. "No. She's not. She's gone to Dublin for the day, to meet a friend."

"What about Andrew?"

"What's it to you?"

We locked eyes, and I know she was daring me to ask to see him. That was the last thing I needed. When I said nothing, she sniffed out a bitter laugh and started back towards the house.

"Will you just tell Tors I want to talk?" I called after her.

She turned slowly on the spot and took a few steps back towards me. "I'm glad to hear your sister is okay." Her face softened, and looked almost kind. Then just as swiftly she turned and marched back to the sea house.

Unsure what to make of our conversation, I sat heavily into the car and drove back to the hospital. This time I parked not near A&E, but around by the separate out-patients' entrance. Inside, I asked for Dr

Stevens, impressed that I could recall his name after the trauma of the day before.

A tall, slightly balding man emerged within minutes and thankfully recognised me immediately. He shook my hand firmly and asked about Katie.

I answered him and then added as casually as I could, "I'm looking for Tors Shaw, actually, Dr Stevens. Is Andrew Shaw still in hospital?"

"What? Yes, we decided to keep him in, since he's due back in for his next round of dialysis tomorrow anyway. Is there a problem?"

"No, not at all. I was just visiting my sister and thought I would drop in to Tors if she happened to be here. She mentioned that Andrew might be kept in for another day or so."

He looked unconvinced and cocked his head to the side before he answered. "Tors isn't here at the moment. She was in this morning but that was a couple of hours ago. Andrew's mother is due in shortly. Tors won't be back until tonight, I believe."

Delighted that he was talking to me about it, I decided to use the opportunity. "Dr Stevens, I hope you don't mind me asking – but I don't like asking Tors about it, she gets upset. What's Andrew's prognosis?"

He surveyed me over his glasses almost as sceptically as Karen Shaw had back at the beach house. "You must know I cannot discuss his health with anyone other than family."

Hardly believing I was saying it, I countered quickly before I lost my nerve. "You must have heard the story, Doctor. I *am* family."

He considered me for another moment before he shook his head. "I'm sorry, Seán. You haven't even been to see him. You know I cannot give you information about his health."

"I understand," I nodded, suddenly terrified my inquisition would get back to Karen. "No problem, I just thought I'd ask."

I shook his hand and turned. But as I walked across the car park, I heard him call my name. I looked around as he jogged up to me. "Seán, it's not my place but I'll just say this. Visit him."

Slightly taken aback and not knowing what exactly he meant, I just nodded. I drove around for about an hour, pondering on this cryptic message. Had Andrew said something to the doctor? Did he want to see me?

By the time I got back to the house, Mum and Lizzy had already returned from visiting Katie. As soon as I set foot inside the door, I knew I should have got my story straight before coming back.

"Where were you?" Lizzy ran up to me and kissed my cheek.

Over her head I saw Claire standing in the kitchen, probably left mid-sentence by my sister. I panicked. "I . . . I decided to call to the shops to pick up a few things and then I went back to the hospital to see Katie."

"But visiting hours were over ages ago!"

"Yeah, I know. I mean, I only realised that when I got there so I just came straight back here. Hi, Claire." I ducked around my sister to peck Claire's cheek, just as Lizzy had kissed mine moments before.

"Oh you're back, Seán! We wondered what happened to you." Mum shuffled down the stairs and into the kitchen in her dressing gown. "Claire was just telling us she's heading back tomorrow."

"Yes, I booked my flights. I fly out first thing."

Mum took Claire's hand, and I watched uncomfortably. "Claire, I'm really very sorry that we haven't given you a decent reception here – look at me, I'm not even properly dressed! It's just all a horrible mess at the moment, but I'm sure Seán is very grateful that you came all the way over here. I'm glad he has friends in New York as thoughtful as you to look after him."

I could practically feel Lizzy sneer derisively behind me and I suddenly wanted to get Claire out of there.

Claire was happy, at least, with Mum's speech and waved goodbye to my family with something approaching cheer as we drove off later that day. As we pulled out of the driveway, I spotted Mark's shiny car racing towards us, Niamh at the wheel. I had mixed feelings about her coming back. Of course, Mum would be over the moon, and it was only right that Niamh would see Katie and attend Mrs Boden's funeral – I shuddered again at the tremor of guilt that ran through me – but I was still angry at Niamh for leaving so abruptly and though I was not adverse to Lizzy making life difficult for her, as I knew she would, I dreaded further tension in the house.

I had decided to take Claire to Dublin the night before her flight and Mum insisted I take the car, even though it meant Pat O'Hara having to ferry Mum and Lizzy over and back to the hospital. No one questioned my motive for going to Dublin the night before the flight – as it was the early red eye, the alternative was driving her in the middle of the night. But my real purpose was to get her away from my family, before Mum got too attached or Lizzy let something slip about Tors. There was also another reason. Even though I could feel nothing but frustration towards her for the timing of her arrival, the logical part of me remembered well how much Claire had meant to me while I was in New York and how kind she had been when Dad died. I knew I had treated her badly, and I suspected that she wanted something before she left, something I couldn't give her in a teenager's single bed in my mother's house.

So rather than book us into an airport hotel which would have made more sense, given the time of her flight, I took a suite in the Gresham Hotel on O'Connell Street. Despite the disaster of her visit, Claire could not help but be thrilled by the notion of staying in the famous hotel on Dublin's main street. It would be something positive for her to boast about with her gossipy friends. Still, the evening was nothing short of uncomfortable. I took her to a posh restaurant in Dublin city, similar to those we would frequent in New York. She pushed her food around her plate and joined in my inane conversation reluctantly.

When we settled into the hotel room it was almost midnight and I was unsure what to do. It was partly irrational anger at Tors' avoidance of me that pushed me to spend the night with Claire. She wouldn't even give me a chance to explain myself.

But it was easier to make the decision than see it through. When the moment arrived, it felt wrong to be with Claire just to get back at Tors. There was also the problem that I did not want Claire to think I was just using her before kicking her out of the country. But to leave without spending the night with her would definitely upset her. As an added complication, I knew Claire must be worried that Tors was more than just the 'family friend' she pretended to be that day. Claire had not bought my excuse about shopping earlier that day any more than Lizzy had. I knew she needed reassurance that I still wanted her. I hesitated too long, and eventually Claire moved towards me and kissed me fiercely.

I responded, relieved that at least I knew what she wanted, but feeling her too tall in my arms. Ignoring the immediate sense of betrayal, I pulled her onto the bed with me. Tors and I were only together once while Claire and I had been lovers for nearly a year. Feeling guilty was ridiculous. Claire took my hand, and placed it purposefully above the inside of her right knee, where she liked. Where I *knew* she liked – so why did she need to show me? I needed to stop thinking about Tors, I needed to focus. Focus? How romantic.

It was a pathetic half an hour, but we got there. I don't know how she felt about it, but she allowed me to hold her as she fell asleep. I stayed awake for most of the night, looking down at her pale, smooth skin. It was so confusing, having Claire in Ireland. Only yesterday, she seemed like she belonged to a distant dream, from another life, long ago. Then she was there, melding my two worlds together and forcing me to accept that Tors and I were not a couple. Still, Tors ran from me when Claire announced herself. It must have been more than a one-off for her too. I watched the darkness of the night evaporate into the yellow hue of morning but must have drifted off because Claire was suddenly shaking me awake.

The rush to make her flight was compounded by city-centre traffic and a last-minute panic that she had left her passport in Ballyloughlin. By the time we found it at the bottom of her overstuffed handbag, weaved through road works and accidentally stopped at the wrong terminal, there was only time for a quick goodbye, I'm sorry and thank you, before her boarding card was whipped out of her hand by an irate security official and she was shunted forwards out of sight.

Pity for Claire compounded my own selfish reaction to her visit. I know she would have bragged to all her friends about the wonderful romantic gesture she was making, in anticipation of flying to Dublin. To have me pack her off as soon as she arrived would be humiliating, even with the legitimate excuses of Katie and Mrs Boden.

However, once I returned to Ballyloughlin, I barely gave her a second thought. I spent the rest of the week in mourning for Mrs Boden and made more attempts to contact Tors, though I stayed clear of the sea house. But I did begin to think about Claire again during my guilt-ridden flight back to New York.

* * *

It is now obligation more than desire that forces me to pick up the phone and call Claire. The light wind in the park whistles and I can't hear her very well. Although it is the last thing I want, I tell her to call over tonight then trudge home feeling miserable and utterly sorry for myself.

"Look mate," Sam tries to catch my eye as I rummage around looking for decent place settings, ignoring frustrated grunts from Jerry that I am in his way. "You like Claire. A lot. All right? I know these past few weeks have been rough on you and that you think you have feelings for this non-sister of yours," (we ignore a snort from Jerry) "but don't ruin everything you always wanted with Claire."

I straighten up. "Look Sam, it's just that –"

"Get the hell out of my kitchen! You're in the fucking way!"

"Sorry, Jerry," we both mutter, catching each other's eye with a grin.

Taking a bowl of freshly chopped salad over to the table, I smile playfully at Sam. "She's probably only coming over here because she knows Jerry's cooking anyway."

Ignoring Jerry's "Right too" response, Sam is resolutely serious, as though trying to talk me down from a ledge. I barely have time to convince him that I know what I am doing when the buzzer sounds. Jerry jumps and curses about guests being early.

I make a huge effort to be welcoming, but think I overdo it. I see Sam throwing his eyes up to heaven at my awkward hello and clumsy hug that just ends up squashing her arms into my chest. Jerry does his best to contain his frustration when Claire ambles into the kitchen, snooping around to see what we're having for dinner. Before long, they have enough and bolt for the pub, Jerry leaving strict instructions about heating and cooling temperatures which we promptly forget.

"He's wasted in that low class diner. He should be in a Michelin-star restaurant." Claire lifts the lid on one of the steaming pots and sniffs at the bursts of spiced air puffing out.

"He will be some day," I answer, watching her as she moves gracefully to the table and sits opposite me.

I reach across and take her hand. I try to say how sorry I am for what happened in Ireland, why she had to leave. I start to explain again about Katie, but she just shakes her head and pulls her hand from mine.

"I understand all that, Seán. I have a family too, you know. That's not the issue. The problem is that you didn't seem to want me there. I think, even if your sister was fine and your neighbour hadn't died, you still would have wished I hadn't turned up."

She is right, of course, though I start to deny it. Seeing this has no effect, I change tack. "Look Claire, my head was a mess. It's not that I didn't want you there, it's just that you are from my life in New York and it was confusing, on top of everything else, to have you there in the middle of it all."

Her eyebrow twitches as it does when she's contemplating how to react. I barely breathe. But she says nothing, and after a few minutes we simply continue eating. I don't mind the silence – my mind is occupied in a brutal tug of war between reality and dreams. I came back to New York. I made the decision to leave Tors behind when she wouldn't speak to me, wouldn't even hear me out. What I did with Tors wasn't cheating on Claire, really. I never had that kind of steady relationship with Claire which seems to characterise all relationships back home. Okay, I was never with any other girl while we were dating, but that was only because I wasn't interested in anyone else. I'm convinced it wasn't always the same for Claire. If Tors had just let me explain . . . But she didn't, and I didn't force myself on her. I left to come back to America where Claire lives. She obviously cares for me more than I thought and I should give her a chance.

Decision made, I start up a light conversation and stay as engaged as I can. It was not my original plan, but she stays the night. Maybe it is the fact that I'm back in my usual bed with her, or that I have not seen Tors for so long, but it is easier and better than that disastrous night in the Dublin hotel. We move as one and this time I enjoy the feeling of her skin against mine, her breath on my neck.

Later, she sighs contentedly in her sleep as I pull her close to me, knowing she is unaware that I am clinging to her not like a lover but like a child, squeezing my eyes shut to hide from a tall woman with long hair and angry blue eyes.

Chapter 17

Seán

Claire is up and gone by five in the morning. At first, when I feel her squirm gently out of my arms and begin to patter around the room, I worry that I have somehow offended her. Did I say something in my sleep? But then I remember that public relations can be even more demanding than business consultancy. I'm sure taking time off to come to Ireland didn't help her chances of that promotion she has been chasing, but she did it anyway. Great. More guilt before dawn has broken. Feigning sleep, I lie resolutely still as she places a light kiss on my lips and tiptoes out of the apartment.

I sit up when I hear the door close, the dull greyness of the once pristine white ceiling my only stimulant. For the first time, I begin to feel nervous about going back to work. While I used it as an excuse for returning, in reality I have so far ignored the ramifications of having missed three full weeks. It was easier to shut out Marx's pressing emails with the slam of a laptop cover in Ballyloughlin.

But the truth is business moves fast, at the pace of New York City, as Marx likes to say. Listening to the chatter of men on mobile phones and honking of cars on the street outside, even in these early hours, his words take on real meaning. In the safety of my bedroom, I allow myself to admit that it is going to be stressful, trying to catch up on what I have missed, both with my clients and in terms of market flux. Never mind re-focusing all my energies on the job.

I had been so excited when I was accepted onto LL&T's graduate programme after college and beside myself when they offered me a full-time position. It meant I could stay working in America, and I felt I had earned it. It wasn't because I was a Murtagh that everyone in the office knew my name, it was because I was good – actually, if I'm being truthful, really great – at my job. Still, I knew the chance wasn't something to take for granted and I threw myself into the work.

Meeting clients, analysing business problems and developing solutions to money-losing ventures – it is busy, high-end and it gives me a real buzz. There is also the compliance side, ensuring our corporate clients don't stray from the law in pursuing new and often ambitious projects. Really, that's the work of the legal teams, but my input on the business-consultancy side has to take account of their advice.

Dad always became excited when I spoke to him about that aspect of my work. He liked to think I followed in his legal footsteps, even a little bit. Thinking about Dad makes my breathing come heavy. In the past few weeks, I've gone from devastation to shame to extreme fury. It wasn't his fault he died, but everything that's happened since – Andrew, Katie, Mrs Boden – it's all because of him. Even the mystery of what he was doing at dawn on the old Cork road leaves me unsettled, though no one else seems to be aware that it's odd. When we first found out about Andrew, I thought he might have been on his way to see him but, as Michael pointed out when I confessed my suspicion, neither the old Cork road nor the new Cork motorway would have been a sensible route to north Kerry. Anyway, Karen Shaw made it clear that Dad played no part in Andrew's life so why would he suddenly try to visit him? I feel my hands start to tremble as they do when I let these thoughts run free. I force my mind away from my cheating, lying father back to the office.

Permanent employment was not the only reward of the long hours and tedious training. It was through work that I first met Claire. Her company was representing one of our clients in the promotion of a new financial management project. I don't remember much about our first team conference because I spent the meeting staring across the boardroom table at the tall, beautiful woman who twisted her shiny black hair around her perfectly manicured fingers as she took notes. It took a second meeting before I plucked up the courage to speak to her directly, but by the third meeting she was playing footsy with me under the table.

Remembering that makes me smile slyly, bringing back some of my earlier feelings for Claire. But they don't last long. Tors is never far from my thoughts these days.

Though nervous, I am also impatient, almost anxious, to get back to work. There is a new angle to my sense of urgency. Dad's death has made me feel strangely alone. Quite apart from the monetary problems that come with Dad's will, the fact that I have lost a parent panics me. I am not going to have people to look after me and provide for me forever. I have to take care of myself. I curl up against a tightening in my chest and lie like a statue for a long time, until a gentle tapping on my door rouses me.

"Seán, lad, wake up!"

The light from my phone flashes up six a.m., and I all but leap out of the covers. Time flies when you're lying in bed depressed, I think bitterly. If I am late for work on my first day back, it will just be another disaster for which I can blame Dad. I think of him driving, alone, at this time only weeks ago, with no inclination of what awaited him down the old Cork road. I shake him from my head and refocus on the day ahead.

We start early in work, nobody comes in any later than eight, and I like to be in before that to get a jump on the day. Early mornings are one of the most moaned-about aspects of the job, but I don't have a problem with them. Although we let out the farm lands of the estate, Dad liked us to get up before sunrise to help the O'Haras with their farm. I smile now when I think of the arguments we used to have.

"Seán Murtagh, you big lump, get out of that bed this instant and get dressed."

"Dad, it's seven in the morning. School doesn't start until nine. Go away!"

"Your mother told Kevin and Pat we'd help with the hay for an hour before school. We're leaving for the O'Haras' in five minutes, and you know you'll have to eat your breakfast before then or your mother will lynch you. And me."

"They have four boys. What do they need us for?"

"If you moved your legs as much as you flapped that lip we'd have been there by now!"

More than once it ended with him dumping a basin of cold water over my face while I lay stubbornly in bed, with my mother chastising him while trying to keep from laughing. Despite my anger at Dad I grin into the shower, giving in to a normal memory, and twist the knob, turning the water icy cold.

Jerry is yawning widely when I walk into the kitchen, sniffing the air.

"Are those Irish sausages you're cooking?" I look down at the frying pan as he takes a pile of white bread from the press and starts buttering the slices sleepily.

"Yes, indeed. Got them from that shop in the Village that imports from home. Only the best for our Seán!" He grins as he flicks the sausages expertly from the frying pan onto the plate with the bread and thrusts it into my hand.

"Legend, thanks." I begin wolfing them down immediately. "Are you on the breakfast shift at the restaurant?" I manage through a particularly large mouthful.

"Nah, heading back to bed now."

I swallow quickly, coughing my astonishment. "You got up at six in the morning just to cook me breakfast?"

"You gotta be fed and watered before the big day back." He claps me on the back and slopes lazily back to his room before I can say another word. Heartened, I slow down and savour every bite, until once again I realise the time. Choking back the last of the sausage sandwiches and a cup of scalding tea I am out the door within five minutes.

The mildness of the weekend has given way to a biting cold and I pull my coat around me to protect against the wind. Spring is late in coming this year.

My normal trek to work is a fifteen-minute walk to the underground subway station, waving to Alek in the drycleaner's and smiling at the woman with the pram who I always pass just outside a corner Starbucks where I usually pop in and down a shot of espresso. This morning, I almost miss the subway. The woman's baby is transforming into a toddler and the pram is now a buggy. Her eyes light up when she sees me, and we smile at each other like long-lost friends, although in the year since I've been passing her, we have never said a word to each other. The line in Starbucks is long and I have to run to make the 6.57 train. Not as packed as it will be in an hour, I manage to get a seat for the half-hour journey that brings me right into the centre of Manhattan.

Trudging up the steps from the subway station at the Lincoln Centre, I take a deep breath and exhale contentedly. It's not the fresh, rejuvenating air of home. It smells of petrol fumes, coffee and perfumes as commuters bang against me, muttering in frustration at my standing still, taking it all in. This is my world, the world I've created for myself. It might not have my family, the O'Haras, or Tors (I think of her before I can stop myself), but it is mine.

Another fifteen-minute stroll brings me to Angly Towers. I stop outside the door and, just as I did on my first day three years ago, I tilt my head up and with the dropped jaw of a tourist, stare up at the shiny, sixty-storey building. The size is not unusual for this part of Manhattan but is still incredible to me. I look down the street in expectation of seeing any of my colleagues. It is only starting to get bright but the street is packed with early-morning workers, weaving in and out of each other, swinging briefcases in one hand and clutching sloshing paper cups in the other. Every now and then, a young couple will stumble drunkenly through the crowd and I smile as I avoid a particularly potent-smelling pair, remembering my old college days in Dublin, until I realise these are not party-all-night students, but two of the many New York homeless. Taking a deep, steadying breath, I walk purposefully in the door of my workplace.

It is not yet swamped, but groups of suited colleagues mill around the reception area, some rushing towards the elevators, others deep in conversation, sipping coffee. I don't recognise any of them, but this is not unusual as Angly Towers is home to not just LL&T but also many other businesses, banks and firms. I look towards the barrier, expecting to hear the usual booming greeting from Hank, the young and overly enthusiastic security guard. But when Hank is nowhere to be seen, I am forced to accept that this is not going to be a normal working day like any other.

I ride up to the thirty-fifth floor alone in the lift, my tongue sticking like sandpaper to the roof of my mouth.

The first person to greet me when the elevator door opens is Sandy, Marx's secretary. Sandy is a large, black woman in her fifties who adores me and spent much of my first year here trying to convince me that there is Irish blood in her family too. She shrieks aloud when she sees me and pulls me into a massive bear hug. Despite the dread of the drama inextricably linked with my return, I can't help but smile into her big embrace.

"You know Sandy, a *real* Irish person would gasp politely if they were surprised, not scream the house down!"

She ignores me, gripping my arm in a vice-like grasp and dragging me towards Marx's office. Secretly glad for an excuse not to answer the calls of welcome from all sides, I merely smile and gesture patronisingly towards Sandy as she marches me unceremoniously down the corridor.

At the end of the wide hallway is the boss's large corner office. Marx moves to the door on hearing the commotion. Since he is the only person I informed of my sudden decision to return to New York, I imagine he has guessed the cause of all the excitement. Breathless, Sandy tosses me in front of her and shoves me inside the office door.

"Mr Marx, it's Seán! He's back!"

"I know, Sandra, he told me he was coming back three days ago." And with perfect comedic timing he pushes the door closed, leaving poor Sandy gaping on the other side. Marx thrusts his hand into mine and shakes it vigorously. I return the gesture with gusto.

"Really, sir, are you ever going to call her Sandy? You know she hates 'Sandra'."

"Well, I don't much enjoy 'sir' but you've never been able to break that habit."

I nod and sit where indicated, while Marx perches himself on the side of his meticulously tidy mahogany desk. He eyes me for a moment and I admire, as I always do in this office, the breath-taking vista of New York from the long windows.

"I'm very sorry about your father, Seán. I haven't seen you in person since it happened to be able to tell you that. I understand from some of the boys that there were other difficulties at home too?"

I have not told anyone in work about what happened at home. In fact, aside from Marx and my two best friends from the office, Gary and Mary-Anne, I have not been in direct contact with anyone in work. But Claire, Jerry and Sam all know people in my office and I'm sure there has been idle chat, gossip and rumours flying about that Marx will have heard, some more true than others. I expected this and am prepared for it.

"Sir, there was a lot going on and I'm sorry I was only able to come back now. But I'm here, ready and able, and I just want to get back to work."

Marx observes me contemplatively, twisting a miniature American football in his hands. "Seán, you know I like you, but you've taken almost a month off and we've had to assign people to your accounts, to your clients. I'm glad you're back and, believe me, it's only because I stood up for you with the powers-that-be that you're not out on your ass right now."

I don't doubt him for a minute.

"Your office is still yours, but you'll be working with Brad and Trevor on the work they've taken over."

At this, I feel my face screw up in disappointment. Of course, I knew my work couldn't just sit in my office untouched until I came back, especially given how quickly our clients need to move on their projects. Brad is a decent guy but Trevor is a notorious climber who would sell his granny if it got him within sight of the next rung of the corporate ladder. I do not expect him to hand my accounts back with a dainty bow. Well, if there is to be a fight, I am ready.

Marx cocks his eyebrow at my obvious displeasure, but I quickly make to appease him.

"Fine, sir. I'll go through what's left in my office and arrange a meeting with Brad and Trevor for later this morning."

Marx nods thoughtfully. "Take your time settling back in. The projects have moved on. There have been changes in attitudes and even personnel with some of your clients. They might be more comfortable continuing to deal directly with Brad or Trevor. Just take it on a case-by-case basis."

I stand, keeping my posture straight and tall to exude readiness. Marx grins patronisingly and ushers me outside into the waiting arms of Sandy.

It takes me another half hour to make it back to my office, as it seems my entire floor has come out in force to welcome me back. Most are genuinely pleased to see me, and only a few of the nosier women ask impertinent questions about home. I distract them from their enquiries with idle chat and, by the time I reach my office, I have fallen back into my New York character.

It was pure luck that I ended up not only with such a spacious room, but also one to myself. While there were twenty young graduates recruited with me, only eleven of us were kept on after the two-year programme was up. About half of those participating in the graduate programme specialised in the stock markets and trading side of LL&T, while the rest of us were immersed in the less numerically-based business development and consultancy areas. My retention was even more impressive as only three of the jobs offered on completion of the graduate programme were in these areas. Marx had taken a shine to me and I know his influence was important in getting me the job.

Every now and then I need to remind myself that his preference for me is not merely down to the well-known fact that everyone loves an Irishman. My work is always up to scratch – at least, it was before I left for Dad's funeral – and while I do not have a particularly great head for figures, my people-management skills are excellent and I know the business inside out. Marx took me under his wing and when a man in his early eighties happened to retire the week I was hired, Marx secured his office for me. The other guys who were recruited into business management share a small, insignificant office at the back of the thirty-fifth floor.

I flop down into the leather, high-backed chair I never felt I deserved and look around at the filing cabinets and shelves lined with folders. My stacks of work-in-progress files have been depleted and my client-contact rolodex is missing from my desk. I have no doubt Trevor has taken it. Before I do anything else, I power up my computer to send both Trevor and Brad an internal email, the tone of which should leave no doubt as to who is the superior, even if it is only by one year's experience.

I lean back in the chair. I always feel so much more in control in this office than in the real world. Yet it feels alien this morning.

A sudden dart of pain pinches my stomach and I realise immediately what it means. I'm homesick. I make sure the door to my office is fully closed before dialling the number. It is just after eight in New York so it will barely be gone noon at home. I wonder if Mum is back teaching in the school. Embarrassed, I realise I never even discussed this with her.

Katie answers the phone and I smile at her soft greeting. She has obviously not gone back to work yet. Her voice brightens when she hears it's me and she proceeds to chat away, something I am still getting used to with her. She is feeling much better. The doctors have cleared her to eat normally again and they are making her talk to a psychologist.

"It was embarrassing at first, I wondered if I really was crazy after all. But the woman is really nice and it's so helpful to just talk through everything that has happened."

I feel a stir of something like failure that she didn't feel she could talk to me. But then I remember the way I left and hang my head into my desk, knowing no one can see my shame. How could she ever confide in me, the way I've treated them all? Before we stray into that territory, before I can even apologise, Katie is telling me she has to go as she is on her way to the hospital for one more test. I press her for particulars, but she won't go into details about it. Unable to get anything more out of her, I write a note in my battered diary (which someone, probably Trevor, has very clearly been flicking through) to follow up on this.

"Is Mum there?" I ask before she hangs up.

"No, she's gone to the grave actually. She's been going every day."

I twist from a pang of misery. Until I left, Mum had not visited the grave once since the funeral. I don't like the thought of her going alone every day. "Just tell her I called, will you?"

"Of course. By the way, Eddie Edwards was down visiting Michael last night so he called over on his way back," Katie volunteered. "He's going to want to talk to you about whether you'll contest the will. I think I'm going to."

"Really?" My tone admits surprise and I can feel Katie give a small smile on the other end of the phone.

"Eddie says that even though I wasn't trying to kill myself, the fact

186

that I thought I needed to swallow all those pills shows that I'm . . .
weak somehow. Apparently, I have the best argument that a small trust
fund is not sufficient. I will probably be able to get the most for Mum
from the will."

I don't respond. I am consumed by a rush of protectiveness towards
my sister. How dare Eddie call her weak, even if it's true! I suddenly
wish I was back in Ireland. But a sharp knocking on my office door
returns me to reality. "Katie, there's someone at my door – I'd better go."

"No problem, I have to head to the hospital anyway. You should
call later – I know Mum would love to talk to you."

"Yeah, okay, bye," I mutter as I hang up, sitting up straight to wave
Trevor into my office.

"Trevor." I deliberately do not stand up, but stretch my arm across
my desk to shake his hand.

Trevor's ambitions are mirrored sharply in every aspect of his
personality. His eyes always seem to pop, as though he might miss
something by blinking. His gait is too quick and his conversation brisk.
I never had a personal run-in with him before, but his over-eagerness
is grating for a rookie.

Full of his own importance, Trevor immediately launches into a
speech about how he has the accounts under control and the clients
are happy dealing with him. "You shouldn't worry," he says. "Take
your time settling back in." He offers sympathy on the death of my
dad as an afterthought.

It's funny how those with the greatest desire to get ahead make it
the most difficult on themselves.

"Trevor," I smile amicably, "did you get my email?"

"Yes." Trevor shifts his stance. "You want to meet both me and Brad
at ten o'clock."

"Right. So let's discuss the ins and outs of handing back the files
then. I appreciate you keeping them ticking over, but we'll discuss it
more at ten, if you don't mind. I have a number of issues to clear up
before then."

Trevor, recognising his dismissal, contorts his face into what he must have thought was an obliging smile and leaves. The truth is that I have no 'issues to clear up' before ten o'clock, but I have no intention of letting my authority slip in LL&T. I don't intend keeping to Marx's plan of sharing work with Brad and Trevor either. If I am to forget the wretchedness that has been the past few weeks, I need to excel here independently. I re-open my now overflowing email inbox and start to filter through the messages, one by one.

Colleagues flit in and out of my office throughout the day to welcome me back but I use my trusted trick of standing almost as soon as they enter to indicate the visit won't be long. They are awkward in their sympathies and just as glad to escape as I am to be left alone. I take a half-hour break at lunchtime when Gary and Mary-Anne call up, armed with my favourite sandwich from the Subway around the corner. They don't focus on the will or my time in Ireland, even though Mary-Anne must know most of the story, being a good friend of Claire's. After quick sympathy hugs, we chat mainly about what I have missed in the office during my time away.

They leave at about half one to go back to work in their offices, and I get my head down for the rest of the day. I work solidly until after half nine that night without a break for dinner. By then, it is too late to call Mum. Secretly glad of this, I push down the familiar feeling of guilt and ring Jerry who is out having a few pints with Sam and some of our other friends in one of the many local Irish bars. A quick subway ride later I arrive, but after one drink they are all ready to leave. I find myself protesting, not wanting to go home to a night of guilt-ridden dreams. I offer to buy a last round, but they look at me strangely.

"It's nearly half eleven, boy," Sam half-laughs. "We all have work in the morning. So do you. Let's go home."

I look at Jerry expectantly. If anyone would be willing to stay out all night, it's him.

Uncharacteristically, he shakes his head. "Not tonight, Seán. I'm working a double tomorrow."

I convince them I won't be long, to go on without me so they reluctantly leave me nursing my pint.

I stay for another hour on my own. I talk amicably to the few good-looking women who approach me, but brush them off before it can go any further. Eventually, having ignored four calls from Claire, I stagger home. A mere five hours later, I leap out of the bed at the sound of my alarm and another day begins.

* * *

It is the end of my first week back in work and I am drunk. Claire is waiting in my flat, watching television in silence with Jerry and Sam when I stumble in. All three glare at me and I am not surprised. The last week has been a series of incidents through which I have managed to alienate nearly everyone around me, including Claire and my flatmates. But the most serious happened today with Marx.

Trevor had been giving me problems all week. I took most of my files back from Brad, though we came to an arrangement that he would continue working on those that were near to closing, so as not to upset the clients by switching handlers again. Trevor, on the other hand, was not so obliging. Having had a calm and, apparently, productive discussion at the ten o'clock meeting on my first day back, Trevor had delayed returning files and was dodging my phone calls. The clincher came when one particularly important client – who I had brought in myself after months of chasing and persuasion – rang me to say that Trevor had informed him that he was taking over the account. Given that Trevor has a year's less experience than me, the client demanded either a discount or me back. Furious, I apologised for any misunderstanding and promised that I would be back on the account permanently by the end of the day.

I was still fuming when I called Trevor to my office. To my own surprise, I started shouting at him. I accused him of stealing my work and lying to clients to make personal targets. His eyes widened in shock by my reaction. I imagine he has never been accused of being a climber to his face, although everyone knows that about him.

"*Seán!*"

I was halted mid-rant by the arrival of a stony-faced Marx at my door. "My office, now! Trevor, go back to your desk, I'll call you later."

Still a pulsing bomb, I stomped aggressively down the hall, ignoring the stares of my colleagues as I passed them. Even Sandy didn't say a word, but sat with her nail file halted mid-use as I marched past her desk into Marx's office and flung myself childishly into the chair. It was only when Marx slammed the door that I felt suddenly nervous, and realised the stupidity of what I had done.

"Sir . . ." I began, hoping to repair some of the damage.

"Quiet." Marx, usually a buddy, could be authoritarian when he needed to be.

I immediately fell silent. Marx walked back and forth behind his desk for a few moments, evidently trying to collect his thoughts. Finally, he glanced knowingly at me and walked over to a filing cabinet in the corner, reached into the bottom drawer and pulled out two cans of beer. He threw one to me and, only for my childhood training with my father and Conn O'Shaughnessy, I would have missed in astonishment.

Marx cracked his open and took a swig. I did the same, nearly choking on it as a warm, fermented taste slid like poison down my throat. Marx didn't seem to notice, or care, and continued drinking.

"Seán," he said slowly, "we have protocols here and you know it. Or at least, you should know it. If you have a problem with Trevor or anybody else you come to me. You don't scream the place down and embarrass them in front of the rest of the office. Now, you may not like it but Trevor, for all his flaws, is exceptional at his job and was a huge help when you picked up and left us for over three weeks."

I stared at the floor and scuffed my feet. I knew the speech wasn't over. I sipped the disgusting beer as a gesture of atonement.

"We're glad to have you back, but you can't just march in here and

190

pretend nothing's changed. In some businesses, three weeks or a month is nothing. You know that's not the case for us. You're not at your peak. I'm sure things have changed in your life too since your father passed away. Give yourself time."

At the mention of my father, anger bubbled up in me again. I knew I had to get out of his office, or I would say something I'd regret. It took all my effort to sound apologetic, as though I'd learnt my lesson. "Sir, you're right. I haven't been sleeping great so I'm a bit wound up. Maybe I should leave early today once I've sorted out the Libermann account. I'll feel better in the morning."

Marx did not appear entirely convinced but was appeased enough to let me out of his office and ignore me for the rest of the day. At six-thirty, I rang straight through to Trevor's voicemail to avoid talking to him and mumbled a quick apology. Then I left Angly Towers for the night. There had been a stretch in the evening so it was only starting to get dark. Unsure what to do with myself, and not in the mood for company, I bought an oversized pretzel from a street vendor and strolled around the streets, down the bright lights of Broadway, through Midtown and down to Times Square. The bustle of hundreds of faceless strangers around me made me feel calmer and I tried not to dwell on any thoughts at all, just walk.

After a while, I began to feel lonely, but had no one to call. I knew that over the past week I had successfully irritated almost everybody.

Jerry and Sam were growing increasingly frustrated with me. I refused to talk to them about what I had been through in Ballyloughlin and while I joined them almost every night for a drink, I couldn't help but lapse almost immediately into a silence they surely found sullen. I spent the week feeling constantly exhausted, but I refused to come home at a decent hour to sleep, afraid of the images that kept me awake and stretched the nights into what felt like years. I wanted, needed, to avoid lying awake at night with the uncomfortable thought that I had abandoned my family when they needed me most, just as Dad abandoned Andrew and, ultimately, the rest of us. But I couldn't bring myself to confide in Jerry or Sam when they questioned my attitude. Their constant teasing about sister-loving has not helped matters.

Claire is barely speaking to me. I didn't phone her until three days after I returned to work and Jerry started pestering me about it. When I finally rang her, it was clear she was furious with me for not contacting her sooner. She didn't hold back, complaining about how self-centred I was to ignore her after she spent so much money on flights, used up her holidays in work and put up with how I had treated her in Ireland. She even mentioned my fawning over the "country girl" but continued before I could defend myself. She ranted at me for half an hour about how she had tried to be sympathetic but had reached the end of her patience. I knew everything she was saying was fair, even her jibe about Tors, so I apologised repeatedly.

Eventually, she agreed to let me come over to her penthouse apartment for a take-away Chinese. We had forced conversation and spent a slow, uninteresting hour in her bed which just depressed me more. I told her I wanted to finish some work at home and didn't stay the night. Claire's eyes brimmed with tears as I left and the increasingly common feeling of self-reproach welled up in my stomach. I tried to let my guard down, explaining as I stood in the doorway, obviously anxious to be gone, that I had been finding it difficult to cope, but that I hoped she would stick by me just a little longer. I could see her soften at this. Though not normally one for getting emotionally attached to the men in her life, Claire appears to have developed a true fondness for me. Her trip to Ireland now makes me wonder if her feelings are turning into something stronger. I suspect the desperate way I embraced and kissed her before I left might have made her determined to give me one more chance. A chance I blew.

Sitting on a bench under the Empire State Building after my telling-off for shouting at Trevor, I watched the tourists flock in and out, all thrilled to be there. It is probably the highlight of their trips to

New York. I usually feel superior around the tourist sites, smug that I am not an outsider any more. At that moment, though, I could not feel any sense of belonging. In the one week since I'd returned, I'd humiliated my junior staff (even if this was only Trevor), angered my boss, pushed away my flatmates and further distanced myself from Claire. I hadn't talked to anyone in my family since my call with Katie the day after I arrived back in New York. Thirsty after my long walk and salty pretzel, I ducked into the nearest bar I could find and didn't leave until after eleven.

So when I drunkenly stumble in the door of my apartment just before midnight, I am pretty pleased with myself that I have made it home before one o'clock. But whatever praise I expected from Jerry and Sam is not to be had. They are sitting awkwardly in the living room, with Claire between them. When I come in, they stand immediately.

"Well, Seán, we're off to bed." Sam flicks off the television, gives an unconvincing stretch and walks straight past me, avoiding eye contact.

Jerry follows, giving me a small, resigned pat on the shoulder as he goes by.

"Claire, before you say anything," I hold up my hand as Claire stands herself and opens her mouth to speak, "I should tell you I'm a little drunk and anything I say can't be used against me in a court of law." I hear myself giggling before misjudging the distance of the kitchen chair and hitting the floor instead. The shock of impact spasms through me and I howl in pain, causing Jerry and Sam to come running out from their bedrooms. But Claire waves them off and I hear them snickering as she pulls me to my feet with some effort. I let her heave my arm around her shoulder and drag me towards my bedroom.

"You're a mess, Seán Murtagh," she admonishes me as she tosses me onto the bed. "You're lucky today is Friday so you can sleep on tomorrow."

"No," I moan into the covers. "Have to go into work tomorrow. Big deadline. Have to go in."

I hear a long-suffering tut.

"Well, just wake me before you go, Seán – I'll make you some breakfast."

Feeling like a real jerk again, I reach my hand up and tug her arm, pulling her to the bed. "You're amazing." I know my words are slurred but I mean them. "I don't deserve you."

"You got that right," she manages to say before I cover her mouth with mine.

I don't wake Claire the next morning, but sneak out early and ride the subway all the way to Lower Manhattan. Aside from not enjoying company and wanting to avoid another heart-to-heart with Claire, there is a particular reason I need some time to myself this morning. Dad is dead a month today. I thought the phone call I received from Pat O'Hara exactly one month ago today was the worst news I could possibly receive. If only I had known the month that was in store for me.

Without consciously thinking about it, I find my legs carrying me towards the Liberty Island ferry. The journey across is busy, but not nearly as crowded as it will be in a few hours. I spend the day on Ellis Island wandering aimlessly, knowing that Claire will probably come to look for me at LL&T and I just can't face an inquisition. No one would think to look for me on Ellis Island and I certainly won't run into anyone I know. As soon as I think these words, I curse myself for tempting fate and look around, half expecting to see a neighbour from Ballyloughlin waving at me. But there is no one, so I continue strolling, head down, reminiscing.

By midday, I can't take my own thoughts any more and I use one of the payphones to call home. There is no answer. Dispirited, I continue to wander around the grounds and eventually arrive back at the famous statue of Annie Moore, the first person to be processed through Ellis Island. I stare up at her marble figure, holding her hat in what looks like a sort of salute. All those people, I think, came here because they had to, looking for a better life. I originally came to

America in search of an adventure, not out of necessity. But now, in a way, I envy those people. When they came here they could get on with their lives – they never had to go back. Suddenly, I feel hugely ashamed. The majority of people who arrived in Ellis Island left behind loved ones they would never see again.

Propelled by shame, I walk back to the pay phone and this time, she answers.

"Hi, Mum," I say quietly into the receiver.

"*Seán!*" she exclaims and I hear her shout the news to my youngest sister.

She sounds genuinely thrilled to hear from me and this makes me feel even more discomfited at the way I walked out on the family. Unable to hold myself back, I broach the subject. "Mum, I'm sorry about the way I left. I didn't mean to say those things . . ."

Mum cuts me off. "Let's not talk about it, Seán. You've phoned now which is great."

Lizzy, when Mum eventually hands the phone over, is less cordial. I guessed she might still be cross with me, and her subdued tone and short, curt answers to my polite enquiries confirm it. The conversation begins to run out, so I ask for Katie.

"She's in the hospital," Lizzy says, but before I can ask her why, Mum is back on the line.

"Don't worry, sweetheart, she's not in the hospital because there's anything wrong with her. She's visiting a friend."

I pause, deciding whether or not to believe her. But since I have no right to question her, I don't push it. "Well," I respond eventually, "she'd better hope she doesn't run into Karen Shaw while she's there." Mum laughs and I feel more heartened than I have done since returning to New York.

On the boat back to the mainland, I sit alone at the back, in contemplation. Just talking to Mum has eased my mind slightly but there is still a niggling in my stomach, knowing I cannot leave it all fully behind. The call also makes me picture Tors more clearly than I have in days. When stepping off the plane, I made a conscious decision not to think about her but a part of me knows that some of the irrational anger I am feeling towards Claire at the moment is nothing other than a frustration that she is not Tors.

I arrive back in Manhattan at nearly four o'clock, wondering if Claire is still at the apartment, or whether Jerry and Sam are there alone, waiting to lecture me. Jumping on the subway back towards my office, I stop off at one of the local bars my colleagues would often drink in together after work. Not believing my luck, I find my friend Gary sitting in a booth in the corner with some friends. I saunter over in that general direction, trying to look casual and act surprised when Gary calls my name and insists I join them for a drink. The first hour is fun, and no one asks me anything about the past month. I do not know the rest of Gary's friends so their lack of poking and prodding is hardly surprising, but after a while I sense myself lapsing back into my usual brooding reverie.

Remembering that it was this time last month that Claire was taking care of me after I received the call about Dad, I make a decision, albeit a slightly inebriated one, to text Claire and apologise again, offering to cook her dinner on Monday night. She sends a rather cool text back reminding me that she has Pilates on Monday nights, which I had of course forgotten. But she agrees to meet me for dinner out on Wednesday instead.

* * *

The next few days are quiet. Both Jerry and Sam spend all day Sunday working and arrive home late. I can't but wonder if they are avoiding me. Taking advantage of the space, I don't leave the apartment all day except to do some grocery-shopping around the corner. I doze off on the couch and watch trashy movies for the rest of the day, flicking quickly over when *Sister Act* comes on in case the lads come home – they don't need any more ammunition than they already have.

The first few days of the week are uneventful in work. I listen to a voice message from Trevor accepting my apology, although I suspect from the tone that he was ordered to make the call. Aware that people are scrutinising my behaviour, I rarely venture out of my office. I make sure to leave work early on Monday night to sit in with Jerry and Sam and watch a game of American football. We don't discuss my family, or what has happened with Claire or anything to do with my mood. We drink a few beers each and sit in companionable silence for the evening, occasionally yelling at the players or making dramatic contrasts with GAA – the 'real' sport.

By the time I meet Claire on Wednesday, I feel like I am approaching a state of normality. I am rested and, for the first time since Dad died, I feel in control of my own life. When Claire arrives, I am already waiting at our usual table in her favourite Italian restaurant halfway between our two offices. We often meet there on weekday evenings, and I revel in the familiarity of the surroundings. I admire her as she weaves her way through the tables of the crowded restaurant to reach me. Her movements are effortless, every step towards me a dance. Her thick black hair is tied back into a tight, high pony-tail, not a whisper of hair out of place. I usually think of her as beautiful, and tonight elegant is the word that flashes in neon lights in my mind. I know I am not the only man watching her. Her mid-length dress is colourful and funky, offset with a flowing black scarf. Before I can stop myself, I think of how Tors, though very pretty, could never pull off such an outfit and furthermore would never attempt it. Shaking Tors out of my head, I bump cheeks awkwardly with Claire as she arrives at the table and takes her place opposite me.

She is still slightly reserved but engages me cordially throughout dinner and I relax into a conversation of easy small talk. Only once we have finished desert and I am looking around for the waiter to ask for the check does Claire start talking for real.

"Seán, I know that you don't want to talk about what's going on at home in Ireland."

197

My body stiffens and my face tightens, but she presses on.

"But this isn't about you. I have things going on in my life too, you know. Look, I can be there for you if you want. But it has to be a two-way street. I got my hair cut last week and you didn't even realise." She puts up her hand to stop my attempted interruption. "I got enough compliments in work, I don't need yours. And you know I don't expect guys to realise when girls get their hair cut anyway. But before you went back to Ireland, you used to notice everything about me. I was a big deal to you. And I'll admit, I took you for granted sometimes. But when you were gone I realised how much I missed you. I want us to be a proper couple. Just the two of us, Seán, no one else."

She reaches across the table for my hand and my thoughts cloud with emotion. Claire is offering me her total and undivided commitment. I've waited for this for so long. Now, I just want to curl up in bed alone.

"If it's too hard for you to be in a relationship right now, I understand. But I've said it before – I went to a lot of trouble taking time off work and buying expensive last-minute flights to Ireland. And I know there was something going on with that country girl which, by the way, I find just weird since she's your brother's sister. You're practically related."

"We're not related!" It is out of my mouth before I can stop myself and Claire freezes. I know immediately that it was a test, and my first reaction was to deny a blood connection with Tors, rather than reject any other kind of relationship. I sit in terrified silence, watching Claire come to a decision.

"Do you remember Karl? From my office? You met him at the Christmas party last year?"

I nod even though I have no recollection of any Karl.

"Well, I'm not related to him either."

She looks down at the table, embarrassed, and I tense at the lick of anger inside me.

"Seán, I want us to be exclusive. Just us. I think I've proved that

I'm willing to make the effort for you. But you have to be willing too. I don't want you to say anything now. Just think about it."

Before I can answer, or maybe before I want to, she stands and glides her way between the tables and out of the restaurant with a poise I could never have managed had the situation been reversed. If Claire had made that speech a few months ago, I would not have had a moment's hesitation about racing after her into the street. But everything has changed now. I have changed as a person, except I'm not sure exactly who I have become.

In work, when situations get stressful I respond well: stress is an impetus for me. Marx has commented on it more than once. But now I am facing the biggest crisis of my life and I have run away; literally halfway across the world to escape dealing with it, with her. But I am not engaging in life here either. Claire was right – before I left I would have noticed if she had chipped a fingernail. Tonight I had seen her across the room and, while aware that she is gorgeous, any further detail escaped me. I just don't seem to care any more.

I rub my temples and let out an exhausted sigh. One way or another, I am going to have to give Claire an answer. I will have to deal with this, just like at some point I am going to have to deal with what is happening at home. I order one more drink before paying the bill.

* * *

I do not see Claire again until the following Sunday, two weeks after I returned to New York. We speak on the phone but any time I tentatively broach the subject of our relationship, she cuts me off, demanding that we wait to have such an important conversation face to face.

She is not my only concern. I have been carrying an uneasy feeling about my family. I phoned home twice this week but no one has answered and none of them have tried to contact me. I thought the conversation I had with Mum from Ellis Island had gone well and cannot understand the sudden halt in communication.

On Friday morning, when there was still no answer, I rang the O'Haras to speak to Kevin. We had a short, depressingly forced conversation, which made me sure he still blames me for Mrs Boden's death. He wouldn't say much about my family, just that he had seen Mum a few days ago and she seemed fine. After hanging up dissatisfied, I contemplated ringing Tors, but I knew she wouldn't talk to me.

Work has not been going well either. By Friday, Marx seemed to have decided I had been given long enough to deal with my personal problems and begins laying on the work. I stay in the office until nearly midnight on both Thursday and Friday and have to work most of Saturday.

By the time dinner with Claire on Sunday evening rolls around I am exhausted again and not inclined to tolerate company.

Jerry, who moans constantly about work but can never resist an opportunity to cook at home, is making another lavish meal of lamb tagine for me and Claire. He puts the finishing touches to the pots and pans while I set the table and insists on giving me some brotherly advice.

"Just be attentive, Seán. Listen to everything she says. Girls like to trip you up by asking you questions about complicated stories they've just told you. So concentrate. You'll never get her if you have your head in the office or back home with your fake sister."

I have to laugh at his sincerity. Jerry is so dramatic about relationships and, since a devastating break-up about a year ago, has remained solidly mistrustful of all women's intentions. Still, it turns out to be good advice. Still tired from the week and unable to get the lack of contact with my family out of my head, my mind begins wandering whenever Claire says something that does not require a direct response from me. I try to actively concentrate on her words, as if I am in work.

About halfway through dinner, a phone purrs. I frown, looking around for the source of the old-fashioned drone. We always use our mobile phones in the apartment, never the standard landline that came with the rental. I had forgotten about its existence but there it is, under a pile of old movie magazines, flashing and emitting a tired chime in the corner. Tentatively, I lift it, wondering who on earth has our landline number.

"Hello, is that Seán? This is Eddie Edwards."

Realising I have been caught in a trap, I take a deep breath and try to stay calm. "Yes – hello, Eddie, this is Seán. Why are you ringing me at eight o'clock on a Sunday night?"

"Oh, I am sorry, Seán." He sounds genuine. "But I was just over with your family having a late lunch, it's not even four o'clock in the afternoon here, you see. I suggested that I would ring you in your office during the week but Lizzy insisted that they work you like a Trojan over there and so I should try your apartment."

I feel the side of my mouth twitch upwards involuntarily. Lizzy knows me so well – knows I would find a reason to avoid a call from Eddie in work but that I would be caught by surprise if called at home.

"Look, Eddie," I say, uncomfortably aware that Claire is watching me, hawk-like. "I'm actually in the middle of dinner here, so I can't stay on the phone for long. Is there something in particular I can help you with right now?"

"Well, Seán, not really, to be honest with you. Your father is only dead a number of weeks so it will still be months before a grant of probate is issued. Hell, it could even be next year, given the size of your estate. So there is no particular rush in deciding whether you want to contest. The thing is," his voice quietened, "I've been over with your family a fair bit recently, mostly at Michael's request, just to put your mother's mind at ease. The fact that the Shaws are still in Wicklow, when even in the best-case scenario for them it will be a year before they could take possession, is scaring Glenda. I've been going through the options with her, talking about other cases. She'd like to have a strategy in place. It mightn't be one that we can action until after the grant, but I'd just like you to get thinking about the pros and cons of your own application. If you decide to contest, as I said, it would be more prudent for you to get your own lawyer. But in the meantime, at your mother's request, I'm happy to talk to the family as a whole. Your sisters all seem happy with that approach."

"Even Niamh?"

"Yes, your mother was in Dublin during the week and had lunch with your eldest sister. She was the most amenable to the idea of a challenge of all of your sisters, I believe. Katie has been chopping and changing her mind. When I spoke to her during the week she was inclined to challenge but, to be honest, it would not surprise me if she comes back from the hospital now with her mind changed back again."

"Katie's in the hospital again?" I cut in hurriedly. "Let me speak to my mother."

"Oh no, I'm sorry, I didn't mean to give you the wrong idea. There is nothing wrong with Katie herself. She is just visiting a friend who is sick. Glenda isn't in the room right now – perhaps you can ring her later. So, as I say, it's just prudent to have a strategy in place so that once the grant of probate goes through, we can move quickly."

I take a long pause. I do not believe for a second that Mum is not in the room. I can easily visualise her with her ear pressed to the phone, practically shoving Eddie out of the way. I know I will have to discuss all this with Mum at some point, but the urgency is lost to the fear that my sister is still sick and no one is telling me. For the first time, I feel a flash of empathy with the plight of Karen Shaw. If Katie is unwell and needs treatment, I am willing to walk roughshod over anyone and usurp anybody's will, whether rightfully mine or not, if that's what it takes to treat her. But I know Eddie will not engage me in talk about Katie.

"Okay, Eddie. Why don't you ring me late Thursday afternoon your time, it'll be lunchtime for me so I should have time to talk to you. Ring my office number – Mum can give it to you."

I hope that will be enough to satisfy him and Mum for the time being, though I have not yet decided if I will actually take the call. I am just getting used to being back in America and don't understand the big rush. Annoying as Eddie is, I cannot deny that he is going out of his way to help Mum – travelling out to our house on a Sunday. My mind travels back to Katie again.

"Eddie," I say firmly just as he is about to hang up, "can you please ask my mother to ring me as soon as possible? I'll be here in the flat all night."

"I certainly will, young man," Eddie replies, a little too cheerfully.

I place the phone back on its large stand and sink into the couch. The conversation spins in my mind and I don't know how long I've been sitting in contemplation when I hear a chair scrape behind me. I jerk around, having forgotten that Claire is sitting there.

"Look, you obviously have things on your mind and you want to talk to your mother." She is clearly livid. I attempt to interrupt but she is already marching into my room to grab her coat from my bed. "It's fine, Seán. I know when I'm only in the way. See you around." She swings her long-handled bag dramatically over her shoulder with such force it flies across her back and lands over her other shoulder. It has such an opposite effect to the dignified exit she was going for that, before I can help myself, I feel a blissful release of tension wash over me and I blurt out a laugh. Furious, Claire storms out of the apartment and I am too distracted sniggering to follow her. Eventually, I calm down and drop back onto the couch.

I am glad she has left. The silence is glorious. I sit there all evening preparing questions for Mum. She never rings.

* * *

The first thing I do when I arrive at the office the next morning is call home. No one answers. I wonder if they have installed a caller-identification system on the phone and are actively avoiding me, or if they are actually all out of the house. Perhaps they are all at the hospital with Katie. A horrible combination of rejection and shame swims uncomfortably in my stomach.

I try to put it all aside, as I have been doing for the past few weeks but the idea of Katie weakening keeps lurching to the forefront of my mind. Even if I am not being lied to by my family, and Katie is constantly just visiting a friend, who is this person? Katie lives a quiet, confined life in Ballyloughlin. Unlike Lizzy who has friends from every county in Ireland, Katie has few close friends. I am likely to know whoever it is who is so sick. Anger overtakes humility until I remember again how I stormed out of the house and know on any objective review I don't deserve to be kept in the loop.

"Seán? Are you listening to me?" Marx is standing by the door with Brad and Trevor hovering in the background.

"Sorry, Marx. Just strategising." I stand up and motion for them to step into my office. Only when I notice Marx crinkle his nose in disdain do I become aware of the disarray that has built up over the past few days.

"You know, Seán, you should really keep on top of your filing even if you're working late. You know you can ask Sandy to help you if you need it."

His tone is not friendly and I suspect this is not a casual visit.

"Is there a problem, sir?"

"We need to talk about your work. I know that you're not back in New York very long but we can't just wait around for you to get back to your normal self. I want you to give Brad the Libermann, Pulsor and Zendman files, and Trevor can take all the files he was working on while you were gone." My two usurpers step forward – Trevor a little too eagerly – to take the files from my desk.

I move to quickly block their way. Even though most of the information is in soft copy, the physical papers have all my notes and I'll be damned if Trevor thinks he can simply take possession of them. As I put out my hands protectively, I find myself only a hair's breadth from Trevor's smug face.

"Those are my files. What am I supposed to work on if I hand them all over?"

"Seán, just give them the files so they can get working and then you and I will talk."

But the adrenaline is beating through me and I don't even attempt to hold onto the last scrap of reason that is floating blissfully out of my head.

"You've obviously filled them in already on whatever you're planning saying to me," I spit angrily. "Whatever you want to say, you can say in front of them."

Marx, who is not one to be intimidated, moves closer and squares up to me. "Just do it."

I hesitate for a fraction of a second more before gathering up the large folders and dumping them in their arms. My desk looks strangely empty. Brad, appearing embarrassed, and Trevor, smirking gleefully, shuffle out of my office. Marx closes the door slowly behind them. Moving deliberately, as though I'm a grenade that might go off, he approaches me and places a hand on my shoulder. Before I can stop myself, I shake him off. He's not my father. I catch him raise an eyebrow for an instant, but when he speaks, his tone is conciliatory.

"You're finding it difficult. You've been working hard but your standard of work is slipping. I know you worked all day Saturday but I had to spend Sunday in here putting out your fires. The clients are complaining that you are short and rude, and you're making basic errors as well as larger ones."

The anger still churns but real fear is now mingled with it. "Are you firing me?" My voice, intended to sound hard, squeaks pathetically.

"Of course not. You were hired in the middle of a recession, we know your value. But we can't have you on the front line when you're performing like this. We want you to take a sabbatical and see a psychologist to help you work through your issues."

I blurt out a harsh laugh. "Oh, sir, you are so American!"

Marx frowns.

"I don't need to see a psychologist, I'm not crazy. And I don't need time off. What I need is for my team to get behind me and off my back. I need Trevor to be gone from this team and I need a Sandy of my own to help with filing. Then I'll be on track."

Marx smiles sadly. "Seán, you can't dictate terms like that. Trevor is excellent at his work. No one at your level has their own secretary. I'm not the only one who has noticed that you're slipping. And when the clients complain, I can't be lenient any more. This is an order. Take the time off and regroup."

He stands and opens the office door, indicating for me to get out.

"You want me to leave right now?" I am astounded.

"Seán, you are a decent guy who everyone in here loves. We all want you to get back to yourself. Now, I know you won't want to cause a scene and make things worse for yourself. Just slip out the door and no one will notice."

Suddenly, Trevor is at the door, wearing an unimaginably superior expression on his face. "Marx, Sandy says there's a call for you."

Something snaps inside me. Sandy would never interrupt Marx during what she must know is a confrontation. Furthermore, Trevor would never stoop to messenger-boy for Sandy. He is using any excuse to witness my humiliation.

Over the humming in my ears, I hear myself shout. "How can things possibly get any worse for me, Marx? You haven't a fucking clue what's going on in my life!" I march past my boss, who I have never before referred to by any other name other than 'sir' and, without even realising I am doing it, violently shove Trevor out of my way. Trevor steadies himself a moment, having been knocked against the wall, then moves to retaliate.

"Seán, Trevor, stop it *right now*!"

Marx is suddenly between us, his breath on my face, and I feel myself sweating as I irrationally reach around him to try to get to Trevor. Marx stubbornly blocks my way and shouts my name once, loudly. It has the desired effect and I realise heads are peeking out of office doors to witness the scene. Panting, I turn on my heel and stalk out without looking back.

I stride three blocks before whipping around and marching back to our usual coffee shop, just across the road from Angly Towers. As I anticipated, it hardly takes Gary even fifteen minutes to hear the news and ring my mobile. I tell him where I am and have already ordered cappuccinos and muffins for him and Mary-Anne when they arrive. Gary claps me on the back before taking his seat while Mary-Anne reaches in to kiss my cheek. I feel a debt of gratitude to her. Although Claire must have unloaded onto her about my unforgiveable behaviour over the past weeks, she has never stopped being a friend to me. Neither of them says a word, and their silent solidarity reminds me so much of home that I am horrified to feel tears well up in my eyes. Keeping my head down, I gulp my coffee, trying to choke back the lump in my throat with it.

Mary-Anne is the first to speak as she swishes low-fat milk around in her drink and breaks off a piece of her double-chocolate muffin. "Seán, I never allow myself to eat this kind of junk food early in the morning – it's only for you I'm doing it. You should go on sabbatical more often, you know!"

We all laugh, relieved that the ice is broken, and I wonder if maybe these two, of all people, will understand. "I don't know if they'll let me just take a sabbatical now. I think I might be fired." I watch them exchange worried looks and continue. "I assume by now you've heard what happened with Trevor?"

"Look, mate," interrupts Gary, "do you remember Ben, from Accounts? He started under-performing after his sister was killed in that fire. They fired him within a month." Mary-Anne thumps Gary on the shoulder but he just laughs. "You know what I mean, Seán. Ben was never fully committed to the job even before his sister's death. They just needed the under-performance as an excuse. If they were going to fire you, they would have done it when you didn't come back from Ireland for weeks. Or when you mouthed off at Trevor in your office. Don't look so surprised – word travels fast in LL&T, you know that. Look, they're giving you time off because you need it. They'll want you back. Just take it, go on holidays, try and sort out your head. If my dad had just dropped dead, I'd have snapped long before you, especially if Trevor was on my case."

I drink in their expressions of genuine concern and decide they deserve the truth if they're going to stick by me like this, when I know everyone else will run a mile rather than risk being tainted by association in the eyes of the company. I address my mug rather than face their looks of sympathy.

"It's not just my dad's death. We found out that he cheated on my mother when I was a kid and has another son. He left everything to him. Mum is left with next to nothing. My sister is taking it really hard. It's all gone wrong."

I look up tentatively.

Mary-Anne pauses, her mug halfway to her mouth in undisguised astonishment.

Gary's eyes swell in shock but he moves immediately to put a hand on my arm. "Mate," his voice is forced, "what are you doing here? Why aren't you at home?"

"I have to work, Gary." I know my voice is accusatory, but I don't care. I've been having this argument for days in my own head so the words come quick and harsh. "I have a life here. I can't just sit at home forever waiting for things to go back to the way they were."

"Seán, Gary didn't mean it like that."

Mary-Anne's voice tries to be soothing but I am already enraged, re-infused with the fury Trevor set off in me. I sit in an unforgivably stubborn sulk for another half hour, while the others try to reassure and cajole me. Then I walk them back to the office and accept handshakes and hugs. They promise to keep in touch. I want to apologise for my aggressiveness, and to tell them how much their support means. But I am afraid my voice will betray my true vulnerability so instead I hold onto their handshakes longer than usual and try to convey it with my eyes. Hopefully they understand.

I spend the rest of the day walking in a daze, fighting off the bitter chill in the air, moving from quiet contemplation to panic that now I have no work to take my mind off my life, or income to pay the rent. I am surprised I'm not hit by the unpredictable New York traffic as I move without direction, up, around and through Central Park until eventually I find myself on the subway, heading home. I make it back to the apartment late in the afternoon and spend an hour in the shower, scrubbing myself and trying to get warm. I stare at the blaring television without really watching it as the sun goes down outside.

At about seven o'clock, just as complete darkness sets in over the city, there is a knock on the door. It is Claire.

With no other choice, I stand back to let her in, but for some reason I cannot pinpoint, I already know what is coming. Maybe it is just a day of endings.

When she says the words, I find I don't particularly care and this saddens me. I have no argument, no defence so I just listen and try to concentrate on her words as she lists the hours she has spent crying over me, the effort she has put into keeping our relationship alive even after I retreated into my own selfish shell. She actually counts on her fingers the number of occasions she has attempted to talk to me about my 'home issues' and the many ways I have cast her aside.

I wait for her to mention the trip to Ireland, to mention Tors, but she does not. I suppose it has all been said already. At last she stops talking and looks at me expectantly. I wish I could say something, anything, to make her feel better, to explain that she is amazing and deserves so much better than me. But anything I say will sound practised and trite so I just take her hand and kiss her softly. She leans in for a second, then pulls away gently.

"You haven't even put up a fight, Seán. I think we both know this is over."

A tear slides down her cheek and I lift my finger to wipe it away, but she gets there first. I watch despondently as she walks to the door and looks back one last time.

"I'm sorry," I say, and I mean it. I'm sorry it's over, that our lives will no longer intertwine, that I've changed into someone who isn't compatible with her.

She sighs and I recognise the resignation in it. With one last toss of her head, she walks out the door and out of my life.

How long I sit there, I do not know, but a knock on the door rouses me. I lift my head from my hands, wondering if she has changed her mind. I open the door but the woman standing there is not Claire. My jaw drops.

Chapter 18

Tors

I have been standing outside for about fifteen minutes when I see her walk in. She comes from the left, on the other side of the road, the side with his apartment. She doesn't notice me propped up against the wall on the opposite path, watching her fix her hair in the side mirror of a parked taxi before striding up the steps.

I don't know why I continue waiting. It is obvious to me that she will stay the night. Or at least, that they will both emerge together, dressed up to the nines, strutting off to some restaurant or club. But I stand there anyway, watching the upstairs windows, though I don't know which is his, or even if his looks out this side of the building. What do I expect to see – two naked bodies kissing before pulling the curtains? Is that what I want to see? Would it make approaching him easier, casting him as the villain?

As I stand there, wondering how to interrupt them, as I know I will have to, she comes back out. Alone. It can't have been more than a quarter of an hour. As women do, she senses my gaze. I do not look away when she glances over with a very obvious double take. Her eyes narrowed in disbelief, she walks warily over to me. I straighten up from leaning against the wall, meeting her stare boldly.

For a few moments, we simply look at each other.

She breaks the silence. "He's waiting for you."

"I . . . he doesn't know I'm coming."

She bends her head disbelievingly to one side and I feel a rush of pity for her. I never wanted to be the other woman.

"It's not what you think," I say.

She doesn't laugh, or even smirk. She simply waits, considering me, and I see in the streetlight that her eyes are red and swollen. She controls whatever she is feeling well. "He's a good guy. Take care of him."

Before I can answer, she turns on her heel and marches back down the street, her head held high. I stay where I am, staring after her. Then I turn and gape up at the three-storey building. Red ivy trickles down the side of the brown bricks. It looks quite well-to-do from the outside. Taking a deep breath, I steel myself for what is coming next and slowly walk across the road. Just as I make to ring the buzzer, a man leaves the building and I duck inside. Following the numbering, I make my way up to the second floor and face his apartment. Another few moments pass before I calm myself. My heart is racing and though I have rehearsed what I will say a million times, my mind keeps blanking.

Eventually, tentatively, I knock. If I were not such a bundle of nerves, his expression would be pure comedy.

"Tors?"

Hearing his voice say my name makes my whole body tingle with a mixture of elation and relief. I keep my face expressionless as I lock eyes with him.

"Can I come in?" I ask eventually.

He jumps back as though burned and waves me in with an overly enthusiastic swing of his arm. "Of course!" He takes my coat hastily as he ushers me over to a low, bumpy couch. My first impression as I look around the boxy living space is that he must have found this place utterly minute after his Ballyloughlin mansion. I swivel around on the couch, taking in the surroundings. A large television is perched in the corner and three mismatched sofas huddle around it in what is left of the space.

Seán disappears down a narrow hall, so I walk over to the kitchen area and see that it is much larger than the living area. This is probably a good thing, with three grown men trying to feed themselves. I poke my head around the corner into the hall and see him in a small room at the end, flinging my coat unceremoniously onto a bed, before turning to jog back.

"Tea?"

I stand back and take him in as he goes to put the kettle on. He looks terrible. He might have lost weight, but it could just be the old, loose-fitting clothes hanging off him. His hair needs a cut and there is a sunken curve to his slightly bloodshot eyes. But more than any one physical aspect, he looks generally beaten down. Diminished, somehow, from the man I first met in Ballyloughlin. I shouldn't feel sorry for him; his woes are nothing to mine, to Andrew's. But I do.

"I'm not thirsty." My voice sounds somewhat strangled but I can't help it. I am raging at the feelings welling up at the sight of him. It hits me now how much I missed him all this time.

He stops and looks at me from the kitchen. For a few moments we merely stare at each other and I notice with some perverse satisfaction that he looks scared. His mouth twitches a few times, as though he wants to speak, but is afraid he might say the wrong thing.

I have to explain myself. I can't let him think I'm here for him. For us. I feel my knees begin to tremble. "Can we sit down?"

Again, he nearly leaps to comply.

Sitting on separate couches, we are still near enough to touch.

I force myself to continue. "I need to talk to you."

"Tors, I'm sorry. I wanted to tell you but you didn't return any of my calls. I even went to the sea house looking for you, and to the hospital –"

I hold up my hand to stop him. This is exactly what I was afraid would happen. "I'm not here for that."

"But I want to explain. Claire and I –"

"She says you're a good guy." I can't help myself and watch as his face registers confusion and horror at the thought of my conversing with her. I sigh. "I saw her leave your building as I was waiting outside. She told me that you're a good guy. Is that true, Seán?"

He looks utterly anguished and a vindictive sense of triumph stirs inside me.

"Tors, Claire and I . . . we are not together any more." His eyes bore into mine, willing me to believe him. "Seriously. It's been a long time coming. We're over."

When I do not respond, he frowns slightly. "What were you waiting for?"

"Sorry?"

"You said you saw her while you were waiting outside. What were you waiting for?"

"Courage." I do not even consider trying to save face. This isn't about me. "It's been a difficult few weeks since you left Seán. For everyone."

He squirms a little in his seat. He wears his guilt like a badge but it does not enhance the sliver of compassion I felt at first sight of him. On the contrary, it triggers a burst of anger and self-righteousness, and not only on my behalf.

His voice quivers. "Are you still in Ballyloughlin?"

Something snaps. My last few weeks only compounded the horrendous month before. That he does not even know where I have lived, never mind what I have been through, when he is the very person who should have been there . . .

"You are the most selfish person I think I've ever met, Seán Murtagh!"

214

Barely registering that I am already on my feet, I watch him rise slowly in horror. This place is tiny. I feel claustrophobic as I try to pace out my anger.

"Tors . . ."

"No! Just shut up, Seán. Of course I have been in Ballyloughlin since you left. But you haven't a clue, do you? You think Andrew has a cold? A flu? He's on the brink, Seán. You think I'm here for you? It's all about Andrew, not that you'd care. You never even tried to meet him!" Feeling my face turning puce with rage, I stop only to take a massive breath, before plunging on. "You don't like the idea that your father cheated with my mother, so you just ignore the consequences! It's all a plot to upset you, isn't it? Katie overdoses, but poor Seán has to clean up the mess. Your mother tries to hold the family together when she's the one who's been betrayed, but God forbid she lean on you even a little. Poor Seán, having to help his family! You ran away when they needed you, when Andrew needed you, when *I* needed you. You're selfish, and you're a coward, just like your father!"

It all happens in an instant. I see the flash of hatred in his eyes, whether because I called him a coward, or his father one, I don't know. But it is there and it's more than dislike – it's revulsion, loathing. He is moving towards me, channelling that anger in a way I've seen before. His face becomes Claude's and I automatically cower and throw up my arms to shield myself, crying out in a fraught, base way that disgusts me.

But the blow never comes. Not daring to look, I stand stock still, my breath coming quick and shallow. I flinch violently as his hands gently take hold of my arms and lower them. Reality comes flooding back. Three times I have seen my old boyfriend's face when looking at him, and this time it showed. Mortified, I see no hatred in his eyes now, only a mixture of concern and something like indignation.

"Tors," his voice is soft, "what was that?"

I say nothing, feeling the tears begin to flow, but when I try to wipe them away, he holds my arms down, searching my face.

"Tors?"

This is it, the moment to admit what I have told to no one but my brother, the sick patient who needed proof that he is stronger than me. I hesitate one last time, but then remember what I came here to ask him. He deserves the truth from me. Aware that I am still shaking, I start to whisper, glad he is still clasping my arms, steadying me.

"When I spent that year in France, I met a man. He was wonderful, attentive. Rich and powerful. Used to having his own way. The first time, it wasn't a . . . blow . . . it was just a grab. I had let him down at the last minute. He was right to be angry."

"Tors!" The exasperation in his voice does nothing to help.

"It wasn't all the time. He was always sorry afterwards." There is a silence, as I will my lip to stop trembling. "The last straw came when I got a call that there was a donor for Andrew and that I should come home. That's what he really needs, you know." I look up guardedly. "A transplant."

Seán nods and listens as it all comes tumbling out.

"I was so excited I could barely stand still. I paced Claude's massive penthouse apartment, one minute laughing out loud and whooping like a mad woman, the next keeled over in fear. I knew it was a serious operation. But he needed it – he needs it. That's why I booked flights home straight away; why I didn't give Claude, or the important evening he had planned, a second thought . . ."

* * *

I was lucky. I got a seat on a flight that was taking off in just over four hours. I needed to pack. Just a small bag would do – I didn't want to waste time waiting for checked luggage on the other side. The operation would take place in Dublin as soon as Andrew arrived from Kerry. It would happen soon, in the next few hours. These operations always took place quickly, while the organ was still fresh. I knew I probably wouldn't make it back before he went under, and allowed myself a second to think of him now, sending him brave thoughts as I stared longingly out the floor-to-ceiling windows, watching the early evening sun fall, dulling the spectacular Parisian landscape.

A sudden realisation hit me. This kidney was coming from another person. Another sister had lost her Andrew. I felt nauseated, and took a long deep breath through my nose. The luxurious waft of oranges and zest – the smell that always overwhelmed me in Claude's apartment – filtered through me. Excitement returned.

Within minutes, I had pulled half the wardrobe onto the floor, looking for any clothes I might have stashed there over the past few months. I rarely slept at the apartment I rented any more and I certainly wouldn't have time to return. I thought vaguely that I must text the girl I lived with to tell her I was leaving the country. Not that she'd notice, as I practically lived with Claude.

I heard his key in the door, and I called to him.

His voice sounded strange. "Victoria? Why is your dress on the floor?"

I remembered then that I had dropped it in shock as Mam broke the news about the operation. I ran out and he was standing there, his face like thunder, my red-velvet dress hanging limply from his hand. But for once I didn't care about pacifying him – he would, understand this.

"Claude, *je suis desolé*, but Andrew is getting a kidney! A kidney, Claude, a transplant! It's what he needs – he's going to be well again!" Tears of joy streamed down my cheeks. I could barely believe I was finally saying these words.

"That is wonderful, Victoria. I am very happy for you, and your family. We will toast with a glass of the most expensive champagne to celebrate tonight. But you must get dressed, as must I. We need to leave in less than half an hour, *ma chérie*."

I laughed. "No, Claude, you don't understand. The operation is happening tonight. I have to go home."

The grab came swiftly, as usual. I was so used to it, it was hardly sore any more. I immediately realised my mistake. This dinner was for his most important clients and I was leaving him without a date at the last minute. That was exactly the sort of carelessness on my part that set him off before. But it seemed so trivial compared to the news I just received. I tried to feel sympathy for Claude but all I could see was my brother's face.

"Victoria, you cannot leave me alone tonight. You know I need you there." His voice was calm, but threatening.

His hand tightened and I felt like a rag doll as he clasped his fingers around my wrist.

"Come on, Claude!" I hated the wobble in my voice, but I always felt so vulnerable when he had me in his grip like this. "Please, he's my brother, this is more important . . ."

I shouldn't have said that. I pressed my lips tightly shut, wishing I could suck the words back into my mouth, but it was too late. His arms, so tender when he held me in our lovemaking, were tense boulders now, just waiting to strike. And strike he did.

He had never hit me before. It was always just menacing words, a violent grip, a carefully placed shove. Nothing really bad, just a warning not to test him further.

The punch landed hard. I didn't even see his arm rise, but his tight row of knuckles collided with my cheekbone with such force that I stumbled backwards into the orange sofa and rolled right over it, tumbling to the floor in a heap. Before I could attempt to move, he was upon me, bundling the front of my dressing gown into his balled fists, dragging me upwards. I shuffled my feet under me, trying to find the ground, but his strength kept me upright without my support.

I heard him curse as I whimpered his name. One hand still on my robe, he tugged at my hair, so neatly curled for the evening, with his other and dragged me into the bathroom. The combination of pain and humiliation allowed my voice to return and I screamed as he pressed me forward, hard against the sink.

"Look, you bitch!" He pinched my face with his whole hand, forcing me to look in the mirror.

Even then, in that moment, I knew it was an image that would haunt me forever. Blood trickled down my face from a cut under my eye. Already the bruising was visible on the raised puffiness of my cheekbone.

In the mirror, his eyes, horrible with rage, bulged viciously behind me.

"Look what you made me do!" Claude's face flushed a deep red and his hands shook as they pulled me from the mirror and shoved me backwards into the pristine white bathtub.

I let out a shriek of agony as my back slammed against the tap jutting out from the head of the tub. Claude's hands were there again, but not to help. Yelling curses, he spun the tap and a gush of water pumped from the showerhead above, almost choking me. Distracted, disorientated, I didn't recognise what his hands were doing. Before I knew it, he was away from me, my robe in his hand, watching as I spluttered, naked, out of the reach of the pumping showerhead.

"Claude!" I gasped.

"I cannot bring you to the party now, you ugly bitch! Look at you! Clean up and I will deal with you when I come back tonight."

Clambering out of the bathtub, I called his name weakly. A dizziness unbalanced me and I tottered in an almost drunken state to the bathroom door and fell against it. But I had heard the key turn already and knew my pathetic twists of the doorknob would not work. Feebly, I continued to bang on the door, crying out for him. I listened to him moving around the penthouse, opening and closing doors, using the electric razor in the other bathroom. Eventually, I heard the front door opening, but there was a pause in his footsteps, and the door did not close.

He's changed his mind, I thought, stupidly.

His slow, deliberate treads grew louder and stopped just outside the bathroom door.

"Claude, I'm sorry!" I could hear the desperation in my voice, but I didn't care.

I wasn't even thinking of Andrew then – I just wanted to get out of that tiny en suite where I was curled weakly against the door, shivering and injured.

I realised what the sharp snap of the light switch on the other side of the door meant in that split second before it took effect and I cried out again as I was plunged into darkness.

* * *

I look up tentatively. Seán is staring at me with an expression of abject horror and I immediately wish I hadn't told him. He is waiting for me to go on, but it is too hard. I am still recovering from the expectation of another blow.

"Look, Seán, it was fine," I breathe. "I got away. He left the key in the lock and I managed to wiggle it out using a hair clip. It fell on the floor just outside the bathroom door and I managed to scoop it inside. I was gone before he came back and I never saw him again."

"Jesus Christ, Tors!"

"It wasn't even what he did to me – it was that he would stop me seeing Andrew when I needed to. I texted him, telling him not to contact me again, and he never did. Scared, I suppose. It was too vicious an attack for him to get away with if I had reported it. He was worried, I was sure. Knew he had gone too far. He transferred some money into my bank account. A good sum of money by my standards, but cheap and insulting knowing what he could afford. But I couldn't even be angry that he was trying to buy me off. I was just glad to be away from him. I wanted to send it back, but Andrew insisted I keep it. I suppose I earned it." I try to smile as I stretch the skin under my eye, revealing a healed scar that normally blends into my laughter lines. It tingles as I touch it.

Seán stares at me in disbelief.

I bow my head, not knowing how I feel. A little better, having said it out loud. But embarrassed that I had let myself be demeaned by Claude. And worried that he might think less of me, think I'm weak. Leave me. Again.

After a moment, he speaks. "What did your mother say?"

"She doesn't know. No one does, except Andrew." I'm done with this story now. A weight is slowly lifting from my shoulders, and I want to start talking about the reason I'm here. "Seán." He is still looking down on me with a mixture of pity and shock. "I didn't come here to talk to you about Claude."

But I am silenced. His mouth covers mine in a deep, searching kiss that reverberates through me. I can't believe he would still want me after hearing about Claude and, before I realise it, I am returning his embrace with passion.

Then just as suddenly, he pulls away. Astonished, I realise he is almost in tears. Turning his back on me, he walks the few steps to the other side of the room, pushing his hair back off his forehead with both hands. "Do you think I am the kind of person who would treat you like that?" He doesn't sound angry, or even self-pitying. It is a tone a teacher might expect from a curious student.

"I'm sorry." I'm suddenly aware what an insult it was to have ducked away from him that way. "It's just instinct."

"But you think I'm selfish. That's what you said – I'm a coward. What's one step further? A bully? A man who hits women?"

"I . . . I don't think that . . . I'm sorry . . ."

"Stop apologising!" his voice is loud, but not angry. "You didn't need to apologise to that bastard, and you don't need to apologise to me." He is sitting now, with his head in his hands and I see that he is shaking. He looks up. "Why are you here?"

Taken aback, I just stare down at him.

"I mean it. You normally never leave your brother for more than a couple of hours at a time. Why are you here?"

Drawing in a deep breath, I know this is it. There will be no more

221

interruptions. No Katie, no Claire, no images of Claude. Just me, asking the very thing I should have asked the moment I met him.

"The donor that became available for Andrew when I was in France didn't work out. It was pure misfortune because he hadn't been sick, aside from the kidneys of course, for months. But the day before Mam got the call, he contracted the flu. By the time they got to Dublin, Andrew was running a fever of over one hundred. There was no way they could operate, and the kidney went to a thirty-year-old mother of two instead. Andrew said that was better – that she deserved it more. Mam was devastated, we all were. It made me realise how dangerous the surgery is in itself if they wouldn't operate because of the flu. But I knew he couldn't stay on dialysis forever and he wouldn't last long without a new kidney. He needed someone to look after him, and he deserved a real friend, not some stranger who was likely to hand in her notice within two months. That's when I decided to become his carer. Not to escape France, but to spend as much time with him as possible. Because even if another kidney shows up, there's no guarantee he will survive the operation."

Seán is looking at me in earnest now. "So, you just have to wait until the right person dies?"

I choose my words carefully. "It is possible to receive from a live donor. In fact, it's becoming more and more common. But it can be hard to find a match, particularly in Andrew's case. The problem is his blood type. He's O negative."

"That's a good thing though, isn't it? Most people are O."

"Yes, almost half the population of Ireland are O . . . but not O negative." My smile is sour. "The ironic thing is that anyone, no matter what their blood type, can receive O negative blood. Andrew is a universal donor. He can give to anyone but only take a kidney from someone with his own blood type, and O negative is rare."

Seán frowns in concentration. "Could Andrew receive from a live donor if he was well enough?"

"Yes. Relatives are the most likely to match. I'm A positive. My parents were tested years ago, but they both have an A blood type too. Mam and Dad are only children and all the grandparents are dead. It doesn't have to be a relative, but we can't just ask strangers in the street. Anyway, blood type is not the only hurdle a donor would need to overcome. Tissue type has to be compatible too and the donor has to go through about a million tests to make sure they are healthy enough to give a kidney. And of course, Andrew has to be well enough to receive it. No colds, flus or temperatures."

"Tors, Andrew has been getting worse, hasn't he? In the weeks before my father died, he went downhill."

"Yes. His AVF blocking was a huge blow." Suddenly, an important question comes to me. "Why did you never visit Andrew?"

He stands suddenly, shaking his head. "Because I never wanted a brother! I never needed a brother. I don't want him in my life!" It's out of his mouth before he can stop himself, and he looks at me terrified that he's said the one thing that will make me walk out the door and never come back. But I'm over it now, over being considerate and sensitive. So I finally ask the question. When I say it, my voice is strong.

"I need to ask you something. I want you to come back to Ireland and get tested. If you're a match, I want you to give Andrew one of your kidneys. I truly do appreciate what a massive request this is, but please understand, we are desperate. Will you do it?"

In the tense wait where neither of us speak, every mediocre sound reverberates – the dripping tap, a slight buzzing that might be the electricity.

"I know it's unfair to ask," I say, "but I told Andrew I would put it to all of you – your whole family – when we first moved to Ballyloughlin."

He gives a gentle laugh. "What did Karen think of that?"

"We never discussed it with her," I answer openly. "She never suggested it and, to be honest, I don't know why. The only possible explanation is pride. Demanding money that Andrew has been left legally is one thing, but begging for body parts for her son from his father's other family – maybe it was just too hard for her. Andrew and I made the decision to ask you ourselves."

"So why didn't you? Why are you only asking now?" His voice is curious and gives nothing away.

"Because of you," I answer honestly. "Giving up a kidney is serious. It's not a sacrifice we can ask of just anyone. But we knew there would be no more blood relatives. Andrew and I agreed to approach Liam's children because family – even an unwanted, wronged family like yours – might be willing to step up and help. But then I met you."

I bow my head: declarations of love do not come easy.

"There was something about you," I go on. "Right from the start, I knew you were special to me, though I couldn't quite figure out why. So I stalled. I didn't realise why at the time, but I see now. Giving a kidney is dangerous. I know what it's like to have a loved one whose health is constantly at risk. I didn't want to put you in that position. I care about you too much."

Sean looks at me with an expressionless face. Our conversations about Claire and Claude seem like years ago.

"But now things have changed." My voice comes out stronger, but trembles again as I continue. "I don't know how many more times he can fall ill before . . ."

My voice trails away and Sean sits, lowering his head into his hands again.

"I'm sorry," I say, tears now pooling in my eyes. "I shouldn't have yelled at you when I arrived here or called you selfish. Of course you've had a lot to deal with. It's just that I'm so tired and we've been through so much – much more than you. And I am running out of options. You are the only one left I can ask."

Sean lifts his face to clarify. "Me and my sisters."

I look at him, surprised. "You really haven't been in touch with your family at home, have you?"

He starts at this.

"You know Katie visited Andrew before you left. Well, they're practically best friends now. She's in with him every day, and over in the sea house when he's not in the hospital."

Seán smiles oddly, like he's just solved a puzzle. "What does your mother have to say about that?"

"She doesn't have a choice. Andrew has insisted. She is his biological sister as much as I am. The thing is, the week after you left, he had a seizure."

"A seizure?"

"Yes, which he has never had before. He'll get infections, throw up, sleep for days on end, but he's never had a fit. They don't know if it's a new disease on top of everything else, or if his body is just reacting in a more serious way to the sickness. Either way, Seán, he is getting worse. We hope he can start using his AVF soon – it provides better dialysis performance and the temporary line is more susceptible to sepsis. But we're all terrified that it won't have developed properly and that he'll need more surgery. The need for a donor is becoming more urgent." I pause. "Katie has become quite devoted to Andrew. She's been tested, but she's not a match. She's convinced Lizzy and even your other sister Niamh to take the test too."

Seán is standing as though frozen, and I know what he is thinking.

"Oh, it's been another world since you left, Seán. Katie has galvanised everyone. Your mother wouldn't let her ask anyone outside the family but when the four O'Hara boys and Michael Undersky heard what the girls were doing, they all insisted on all least getting their blood type checked. None of them were a match, which is just Andrew's typical bad luck."

"What about Mum?" he asks, a worried lilt to his voice.

I shake my head. "She didn't need to get tested. She donates blood regularly and knows her blood type. She's not a match." I don't tell him about the look of horror on Glenda's face when Katie suggested she give an organ to Liam's other child, or how her whole body seemed to shake with relief when, only moments later, she discovered the key was having O negative blood.

225

"So no one else is a match and now you want me to get tested?" Seán speaks slowly, buying time.

"Yes. It makes sense, in a strange sort of way."

"What do you mean?"

"It seems right somehow that you would be a match. You are the only other Murtagh boy. You and I have this . . . attraction." I feel a blush wash over my face, but I don't look down. I have to be strong, like I never was with Claude. This isn't about me, it's for Andrew.

Seán moves towards me and takes my face in his hands. I close my eyes to the warmth of his touch.

"It's more than an attraction, Tors. I have to tell you now, or I'll explode. I love you. I do, I love you."

I keep my eyes pressed closed, though his words knock the wind out of me. I know what I want to say back to him, what he wants to hear. Can we survive it, can he ever forgive me if I make this moment, this declaration, about someone else? I grip his strong arms, refusing to let myself be distracted from Andrew. Not now.

My voice comes out a whisper. "Then help me. Save my brother."

He lets go of me with a shudder. I say nothing as he walks into the kitchen area, takes a bottle of whiskey from the press beside the fridge, and pours himself a glass. Knocking it back in one gulp, he sets the glass down on the counter with such force that it smashes. I jump. Something stops me asking if he is all right. His hunched figure and heaving torso suggest this is not over.

It happens very suddenly. I only just move out of the way in time, ducking behind the couch. He's throwing plates, glasses, utensils – anything within his reach. Not at me, but onto the floor, into the sink, any direction his arm happens to jerk. With a roar, he picks up one of the wooden kitchen chairs and flings it towards the wall.

I shout his name, but he doesn't seem to hear me. He's kicking the table now, grunting and panting, his face a deathly white under the flush of adrenaline. I stay crouched, not wanting to move out from behind the couch, but he's growling, whimpering. He's in pain. I can see imprinted in his twisted face every guilty thought, every torturous moment he has buried since Liam died. It erupts from him, taking over. Gasping in a deep breath, I do the only thing I can think of to stop him. I run at him and before he even recognises my presence, I kiss him. I have to jump slightly to reach him, but I wrap my arms around his neck tightly and don't let go.

Come on, Seán, I think earnestly, trying to put it all into the kiss. *Don't give into it, come on!*

Then he is responding, not violently, not passionately, but slowly, then softly until he's weeping in earnest, burying his head deep into my shoulder as we rock, or really teeter, on the spot for the longest time.

When he lifts his head up, I'm surprised to see he's not crying any more. He brushes my hair back off my face and I relax slightly. This is the Seán I know.

He looks at me intensely. "I'm sorry. Tors, I'm sorry. I don't know what came over me. You weren't even here . . . I didn't know . . ." He sways on the spot and I move him gingerly back to the couch. He blinks furiously. "I feel a little lightheaded."

"Seán, I don't know what you just went through but –"

"Tors," he interrupts me. His voice is different somehow, deeper, more in control than I have ever heard it. His face is clear of the worry lines of earlier this evening, as if the storm that possessed his body has swept them all away. "I've been feeling . . . I don't even know how I've been feeling since Dad died. It's like I don't know who I am any more. I don't know who my dad was, what my Mum went through, what my sister was thinking when she took those pills. I got fired from work. My friends are barely speaking to me. I'm sorry. I never gave Andrew a second thought."

Underneath my pity for his pain, I feel a bubble of excitement.

"Seán, they don't just let anyone donate, even if you pass all the medical tests. You have to be prepared for the long-term consequences of giving away part of your body. They have to be satisfied you weren't coerced, and that you have an emotional connection to the recipient.

This isn't a way to . . . I don't know, *buy* my love. I already love you, I can't help it. But I'm asking you . . . I'm asking you to try. I can't save him alone. Help me."

He smiles properly now. "Of course I will. God, I'm still out of breath!" He looks sweaty and tired, yet calm.

I know whatever it was he just went through, he has come out the other side. I got him out.

Looking around at the mess in the kitchen, he suddenly turns back to me. "Tors, you know I'm not like this usually. I'm not violent, I'd never hurt you, or anyone . . ."

"I know," I take his hand, understanding what he is trying to say, but Claude has never been further from my mind. We lean in, foreheads touching.

"My father was a good man. But he did nothing for Andrew for most of his life, and he left the rest of us to deal with his mistake without him. He made sure the truth wouldn't come out until after he died. He knew he wouldn't be there when we would need him most. I'm just like him."

"No . . ."

"Yes, Tors," he says emphatically. "Yes, I abandoned them. I left Mum to fight the will with no one but some city solicitor she barely knows for help. I left Lizzy to look after Katie and you to take care of Andrew, when I should have stayed. I shouldn't have come back here."

"You've built a life for yourself here . . ."

"But that doesn't mean it's important. Family. You. That's what is important to me, Tors." He pauses. "When is your flight back to Ireland?"

"Tomorrow morning." I tell him the details.

"I'll book onto that flight too . . . if I can." He stands up immediately and walks into his bedroom. "Just let me fire up the laptop!" he calls.

I lean back into the sofa, closing my eyes. Before I know it, rays of morning light are streaming in the window and he is shaking me awake to go catch our plane home.

Chapter 19

Seán

Tors is sleeping, again. She passed out last night as I booked the flight home and didn't stir while I cleaned up the mess in the apartment, or when Jerry and Sam bustled in the door at close to midnight, chatting and laughing at the tops of their voices. She dozed off in the cab on the way to the airport and now that the plane has lifted off she is either snoring lightly or breathing heavily. Either way, it is adorable.

I recline my chair ever so slightly and gaze contentedly at her. As a couple, we are far from a sure thing. We did say we loved each other last night, but since it was hidden in conversations about violent ex-boyfriends and sick half-brothers, I don't dare pin all my hopes on it. Of course, given both our 'episodes', it is arguable we were nothing but honest last night. My mind reels.

I have no desire to sleep myself. For the first time in weeks, my demons did not keep me up last night. Besides, I am too full of nervous excitement to drift off now. The thought of seeing my mother and sisters again is suddenly thrilling. Even the childish, bitter way I left them is not hampering my spirits, since I know I'm about to fix that. I'm scared to meet Andrew, but I know offering to do this, to give him something that could save his life, will instil in me the sense of purpose I have been missing ever since Dad died.

I am tired in a different way though. After whatever happened to me last night, I feel like I have run a marathon, or worked through the night. My body is drained, and I realise part of the reason I keep staring at Tors is because I am too lethargic to move my head.

I honestly do not know what came over me. My only guess is that there were too many emotions for me to cope with. I believed I was a failure and could not picture my future after being fired. I was relieved at having broken up with Claire, shocked at seeing Tors, horrified at hearing what that bastard did to her in France, and then, the final straw, guilty at her having to beg for my kidney for Andrew. There has been so much shame and self-reproach over the past few months that I just couldn't take it anymore. I don't recall trashing the flat, though from the looks of the place I really went for it. I remember the glass smashing against the counter and then pure fury like I have never felt before was coursing through me. The next thing I remember is Tors kissing me. I stumbled slightly, because I had forgotten she was there.

I know that I must have frightened her. That was unforgivable, after what she had confided in me. But she brought me out of it. She must have known that I am not like that, like him.

Her face is relaxed as she sleeps and I feel a rage building up inside me again that anyone could treat her so badly. I can't believe he got away with it. I wonder where he is now, and whether I could find him. I clench my fists in my lap with a sudden urge to thump something.

I think then about my mother. She mentioned, only in passing, that the man she married, George, had been violent when drunk. She never went into more detail and, ingrate that I am, I never asked. I wonder if the girls probed her for details. If any of them did, it was probably Katie. I wish I had been a better brother to that girl. She's so vulnerable, yet in many ways she is the most mature of us all. The way

Mum described it, Dad saved her from George, taking her away to Ireland. If only someone had been around to do that for Tors. If only I had been. Maybe I am more like my father than I thought. And maybe that is not the insult I have recently taken it to be.

The plane journey passes relatively quickly with such thoughts to distract me. Tors sleeps right through until we touch down and I think again, as she stirs on landing, how little she must have slept in the past week. She probably did not rest on the flight to America, being too nervous about whether I would say yes to the transplant.

For some unknown reason I, like Tors, am convinced that I am a match for Andrew. I don't know why, when so many other people are not. I reflect on what would have happened had Tors' father had the same blood type as Andrew. Further tests would surely have uncovered that he wasn't Andrew's biological father. I conjecture that Karen Shaw must have felt both dismay and relief on learning her husband could not donate. I glance swiftly at Tors, wondering how different our lives would have been if this secret had been exposed earlier.

Tors has left her car in the short-term car park and the journey home does not take long. We travel most of it in a sleepy silence.

As we approach Ballyloughlin, worry churns inside me once more. Maybe Mum, Katie and Lizzy will not welcome me back, after the way I left. But before I have a chance to calm myself, we are pulling up in the driveway.

"Tors, I'm all over the place. What day is it?"

She laughs. It is a wonderful sound. "Tuesday. It's late. They should be in there."

"Will I see you soon?"

"Tomorrow. Andrew has dialysis this evening so I need to be with him. I'll call you."

She reaches across the car and brushes her delicate fingers lightly across my face. "You should really shave." I lean over to give her a scratchy kiss and she laughs again. "I'll ring you later."

Before I know it, I am standing alone outside the door, feeling like the past month was a dream and that I never left for New York. I feel uncomfortable using my key when I cannot be sure of a warm welcome. So I raise my hand to lift the brass knocker, but stop myself. My pulse is racing and my mouth fills with a pool of saliva. My fingers are shaking.

But I have no time to compose myself as the door is suddenly pulled open from the inside and there is my mother, in her coat and scarf. She starts, not expecting to see anyone, let alone me, standing in the doorway. A second later she registers who I am, and before I can apologise or even say hello, she is hugging me, caressing me, squeezing me to death.

"You're back! Oh, Seán, you're back! Katie! *Katie*!"

My whole body burns with relief as I hug her back tightly. Then a high-pitched squeal that I would usually associate with Lizzy reverberates from the house and Katie is upon us. I try to say I'm sorry, but they will hear none of it.

"Come in!"

"Give me your bag!"

"When did you get back?"

They don't let me answer as Mum pulls off her coat and scarf and Katie disappears to ring Lizzy.

I try to object – "I'll see her when she gets home later" – but they ignore me and soon we are sitting around the kitchen table talking about everything and nothing. No mention of Andrew or Dad or the way I left. It's mundane, beautifully normal, full of affection and hand-holding. I am ashamed that I ever thought they would not welcome me back with open arms.

It's not long before the front door bangs open and Mum is calling out to Lizzy. I stand up, beaming, ready to embrace my youngest and closest sister, but she stops in the doorway of the kitchen. Leaning pointedly against the frame, she folds her arms and raises an eyebrow at me.

I glance down at my mother who is looking concerned, and Katie's fallen face.

Katie tries to placate our sister. "Lizzy, he's back. He came back."

"Yeah," Lizzy's voice is cutting. "Back from having left us."

"Let's go for a walk, just you and me," I say.

Without waiting for a reply from any of them, I call out goodbye to Mum and Katie over my shoulder and, gripping Lizzy firmly by the arm, lead her to the door. She shakes out of my grasp resentfully, but walks with me as we set off on her favourite walk around the back of the house and up towards the stables. It is a difficult path to follow in the dark, but that doesn't stop her.

We walk without speaking for a full five minutes. Eventually, I begin to talk but she cuts me off immediately.

"Look Seán, I'm glad you're back and everything. Mum will be over the moon. But don't expect that you can fix things with me in one conversation." She stops walking and looks up at me, her face hard. "You don't know what it's been like. You and Niamh gone. Katie has been obsessed with Andrew Shaw. Mum's a mess. The doctors have her on medication and she's crying all the time. I've been trying to help her but nothing I say or do makes any difference." Her eyes water and she marches on, determined to hide it. "I don't know why you came back when it's obvious you hated it here. We were just holding you back from your *real* life in America, with your fancy job and your Barbie-doll girlfriend –"

"She's not my girlfriend any more."

There is a pause and Lizzy turns slowly on the spot.

I rush on. "We broke up, before Tors even came over."

"Tors? Came over? To America?"

"Of course. You didn't know she was coming?" I falter, not understanding how she could not know.

Tors had my address – who else could have told her but Mum or my sisters? Of course, there is Kevin. If he was at the hospital getting blood tests for Andrew's transplant, he could have got talking to her.

Maybe Michael Undersky? He is exactly the type of calm, fatherly person someone like Tors would confide in. I look down at Lizzy. It is clear she did not know.

I pull myself up tall, knowing I have to be the sort of strong son and brother my family needs. I might as well start now.

"Look, Elizabeth –"

She frowns at the use of her full name.

"I made a stupid mistake leaving when I did. I was confused and upset and I took it out on the rest of you. I'm not proud of it, but I have come back to try to make amends and to be here for all of you. I don't expect you to forgive me, or trust me straight away. But I'm going to be here, helping, from now on and I'm going to need you on my side. Okay?"

Maybe it was pompous, but it does the trick for the moment. Hesitantly, she reaches out and shakes my outstretched hand. I pull her forward into a hug.

"A gentleman's agreement, then," I whisper into her hair, as she lets me embrace her and even squeezes me back a little. It's what they need – a leader, a protector. That is what I always wanted to be to the girls, and now I will be.

Back in the house, Mum and Katie look surprised to see us return so soon. Feeling tired, hungry and craving my bed, I take a strange sort of pleasure in casting that aside and batting through for their sakes. I gather them all around me in our sitting room, warmed by its smell of Mum and home.

They stare at me expectantly and I feel like I'm in court. Relishing it, I look earnestly around at them.

"First of all, I'm sorry, truly sorry for the way I left the last time. I was seriously messed up, but that does not excuse it. I'm sorry."

I pause here, and get exactly the reactions I expect. Lizzy says nothing, Katie rushes to appease me and Mum merely grips my hand in hers and smiles.

"I got fired yesterday."

"What!"

All three mouths drop and I grin.

"Yeah. Initially, they just asked me to take a sabbatical, but after I yelled at my boss and shoved a colleague into a wall, I think any chance of my returning is pretty much zero."

I give them a minute to process this but cut them off as soon as the questions begin. "Look, it just goes to show what a mess I really was."

"And you're better now? Twenty-four hours later?" Lizzy's voice is dripping with sarcasm.

"Actually, yes. I wasn't doing well at all. Claire and I broke up, I had just been fired, my flatmates were barely talking to me because of the way I have been acting. Then last night, I had . . . an incident. It was like I was under some sort of a spell. I don't remember it all, but I started throwing things around the flat. I just lost it." My voice starts to crack, but I don't stop. "Just . . . everything came crashing down – Dad, the will, Mrs Boden . . ."

"Are you all right?" Katie's voice is a whisper.

"Yes. I'm fine. I had a visitor, and she snapped me out of it."

Lizzy's mouth falls open but it is Mum who speaks. "Your friend Claire?"

"No. Tors Shaw."

Stunned silence permeates the room.

"She flew to New York yesterday. None of you knew she was coming?" The gaping looks of disbelief give me the answer. I focus on Katie. "She said Andrew needs me. That loads of people have got tested but no one is a match. So she came to ask me."

"She . . . she asked you to get tested?" Mum's voice quivers.

"Yes. I'm his half-brother. There is a chance. She told me that you have been quite the crusader for Andrew." I smile at Katie and she moves to sit beside me, her eyes bright with enthusiasm.

"He's a great guy, Seán," she says. "Funny and very outgoing, considering he spends most of his time cooped up in hospital. He's blunt – he tells it like it is, but he's got a good heart. We've all met him, even Mum. He didn't want me to ask anyone outside the family, but I did some research and it doesn't *have* to be family who can donate. Anyone can, it's just that the odds are greater of finding a match amongst blood relatives."

"Like us."

"Exactly, like us."

But I am not looking at her any more. I am concentrating on Mum, who is staring resolutely down at her hands.

Looking anxiously between us, Lizzy interjects. "Seán, she obviously convinced you to come back. How long are you staying for?"

I sit forward. "Lizzy, Mum, Katie, it is very important to me that you understand this. I agreed to get tested and, if I'm a match, I will donate my kidney to Andrew. But that is not why I came back. I came back to be with you. We still have Karen Shaw to deal with, and the will to finalise. But even aside from all that, we're still in shock that Dad is gone. I feel betrayed by what he did and, Mum, it's hard for us to deal with the fact that you and Dad never married. We need to be together for a while. Just live with each other and cope as a family. I'll probably go back to America sometime. Or, if not, then maybe to London, or at least to Dublin. But for the moment, for the foreseeable future, I'm here. With you."

With a wracking sob, Mum is upon me, hugging me, and I press against her tightly.

Later that night, having spoken to Tors on the phone, I hear Mum close her bedroom door to go to sleep and I knock lightly. Entering her room, I realise with a jolt that I still expect to see Dad sitting up on his side of the bed, reading his *History of Gaelic Football in Wicklow* hardback that he's had since I was a kid. I think I gave it to him one Christmas or birthday. I squash down a sadness that memories are fading, and go to Mum.

She looks tired, but smiles brightly as she beckons me to come and sit beside her on the bed. Crossing my legs, I pick at the duvet for a while as she tells me how she rang Pat O'Hara earlier and that they are all delighted I am home.

"Mum," I interrupt, "I'm guessing you're not thrilled at Katie's sudden affection for Andrew Shaw."

She doesn't hesitate. "No. I'm not, Seán. And while we're on the subject, I hope you don't feel pressurised into giving up a kidney. Transplants have long-term risks. I don't want you to compromise your health for anyone else. Least of all the child your father conceived with Karen Shaw. Look, of course I don't want the boy to die, but at the same time I just want him gone, out of my life. But, unless we successfully challenge, we're the ones who will be gone! Cast out of Ballyloughlin, possibly. I don't like seeing our friends rallying around him, around the Shaws. Offering up vital parts of their body to keep him alive! And I don't like that Katie is spearheading it. She has this notion that she and Andrew are like twins because they were born only a few months apart. I keep telling her that Liam loved her for her, but ever since she took those pills she's become fixated on Andrew Shaw."

"How is she doing?"

"Much better. She's back in work and physically she's recovered. The O'Hara triplets are even more protective than usual – she can't go anywhere or do anything without at least one of them traipsing after her. In one way, befriending Andrew Shaw has done her a world of good – she's really come out of herself."

"You've met him?" I am eager for any details.

"Yes. Katie really wanted me to and I would do anything to keep her happy and positive at the moment. He's a nice young man. He looks nothing like you or Liam." Her relief at this radiates though she tries to hide it.

"Did he mention the will?"

"He tried to bring it up. He started to say he was sorry but, to be honest, Seán, I'm just not strong enough to have that conversation with him. We talked mostly about his health and about Katie. It was only for a few minutes. I didn't want to run into Karen Shaw. I can handle

Andrew, but I just can't deal with that woman, ever."

The harshness of her tone upsets me. But despite being obviously devastated by the whole situation, she seems strong. Mum has always been strong. I wonder if she'll talk about it.

"Mum?"

She looks up at the hesitation in my voice.

"Can you tell me a little more about your life before you met Dad?"

She smiles, somehow knowing exactly what I am asking. "Your father and I met when I was twenty. I had been married to George for two years, the first of which passed by uneventfully. When his father lost everything, he began drinking. Mostly it was just unpleasant – we were young and hot-tempered so there was a lot of yelling and tantrums."

"But you said that he was violent with you?"

"It started getting bad, yes. My parents were no help. As far as they were concerned, I was married and had to deal with whatever that brought."

"That's ridiculous!"

"I know, sweetheart, but it was different times. My parents were old-fashioned – it was a different era. I had no money of my own, no income, no way of escaping. Then I met your father. I couldn't go through the hell of a public divorce – it just wasn't what was done. So we ran away to Ireland. Your grandparents were staunchly Catholic, as you know. It was bad enough that he married a Protestant from England, but they would never have accepted me unless we were married. So we said we were. We just had to be careful, as I said, with bank accounts and the like. To be honest, I liked that I had my own money from teaching – it gave me that sense of independence I never had in England. I was happy for us to keep our assets separate in that way. All in all, there was never any need to get married."

I shake my head. "You and Dad did so much to keep other people happy."

"It was a different time, Seán – it's not like that nowadays. You know none of us are crazy about Mark, but Niamh likes him so I certainly will not impose my views on her."

I look up sharply. Will she be so accepting of Tors? Has she figured it out yet? Lizzy has, I am sure. I'm exhausted after the day – now is not the time to discuss it. I veer the conversation back to Mum's past.

"It sounds like medieval times, but it wasn't that long ago."

"It was long enough. Don't look so upset, sweetheart, that's life. These things happen and we just have to do whatever we can to cope."

"Like Katie."

"Exactly." She looks resigned. "If Andrew is what Katie needs, then fine."

"That doesn't make it any easier on you." I look at her intently, determined to make her see that I am on her side. I will be the man her husband should have been – the one who will never desert her.

She takes my hand, smiling. "Having you back makes all the difference in the world, love."

"I'm going to see Dr Stevens the day after tomorrow. Tors has made me an appointment. He is just going to check my blood type first, and if I'm a match I'll need to go to Beaumont Hospital in Dublin for further tests."

Mum just nods. I want to tell her how much I love her. How no one, not Claire or Tors or any other woman could ever take her place. How I will never let her down like Dad did. But I can't say that, because I already abandoned her when she needed me most, just like Dad. The only difference is, I came back. I squeeze her hand and hope she understands.

* * *

Driving to the hospital the afternoon of my appointment with Dr Stevens, my mind could not be further from Andrew. I had met with our solicitor in the morning, and the conversation continues to echo through my head.

Eddie Edwards' offices were just as I expected. Everything, like the man himself, was large and overstated. As I sank into one of the plump, leather sofas in his waiting room, I shook my head at the lavishly furnished reception area and the moose head mounted on the wall beside a small television. Classical music floated from the speakers as Eddie came bustling out of his office and thrust his hand into mine.

"Seán, come on in," he said loudly as he led me to a small conference room and settled himself behind the shiny, brown table. "As I said on the phone, I'm happy to talk to you about the will, but I really would recommend you get independent legal advice should you and the girls decide to contest separately to your mother. In any event, as I told you, we won't need to move on it until after the grant of probate has issued, and I would expect that to take at least nine months, depending on how fast Michael moves as executor. Coffee?"

It's instant coffee but, feeling exhausted, I sip it gratefully, realising that what I miss most about New York is the real, strong coffee Sandy used to make. I make a mental note to tell Jerry and Sam that they are second to caffeine. They'd get a kick out of that.

I spent about an hour with Jerry and Sam when they returned from the pub on the night Tors arrived. I had to physically shove them into Jerry's room as they ducked around me and strained to get a look at Tors asleep on the couch.

"That's the sister? No fucking way!"

"You're messing, boy! What's she doing here?"

I ushered them forcefully away from Tors, towards our bedrooms. "Shut up! You'll wake her. Get into Jerry's room, we need to talk."

I felt guilty to be leaving them in the lurch. I offered to pay the rent for as long as they needed, but they shot that down immediately. For all the hassle I had given them over the past few weeks and for all their taunting about my relationship with my 'sister', they understood.

"You've no job now, you mad eejit," Jerry shook his head. "Where are you going to get money for rent?"

"I've got savings –"

"Which you need to keep saving," Sam cut me off, his eyes – which had been darting down the hall, trying to get another look at Tors – reverted to mine. "In a few months down the line, when things calm down, you'll look to move out of home again and you'll need your savings." He continued as Jerry nodded furiously. "Look, you're paid up for another two weeks. If we haven't found someone to take your place by then, we'll let you know – maybe we'll split your rent three ways for another month or something, if it makes you feel better."

"Except it's not going to come to that," Jerry grinned wickedly. "You're not the only one who's been dumped recently. John Parsons has been kicked out on his ass by the girlfriend – he'd be only delighted to take your room. Simon O'Keefe is moving over from Galway in three weeks and hasn't found a place to stay, so he'd do . . ."

"Or Linda Thompson from work is always saying how much she hates her flatmate, maybe we should branch out the bachelor pad . . ."

I watched Jerry and Sam turn from me, discussing the future amongst themselves. While grateful, there was also a flutter of sadness in watching them plan my replacement. I moved in with Jerry when I first came to New York, into a pokey hole of a flat with peeling paint and electricity sockets hanging out of the walls. Within six months, we'd had enough of it and were able to afford a better place. We were initially only supposed to move in with Sam for a short time while we looked for a bigger apartment, but, though a bit too small for three grown men, this flat felt like home from the beginning. Knowing I would be leaving it, and the boys, might have been enough to make me rethink were it not for Tors asleep on our couch.

Eddie pounded his mug onto the table with a smack of his lips, jerking me out of my reverie. "So what would you care to know, Seán?"

"Everything," I answer firmly. I want to be all over this information. Now that I am back, this should be off Mum's plate.

"Well, as executor, Michael prepares the paperwork and liaises with the various offices . . ."

"What offices?"

"Well, there's the Revenue Commissioners and the Probate Office mainly. He also had to get in touch with the banks your father had accounts with . . . and so on. Between you and me, I gathered Michael was going to take his time on all this, stretch out the process as long as legally possible for your mother, but she said she doesn't want it hanging over her any longer than necessary. She told him that if she has to give up the estate, then she'd rather know now, than wait around in purgatory. So he's ploughing ahead."

"You have talked to all of my sisters, I understand?"

"Yes. They are all inclined to contest the will. Given recent events, Katie has the best shot at it."

"Eddie, I don't appreciate you telling her she's weak."

"Ah now look, I didn't say it to be a bully. I'm just doing my job. Like it or not, the overdose demonstrates that she *is* more frail than the rest of you and, by all accounts, she was extremely close to your father. We can argue that he should have been aware that she would not handle his death well, even aside from the revelations about Andrew Shaw, and that he should have made provision for that in his will."

I stood up roughly and twisted away from Eddie. When he spoke again, his voice was softer.

"Look, Seán, this process is not going to be easy. If you decide to take this route, you are going to have to argue that your father did not adequately provide for you. I don't know if that's something you believe, but it's something you are going to have to show with conviction. Your sisters are willing to do it, though I believe it is more with the intention of being able to help your mother than anything else."

I turned back to him then, to ask him the one question I had prepared for this meeting. "Eddie, I'm heading to the hospital after this meeting to see if I am suitable to be a live kidney donor for Andrew Shaw. If I am, would the fact that I am helping him affect a challenge to my father's will?"

He sat up, surprised, and looked at me thoughtfully for a moment before answering. "This area of law is not black and white. On the one hand, you could argue that how your father provided for you, rather than your relationship with his other children or what he left to them, is the most relevant factor. But if you give the boy an organ, you can hardly turn around in court and claim he doesn't need help. I should warn you that of all the children, your argument will be the toughest to make and giving him a kidney will only demonstrate that you believe he needs all the help he can get, more than you or your sisters."

"Why do I have the hardest argument?"

"The court will look at whether your father failed in his moral duty to make proper provision for you not just in his will, but throughout your whole life. It will look at your circumstances, which are currently good. You have a degree and experience at a top consultancy firm in America. You are essentially self-sufficient. Your father provided for you when he was alive. He gave you a good education and never left you wanting. Compare that to your siblings – your youngest sister has not been university educated, although that was her own choice. Niamh is a student, living off your parents mostly. Katie's recovering from an overdose. And then there's Andrew, who is too sick to work and dependant on a mother and sister who between them barely make enough to keep the family ticking over. How much would *you* award to you?"

My hand twitches involuntarily. I don't have a shot in hell when he puts it like that. I wondered what my father would do if he were alive.

"Look, Seán, why don't we finish up for this morning?" Eddie had a strange look on his face – it might have been pity. "Think about it. You have plenty of time. It's an individual decision to be made separate from your sisters. Don't let them or your mother, or anyone else for that matter, influence you."

In other words, be a man.

Well, I think now, as I pull the car into the hospital grounds, that's what I came back to Ballyloughlin to do.

The hospital smells of that awful disinfectant so I wait outside by my car until I see Tors pull up. She looks much fresher and rested as she all but bounds up to me and kisses me lightly on the lips.

"How's Andrew?" I ask, as we determinedly hold hands and walk into the hospital.

"He's good. Dialysis went fine this morning. Don't worry!" She squeezes my hand. "This will only take a couple of minutes."

Before I can respond, we have arrived at a busy nurses' station with doctors, nurses and patients all milling around. We loiter for a few minutes until Dr Stevens shows up. I am mesmerised by the pace and noise of the ward. He is talking animatedly as he leads me to a chair in the corner and pulls up another beside me. Tors looks on and I feel like a small child being watched over by a mother. The colours, clicking machines and constant movement of the ward continue to distract me and I barely notice Dr Stevens take my hand in his and place it on the table in front of him.

"Right – now, Seán, this will only sting for a second. We merely need a drop to determine blood type."

I look at Tors as Dr Stevens tightens his grip, but before I can feel nervous a sharp scratch pricks my index finger and a flesh-coloured plaster is taped around the tip.

"Well done, Seán. We should have your results in no time. I told Andrew he could wait in one of the rooms two floors up – it was vacated this morning. You can go up to him if you like and I'll come get you when I'm ready?"

I can't hide the surprise from my face but let myself be led out of the room by Tors. "Andrew? But I thought he had dialysis this morning. Is he still here?"

"I asked him to stay behind for a while." Tors looks resolutely ahead. "It's about time you two met."

She's right of course. I've started the process of testing for donation. I knew I would meet him soon. Still, I'm unprepared and my stomach contracts with fear as we reach his floor.

Before I can prepare myself, Tors is pushing open a door and steering me into a small room. A single bed is pressed up against the window with a young, slender man sitting on it. He looks up from a large white sheet of paper on which he appears to be drawing. I see Karen Shaw's eyes and Tors' chin. Mum was right. There is not a spot of Murtagh in his face at all. A soft clunk reverberates as Tors slips out, closing the heavy door behind her.

Alone with my brother for the first time, I can only stare. I always knew Andrew was ill yet I am taken aback at his sickly appearance. In my mind, he was big and burly. I don't know why – it must have been because I always saw him as a threat, to my family and to the memory of my father's love for me. Physically he looks small, though Katie told me that he is exactly the same height as her, which isn't much shorter than me. Black circles loop under his eyes and his fair hair is thin and straw-like, not unlike Tors'.

Casting his pencil aside, he swings his legs over the side of the bed and stares at me. I have lost all capacity for speech. When it looks like he is not about to break the ice either, I pull the single, straight-backed chair from the corner of the room over towards the bed so I am face to face with him. His eyes bore into me, and I wonder if he too is looking for a similarity.

"Andrew," I say eventually, feeling his name twist on my tongue, "I'm Seán."

He smiles sadly. "Thanks for stopping by."

I can tell this is not a dig, but I wish it was. A fight would be so much easier. "How are you feeling?"

"Ah, you know," he relaxes into what is clearly a common conversation, "not too bad considering the move and everything. They're a great team here."

Just glad he's talking, I nod along.

"Katie showed me pictures of your father," he continues, not taking his eyes from mine. "You look a lot like him."

"Thanks," I say, automatically.

"My dad died three years ago. My real dad, I mean. I'm sure your dad was a good man, but I already have a father."

I do not understand why he is getting so defensive. He's the one with the inheritance. Remembering what Katie said about him being blunt, I try to give him the benefit of the doubt.

He keeps talking. "And I already have a brother. Listen, Seán, I know Tors would like us to be buddies, but you don't need to be here if you don't want to be."

"You know I'm getting tested, don't you? Dr Stevens is checking my blood type as we speak." It is important that he knows what I am willing to do for him.

"Seán," he leans forward solemnly, speaking very clearly, "giving away an organ is a big deal. I understand if you don't want to do it."

"I do want to, Andrew."

He sits back, smirking. "Not that I care why, but it seems to me a bit dramatic to be giving away an organ just to impress a girl. Surely you could just buy her some flowers?"

I open and close my mouth stupidly, goldfish-like.

"Seán, my sister and I have a truth pact. We don't keep things from each other. That's how it works. No dignity. She can work out my temperature from the colour of my vomit, and I know when she's about to hop on a plane to bump uglies with my new half-brother."

"Andrew, hang on. She came to New York to ask me to do this for you and we didn't . . . I mean she was only there for . . ."

"Relax, Seán. I'm not trying to freak you out. I'm just saying that if I end up with your kidney inside me, *I'll* be the one indebted to you, not her."

Whatever I expected from my first conversation with Andrew Shaw, this was not it. I gawk at him. Blunt is the word: he's an open book. Does Tors really tell him everything? I mean, everything? I feel a strong desire to prove myself to him.

"Andrew," my voice sounds stronger, "Tors confided things in me too. She told me about Claude."

246

To my surprise, Andrew looks down at his hands, his tone softer. "It's strange, you know. All the times before when I've been so sick it seemed like I could kick the bucket, and I always fought to live. Not for the sake of living, not because I had any unfinished business in this world. It's been a different feeling since I learned about Claude. Wanting to live, to improve, to grow stronger – just so that someday I can kill him."

He meets my eye again and I see pure hatred festering in him. Before I know what I am doing, I stand up and move to sit beside him on the bed.

"Andrew, I'd never hurt her."

"You left her. You really freaked her out in New York when you went ballistic. How can I know you're not like him?"

"I'm not." It still seems unreal that I am having this conversation with Andrew Shaw. I continue, desperate for him to understand. "Andrew, I have sisters too."

At this he looks at me and I think I see something like acceptance in his face.

The door opens and Dr Stevens enters with Tors just behind, her beaming smile telling me the result before the doctor can open his mouth.

Chapter 20

Tors

I stretch long and yawny, like a cat on hot concrete. Rolling over, I bundle my pillow into a ball and curl up against it, unsure what time it is. The rays of light that creep over the top of the curtain rail suggest it is well into the day. I try to remember when I fell asleep.

I told Andrew everything during his dialysis on Tuesday. The next day we filled Mam in on the trip. I hadn't hidden from her the reason I was going to New York and she was not happy about it. I could not blame her. The blistering row they had at the sea house cannot have been far from her mind. She was initially angry at Katie for talking people like Michael and the O'Hara triplets into getting tested.

"We're not a charity case!" she kept saying, and it took Jack piping up with "We are charity – Andrew's sick!" that finally made her accept it. Ultimately, she found their support a little overwhelming and it probably complicated her feelings about the will. Not enough to convince her to move back to Kerry though.

I tried to stay away from Roger Nestor, not wanting to get involved in the legalities, but I did accidentally answer the phone to him one day when Mam was in the shower. The number that flashed on the screen was Dublin, and I thought it might have been Beaumont Hospital with news of a potential donor for Andrew. When I heard with a sinking heart that it was the solicitor, I tried to end the call immediately, but he was anxious to continue the one conversation I had with him before leaving Kerry.

"Tors, I've tried talking to your mother but I'm not getting through to her. She doesn't seem to grasp the reality that grants of probate are not issued in a day; far from it. And even if it does go through quickly, which is unlikely, there is a concept called the Executor's Year which I have told her about several times. You cannot go to court to force Michael Undersky to distribute Liam's estate until a year after his death. So unless you want to remain in Wicklow for Christmas, and well after it, she should consider moving back to Kerry."

I thanked him, but I didn't bring it up with Mam. She has no problem understanding harsh realities, even in an emotionally fuelled situation like this. It pains me to think about it but deep down I know the real reason she is keeping us here. She wants to keep pressure on the Murtaghs, disarm them, make them feel so uncomfortable in their own home that they just give up. She wants to bully them into not challenging the will. But she's not a tyrant by nature. I thought that when the Murtaghs and some of their closest friends considered donating their kidneys to Andrew, the gesture might be enough to soften her, but her pursuit of Liam Murtagh's will is unyielding.

Andrew refused to give an opinion on Katie's campaign to find him a kidney until the last negative result came back and he admitted he had been hopeful. I resolved to fly to New York. I brought up my decision with him before telling Mam. Firstly he deserved to know and secondly we have the truth pact. Besides, it has proven in the past to be a wise idea to present a united front to Mam.

As usual, he was noncommittal, even though it had been his idea to ask the other Murtagh children in the first place. Mostly, he was nervous about me going, and it made me realise just how dependent on me he has become in the past year. Just as he had insisted to Katie about other potential donors, he made me promise that Seán wouldn't be forced into it.

"I don't like it, but I need a kidney and the deceased donor route just isn't working out." His desperation unnerved me.

Mam wanted to know why I couldn't just ring Seán. Or why Katie couldn't talk to him since she was the apparent ringleader. I tried to explain that he was having trouble coping since his dad died and that's why he left. He was not going to be persuaded to come back over the phone. I left out the part that even though I didn't want to talk to him again after he lied to me about Claire, I still craved him and this legitimate opportunity to see him was too much to pass over. I wondered if I was going crazy, but decided it really didn't matter. It's all about Andrew.

Mam still did not accept my journey without a fight. "Well, if you think he won't do it, why bother spending all that money on flights?"

I knew her real problem. I never defined for her exactly what happened between me and Seán, and a part of her does not want to know. She is an astute woman so I'm sure she suspected an attachment on my part at least, but I guess the idea of another connection between our family and Liam Murtagh was just too much for her. She suggested if I wanted to do something useful, I should wield my new-found favour with the Murtagh family to convince them not to challenge the will.

"I'm still researching, Tors," she told me in a whisper while Andrew was in the bathroom. "There are so many new advances in America all the time, new trials being run where non-matching donors are used. Once we get our hands on Liam Murtagh's money we can organise Andrew to fly out, meet with some consultants. You never know what might come of it." Her eyes darted to and from the bathroom in case Andrew might hear and I did not bother reminding her of our truth pact.

"I won't try to talk the Murtaghs out of something we don't even know they're doing yet. They know all about Andrew and, if they decide to contest the will, there's nothing we can do about it. I'm going to New York, Mam. I think a live donor is a better option than flying Andrew abroad on a fishing expedition. I'm going and you can't convince me otherwise."

* * *

I am convinced that Seán will be a complete match. I can't explain it, but since his blood test deemed him O negative, I feel certain he will make it to the final donation stage. A tingle of excited anticipation rushes through me every time I think about the next round of tests. It just seems to fit. He had such a hard time dealing with the bombshell of his father's other son, and this would be a way for him to come full circle somehow. I am so convinced it will work, I find myself less and less worried about how the operation and loss of a kidney might affect Seán's health.

I can see him and Andrew becoming fast friends. I imagine Mam being so grateful to him for saving Andrew that she forgives him. I can visualise Glenda Wilson accepting that Andrew deserves what was left to him in the will, allowing our mam to make a more comfortable life for her and Jack. She deserves that, after so many years of looking after Andrew. Mainly, I picture Seán and me being able to give it a real shot, the air having been cleared between our families.

It all hinges on him being compatible. It is our way out of this mess and towards a future together. A future that includes Andrew, as it must.

Mam said little on my return, but Andrew was itching to know the details. Although I had already told him everything in the hospital, he was raging when I collapsed into a long sleep as soon as I brought him home from dialysis on Tuesday. The next day, we sat in the living room of the sea house, Mam and I drinking tea while Andrew sipped his healthy apple juice, watching him bathe in the early afternoon rays. The room is a suntrap and I know it's going to be difficult for Mam to move us away from here. She likes to see the sun on his face, even if it is through the double-glazed door.

"So, he actually said he *wanted* to be tested, Tors?"

"Yes, Andrew, I've told you a million times and you know I'm telling you the truth. He has been feeling guilty about a lot of things since his dad died, and I'm sure it was difficult for him that he wasn't here at the time."

"Does he blame us for everything that's happened?" Andrew asks.

Mam glanced up but said nothing.

"No. He knows the will isn't your fault, or Mam's fault. And honestly, I don't think you are the only reason he is coming back. You know that elderly lady died and Seán was supposed to have been visiting her. He's devastated about that. And he left things badly with his mam when he went back to New York. He was messed up and this was the perfect push for him to come home and make things right. For himself as much as for you."

"I'm tired." Andrew gave me a significant look. "I'm going to lie down for a while."

Mam ignored us as we moved the conversation away from her.

We stayed in Andrew's room until dinner time, reviewing the details I couldn't tell Mam. About Seán's meltdown in the apartment, how he'd been fired, how I'd talked to his beautiful girlfriend who seemed to confirm that they had, in fact, broken up. Andrew, not known for his tact, confronted me head on.

"What are you doing, Tors? Are you in love with him?"

I bit my bottom lip. The answer was yes, I am. I hesitated only for a second, remembering that he was my baby brother, and that it should be weird to talk to him about guys. But, like it or not, we were different from other siblings. This whole situation was strange anyway, with Seán being as related to him as I am. I looked up coyly, conveying my answer with a sly glance. He held his hands up in surrender.

252

"Actually, this needn't be part of the truth pact. You need to talk to a girl about this gross love stuff."

I had talked to another girl about it. The day after Claire arrived at the hospital, I was still devastated. I couldn't believe my luck when I texted Debbie to find she was due in Dublin for the day with work. She had an hour for lunch so I drove up to meet her. For tea and sympathy, as she put it.

Debbie and I have been fast friends since we were thrown together in the careers' course the hospital provided for bored teenage relatives of sick children. It happened to be mostly boys who did the course with us and they seemed to think Debbie's baby sister being born with her heart on the outside was cool. Debbie and I bonded immediately over how stupid boys are.

She is now engaged and living in London with her fiancé. The thought of speaking to her about all this made me want to cry with relief. In truth, I do not have many people I can talk to outside of my family. I essentially cut my old friends from school out of my life when I started dating Claude and they never responded to my attempts to get back in touch this year. Most of my college friends were just drinking buddies at the time, and are now scattered all over the world. Aside from a few group emails, we are not in touch. The only women my age in our town are either new wives and mothers who cannot believe I have not yet snagged myself a man, or college dropouts who look down on me for thinking I am above them.

But Debbie has been a rock. I thought if anyone would understand my relationship with Seán, it would be her.

As it turned out, she did not. But she listened anyway. I ate reluctantly while she sat frowning, ignoring her own plate of food to focus all her attention on what I was saying.

"Tors, here's what I want to know. Before this girl –"

"Her name is Fat and Ugly."

"Okay," she laughed. "If that's what you want to call her!" She leaned in, whispering, "Is she really fat and ugly?"

253

"No," I sighed. "She's skinny and beautiful."

"Right," Debbie continued matter of factly, "before Fat and Ugly showed up at the hospital, how did you feel about Seán? Honestly."

"I felt that he's the man for me the way Joe is for you." I knew I sounded like a gushing schoolgirl, but I felt a real release at being able to talk about this with another woman. I tried to ignore her raised eyebrow as I took a small sip of my soup. "Imagine you found out something about Joe that you didn't know before. Something weird . . ."

"Like that he's related to me?" she grinned.

"No, because Seán is *not* related to me. Debbie, forget about Andrew and Seán's father and all of that for a minute. Taken in isolation, I've never felt so strongly about another man."

"But, Tors," Debbie leaned forward again, her forgotten salad wilting on her fork, "you don't know him in isolation. The two of you have only ever existed together in situations of the highest stress. I mean, have you ever had a conversation about music, or sport, or even television programmes? Have you ever laughed at something stupid?"

If it had been anyone else, I would have shaken off such questions impatiently, but Debbie wasn't asking them to be nosy or to get a rise out of me. She was genuinely curious and was trying to help. So I thought before I answered. "No. Debbie, you're right we haven't. And maybe that's why things ended the way they did." I felt tears prick the corners of my eyes. "I really thought we had something. Why didn't he just tell me about that other girl when we first spent all that time together on the beach?"

"Oh honey, when do men ever tell you about the other girls they're seeing behind your back?"

"But he's different, Debs. I really didn't think he was like that."

She looked at me earnestly. "So what are you going to do? Are you going to talk to him?"

I stared at her. How could I explain my sense of loss to someone who had never lost a love in that way? Words seemed utterly inadequate. I pressed my hand against my chest.

"I feel like there's a slab of metal pressing down on my chest. It's not sore, it's just . . . pressure. Sometimes, when I think about him, it presses so hard I can't breathe."

I knew I sounded like a drama queen, but it was true. That was the moment I accepted that whatever I had with him, it must have been real, because of what it was doing to me.

"Honey," my friend leaned back in her seat, "maybe it's for the best. I mean, how could it possibly work out with Andrew being Seán's brother, and Seán being disinherited because of your family?"

"But it's all so irrelevant!" I knew I was grasping at any solution, and contradicting myself, but I didn't care. "Just because of Andrew, does that mean we're not right for each other? Would it matter how you had met Joe? I bet nothing would have stopped you ending up with that ring on your finger."

"I don't know, Tors. When we first moved to London, I was unpacking his stuff and I found pictures of him when he was seventeen. He had sideburns, Tors. *Sideburns.*"

I snorted into my plate.

"I'm telling you, honey, if he had sideburns when I met him, I wouldn't have given him a second look!"

We laughed noisily and I felt better immediately. The conversation eventually switched back to Debbie's sister and I began to relax.

But later that afternoon, as I drove back to Ballyloughlin, I thought about what Debbie had asked and I knew I could not see Seán.

When I arrived back, Mam told me he had called to the sea house for me, but I had already made up my mind. I would never see him again, as long as I could help it. I had told Mam we had a fight and thankfully she just accepted it. She was probably glad of a reason to be angry at any of the Murtaghs.

My resolve lasted just under three weeks until the last person Katie had convinced to be tested as a live donor was rejected. Dr Stevens said it had always been a long shot, especially with the O'Haras and Michael. Relatives have the best shot.

* * *

I roll over in bed again, squeezing my eyes shut, thinking about the past few days. I can't believe how much has happened. I convinced Seán to come home; he's broken up with Claire and met Andrew; his blood's a match; and yesterday he travelled to Dublin to meet with consultants.

We spent most of the past weekend together. We walked the beach countless times and talked about everything from Andrew to his life in America, from my Dad to our childhoods. It was the start of what Debbie would have called 'normal conversations'. We spent time huddled together in the dunes until a breezy Saturday evening when Mam decided to brave the weather and take the boys out for a post-dialysis dinner.

We made the most of the empty sea house. The wind bashed the walls in a howling storm, competing with our own cries of elation. It was more wonderful than the first time because it was not merely a desperate fusion of two broken souls. This time, we had time and tenderness. We explored each other, wanting to learn and discover because it was a pleasure we expected to repeat for many years to come.

I indulge myself for a few minutes in the memory, grinning mischievously into the pillow, then roll back over to pick up my watch. It's past noon. I have been asleep for almost fourteen hours! Leaping out of bed, I barge into Andrew's room but it is empty. With a jolt of panic, I race to the kitchen and to my relief find them all sitting around the counter that separates the living area from the kitchen, on the high stools.

"Hiya, sleepy head!" Jack calls from over his comic book as the others smile at me.

"Did you have a good rest, sweetheart?" Mam slides across the wooden floor in her socks and kisses my cheek.

Andrew grins. "That's the second night in a row that you slept more than I did, Tors. That's got to be a record!"

"Tors! Tors! Are you coming to my match, Tors?" Jack is up and pulling at my pyjamas top.

"Actually, love," Mam says, "it would be great if you could take him to the club. They have practice for an hour and then a match."

Still recovering from my sudden panic that I had abandoned Andrew for fourteen hours, I nod listlessly.

"Yay! We're going to win!" Jack runs off into his room, his excitement catching. Enlisting Conn O'Shaughnessy to include Jack in the GAA was the best idea I've ever had. He's been so much happier since he started playing with boys his own age again, and his glee radiates through the house.

I yawn and ease myself onto the stool beside my brother. "Are you guys coming to the match too?"

"Nah," says Andrew. "I'm going to hang out with Mam for the day."

Mam pushes his hair back from his face lovingly. "It's been a while since we've had an afternoon, just the two of us."

"You know what?" Andrew's face is suddenly alight. "It's been ages since we've had a fun day with all four of us. You know, a day that didn't involve hospitals or solicitors. The weather's breaking and it's supposed to get much warmer over the next few days. I've dialysis tomorrow but why don't we do something fun on Friday?"

Immediately, I reject the idea. "You've had a few nasty turns in the past month, Andrew."

"Yeah and it's been lousy. Really crap. I miss home. Why don't we just do something fun, without all the drama. Nothing wild, oh Sensible Carer. Just a picnic on the beach."

"We'll talk about it tomorrow." I hop off my seat and kiss him lightly on the cheek.

This is one part of being his carer that I despise. It's fine when we have our truth pacts and gang up on Mam, but I hate having to be like a mother or a teacher to him, when he just wants to be a normal guy.

257

It's easy to forget that he's a young adult, and it must be so frustrating to be stuck inside all the time. He must be desperate for company other than us and the doctors. For that, I'm so grateful to Katie and the O'Hara triplets, who, since Katie's incident, have not let a dialysis go by without stopping in. Katie has even been to the sea house a few times.

Poor guy. His idea of a fun day is a picnic on the beach with his family. I turn back and gesture to the beach out the window. "Well, if the weather continues to improve, I'd say you'll be fine for a trip to the beach by Friday. After all, it couldn't be closer."

He smiles gratefully and I feel instantly better. After all, once Seán's tests come back, the transplant can take place within a few months. I shake myself angrily as I go back to my room. Certain as I am that Seán is a match, I can't get too caught up in it until we know for sure. Still, I allow myself another sly grin as I flop down onto my bed.

Dying to hear all about how Seán got on with the consultants yesterday, I drop Jack off a little early at the club. He jumps out in excitement, barely hearing me call that I will be back in an hour after his practice to support him in the match. Then, just as giddy as my little brother, I set off for the Murtagh residence.

As I pull up in their driveway, I tilt my head up at the magnificent house and imagine it belonging to Andrew. How amazing it would be for him to be able to recuperate in such a secure place, surrounded by fields and fresh, country air!

"Tors!" Glenda steps back immediately to let me in, a glowing smile on her face.

Remembering the devastation she would suffer should Andrew take this house kills the joy of my fantasy. It amazes me still how her gratefulness for the help I gave Katie on the morning of her overdose seems to have made her completely forget that I am Karen Shaw's daughter.

"Come in, come in. *Seán!*"

I hear him thudding across the landing to the stairs and my face breaks into a smile when he arrives down. He looks well, relaxed even. All too aware of Glenda's presence, and unsure of how much she knows about us, I suggest a quick walk before I have to go back for Jack's match.

Outside he leads me around the back of the house and up towards the stables.

"This is one of Lizzy's favourites," he says eagerly. "We'll do the short version so you can get back to the club."

"It could do with a trim," I smile, as we duck and weave our way around thorny bushes and long nettles. Still I don't have to work as hard as him to avoid the stings, his tall frame fielding the brunt of it as he leads the way. It has taken all my restraint not to bring it up yet, but I'm about to burst so I grab his arm, swinging him around. "How did it go, Seán?"

He grins down at me, wrapping his arms around my waist and pulling me closer. "I spoke to the co-ordinator. I explained my relationship with Andrew and she was very taken aback, as you can imagine. I reckon I gave them a few hours of gossip if nothing else!"

"What else?" I press.

"I think I managed to convince her that I wasn't coerced into it, but there'll be proper psychological tests later if I'm deemed physically compatible. They took my blood to test for tissue-type compatibility. Tors," he stroked my hair, "you know it'll take at least six weeks before we know the answer for sure. But yesterday went well. I'm confident."

I look into his eyes. "I am too."

In the shade of the trail, we fall to the ground. Relaxing into his arms, I feel utterly content that all the pieces of my life are finally coming together. I lean into him, hearing his breath in my ear over all the other sounds – my beating heart, the unusual caw of a rare bird that I once heard on a camping trip with Dad, and the delicate crunch of the strangely autumnal dried leaves under our bodies.

Chapter 21

Tors

It happens quickly. We get the call and, like always, rush in. Same sense of foreboding. Same knot of fear clenched in my stomach. No different to the dozens of other times.

It takes maybe twelve hours for the infection to win this tiny battle and with it, the war.

We watch in horror as the sepsis takes hold, his blood pressure spirals and, sooner than I could have imagined, his heart fails. I think maybe he senses it, the way he grips my hand so tight, digging his fingernails into my palm as though trying to break the skin, trying to bury inside me where he could be safe.

He is asleep.

I used to like it when he had a good stretch of sleep. Too often he'd wake up at night in pain, or just uncomfortable. A long, deep sleep meant he was doing well, that his body was repairing itself. This time it means something different. The doctors and nurses have backed away, leaving him in peace.

In the end, it is perfect. We are all there, even Jack. It was a decision we had hoped we would never have to make. Maybe it is cruel for him to have to witness it at such a young age. But he has lived with Andrew's diseases his whole life, and he knows what death is. He deserves to be there for the end.

So we all say goodbye, I love you, I'll miss you, thank you. I bay in agony as the muscles of my heart pull and tear in every direction, crumbling within me. Jack nuzzles into Andrew's ear, telling him to say hello to Daddy and Holy God for us. At this, Mam's sobs turn to heaves, coughing, choking. A nurse thumps her on the back and makes her lie down flat on the floor. I think of my paper bag sitting in the glove compartment of my car.

Then, just like on TV, they flick a switch and the pulse rising and falling on the monitor screen slips to a long flat line. Mam screams at the sight, gripping her hair in her veiny hands. All three of us lean over him, vying for room. We stroke his arms, his face, telling him not to be scared. We speak loudly. We practically shout it at him, desperate for him to hear one last word of love from us.

After all those worries that we'd miss it, that he'd die alone in the bathroom after a fall, or choke in the middle of the night, unable to call anyone, it is the most soul-destroyingly perfect goodbye we could have had.

Amazing really, that such a gift is no comfort at all.

Chapter 22

Seán

Like a child with a spinning top, my world is once again stopped abruptly, only to be whirled in a new direction. Dad, Mrs Boden and now Andrew, each taking with them a slice of my heart. Lizzy's soft hand on my shoulder, reaching forward from the back of the car, strengthens me enough to step from the car. I walk ahead, leaving the girls to help with Katie, whose wretchedness has consumed her.

There was no removal, at Karen Shaw's request. It is a small funeral and I am conscious that I don't know the people who have gathered outside to watch as the tiny family follows Andrew's body into the church. Tors smiles weakly when she sees us, but Karen Shaw does not. Katie, in a sudden burst of energy, rushes forward into the church and to my dismay I realise she is making for the front of the church, where the family sit. There is all but a coffin-side brawl as Karen screams at her to get away. I never would have believed it of her a few months ago, but Katie starts shouting back, immune to her surroundings.

"Andrew is my brother too – I've just as much right to be here!"

Karen roars in frustration and tries to launch herself at Katie. It looks like she will succeed and I hear Mum cry out as two men grab Karen's arms while gaping at our family in utter disbelief. Tors moves around her mother to Katie, with Jack bawling and clinging to her side.

"Please, Katie," she says, "Andrew would have wanted to make this day as easy as possible on my mother. Please."

I use Katie's momentary pause to grab her upper arm and drag her past the pews of open-mouthed mourners to the back of the church. As we sit in tense silence in the last row, waiting for the funeral mass to begin, I think how close we had been to becoming a family. Had Andrew been able to hang on a few months, he would have had my kidney inside him.

I wish Katie had not made a scene. I had hoped I could be of some comfort to Tors today, since I have not been able to find her since the night Andrew died – since she came to us with the news, wild with anguish.

* * *

It was late, almost eleven, when Tors appeared at the door with a tall, skinny man in his thirties who was all but holding her upright. Mum answered the door in her dressing gown as I pattered down the stairs, hoping the knock on the door was Tors. She had promised she would ring me earlier but I had heard nothing from her all day. I took in her shaking frame as my family converged on the front door, as if Andrew had called us all there.

Katie came skidding across the hall with her coat on. "It's for me – it's the triplets – we're going for a late one in Keogh's."

"A bit of quiet, please!" Lizzy popped her head out of the living room where she was frantically trying to finish off an article for an equestrian journal, which was due the next morning.

They both stopped short.

Tors' eyes bulged and flicked over the faces of each of us, settling on me.

Her companion stuck out his hand awkwardly to introduce himself to Mum. His name was Peter, he said, a volunteer who had helped Andrew in Kerry and was called to Wicklow by the hospital. I ignored him. I was staring at my girl. She was clinging to this man's shirt to keep from dropping to the floor. He managed to manoeuvre her across the threshold, but tripped in the darkness, and the two of them collapsed in a heap.

He stood and tried to pull her upright but she stayed down. After a moment, her mouth opened slowly, crooning on a high-pitched note. No one moved. No one tried to help. It was too feral, too wrong to be fixed with a kind word or a helping hand.

Katie guessed first, and crumpled, screaming. My own heart plummeted to my stomach. Andrew. His face swam before me, the details fading as I tried to hold onto the image. Everyone was wailing and I felt darkness narrow my vision. Tors couldn't speak and Peter relayed the truth in broken details. Tors' cries turned to shuddering gasps as we looked on and I tried to move my clenched legs to go to her but Peter was already lifting her from the floor. I tried to call "Wait!" but I choked on the word and only an indistinct breath gurgled from my throat. I gripped the staircase hard and watched as Tors was led, staggering, from our house.

* * *

It has been four days since the funeral and I still have not managed to get in touch with Tors. The Shaws have gone home to Kerry, I'm told.

I am sitting in the living room with Mum and the girls, sipping tea and eating a scone at Pat's insistence, without tasting it. My last image of Tors replays constantly in my mind. The priest had, with open arms, invited everyone back to a local hotel for sandwiches after the burial. Knowing we would not be welcome, we had slipped out of the church at the end of Mass, past Karen Shaw while she was in the embrace of a friend, and went directly to our car. Lizzy managed a quick ruffle of Jack's hair as we passed and he gave her a watery smile. I tried to meet Tors' eye but she was weeping steadily in the arms of another woman and I felt Lizzy pull me on. I wish now I had stayed.

The house feels empty, like it has lost another member, though Andrew never set foot here. Satisfied that we have been fed, Pat stands to leave and I walk her to the door like a zombie. She has come every morning for the past few days to take care of us, arms loaded with home-baked goods. Though we barely speak to her, she is not offended. She hums as she potters and now, as I open the door for her to leave, she presses her hand hard into my shoulder, sighing.

I have to steel myself to return to the living room where the atmosphere hangs heavy and not a word of comfort can be dredged up from the misery. I look around as I sit and I can see that Andrew's death has affected my family just as much as my father's passing. For Katie, it is probably the combination of the two that has pushed her over the edge. The doctor explained to Mum that Katie used her newfound friendship with Andrew as a way of dealing with her father's death. With him gone too, there is nothing to halt the onslaught of grief.

Mum is now living in constant fear, as are we all, that Katie might try something dangerous again. Aside from her anti-depressants which are under lock and key in Mum's room, the house has been cleared of any medication. Pat O'Hara gives Mum one sleeping tablet every day and there is not even paracetamol to ease my thumping headache. I watch Katie sniff and pat her eyes with a tissue and feel a rush of annoyance towards her. We are all devastated about Andrew but at least the rest of us are making an effort to cope. I wish she would try to pull herself together, even just a bit, for Mum. But Mum would skin me alive if I suggested it and even Lizzy came to Katie's defence when I mentioned that I was thinking of speaking to Katie about it. "She can't keep it inside! Look what happened the last time."

I turn from Katie to Lizzy, who is sitting on the floor, scrolling through her phone half-heartedly. She might be the youngest, but she acts like a mother hen. Lizzy and I have taken over the running of the house, with some help from Pat O'Hara. We do the shopping and the cleaning and make sure someone is always around Mum and Katie. We never discuss why this is necessary, but we know it is. In the space of mere days, we have become a little couple, fussing over our girls and worrying about the future.

Time passes slowly as I sit musing and thinking of Tors, but eventually the doorbell rings and I stand quickly, knowing it will be Michael with Eddie Edwards. I cast an angry glance at Niamh who is sitting in the corner with her sociology notes spread around her. Locked in her own world, she appears oblivious to the intense sadness seeping from her family. I am particularly frustrated with Niamh as I walk to answer the door, since it was her meddling questions that resulted in Eddie Edwards being invited here today, and I just can't stand that man.

Niamh blurted it out last night when Michael called over to, in his own words, help us make a dent in all of Pat's cooking.

"So I assume all this hassle with Dad's will is sorted now? I mean, since Andrew can't get anything now, surely it'll go to Mum?"

Michael choked on his slice of bran cake. "Niamh," he threw a nervous glance at Mum, "I'm not sure that's the way it works. We'll talk about it another time."

"What do you mean, you're not sure?" Mum snapped. "You're a solicitor, aren't you?"

Lizzy and I locked eyes to sustain each other during the embarrassing silence that followed. Since Andrew's funeral, poor Michael and Pat have been getting the brunt of Mum's sleep-deprivation.

"Niamh," Michael turned to her, "everything was left to Andrew. His death doesn't change anything. He was alive when he became entitled to your father's estate. The moment your father died, it fell into his power, if not his immediate possession. He can do what he likes with it in his own will."

Niamh ignored my glare. "What if he didn't make a will?"

"Well, since he's not married and has no kids of his own, then his mother gets everything."

I looked down at my plate of Pat's delicious cooking, my mouth suddenly dry. If I could be certain of anything, it was that Andrew would either have no will, or one leaving everything to his mother. Either way, Karen Shaw was now entitled to our family estate. The idea of another son inheriting his fortune had been difficult enough for Mum, but the realisation that Dad's will had indirectly left everything to the woman with whom he had been unfaithful, was too much. In the chaos of tears that followed, Michael promised to arrange for our solicitor to talk to us without delay.

Now Eddie bustles in the door with too much cheer and I frown angrily at Michael, as though it is his fault. He makes a downward motion with his hand, signalling me to stay calm. Eddie embraces Mum in the living room and makes himself at home, taking the last of Pat's latest batch of fruit scones from the plate with something akin to glee.

I glare at him. Michael in turn shoots me warning looks and eventually beckons me to follow him into the kitchen. He knows Eddie's blustering manner rubs me up the wrong way but has no time for my impatience today.

"He's doing this as a favour to me, Seán. Be decent to him."

"He's getting paid, isn't he?" My temper flares, as it has often since Andrew died. The loss and loneliness that engulfed me when I fled to America have been dragged to the surface once again. But I look at Michael's appeasing face and take a breath to control myself. "I'm sorry Michael," I sigh.

He claps my shoulder in a fatherly way and we proceed back to the others.

"You know," I whisper as we walk, "I can't believe we didn't figure out until yesterday what Andrew's death would mean for the estate."

"You had Andrew on your mind, not the inheritance," Michael

replies softly and I think about the way in which Tors always seemed to be consumed by her brother with a sudden rush of understanding. Some things are so immense that other considerations are swallowed up and forgotten.

Eddie is busy lecturing the girls in his booming voice. I sit beside Lizzy and am soon tapping my foot impatiently as he harps on about affidavits, rules and judges. I know I should concentrate on what he is saying but instead I am making a mental list of what annoys me about him. It is therapeutic to have one person at whom to direct all the anger that has been building up inside me. I am almost waiting for him to tell Katie she is weak again so as to have an excuse to attack him. At the moment he is merely telling us what Michael has already relayed. We can still challenge the will but, with Karen Shaw running the show, it won't be an easy journey. We already know this. I add '*States the bloody obvious*' to the list.

My own thoughts take over once more. There is no way Karen Shaw will give in. There will be legal appeals if it comes to it. All my hopes for my mother's security are dashed. I'll have to think about moving away soon to get another job. I'll need to support her, and my sisters. If nothing else, there will be doctor's bills for Katie. Andrew was like a rope, securing her from grief and in his death she became not only loosened but entangled in a web of despair. As Eddie talks on about challenges and court appearances, a further gloom descends upon me. His analysis confirms my greatest fear: any chance for harmony between us and the Shaws is now over. Tors and I have no chance.

* * *

A scrape of tyres on gravel signals that we have a visitor. Michael stands and peers through the window impatiently. "Who is this for heaven's sake? I told Pat not to let anyone . . . oh, good Lord!"

Lizzy and Mum jump up and run to the window, and even Katie

turns her head. I am on my feet, but before I reach them they all look back at me, almost fearful. I know of only one person who could have secured that reaction from my family and I run to the door, my heart pounding with trepidation.

She looks good. Better than I expected, at least.

"Come in, Tors." I stand back eagerly. "Everyone's dying to see you." Her eyes dart from her hands to my face as I curse myself for my choice of words.

But, typical Tors, she does not take offence.

"Actually, Seán," it seems to be costing her some effort to say my name, "can we go for a walk first, just the two of us, before I come in?"

Anyone looking at us strolling around the rose garden by the stables would think we are an ambling young couple, without a care in the world. But my palms are sweating and my back is so stiff I must be arching backwards. I am aware that this could be the last time I ever see Tors, and it makes me realise with a perfect clarity that I love her. Everything about her, from the way she is just that bit too short to fit neatly under the crook of my shoulder to how her round eyes used to sparkle when she talked about Andrew. I love her in a way I never loved Claire, and it takes all my effort not to grab her and kiss her right now.

But I hold it in. Just like always, it won't be me on her mind. Even now, as she would say, it's all about Andrew.

"How are things at home?" I manage, looking down to catch her eye, but she's staring far into the distance.

"Oh, you know," she sighs, then turns her face to me. "I have to tell you something."

We stop walking and I realise I'm not breathing.

"Andrew left me a . . ."

She breaks off in tears, then stamps her foot and wipes her eyes furiously. I long to put a comforting arm around her.

She takes a deep breath and starts again. "Andrew left a letter, addressed to me." She blurts out a bitter laugh. "At first I thought it was a goodbye note, written in case he died and I was furious because I had told him I never wanted him to write something like that. It would mean he had given up. But it wasn't a letter, it wasn't a note . . ." There is fire in her eyes. "It was a will."

Our eyes lock and I feel my knees tremble.

"Do you want to know what's in it?"

I look down at her pale, tired face. Then my resolve breaks and I grab her and press her tight to my chest. Of course I want to know. Of course she has to tell me. But first I want to hold her, feel her warm body against mine, one last time.

* * *

Arriving back at the house, I am glad to see Eddie is still here. Annoyed though I am that he has clearly overstayed his welcome, I want to hear his opinion on what Tors has to say.

Mum beams with delight and even Katie has perked up at the sight of Tors. Michael plants a tender kiss on her cheek and looks at her fondly. But for all of the warmth of the welcome, it is still awkward until Lizzy's bear hug almost knocks Tors over and the ringing laughter echoing throughout the hall breaks the tension.

After tea is poured and more condolences offered, Tors becomes business-like. Her voice is slightly croaky and her whole demeanour is more fragile than I remember but she holds herself straight. I glance at Katie, wondering if she could be inspired to be strong by example. Tors, ever thoughtful, directs what she has to say to my mother.

"Glenda, my understanding of the situation from Roger Nestor is that even though my brother died before he actually received anything, he is still the person legally entitled to everything Seán's father left him."

To my disgust, Eddie butts in. "That's correct, Tors, dear."

"Right," she nods. "Well, you'll remember my brother had a number of very serious turns while here in Wicklow before . . . the

270

final one. It transpires that after the first, he decided he should make provision."

I look around at a room of widening eyes.

"He made a will. I have a copy in the car which I can show you, Mr Edwards. But, in a nutshell, he has undone Liam's will."

My mother's hand grips mine.

"He leaves everything to Seán, on two conditions. First, on the understanding that Seán will take care of Glenda. Andrew says that he would have left everything – or really, given everything back – to Glenda except she would have been hit with a massive tax bill, because she is not related to him by blood. The amount taxed on gifts left to siblings is substantially lower and, for the purposes of inheritance, Seán is legally his brother. The second condition is that my mother is taken care of financially. Andrew is quite specific. He wants Mam to get an up-front lump sum, and an amount paid annually in perpetuity. He's done his homework, though when he had the time is beyond me. With some careful investment, Mam can be looked after without this house being taken from Glenda, but some of the lands will probably have to be sold.

"You can work it out in your own time, but I would ask you to accept this, and not challenge your father's original will. Not just because I believe it is fair, but because this is my brother's last request and, frankly, if you don't honour it, I will fight you with everything I have."

Her look is determined, yet her eyes brim with tears. A deathly silence hangs over the room, broken, of course, by Eddie.

"Tors, dear, if you have no objection, I would like to see a copy of this will."

"Of course," she stands quickly, eager to be out of the room if only for a moment.

Though I am still struggling to digest this news, I am not in such immediate shock as my family and I take in their expressions with interest. Katie is weeping into her hands while Niamh is standing with

271

her hands on her hips, her eyebrows having flown up into her fringe. Mum and Lizzy sit rigid, like stone, their expressions unfathomable.

After a moment, in which no one dares utter a word, Tors is back, holding an envelope, a package wrapped in brown paper, and a small backpack thrown carelessly over her shoulder. I frown, puzzled. Everyone watches as she moves consciously to Eddie and hands him the envelope. He pulls out the contents and sits, apparently enthralled.

Tors sits beside Katie, who lifts her face from her hands and gulps.

"Katie," Tors says kindly, indicating the large brown package. "Andrew also left this." Slowly, as if handling a bomb, Katie unwraps the paper to reveal an unframed picture, clearly hand-drawn, of two people who, aside from their identical heights, do not look anything like brother and sister.

Katie stares at it in awe, and before she has a chance to burst into tears again, Tors hands her a small envelope. "He left you this note with it."

Katie's eyes shine with something other than gloom for the first time in days and she turns away, immersing herself in the gift. Tors stands up and, indicating her backpack, faces Mum.

"Glenda, would you mind very much if I stayed here for a few days? I had nothing to do with Andrew's will, truly. But my mother does not believe me, and she has thrown me out of the house."

Chapter 23

Tors

Seán's reaction is indignant. "What? She kicked you out?"

To my surprise, it is Glenda who comes to my mother's defence. "Seán, Karen has just lost a son. She isn't thinking rationally. Tors, of course you can stay here for as long as you like. You can take the spare room beside Seán's bedroom. Lizzy, help Tors with her bag."

Lizzy jumps to be useful and I follow her sheepishly out of the room.

Seán does not move. "Mum . . ." I hear him say.

"We've just had some important news, Seán. Let's not say anything rash."

I close my ears to their conversation as I follow Lizzy up the winding staircase. She places my bag down gently by the bed and opens a window. A gust of fresh wind immediately cleanses the dusty room.

"No one has stayed here for a while, Lizzy says. "It just needs a bit of air through it. I'll put fresh sheets on the bed for you."

I say nothing as she leaves, wondering vaguely if this was Claire's room when she stayed. Before I can dwell on it, Lizzy is back with pale-pink bed linen bundled in her arms. She holds a sheet out to me, dropping the rest of the pile onto a chair. I take one end and together we shake it out and begin to make the bed.

Never taking her eyes from the sheets, she speaks softly. "I know it's been said already, but we're all so sorry about Andrew. I met him a few times after Katie introduced us, and he was a good guy. He didn't deserve what he got."

As usual, with any mention of my brother's name, air catches in my throat and my body freezes. It takes real effort to force myself to move, to just physically respond without collapsing.

I'm doing all right in general. I can function. Until someone mentions his name. This time a week ago, my brother was alive. It feels like decades ago. His voice is a distant echo and my memory of his face is blurry.

* * *

I always knew it would be most difficult for Mam. It is far crueller to lose a child than a brother, even though right now I cannot imagine anything making me feel worse. She took it badly at the start, as was to be expected, but she has not improved. At first she just cried and was not able to sleep. By the third day, the morning of the funeral, she could not speak and I had to help her to shower. Then, of course, there was the incident at the funeral when she tried to attack poor Katie Murtagh. By the time the funeral was over, she was so spaced out she seemed to have forgotten that the confrontation took place.

I'm glad I was able to keep it together, both for her sake and because someone had to handle the practical arrangements for the funeral. I'm surprised I haven't gone to pieces, but from the moment Peter put us in his van and began driving us out of Ballyloughlin back to Kerry, the tears stopped and I have just been numb. Sad, of course, but able to keep going, once I do not think of him. And it has not been difficult because I cannot conjure up a clear memory of him. I don't try too hard. Someone needs to keep a clear head during these first few weeks, not just for Mam but for my other brother, who is taking it all a little too well. Mam terrifies him, the way she is acting. So he avoids her, playing with his toys, not causing any trouble but following me around like a shadow.

The day after the funeral, Debbie called before heading to Dublin to catch her flight back to London. I shooed Jack out of the room so we could talk, but Debbie, as usual, was right on the button. "Poor mite, he's scared that if he leaves you alone, you'll go next."

Realising she was probably right, I told Mam we should consider booking him in for a session with a psychologist who specialises in children who have suffered bereavement. Mam agreed and began suggesting other ways of making the transition easier on Jack. It was the first time she engaged properly with me since my brother passed away and I wondered then if she would start to come around.

But any chance of that was ruined when we found the will.

In the first few days we hadn't had the strength or the courage to clear out the backpack he had with him in the hospital, the one he took everywhere. But it was starting to smell so I steeled myself and opened it to find a half-eaten sandwich. Then, as I rummaged around, looking for anything else, I saw it. A large brown envelope with my name on the front.

My legs gave way and Mam rushed over to me. I let her lead me to a chair, my heart pounding. Surely he hadn't given up and written me a goodbye note? We had agreed years ago he would never do that. Mam dived into the bag to look for a note addressed to her, but there was none. So she dropped back down beside me, engrossed in my actions as I opened the envelope with care.

There was no note with it, no explanation or qualification. Just the will. It took us time to plough through the legalese of it but we understood. We stared at each other in shock for a few moments before Mam lost it. She jumped away from me, knocking the will from my hands. Her fierce, almost mad look reminded me forcefully of Seán's episode in New York. Seán. Just thinking of him made me want to cry again.

Mam was in front of me, screaming in my face. "You must have known about this, Victoria! You and your damn truth pact! How could you let him do this?"

"I . . . I didn't know. Really, Mam. He didn't tell me. I don't know why –"

"Oh, I'll tell you why! It's because he knew we'd talk him out of it! I bet it was that Katie Murtagh, always whispering in his ear . . ."

"Mam, stop!"

But she was a spinning top, fidgeting as she turned and twisted around the room.

"Oh, don't think Katie Murtagh wasn't influencing him, Tors. He drew that picture of the two of them like they were family. She made him think he owed them. Made him feel guilty for inheriting money he was entitled to. And if they had just decided outright not to contest Liam's will, and insisted he got his money straight away, maybe we could have done something with it – saved him."

Even though I knew I should not upset her even more, her blaming the Murtaghs struck a nerve and I could not help but fight back.

"He might have been sick, Mam, but he knew his own mind. If he didn't even tell me about it, it must have been his own decision and no one else's."

"You sure about that, Tors? Are you sure you didn't help him with this? You and Seán and the Murtagh women all colluding behind my back, trying to take my boy away from me! My sweet, innocent boy who would *never* do this to me!"

"Mam, stop it right now! He hasn't done anything to you. This will is more than fair on his part. You should be proud of the way he handled this."

But she clawed at her face, hysterical.

"How *dare* you speak to me like that! You'll all do anything you can to blame me for this. Well, you can get out of this house. I mean it,

276

Tors, I don't want to look at you. *Get out!*"

I tried to interrupt but she was possessed.

"*Out!*"

"But . . . Jack . . ."

"He's my son – I can take care of him. I said get *out*!"

In a daze, I walked to my bedroom and began to pack, waiting for her to come in and tell me she'd changed her mind. When Peter dropped Jack home an hour later from a trip to the shops, I told my little brother I had to go away for a few days to sort out some boring adult stuff and that I'd see him soon. As I expected, he panicked. My heart ached as he clung to me, begging me not to leave. Mam wouldn't look at me as she pried him from my waist, my distressed attempts to comfort him lost in the shrieks of his pleas.

"I'll be back soon, baby, I promise. Mam . . ."

"*Go!*"

In the rear-view mirror, I caught sight of Jack's arms stretching out from behind Mam, reaching for me as she lugged him forcefully back into the house. Tears flowing, I drove to the only place left on this earth where I knew I would find someone who loved me.

* * *

"Thanks, Lizzy." I acknowledge her words of condolence with as much of a smile as I can muster, pushing the dreadful parting scene from my mind.

"It's just . . . when Katie nearly . . . I don't know what I would have done if she had . . . Tors, if there's anything I can do . . ."

I cut her off. It's too much. I tell her some restful quiet is what I need and she backs from the room, eager to help even if it's only by leaving.

Once she has gone, I flop down on the bed, utterly spent. I know Mam is just angry, that she will come around, but it's still hard. I nuzzle into the freshly laundered sheets – they smell of fabric softener. We rarely use fabric softener. It's expensive.

I can understand why Mam still wants Liam's money. It would have made life so easy if she had been able to get help from Liam all those years ago. She struggled on without it, usually Andrew the one suffering when Dad was out of work and the prices of medicines soared.

The smell of the sheets is warm and comforting. Two days ago, I made myself get up early and found Mam in Andrew's room, kneeling by his pillow. She was taking deep breaths because, even though we hadn't lived there in months, a trace of him still remained. She smiled sadly when she saw me and threw me one of his pillows. I brought it back to my room and buried my face in it. Now, breathing in the Murtaghs' sheets, I can't smell him at all. Waiting for a wave of pain, I close my eyes and succumb to sleep.

It must be midnight when I wake up. The curtains are still open and it is pitch black outside. I rummage around in my bag for my mobile phone and feel my heart leap with excitement when I see there is one text. But just as quickly a bitter taste invades my mouth as I realise it is not from Mam, but from Seán elsewhere in the house. I have never been sorry to hear from Seán before and I sigh as I open the text. He says no one wanted to disturb me but that if I need anything during the night to call in to him or any of the girls.

I lie back on the bed. I have not thought much about Seán over the past few days. I could not bring myself to answer any of his calls. A week ago, I had allowed myself to believe that everything could work out. But without my brother, it's hard to care about anything else.

I still want Seán, I think. But the sorrow is all-consuming. It's a grief even worse than when Dad died. My brother had become my whole life. I have no job now, no purpose, no direction. I'm lost, and the one person who I could always turn to is no more. Though I must have been asleep for nearly eight hours already, I am exhausted again and before I know it, the morning sun is streaming through the windows.

* * *

Glenda is all over me when I arrive downstairs looking dishevelled and still feeling tired. I realise with a jolt that it is exactly a week since my brother died. I have not lasted more than a couple of days without him in the past year and a half. That I even survived the week is unbelievable.

"Tors, love, come in and have some breakfast."

The entire Murtagh family is seated around the kitchen table, staring up at me as Glenda leads me to a spare seat beside Niamh. She says nothing as I sit down, but Seán, sitting opposite me, gives me a wide smile.

"Thanks, Glenda. I've been asleep since the second Lizzy left my room yesterday."

"You obviously needed it, love."

Strangely, I don't think I did. Unlike Mam, who is struggling with insomnia, I have slept full nights over the past week. Still, I have been constantly tired during the day and have to force myself to get up at the sound of my alarm in the mornings. I'm completely sapped of energy, like I've not slept in weeks, and it is only getting worse instead of better.

Glenda is piling my plate with sausages, rashers, toast and eggs, while urging Lizzy to pass me the butter and jam. All I can think is that I wish my own mother was here.

"How long will you be staying here?"

"Niamh!" Glenda snaps. "She'll be staying as long as she needs to. Right, Tors?"

I smile again. It's a very tiring gesture. "Thanks, Glenda. I hope it shouldn't be more than a couple of days. Mam will come around. I'll ring her later today."

Seán is looking at me intensely. I wish he wouldn't. I didn't come here to cry on his shoulder. In one way, I would like to tell him that but the thought of another deep and meaningful conversation, which is bound to come back to my brother, is something I do not think I can handle.

I end up not having much of a choice. As the family stand up one by one from breakfast, Seán invites me to take a drive with him.

"Go on, dear," Glenda says decidedly before I can answer. "A bit of fresh air will do you good."

Without the wherewithal to argue, it is not long before I am sitting in the passenger seat of the Murtagh family car, my fingers twisting uncomfortably in my lap.

"Are you all right, Tors?"

"Look, Seán," I need to be straight with him from the start, "I know we need to talk and I'm sure you would like to discuss my brother as well as us, but I just don't think I have the strength this week."

I expect him to say that he understands, that we don't need to sort anything out now, but he does not. On returning from America with me, he became instantaneously more decisive. It appears he has not reverted back to the old Seán.

"I thought that's why you came here. To talk to me."

I pause. Of course I came here to see him, but I can't admit it. I won't let myself be vulnerable with him now. I'm afraid of breaking. "I wanted to show your family the will."

"But you could have done that anytime. There's no rush. I'm sure Roger Nestor would have contacted us for you. Your mother kicked you out and you could have gone anywhere, but you came here. Why is that?"

"Because I had nowhere else to go, Seán!" The words are out of my mouth before I realise their truth. We do not have other family and I would rather sleep on the street than move in with one of the nosy neighbours. Peter has been a rock, but he is only a volunteer, and I cannot impose this family tragedy on him. Debbie lives in London. The truth is, while there were plenty of people in our lives, I cannot turn to any of them in this situation. Except Seán.

We travel in silence until eventually Seán pulls into a small, deserted car park. The salty air hits me forcefully when we step out of the car but I don't recognise the area. Following Seán, I make my way down a narrow trail, eventually coming out onto a long stretch of stony beach. The sea is choppy. There are no giant waves like the last time Seán and I went strolling by the shore, but it is far from calm. It is a massive pot of boiling water, bubbling from deep within. The wind whistles gently, but does not blow us over.

Seán takes my hand and I don't stop him. Mostly because it's easier than starting an argument. But it is not long before I wish I had never taken it.

"Conn O'Shaughnessy was asking after little Jack when we got back from the funeral."

"Was he." I keep my tone clipped, wishing he would take the hint.

"How is Jack doing?"

"As well as can be expected, I suppose. So, have you heard any word from your old flatmates in New York?" I can hear the falseness in my voice and know that Seán will not buy my weak attempt to change topic.

He stops and stares into the distance.

"I didn't want to drive directly there, in case it upset you, but we are only about a twenty-minute walk from the sea house. If you wanted to . . . Tors?"

It happens without warning, but the mere thought of being so close to the last place we all lived together, the spot on the beach where we picnicked that wonderful last afternoon, just the four of us, makes me feel physically ill. My stomach leaps and I keel over, gripping Seán's arm for support. With a few deep breaths, I manage to stand upright and push him away.

"What are you doing? Why did you bring me here?"

He looks confused. "I just thought you might like to . . ."

"I didn't come to Wicklow to lean on you. I don't need you to bring me to places that remind me of my brother so I can have a meltdown and you can comfort me!"

"No, Tors, come on, that's not why . . ."

I cut him off again. "I'm dealing with it, okay? I'm dealing with everything. If my staying in your house is going to confuse you –"

But suddenly he is right beside me, pressed up close. I shut my eyes automatically, knowing what to expect, but the image of Claude does not appear. When I open my eyes to the light, Seán is still there.

"It does confuse me, Tors. Before Andrew . . . a week ago, we were a sure thing. I know you're upset about Andrew, of course, and I'll give you as much time as you need. But I need you to know that I'm here for you, just like I was going to be there for Andrew . . ."

"Will you stop saying his name?"

A wave of nausea washes over me again, and this time the reason becomes clear. It is the very thing I have been fighting since my brother died. I do not just feel sad, or lonely, or bereaved. I feel guilty. And I have just realised why. I think my insides are going to rip me to shreds and I bend over and throw up violently.

I barely feel Seán beside me, touching me. The images and memories of my brother that have been evading me all week come flooding back, with one jumping to the forefront. I look over at the direction of the sea house, and the beach where we spread out a rug on that last afternoon, scoffing biscuits and cakes like real holidaymakers.

"He wanted to go to the beach." I am talking aloud but Seán has to bend to hear me. "He was feeling better and I thought the transplant would work so I stopped being cautious. I let him come to the beach with us that afternoon, for a picnic. We must have been there for two hours. How could he have withstood it? He probably should not even have been out of hospital. If I had just told him no, done my job as his carer . . ."

It is all falling into place, yet the truth is far, far too much to bear. This is what has been keeping my brother's image at bay, this is why I have been able to be the strong one all week. I have not let it in, I have not let myself know the truth. As a whirring darkness narrows my vision, his peaceful, white face barrels towards me and the truth screams in my head. He's dead because of my carelessness.

I killed my brother.

Chapter 24

Seán

It is the most terrifying reality I have ever experienced. Someone I love is in pain, and I have no Tors to help me, because she is the one falling apart.

At first, she merely leaned over and threw up. I held back her hair, sorry that I had upset her. I thought about everything she has suffered. Losing her father at such a young age. Taking on the burden not only of little brothers, but a sick patient. Trying to find love only to be locked, beaten, in a dark room. Andrew's death. The inadequacy of my compassion swims with my usual churning shame in my stomach.

I try to pull her upright, but she is unresponsive.

A memory smacks the back of my eyes. I got a whack with a hurley during an under-tens match. They were all screaming at me to get up – my coach and Dad from the sidelines, my teammates encircling me. Eventually, they realised I wasn't faking, or being a cissy. A broken ankle, they diagnosed in the hospital. I was told over and over what a brave boy I had been. But I don't remember being brave. I only recall a pain so intense I couldn't cry or ask for help. I just wanted to be left alone, in my little world of agony.

It was a mistake, bringing Tors here. The memories are pushing her over the edge and she is not listening to my attempts to comfort her. I am suddenly anxious to get her out of here. She straightens, murmuring something I cannot hear. She shoves me away but it is too weak to have effect, so I take a step back and allow her to totter drunkenly towards the shore. For a terrifying second, I think she is about to run straight into the water. In the corner of my eye, I see the red warning flag beat furiously in the wind. "Tors, wait!" I run up behind her, alert to the thrashing undercurrent that the choppy surface masks, ready to whip her legs from under her.

I reach her just as she stops. Her eyes, which only moments ago were wild with something like fear, are now vacant. With a huge gasp, she drops to the ground.

She flails from side to side, as though she is being electrocuted. I try to take her hand to soothe her but she beats me away. Whimpering cries escape her lips as she twists painfully, her eyelids opening just enough so I can see her pupils rolling back. Terrified, I pull my phone from my pocket but I already know there will be no signal on this remote beach. Cursing wildly, I crane my neck in every direction, even out to sea, searching for help. But we are completely alone.

Suddenly, Tors stops moving. I stare down at her, waiting for her to awake. But she does not. She jerks slightly, moaning. A flush creeps down my spine. This is worse than the excessive floundering moments ago. Now she looks weakened. Tors: the loser of a bloody struggle.

"No!" I shout aloud.

I pull her arms towards me, hauling her limp body into an upright position. Using all my strength, I heave her into my arms. She does not resist and although her body continues to spasm involuntarily, she is a dead weight. I keep my eyes ahead, focusing on the car, too scared of what I will see if I look down at her face. The swish of the wind and water recede as I stagger from the beach to the trail leading back to the car park. I call out for help but the place is as deserted as when we arrived. A drop of rain lands on the top of my head. Curling my arms upwards to pull Tors tighter to me, I start to run, as if protecting her from the rain could possibly help.

She shudders as I lay her gently in the back seat. Screeching out of the car park, I automatically head for St John's.

"What the fuck are you doing?" I shout aloud at my own stupidity, wrenching the car into a dangerous U-turn, ignoring the beeps from oncoming cars, and rev forward towards my house. Tors moans again and I try to comfort her from the front seat but it doesn't sound like she can hear me. We are about ten minutes from home when I spot Kevin O'Hara sauntering along the road, seemingly oblivious to the rain that has started to fall in earnest. My heart leaps and I skid the car to a halt, almost crashing into him.

"Kev, take the wheel!" I leap from the car and climb into the back seat with Tors. He looks into the car quizzically and I scream at him to hurry up. Tors' unconscious but jerking body snaps him into action and he takes off at twice the pace I consider speeding. I murmur soft comforts in my girl's ear, but she does not respond. Within minutes, Kevin careens right up to my front door and helps me bundle Tors out of the car.

My mother and sisters can only gape as I burst in the door with Tors, Kevin at my heels. Seeing them all has an immediate calming effect. I no longer feel Tors' weight as a burden. Even with her tossing, I am confident that she is secure in my arms.

I turn to Kevin. "Go get our GP, Dr Cassan. Tell her it's an emergency."

"Do you not want to take her to the hospital, Seán?" he asks.

"No." I know what is wrong with her. "She's not sick. She's lost in the grief. The worst possible thing would be for her to wake up in the same place Andrew died." Tors convulses in my arms and I turn to Mum, grateful that Kevin is not arguing back. "Mum, ring Karen Shaw. Michael will have her number. She needs to come here. Lizzy, get me towels and some warm clothes for her. Katie, come with me, I need you to help me calm her."

No one says a word as they all jump to follow my instructions. Mirroring another moment of agony when I ran down the stairs with Katie in my arms and Tors in tow, I start up with my sister behind, clinging to the shell of the woman I love.

Chapter 25

Tors

Something is happening, but I really don't understand what it is. Seán is here, I know that much. His voice is very loud, but the words do not have any meaning. It doesn't matter. Nothing really matters.

* * *

I have been transported to another world, where all the shapes and colours and sounds mesh together. It is interesting really. And there is a niggling in the back of my mind. I know that I was upset but I can't remember why. In a way, it is not important. Just interesting, niggling. I cannot tell if I my eyes are open or closed. Sometimes the lights get brighter and what might be different voices weave in and out.

* * *

I think I am still now. At first, there was definitely movement, though

I could not define the motion. I was swinging, in a way, then still. And I have been warm for a while. I was cold, then hot, much too hot. Now, I am just warm.

* * *

It takes a while, I don't know how long, but I begin to place the sense. It's touch. Someone is touching my arm. There is a stroking sensation, and I recognise the feel. It is a hand. A small, smooth hand that has stroked that arm for years and years. I like it, so I focus on it. I start to distinguish a voice. A low, calming voice. I think it's saying my name. And it's saying other things too. Nice things. I like this. Yes, I can attach myself to this . . .

"Oh good Lord, she's opening her eyes! Glenda, Lizzy, all of you, come here!"

"What is it?"

"What's wrong?"

"Nothing, nothing is wrong! She opened her eyes, I'm sure of it! Yes, look, she's doing it again. Oh, Seán, come in, look, she's opening her eyes! Tors, Tors, my love, can you hear me?"

The voice says other names I recognise from a distant dream. I know, somehow, that these names are good, that I should be happy just hearing them. But I can only fixate on the voice saying them.

"Mam?" I think that was me speaking. It didn't sound like me, but it must have been.

"Yes, my angel, it's me, I'm here. Don't worry, everything is all right."

"Tired." Again, was that me?

"You sleep then. I'll be right here when you wake up. Go on, now, do as your mother tells you."

I've heard that before, many times. And though everything else is still hazy, I know that instruction is not to be argued with. So I close my eyes and let a dreamless sleep wash over me.

Chapter 26

Tors

Katie is putting the finishing touches to my hair as I admire myself in the mirror. She really has quite the artistic hand. Just like Andrew.

"Okay, Tors, I think you are nearly ready. How does that dress feel?"

I glance down at myself and try not to grimace. I had grabbed only a few items and stuffed them in my backpack before I left Kerry – I was too upset to do more. Once I started feeling better two days ago, Glenda went shopping for some clothes to keep me going. Including this dress, which is too short, too garish and just altogether too fancy. I can picture Niamh in it all right, on a night out in town, but for a casual dinner tonight in the dining room, it's not what I'd choose. I make a face at Katie and she laughs.

"You don't have to wear it, you know. Mum won't care. She also bought you jeans – why don't you put those on with the light-blue top?"

"I think I'll have to, Katie," I sigh at her.

She laughs again. It's great to see.

"I'll go and see how they are getting on with dinner. It shouldn't be long now. I'll call you when we're ready."

I continue to stare at the door after Katie leaves. I never asked her what Andrew said in his note to her. According to Glenda, it had a profound effect. She is still upset of course, we all are, but apparently she started to come around even before I was taken ill. The only plausible explanation I can imagine is that it was not a note he intended her to read after he died. He must have been planning on giving the sketch to her himself, with a note that was probably light-hearted and fun.

I take my time changing. I feel so much better. Physically, I have definitely improved. The only indication that I have been unwell is my sluggish movements. When I try to do something quickly, I can't. My body reacts more slowly.

Dr Cassan, the Murtagh's family doctor, has told me that this is to be expected. She is not sure what happened to me. I certainly do not remember.

* * *

I came to properly the day after Seán took me to the beach, to the sound of my mother's voice. I lay there for a while, looking up at Mam, trying to remember where I was. Then it all came crashing down on me. Andrew. Dead. Because of my neglect. Huge choking sobs that shook my whole body and turned to screams for Andrew. Mam held me tight and whispered in my ear. Other voices were also speaking softly. I could pick out Seán. But I ignored him, burying my face in my mother's chest and howling for her forgiveness.

"He's gone, he's gone!"

"I know, baby. It's okay."

"I killed him. He's dead because of me, Mam, I'm so sorry." My words were slurred, meshed between long, snivelling gulps of remorse.

The voices hushed, the comforting words stopped abruptly and Mam leaned back to look into my face. I had to say this, Mam had to hear it, but my thoughts were confused and it came out all wrong. "I should have kept him indoors. No picnic. His immune system. He couldn't handle a beach! Grit and damp. Diseases everywhere, on us, in the air. I should have locked him in his room, made him stay in the hospital."

I would have gone on, maybe forever, but Mam took my face in her hands and said the last thing I expected. "I'm sorry."

I took a shuddering breath.

"Oh sweetheart, I'm sorry I left you alone with this. It's not your fault, of course it's not. If he was that bad, the doctors would never have let him out of the hospital. It was not up to you to imprison him until the day of his transplant on the off-chance he might catch something. It's not your fault. I promise you it's not your fault."

We looked into each other's eyes, both searching for him.

"Say it," she whispered, our foreheads touching. "Say his name."

I gasped it out. My fingers stiffened around Mam's arms, gripping her like the lifeline I should have been for . . . "Andrew." Then blackness descended once more.

When I woke again I felt drained and weak, but not tired for the first time since Andrew died. Suddenly, I could picture his face clearly, and thinking his name did not paralyse me. Mam was still there, with a new person. Dr Cassan talked to me for hours that day, while Mam sat holding my hand. She listened while I spoke and she explained things I already understood. To protect myself from the awful realisation that I had been the architect of Andrew's final turn, my mind shut down any thought of him. Every memory was indistinct. Until Seán took me to the beach.

For a while, Mam wouldn't let anyone besides Dr Cassan in to see me but eventually I insisted on seeing Jack. After a longer cuddle than he would usually allow, I asked to speak to Seán. Mam was reluctant, but in no position to refuse me.

He poked his head sheepishly around the door and moved

cautiously to sit on the bed beside me. I was sitting upright, having spent ten minutes trying to make myself look slightly more presentable with the help of one of Glenda's hand mirrors. It did not work, but I guess Seán didn't notice. He took my hand, his head bowed. He looked tired.

"I'm so sorry, Tors. I really didn't mean to upset you. I thought you would want to go back to the sea house now that you were here."

"Seán, don't. It was not your fault."

"Tors," his eyes bored into mine, "it's not yours either."

I smiled lightly. "I know. Mam believes it anyway, and that's what counts for the moment. Thanks for having her here," I added, suddenly appreciating the enormity of the Murtaghs and the Shaws all living under this one roof. "It can't be easy."

He stood up almost brusquely and began striding around the room. "Of course she had to come. We didn't know what else to do." Then he was back sitting on the bed again, gripping my hand. "Tors, I was so scared when you collapsed. I didn't know what to do."

I dropped my eyes, though I felt him continuing to stare at me intently. My cheeks burned with shame at what I had put him through.

Seán rubbed my leg absentmindedly. "Mum was worried your mother would just hang up on us, but I think she was so surprised to be receiving a call from our family that she couldn't speak for a second and Mum managed to say your name, which got her attention."

I chuckled at the image. The sensation grazed my raw throat.

"When she arrived, it was like she and Mum were long-lost sisters." He let out a short laugh. "It was so weird. To be honest, Tors, Mum loves you after what you did for Katie. And she never had anything against Andrew – she knew it wasn't his fault. But she really loathes your mother. Lizzy and I just gaped like a pair of idiots. Your mother burst in, Jack trailing behind her still half asleep. Mum hugged her – actually *hugged* her, Tors – and helped her up the stairs to you immediately. They *held hands*, Tors! Seriously, I thought I was hallucinating."

I laughed again. I can understand why Glenda hates Mam. I think of the beautiful American, Claire, and how allergic I am to the mere thought of her, when she did nothing wrong. Of course Glenda must despise the woman who had a secret love-child with her husband. I wondered, not for the first time, how my dad would have reacted to all this, had he been alive. I have never been anything other than heart-broken that Dad died, but a part of me feels glad he was spared all of this.

Seán was still shaking his head, clearly stumped by the sudden comradeship that sprung up between Mam and Glenda. He obviously couldn't fathom it, but I understood. They are both mothers.

"Anyway, I'm glad we called your mother. Dr Cassan said having her here really helped you."

I shook my head. "I actually can't believe she came here. I mean, I thought she would have insisted you take me to the hospital, or even back to the sea house. Anywhere but here."

"I think she could tell that we were all really worried and that it was potentially serious. You were Andrew to her then."

I bowed my head and my voice sounded small. "I'm so ashamed that I put her through that, after everything that happened this week. And I'm embarrassed you all had to see me like that."

"Don't be. Anyway, things are going back to normal. Our mothers are avoiding each other again as much as possible. I suppose we should take that as a good sign."

I looked up, and saw that softness I've noticed more and more in his eyes since we returned from New York. My breath quickened and I swallowed slowly, trying to control the panic, but it didn't work. I was still all alone, without Andrew. My mother and Jack are my world now, but it's not enough. I need Seán.

I placed my hand on his arm. "It's something we'll have to work on. Our mothers, I mean. They'll have to get along at some point."

I reached over, and placed a delicate kiss on his slightly open lips. I couldn't bear to look at him as I pulled away but he hesitated only for a second before lifting my chin with his index finger – it was coarser than I remembered – forcing me to look at him. He moved in and wrapped his arms tight around me. I felt his hot breath in my hair as he exhaled desperately.

"I thought that I might lose you, Tors. Properly lose you, the way we lost Andrew. I just can't do it. I'm never letting you go again."

How long we sat there, content in each other's arms, I do not know. I might have fallen asleep. But eventually Jack came bounding in with Lizzy just behind.

"Sorry! Sorry! He got away from me!"

We all laughed.

It was another day before I felt able to get up and about. Dr Cassan came back twice and fed me some sort of medicine. I didn't ask what it was and I didn't complain. I like her; she's gentle. Besides, anything that will get me back to normal quickly can't be a bad thing. I said this to her jokingly and she sat back with a creased brow.

"Tors, grief is not something you ever 'get over'. It's something you learn to live with and after a while, the intensity lessens. But you have to embrace the emotions you are feeling. If you keep trying to hide your pain to protect your mother, you'll end up back in this bed."

* * *

I think about the past two days as I zip up the jeans and slip on a pair of comfortable, indoor shoes. I count all the people who gathered around to help me when I needed them. I have so much support. Yet the only one I really want is Andrew. Well, maybe Dr Cassan will give me a gold star for embracing my emotions, I think bleakly, as I let the tears slide down my cheeks.

After a while, I hear Katie call up to me. Sighing, I leave the comfort of my bedroom and walk slowly down the stairs. Mam is insisting that she wants to get me back to Kerry as soon as possible to recuperate so we are leaving in the morning. Glenda demanded that she be allowed cook a farewell dinner for the two families, which I think everyone is dreading. Pat O'Hara has been over all afternoon helping Glenda get ready – in other words, barking orders at a flustered Katie and Lizzy – but she is not staying. It will just be me, Mam and Jack with the Murtagh clan. Michael Undersky is going to call over later in the evening for coffee. Apparently he has been out of his mind with worry about me.

They are all milling around the table when I arrive in the dining room and I automatically head for Seán, if only to avoid the fuss I know Mam and Glenda want to make over me. It is as if they are vying to be the most helpful. Eventually, we are all seated and tucking into the most delicious roast chicken dinner I have ever tasted. Having eaten very little in the past few days, I am suddenly ravenous and there is a general silence as we stuff ourselves with crispy roast potatoes, gravy-soaked chicken and mountains of vegetables.

In the end, the evening is not as awkward as it could have been. Jack has taken quite a shine to Lizzy. She spends most of the evening joking and playing with him, which entertains us all and keeps everyone in good spirits. Michael Undersky arrives just as we are settling into the living room for Irish coffees and the extra body provides a few minutes of rejuvenation.

Eventually though, the subject of the will comes up. As usual, it is Niamh, talking at the top of her voice to Michael about it, who grabs everyone's attention.

"What is that you're saying, Niamh?" my mother asks and I try to subtly poke her in the ribs with my elbow.

"Mam, it's been a lovely evening," I attempt to get her attention covertly, but everyone in the room is staring at us. "Let's not spoil it."

"I have no intention of spoiling anything, Tors," she says loudly, though her tone suggests the opposite. "I merely heard Andrew's name and want to know what it is in reference to."

Michael looks awkward at first, but then takes control. "Niamh was asking me, Karen, whether Andrew's will had been sorted. I said I was sure that it has not because it is early days yet and, in any case, now is probably not the right time to talk about it."

The mood in the room darkens, and I see with a sense of relief that Lizzy has distracted Jack enough to lure him from the room. I am so grateful to her, and wish Mam would be as sensitive.

"You're right, Michael," I say with conviction. "Let's leave that to another time."

"Do you have children, Michael?" Mam is clearly not finished yet.

Michael looks at my anguished face, and offers up what must be the last topic he wants to talk about, to protect me from more of this conversation.

"My wife Maggie and I were not blessed with children to keep. We did get pregnant seven times, two of whom were big enough to be named and buried. Two sweet little girls. But no, I have no children and certainly do not presume to know what you have gone through this week."

How can an atmosphere switch so suddenly? From relaxed conversion, to tension, to grief. I look around, expecting the red and white tulips on the table to droop, the dull evening sun streaming through the rain to fade. But all that changes is the faces in the room. I can tell from Seán's dropped jaw, Niamh's flyaway eyebrows and Katie's hand jumping to her mouth, that this is news to them. Glenda, I think, must have known about it. I look over at Michael who sits sipping his coffee, perfectly at ease with his memories. I wonder if he sees one of those little girls when he looks at me.

Mam opens and closes her mouth a few times but cannot bring herself to say anything. I do the only thing I can think of to end this conversation and, thankfully, the yawn comes easily. "Mam, I'm tired. Would you please help me to bed?"

Mam scurries to my side. She thanks Glenda more profusely for the dinner than I'm sure she initially intended and wrings Michael's hand vigorously, as though trying to apologise with a handshake, before taking me by the arm and leading me up to bed.

"Jack," Mam calls, "it'll be bedtime soon, so I want you in your pyjamas in ten minutes."

Ignoring his cries of "Aw, Mam!" we continue up the stairs until we hear Glenda's voice calling up after us. "You wanted to be gone early, isn't that right, Karen?"

"Yes, we'll aim to be on the road as soon as we get up." Mam answers without turning around, her grip on my arm tight.

"I'll make sure we're all awake early then so we can see you off."

I turn to see Glenda standing at the bottom of the stairs with all her children gathered around, looking up at us, as though for the last time.

I say nothing to Mam as she tucks me into bed, if only to avoid an argument. I sensed an ending, seeing them all stand around the hall that way. Mam, I know, would like nothing better than to have them out of our lives. Before drifting off to sleep, Seán's image floats before me, smiling. I do not want to think about saying goodbye.

My night's sleep is fitful. Dreams of Andrew and my own dad weave in and out among images that have no relation to anything. A woman I've never met before is tethered to a tall building, almost a skyscraper, and the rope is failing. She's screaming at me for help, but Dad and Andrew just stand there, saying there's no hope. As I try to pull her up, Andrew pushes me aside with a strength I know he never had and starts to gnaw with his teeth, like an animal, at the fraying rope. I'm screaming at him to stop but then the woman plummets, and suddenly I am falling, and I wake with a jerk, my leg muscles twitching, my bed-clothes drenched in sweat.

Mam is there.

"It's all right love," she strokes my head gently and I cling onto her like I am four years old again. "It was just a dream."

"Andrew," I whisper, my voice croaky as though I was actually screaming for that woman.

Mam sniffs stoically. We sit like that for a while, I don't know how long, but slowly I come around and pull back from her.

"Sorry," I mumble, but she shakes her head and starts mooching around the room.

After a few seconds and a wipe of my eyes, I realise she is packing.

"What time is it?" I look around, only then noticing the rain pounding against the window. I look down at my watch and see it is almost nine. "Mam, we're not leaving now, are we?"

"We might as well get on the road, sweetheart. This weather doesn't look like it's going to let up and I want to get you home at a decent hour."

I start to panic. "I don't want to go yet."

She whips around, her face like thunder. But almost immediately it softens and she passes me my clothes from last night, ordering me to go shower. I am still perspiring after the dream so I reluctantly step around her towards the door. Though it's early, I can hear movement in some of the other bedrooms. This calms me a little. I was worried Mam would force me out before I even had time to see Seán.

But just as I make to pull open the bedroom door, her voice rings out, shrill and commanding. "Don't be long now, Tors, love. We want to be on the road soon. We can stop and get some breakfast on the way."

"Mam, come on!" I step back into the room and shut the door as quietly as I can behind me. "You know Glenda would like us to eat with them here before leaving."

"She's been good to you, Tors, I know that. But she's not your mother. She's not family."

My strength comes from nowhere. "I know that! You and Jack are my only family. But aren't you even a small bit grateful for the way she's treated you these past few days? She has welcomed us into her home, when I'm sure it's the last thing she wanted."

Mam lets out a small laugh as she folds a sweater vigorously and stuffs it into my bag. "It's not about that."

"Then what is it about? No, I mean it." I grab her wrist, forcing her to stop moving around and stare directly at her. "I don't understand why you are still so angry with them. What do you want from them?"

"Tors, do you really think your brother was in a right state of mind when he wrote that will?"

My eyebrows crease in horror. "Are you saying you want to contest your own son's will?"

"He was unwell. Why would he leave anything to the Murtaghs?"

"His body was sick. His mind was perfect. And you know he didn't feel the same way about the Murtaghs as you did. No one does. Mam, you'll be dishonouring his memory if you try to destroy his last wishes, just because you don't like them. Do you really think Andrew would be happy if you kick Glenda, Seán and the girls out of this house – and what, we move in? Without him?"

"I don't know, Tors. It's so soon after Andrew . . . I haven't got it all figured out yet. But we have to live."

"We can live more than comfortably under Andrew's will. You'll notice he made me executor, not you? He probably guessed you would pull some stunt like this if he gave you any power."

She looks at me like I've slapped her. Ignoring my own sense of shame at speaking to my mother that way, I march out of the room and into the nearest shower room. I never finished counting exactly how many bathrooms they have in this mansion. It's ridiculous, the idea of us moving in here. Besides, I'm a twenty-six-year-old woman. I'm not going to live at home forever. Just Mam and Jack, rattling around in this mansion, is insane.

I splash cold water on my face and stare into the mirror. The bags under my eyes have lightened significantly and a tint of colour has returned to my cheeks. Of course, that could just be from anger. I really do not understand Mam's logic. I spend longer than necessary in the shower, in an effort to calm down as much as to stall Mam. Even over the plunging spray of the shower I can hear the rain beat against the window. A dullness has descended over Ballyloughlin, and it makes me want to curl up by the fire and never leave. I dry myself slowly, replacing the towel delicately on the rack and dressing with care. I don another baby-blue top Glenda bought for me, a short-sleeved cotton jumper that feels smooth against my skin. It has a softness to it that comforts me.

I pull my hair back and am just finishing moisturising my face when a faded picture hanging on the wall behind me catches my eye in the mirror. A photo in the bathroom seems unusual, and I wonder that I did not notice it earlier. I turn to stare at it. A much younger Glenda sits with a baby on her knee. An older boy stands behind her with his arms wrapped around her neck, while a smiling man bounces a toddler on one knee and holds a slightly older girl close to him. There's a beach in the background and it's obviously a windy day; everyone looks windswept, but happy.

For some reason, it's not Seán who draws my attention. It's the man. Liam. He sits with a young Katie on one knee and an empty space on the other. As though Andrew was plucked from there.

Liam Murtagh. Something about him focuses my mind.

A tremor of rage pulses through me. The whole series of events since the day Roger Nestor and Michael Undersky arrived at our house in Kerry to tell us about the will now crystallise into one explanation I should have seen from the beginning.

Storming back down the landing, I wrench the bedroom door open, stomp over the threshold and slam it shut behind me, not caring that I am certainly drawing the attention of the entire house. Mam jumps and swings around.

"It's Liam, isn't it?"

"What?" She gawks at my hard expression.

"It was never about taking what's rightfully ours for Andrew, or even about living comfortably now. It's not because you hate Glenda that you want them out of this house, and it's not because they're fighting the will that you are constantly so rude to them. It's about Liam. All this has been to get back at Liam." I stare at her as though I've never seen her before. I realise I am trembling.

"Why would I want to get back at Liam? He gave me Andrew, the best thing in our lives." But her voice is reserved, as though testing whether I actually know the truth.

"There's something else." I am sure of it. "What did he do? Why are you so angry at him?"

"Tors . . ."

"You're willing to fight this family until the day you die!" I am shouting now. "I'll ask you again, why are you so angry at Liam Murtagh?"

"Oh Tors, why does it matter?" She picks up my packed bag and tugs open the bedroom door, starting down the stairs. She is trying to get away from me, from this conversation, which only convinces me further that I am right.

I follow her resolutely, ignoring the greetings and worried questions of the various members of the Murtagh family I pass on the stairs. I catch up with Mam as she reaches the front door. Before I can touch her, she stops and turns to me, her breathing irate.

"Tors, we're leaving. I don't want to hear another word about this!" Her voice, so naturally low and soothing, is high-pitched and breathless. "I'm going to put this bag in the car while you say goodbye to the Murtaghs. Then we're gone."

Her voice has a note of finality and in a panic I make to follow her outside.

"Don't you come out in this rain, young lady, without a coat – you're recovering from an illness."

She grabs her jacket, pulls it over her head and steps out into the cold, tackling even the weather to avoid this.

"What does it matter?" She says it almost to herself, but it propels me forward.

The rain beats so hard she doesn't hear me follow but I catch up with her and step around her, so her back is to the grand Murtagh home, the way it has always been.

Glenda runs to the door, calling us back.

My mother echoes her. "Tors Shaw! You're getting saturated! Get back inside this instant!"

I ignore her, the rain matting my hair to my head. The cotton in my pretty blue top absorbs the wetness like a sponge and within seconds I feel it weighing me down.

"It matters." I take a deep breath, and see Seán and his sisters move towards the door curiously, almost cautiously. "It matters, because I don't want this family out of our lives. I'm in love with Seán."

I feel her stare at me with such incredulity that she stops pulling me back towards the house but I am looking past her, into the eyes of the man I want for the rest of my life.

"You don't mean that."

My gaze snaps back to her. "I do mean it, Mam. If you weren't so obsessed with pushing them away, hurting them, you would have seen it. You think I *want* to force Liam Murtagh's family on you? Wouldn't it just be easier for us to slip away, pretend these last few months never happened, and remember Andrew as we knew him before?"

"Yes, much easier. Come on, Tors, let's go . . ." She reaches out to me but I step back.

"Not until you tell me the real reason you are fighting like this. Since we found out about Liam's will, when you're with them you are so hard and cold. That's not who you are. What's going on?"

"Karen . . ." Seán is there, beside her, and she jumps. "Please, I want to be in Tors' life."

Mam turns slowly to see all the Murtagh women gathered at the door, with little Jack peeking out from behind Lizzy. Mam's chest begins to pump furiously and a redness flushes her cheeks.

I look at her earnestly, speaking loudly above the pounding rain. "Mam, I love Seán. Andrew and Katie became best friends, and he has included this whole family in his will. Even Glenda welcomed you into this house when I was sick. You are the only one fighting this. I need you to tell me why."

Then Seán is beside me, with his arm around my shoulder. "Karen, I am going to be in Tors' life from now on."

"Oh, you think that, do you?" Her voice drips with disdain.

302

"I know it."

I stare up at him in wonder. All the men in my life – Dad, Claude, now even Andrew – all seem so very far away. The future is standing here at my side.

Mam is speaking again. At first, neither of us listen, we're locked in our own world. But the air carries her words through the rain towards us. Without intending it, our ears catch it and her confession filters through to us.

Chapter 27

Seán

I am taking no notice of Karen, I only have eyes for Tors. There is nothing she can say that can take this moment away from us. Still, her piercing words penetrate. I catch certain sounds, "Liam", "Andrew", "crash". Before I realise it, I am looking back at her.

"What did you say?" My voice trembles. Tors is holding my hand, steadying me.

"I said you are too late, just like your father."

My mouth goes dry and I am vaguely aware of my entire family walking out into the rain to hear this.

Tors' voice sounds distant when she speaks. "Mam, what are you saying?"

Karen pauses, locking eyes with me. The wind whips around us. Her face could be wet from the rain or from tears.

"After Andrew was born, your father wanted to see him. I would never have agreed but he kept pestering me with calls and letters and I was afraid Stuart would find out. So we met, once, and we both agreed that, for the sake of both our families, Liam would have no more contact with Andrew. He was forever badgering me though, offering to send money and always asking to see him."

A particularly vicious bout of winds unsteadies me, but I remain locked in my stance.

"How could I take his money without Stuart wondering where it came from? How could I explain it to Andrew? Liam offered to buy us property, a bigger house in Ireland, a holiday home abroad. He suggested a car, or cold cash. He said we could pretend we'd won it in a competition! But Stuart wasn't stupid and I couldn't take the risk. Liam was trying to force himself into Andrew's life, when Andrew already had Stuart. Our family was more important than money."

I remain frozen, drinking in her words like water. Her voice is cutting.

"Stuart died. Things got tougher so I considered taking his money. But that would have been an even worse betrayal of my husband, of the man who had been a father to Andrew. We managed to get by. Until February."

Tors gasps.

"When Andrew's AVF failed, I realised we could not stave off a transplant for much longer. It wasn't just about being poor any more. We didn't need his money. Andrew was not just sick, his body was rejecting treatment. We didn't have years any more. We had months." She is looking at Tors now, apologising with her eyes. Then she turns back to me. "So I contacted Liam. I asked him to get tested. Dr Jim set up an appointment. In Cork. In the one hospital Andrew has never been in, where no one would suspect or find out. On the afternoon of the second of March."

I gasp. Shaking, I hold out my hand for my mother to take as they all walk around Karen to my side.

I hear my own words, my voice unfamiliar. "My father died speeding to get tested? For a live transplant? For Andrew?"

Karen makes a noise between a rough laugh and a cry of regret.

When she continues, her strangled voice has leapt an octave. "He was my last hope and he let us down. We didn't find out he had died until it was too late. You probably donated his organs. How could I beg the rest of his family after that? Become indebted to them – to *him*. He was too late, and you were too late, and now Andrew's dead. And what are you going to do about it?"

I take deep, steadying breaths but Tors speaks first, quietly, almost a whisper. "That is why you are so angry at Liam Murtagh?"

Karen looks past her to Mum. "The one time, the *one time*, I asked him to help Andrew, and he did not make it. Oh, I sat in that hospital waiting room in Cork for hours, pacing the floors like a madwoman, sure he would come. But he got off easy. No tests, no needles, no transplant. He didn't have to deal with his family finding out and he didn't have to take care of Andrew. He just died."

More than Katie's sob or the look of horror on Niamh and Lizzy's faces, I can sense the pain, the betrayal filtering through my mother. But something else is happening to me.

A flood of memories crash over me. No, more than memories – the emotions they evoked. Finding out that Dad was dead; that he and Mum never married; that he had cheated on Mum with Karen Shaw; that I was not his only son. The feelings of guilt, betrayal, helplessness that engulfed me – I feel them yet they are not taking over.

If I had discovered only a few months ago that my father died trying to save his secret son, I would have blamed Andrew, hated Karen, become bitter at my father. But I do not feel that way now. I understand. He loved Andrew, unconditionally. I squeeze Tors' hand and, for the first time since Dad died, I feel proud. I continue staring at Karen, and she says it again.

"He just died."

When I speak, my voice is steady. "Speeding. He died speeding. On his way to help you. If you told me now there was a way I could bring Andrew back, I'd speed faster than my father did that night. I'm more like him than I thought." The rain lightens, but does not stop.

Tors' hand is slippery in mine, but I hold on. "You are not getting rid of me, ever. Just like you never got rid of my father. You might not have wanted him, but he was there, willing, right to the very end. Willing to die for your family. So am I."

Karen stares, her eyes drowning in angry tears. Without needing to look down I feel Tors shiver beside me. Shock, secrets, hurt. It's about time something good connected our families.

I sigh and speak, to no one in particular. "Dad's will. Andrew's will. What about our will? We're still alive, let's make our own decisions. To start, let's get out of this rain."

Heartened by Tors' firm grip, I step around my family, past Karen and, pulling Tors with me by the hand, walk forward into our dry, warm home.

Epilogue

Karen

I am crouched in the bushes like some class of a stalker, watching him bend and arrange a fresh bunch of flowers neatly by the roadside.

Tors has told me that this place – where Liam lost his life – has become something of a shrine for the Murtaghs, and they visit it often. Shrine is bloody right. There are more plants and flowers than a garden centre.

The road curves around and dips with the bend, like a slide. It is not hard to imagine a speeding car losing control. I watch the spot where Seán kneels and gasp as the image of a car smashing into a truck flashes before me. I shake myself back to the calm evening, willing Seán to leave before it becomes too much for me.

It was only last Sunday night that I first felt a pull to this place, but I was scared of coming during the week. One of the Murtagh girls, or a neighbour, or worst of all Glenda might be there. But I know none of them will come to pay their respects on a Friday – that is Seán's night. Once he leaves – if he ever does – I know I won't be disturbed.

I watch the love of my daughter's life re-organise the shrine and wonder, as I often do, whether they will eventually marry. A quiet, bitter laugh escapes my mouth at the prospect. A second son gifted to me by Liam Murtagh. I push the thought away. I can only wallow in bitter anguish for so long before my chest constricts so tight I feel a sensation of suffocation.

Since Seán took on a new job in Dublin, he and Tors have divided their weekends between Ballyloughlin and Kerry. Seán arrives late after detouring to the shrine and they often take Jack out on Saturdays. So I don't have to see him too much. For Tors, I welcome him to our home, but not the rest of his family.

Finally, he appears satisfied with his handiwork and returns to his car. I have parked mine a few hundred metres back around the bend, well hidden so he won't spot it as he drives away. Carefully, I cross the road and approach the shrine. A grey, stone cross – long, thick and mounted on a raised platform – is adorned by the fresh pansies and orange blossom Seán brought as well as older, more dainty offerings. A legacy is etched in black calligraphy –

Liam Murtagh, beloved father, died tragically 2nd March 2013

I can feel the spite curling my lips upwards. The Murtaghs undoubtedly consider the shrine with its fancy scroll and overloaded floral display a fitting tribute to their distinguished patriarch. All I see is pretentious pretence. Before that dirty cloud of misuse settles over me once more, I force myself to remember why I am here. I kneel, as Seán had, with my shadow blocking the weak evening sun from the engraving. I speak his name aloud.

"Liam."

A low breeze sings in my ears with the twitter of evening birdsong.

"Liam, this is Karen. I came here to tell you – our son died."

In the silence that follows, a deep, wretched sadness engulfs me. Every vile thought about the Murtaghs which I have cradled inside for over a year in fear of losing my daughter bursts out of me. I scream at the unfairness of his escape from the consequences of our mistake all those years ago when I have to live with such pain. I pummel the ugly grey stone with my fists, cursing him for being the person who shaped my life. For being Andrew's father, when I so wanted it to be Stuart. For robbing Andrew of the reality I had created for him by revealing the truth in that cowardly way. And for dying, after I had abandoned all self-worth and begged him for a vital organ for my boy.

Eventually, the power of my aging fists and sagging muscles ebb away and I begin to talk for real.

"It's been over a year since Andrew died," I sigh, slipping sideways onto the dewy grass to avoid the nettles. "He was taken from me and now your family is trying to take Tors too."

My voice chokes as I remember Tors' calm face, so secure in her love for Seán that no pleading, shouting or logic could persuade them to separate. The only other person who seems to understand my disgust at the notion of our families forming a friendship after everything that has happened, is Glenda. She has a soft spot for Tors, but I know she wants nothing to do with me. The couple of days Tors spent in the Murtagh residence after collapsing are still a blur. There had been an unspoken truce between us, as mothers. It ended naturally when Tors recovered – the kids don't understand this, but we do. Glenda and I can't fall back into that fragile relationship any more than a bubble can be unburst or a car can be uncrashed on a country road.

"Nearly losing Tors so soon after Andrew changed something in me," I confess aloud, shivering as the sun dips lower behind the trees. "Throwing her out of the house in a fit of rage was one thing, but getting that phone call from Glenda and hearing the word 'unconscious' shook me. After that, I knew I would do anything to make sure I never lose her like I lost Andrew, and Stuart."

I sit in silence then, listing out in my head all the concessions I have made to keep Tors in my life over the past year, including admitting Seán into our house every second weekend. When he is there, we rarely speak about his father. The few times we broached the subject he seemed frustrated at my refusal to revere Liam's death as that of a tragic hero. Fearing I'll say something that will cause Tors to leave me, I always walk away. Sometimes I let them take Jack to Ballyloughlin on the weekends as a compromise, to ensure none of the Murtaghs encroach on my home.

Some day – soon, I'm sure – Tors and Seán will move in together, probably in Dublin if not abroad. For now, Tors feels it is important that Jack not be deserted by another family member. I wish it is for me that she stays, but I'll take whatever I can get.

There is a reason for my journey to the shrine. Jack is turning ten tomorrow. Double digits – he could not be more excited. He wants a party and he wants Katie and Lizzy to be there. Of course, I refused outright at first when we discussed it last Sunday night. But Tors became militant. She has a real chip on her shoulder about how Jack was affected by our time in Ballyloughlin and she blames me entirely. She told me outright that I have no right to keep the Murtagh girls from the party. They will be welcomed by her and Jack whether I 'allow' it or not.

I felt my power, my position in our family slipping away, but I knew if I didn't acquiesce I'd lose them all.

As Tors stormed from the room, Seán turned to me and asked me to put up with his sisters' presence for just one day, for Jack. He made to leave after Tors, then turned, his eyes searching mine pleadingly. He said, "Just try."

My legs weakened. Luckily, he left straight away and did not see them give way and tears erupt from my eyes. I was transported by those words back to a time over twenty years ago when his father comforted me after a chance meeting.

"You remember, don't you, Liam?" I whisper into the night air. My voice is soft as my fingers trail across his name where only minutes before I had beat at his memory with all my strength.

I have not allowed myself think about the night I met Liam Murtagh since he died. The aftermath and consequences have always been in my mind, but not the night itself. I speak into the night air once more.

"My family seemed to be disintegrating, my whole life falling apart. You gave me what I needed to start again – warm arms, empathetic words and hope. When I cried that I didn't know if I could go on, you looked deep into my eyes, just like your son did last Sunday night, and told me to 'just try'."

So I did.

I will give in and swallow the hate. I will keep Seán's family in my life, for Tors and for Andrew's memory. And for Jack. My final secret is that I will allow myself to remember Liam Murtagh with something other than resentment.

"Our son," I say once more, before standing and backing slowly away.

Tors and Jack are all I have left and I will not give up on them, just like I never gave up on Andrew. If it means suffering through Seán's visits and watching the Murtagh girls enjoy my little boy's affections, I will do it. I have to do it. At the very least, I will take Liam's advice. I will try.